THE
HOUSE
AT
RIVERTON

THE
HOUSE
AT
RIVERTON

A Novel

KATE MORTON

ATRIA BOOKS

New York London Toronto Sydney

For Davin,
who holds my hand on the roller-coaster

ATRIA BOOKS

A Division of Simon & Schuster, Inc.
1230 Avenue of the Americas
New York, NY 10020

Copyright © 2006 by Kate Morton
Originally published in Australia in 2006 as The Shifting Fog by Allen & Unwin
Published by arrangement with Allen & Unwin Pty Ltd

First Atria Books hardcover edition April 2008

ATRIA BOOKS and colophon are trademarks of Simon & Schuster, Inc.

For information about special discounts for bulk purchases, please contact
Simon & Schuster Special Sales at 1-800-456-6798 or business@simonandschuster.com.

Designed by Karolina Harris

Manufactured in the United States of America

10   9   8   7   6   5   4   3   2   1

Library of Congress Cataloging-in-Publication Data

Morton, Kate, date.
  [Shifting fog]
  The house at Riverton : a novel / Kate Morton.—1st Atria Books hardcover ed.
    p. cm.
  "Originally published in Australia in 2006 as The Shifting Fog by Allen & Unwin"—T.p. verso.
1. Women domestics—Fiction. 2. Reminiscing in old age—Fiction. 3. Upper class families—
Fiction. 4. Poets—Crimes against—Fiction. 5. Great Britain—Social life and customs—
1918–1945—Fiction. 6. England—Fiction. I. Title.

  PR9619.4.M74S55 2008
  823'.92—dc22   2008007023

ISBN-13: 978-1-4165-5051-8
ISBN-10:   1-4165-5051-8

CONTENTS

PART ONE

PART TWO

Contents

PART ONE

GHOSTS STIR

LAST November I had a nightmare.

It was 1924 and I was at Riverton again. All the doors hung wide open, silk billowing in the summer breeze. An orchestra perched high on the hill beneath the ancient maple, violins lilting lazily in the warmth. The air rang with pealing laughter and crystal, and the sky was the kind of blue we'd all thought the war had destroyed forever. One of the footmen, smart in black and white, poured champagne into the top of a tower of glass flutes and everyone clapped, delighting in the splendid wastage.

I saw myself, the way one does in dreams, moving amongst the guests. Moving slowly, much more slowly than one can in life, the others a blur of silk and sequins.

I was looking for someone.

Then the picture changed and I was near the summer house, only it wasn't the summer house at Riverton—it couldn't have been. This was not the shiny new building Teddy had designed, but an old structure with ivy climbing the walls, twisting itself through the windows, strangling the pillars.

Someone was calling me. A woman, a voice I recognized, coming from behind the building, on the lake's edge. I walked down the slope, my hands brushing against the tallest reeds. A figure crouched on the bank.

It was Hannah, in her wedding dress, mud splattered across the front, clinging to the appliquéd roses. She looked up at me, her face

3

pale where it emerged from shadow. Her voice chilled my blood. "You're too late." She pointed at my hands. "You're too late."

I looked down at my hands, young hands, covered in dark river mud, and in them the stiff, cold body of a dead foxhound.

❦

I KNOW what brought it on, of course. It was the letter from the filmmaker. I don't receive much mail these days: the occasional post-card from a dutiful, holidaying friend; a perfunctory letter from the bank where I keep a savings account; an invitation to the christening of a child whose parents I am shocked to realize are no longer children themselves.

Ursula's letter had arrived on a Tuesday morning late in November and Sylvia had brought it with her when she came to make my bed. She'd raised heavily sketched eyebrows and waved the envelope.

"Mail today. Something from the States by the look of the stamp. Your grandson, perhaps?" The left brow arched—a question mark—and her voice lowered to a husky whisper. "Terrible business, that. Just terrible. And him such a nice young man."

As Sylvia tut-tutted, I thanked her for the letter. I like Sylvia. She's one of the few people able to look beyond the lines on my face to see the twenty-year-old who lives inside. Nonetheless, I refuse to be drawn into conversation about Marcus.

I asked her to open the curtains and she pursed her lips a moment before moving on to another of her favorite subjects: the weather, the likelihood of snow for Christmas, the havoc it would wreak on the arthritic residents. I responded when required, but my mind was on the envelope in my lap, wondering at the scratchy penmanship, the foreign stamps, softened edges that spoke of lengthy travails.

"Here, why don't I read that for you," Sylvia said, giving the pillows a final, hopeful plump. "Give your eyes a bit of a rest?"

"No. Thank you. Perhaps you could pass my glasses, though?"

When she'd left, promising to come back and help me dress after she'd finished her rounds, I prised the letter from its envelope, hands shaking the way they do, wondering whether he was finally coming home.

But it wasn't from Marcus at all. It was from a young woman making a film about the past. She wanted me to look at her sets, to remember things and places from long ago. As if I hadn't spent a life-time pretending to forget.

I ignored that letter. I folded it carefully and quietly, slid it inside a book I'd long ago given up reading. And then I exhaled. It was not the first time I had been reminded of what happened at Riverton, to Robbie and the Hartford sisters. Once I saw the tail end of a documentary on television, something Ruth was watching about war poets. When Robbie's face filled the screen, his name printed across the bottom in an unassuming font, my skin prickled. But nothing happened. Ruth didn't flinch, the narrator continued, and I went on drying the dinner plates.

Another time, reading the newspaper, my eye was drawn to a familiar name in a write-up in the television guide; a program celebrating seventy years of British films. I noted the time, my heart thrilling, wondering if I dared watch it. In the end I fell asleep before it finished. There was very little about Emmeline. A few publicity photos, none of which showed her true beauty, and a clip from one of her silent films, *The Venus Affair*, which made her look strange: hollow-cheeked; jerky movements like a marionette. There was no reference to the other films, the ones that threatened such a fuss. I suppose they don't rate a mention in these days of promiscuity and permissiveness.

But although I had been met with such memories before, Ursula's letter was different. It was the first time in over seventy years that anyone had associated *me* with the events, had remembered that a young woman named Grace Reeves had been at Riverton that summer. It made me feel vulnerable somehow, singled out. Guilty.

No. I was adamant. That letter would remain unanswered.

And so it did.

A strange thing began to happen, though. Memories, long consigned to the dark reaches of my mind, began to sneak through cracks. Images were tossed up high and dry, picture-perfect, as if a lifetime hadn't passed between. And, after the first tentative drops, the deluge. Whole conversations, word for word, nuance for nuance; scenes played out as though on film.

I have surprised myself. While moths have torn holes in my recent memories, I find the distant past is sharp and clear. They come often lately, those ghosts from the past, and I am surprised to find I don't much mind them. Not nearly so much as I had supposed I would. Indeed, the specters I have spent my life escaping have become almost a comfort, something I welcome, anticipate, like one of those serials Sylvia is always talking about, hurrying her rounds so that she can watch them down at the main hall. I had forgotten, I suppose, that there were bright memories in amongst the dark.

When the second letter arrived last week, in the same scratchy hand on the same soft paper, I knew I was going to say yes, I would look at the sets. I was curious, a sensation I hadn't felt in some time. There is not much left to be curious about when one is ninety-eight years old, but I wanted to meet this Ursula Ryan who plans to bring them all to life again, who is so passionate about their story.

So I wrote her a letter, had Sylvia post it for me and we arranged to meet.

THE DRAWING ROOM

M Y hair, always pale, is now flossy white and very, very long. It is fine too, finer it seems with each passing day. It is my one vanity—Lord knows I haven't much else to be vain about. Not any more. It has been with me a long time—since 1989, this present crop. I am fortunate indeed that Sylvia is happy to brush it for me, oh so gently; to plait it, day in, day out. It is above and beyond her job description and I am very grateful. I must remember to tell her so.

I missed my chance this morning, I was too excited. When Sylvia brought my juice I could barely drink it. The thread of nervous energy that had infused me all week had overnight become a knot. She helped me into a new peach dress—the one Ruth bought me for Christmas—and exchanged my slippers for the pair of outside shoes usually left to languish in my wardrobe. The leather was firm and Sylvia had to push to make them fit, but such price respectability. I am too old to learn new ways and cannot abide the tendency of the younger residents to wear their slippers out.

Face paint restored some life to my cheeks, but I was careful not to let Sylvia overdo it. I am wary of looking like an undertaker's mannequin. It doesn't take much rouge to tip the balance: the rest of me is so pale, so small.

With some effort I draped the gold locket around my neck, its nineteenth-century elegance incongruous against my utilitarian clothing. I straightened it, wondering at my daring, wondering what Ruth would say when she saw.

My gaze dropped. The small silver frame on my dressing table. A photo from my wedding day. I would just as happily not have had it there—the marriage was so long ago and so short-lived, poor John—but it is my concession to Ruth. It pleases her, I think, to imagine that I pine for him.

Sylvia helped me to the drawing room—it still rankles to call it such—where breakfast was being served and where I was to wait for Ruth, who had agreed (against her better judgement, she said) to drive me to Shepperton Studios. I had Sylvia seat me alone at the corner table and fetch me a glass of juice, and then I reread Ursula's letter.

Ruth arrived at eight-thirty on the dot. She may have had misgivings about the wisdom of this excursion, but she is, and has always been, incurably punctual. I've heard it said that children born to stressful times never shake the air of woe, and Ruth, a child of the second war, proves the rule. So different from Sylvia, only fifteen years younger, who fusses about in tight skirts, laughs too loudly and changes hair color with each new "boyfriend."

This morning Ruth walked across the room, well dressed, immaculately groomed, but stiffer than a fence post.

"Morning, Mum," she said, brushing cold lips across my cheek. "Finished your breakfast yet?" She glanced at the half-empty glass before me. "I hope you've had more than that. We'll likely hit morning traffic on the way and we won't have time to stop for anything." She looked at her watch. "Do you need to visit the loo?"

I shook my head, wondering when I had become the child.

"You're wearing Father's locket; I haven't seen it in an age." She reached forward to straighten it, nodding approval. "He had an eye, didn't he?"

I agreed, touched by the way little untruths told to the very young are believed so implicitly. I felt a wave of affection for my prickly daughter, repressed quickly the tired old parental guilt that always surfaces when I look upon her anxious face.

She took my arm, folded it over hers and placed the cane in my other hand. Many of the others prefer walking frames or even those motorized chairs, but I'm still quite good with my cane, and a creature of habit who sees no reason to trade up.

She's a good girl, my Ruth—solid and reliable. She'd dressed formally today, the way she would to visit her solicitor, or doctor. I had known she would. She wanted to make a good impression; show this filmmaker that no matter what her mother might have done in the past, Ruth Bradley McCourt was respectably middle class, thank you very much.

We drove in silence for a way, then Ruth began tuning the radio. Her fingers were those of an old lady, knuckles swollen where she'd forced on her rings that morning. Astounding to see one's daughter ageing. I glanced at my own hands then, folded in my lap. Hands so busy in the past, performing tasks both menial and complex; hands that now sat gray, flaccid and inert. Ruth rested finally on a program of classical music. The announcer spoke for a while, rather inanely about his weekend, and then began to play Chopin. A coincidence, of course, that today of all days I should hear the waltz in C sharp minor.

Ruth pulled over in front of several huge white buildings, square like aircraft hangars. She switched off the ignition and sat for a moment, looking straight ahead. "I don't know why you have to do this," she said quietly, lips sucked tight. "You've done so much with your life. Traveled, studied, raised a child . . . Why do you want to be reminded of what you used to be?"

She didn't expect an answer and I didn't give one. She sighed abruptly, hopped out of the car and fetched my cane from the boot. Without a word, she helped me from my seat.

A young woman was waiting for us. A slip of a girl with very long blond hair that fell straight down her back and was cut in a thick fringe at the front. She was the type of girl one might have labeled plain had she not been blessed with such marvellous dark eyes.

They belonged on an oil portrait, round, deep and expressive, the rich color of wet paint.

She rushed toward us, smiling, and took my hand from Ruth's arm. "Mrs. Bradley, I'm so happy you could make it. I'm Ursula."

"Grace," I said, before Ruth could insist on "Doctor." "My name is Grace."

"Grace." Ursula beamed. "I can't tell you how excited I was to get your letter." Her accent was English, a surprise after the American address on her letter. She turned to Ruth. "Thanks so much for playing chauffeur today."

I felt Ruth's body tighten beside me. "I could hardly put Mum on a bus now, could I?"

Ursula laughed and I was pleased that the young are so quick to read uncongeniality as irony. "Well, come on inside, it's freezing out. 'Scuse the mad rush. We start shooting next week and we're in a complete tizzy trying to get things ready. I was hoping you'd meet our set designer, but she's had to go into London to collect some fabric. Maybe if you're still here when she gets back . . . Go carefully through the doorway now, there's a bit of a step."

She and Ruth bustled me into a foyer and down a dim corridor lined with doors. Some were ajar and I peered in, snatching glimpses of shadowy figures at glowing computer screens. None of it resembled the other film set I had been on with Emmeline, all those years ago.

"Here we are," Ursula said as we reached the last door. "Come on in and I'll get us some tea." She pushed the door and I was swept over the threshold, into my past.

❀

IT was the Riverton drawing room. Even the wallpaper was the same. Silver Studios' burgundy Art Nouveau, "Flaming Tulips," as fresh as the day the paperers had come from London. A leather chesterfield sat at the center by the fireplace, draped with Indian silks just like the ones Hannah and Emmeline's grandfather, Lord Ashbury, had brought back from abroad when he was a young officer. The ship's clock stood where it always had, on the mantelpiece beside the Waterford candelabra. Someone had gone to a lot of trouble to get it right, but it announced itself an impostor with every tick. Even now, some eighty years later, I remember the sound of the drawing-room clock. The quietly insistent way it had of marking the passage of time: patient, certain, cold—as if it somehow knew, even then, that time was no friend to those who lived in that house.

Ruth accompanied me as far as the chesterfield and arranged me in its corner. I was aware of a bustle of activity behind me, people dragging huge lights with insect-like legs, someone, somewhere, laughing.

I thought of the last time I had been in the drawing room—the real one, not this facade—the day I had known I was leaving Riverton and would never be back.

It had been Teddy I'd told. He hadn't been pleased, but by that time he'd lost the authority he once had, events had knocked it out of him. He wore the vaguely bewildered pallor of a captain who knew his ship was sinking but was powerless to stop it. He asked me to stay, implored me, out of loyalty to Hannah, he said, if not for him. And I almost did. Almost.

Ruth nudged me. "Mum? Ursula's talking to you."

"I'm sorry, I didn't hear."

"Mum's a bit deaf," Ruth said. "At her age it's to be expected. I've tried to get her in for testing, but she can be rather obstinate."

Obstinate, I own. But I am not deaf and do not like it when people assume I am—my eyesight is poor without glasses, I tire easily, have none of my own teeth left and survive on a cocktail of pills, but I can hear as well as I ever have. It's only with age I have learned solely to listen to things I want to hear.

"I was just saying, Mrs. Bradley, Grace, it must be strange to be back. Well, sort of back. It must spark all sorts of memories?"

"Yes." I cleared my throat. "Yes, it does."

"I'm so glad," Ursula said, smiling. "I take that as a sign we've got it right."

"Oh yes."

"Is there anything that looks out of place? Anything we've forgotten?"

I looked about the set again. Meticulous in its detail, down to the set of crests mounted by the door, the middle one a Scottish thistle that matched the etching on my locket.

All the same, there *was* something missing. Despite its accuracy, the set was strangely divested of atmosphere. It was like a museum piece: interesting, but lifeless.

It was understandable, of course. Though the 1920s live vividly in my memory, the decade is, for the film's designers, the "olden days." A historical setting whose replication requires as much research and painstaking attention to detail as would the re-creation of a medieval castle.

I could feel Ursula looking at me, awaiting keenly my pronouncement.

"It's perfect," I said finally. "Everything in its place."

Then she said something that made me start. "Except the family."

"Yes," I said. "Except the family." I blinked and for a moment I could see them: Emmeline draped across the sofa, all legs and eyelashes, Hannah frowning at one of the books from the library, Teddy pacing the Bessarabian carpet . . .

"Emmeline sounds like she must have been a lot of fun," Ursula said.

"Yes."

"She was easy to research—managed to get her name in just about every gossip column ever printed. Not to mention the letters and diaries of half the eligible bachelors of the day!"

I nodded. "She was always popular."

She looked up at me from beneath her fringe. "Putting Hannah's character together wasn't so easy."

I cleared my throat. "No?"

"She was more of a mystery. Not that she wasn't mentioned in the papers: she was. Had her share of admirers too. It just seems not many people really knew her. They admired her, revered her even, but didn't really *know* her."

I thought of Hannah. Beautiful, clever, yearning Hannah. "She was complex."

"Yes," Ursula said, "that's the impression I got."

Ruth, who'd been listening, said, "One of them married an American, didn't she?"

I looked at her, surprised. She had always made it her business *not* to know anything about the Hartfords.

She met my gaze. "I've been doing some reading."

How like Ruth to prepare for our visit, no matter how distasteful she found the subject matter.

Ruth turned her attention back to Ursula and spoke cautiously, wary of error. "She married after the war, I think. Which one was that?"

"Hannah." There. I'd done it. I'd spoken her name aloud.

"What about the other sister?" Ruth continued. "Emmeline. Did she ever marry?"

"No," I said. "She was engaged."

"A number of times," Ursula said, smiling. "Seems she couldn't bring herself to settle on one man."

Oh, but she did. In the end she did.

"Don't suppose we'll ever know exactly what happened that night." This was Ursula.

"No." My tired feet were beginning to protest against the leather of my shoes. They'd be swollen tonight and Sylvia would exclaim, then she'd insist on giving them a soak. "I suppose not."

Ruth straightened in her seat. "But surely *you* must know what happened, Miss Ryan. You're making a film of it, after all."

"Sure," Ursula said, "I know the basics. My great-grandmother was at Riverton that night—she was related to the sisters through marriage—and it's become a sort of family legend. My great-grand-mother told Grandma, Grandma told Mum, and Mum told me. A number of times, actually: it made a huge impression. I always knew one day I'd turn it into a film." She smiled, shrugged. "But there are always little holes in history, aren't there? I have files and files of research—the police reports and newspapers are full of facts, but it's all second-hand. Rather heavily censored, I suspect. Unfortunately the two people who witnessed the suicide have been dead for years."

"I must say, it seems a rather morbid subject for a film," Ruth said.

"Oh, no; it's fascinating," Ursula said. "A rising star of the English poetry scene kills himself by a dark lake on the eve of a huge society party. His only witnesses are two beautiful sisters who never speak to each other again. One his fiancée, the other rumored to be his lover. It's terribly romantic."

The knot in my stomach relaxed a little. So their secret is still safe. She doesn't know the truth. I wondered why I had supposed otherwise. And I wondered what sort of misguided loyalty had made me care either way. Why, after all these years, it still mattered to me what people thought.

But I knew that too. I had been born to it. Mr. Hamilton had told me so the day I left, as I stood on the top step of the servants' entrance, my leather bag packed with my few possessions, Mrs. Townsend weeping in the kitchen. He'd said it was in my blood, just as it had been for my mother and for her parents before her, that I was a fool to leave, to throw away a good place with a good family. He'd decried the loss of loyalty and pride general in the English nation, and had vowed he wouldn't allow it to infiltrate Riverton. The war hadn't been fought and won just to lose our ways.

I'd pitied him then: so rigid, so certain that by leaving service I was setting myself on a path to financial and moral ruination. It wasn't until much later that I began to understand how terrified he must have been, how relentless must have seemed the rapid social changes, swirling about him, nipping at his heels. How desperately he longed to hold on to the old ways and certainties.

But he'd been right. Not completely, not about the ruination— neither my finances nor my morals were the worse for leaving Riverton—but there was some part of me that never left that house. Rather, some part of the house that wouldn't leave me. For years after, the smell of Stubbins & Co. beeswax, the crackle of tires on gravel, a certain type of bell and I'd be fourteen again, tired after a long day's work, sipping cocoa by the servants" hall fire while Mr. Hamilton orated select passages from *The Times* (those deemed fit for our impressionable ears), Nancy frowned at some irreverent comment of Alfred's, and Mrs. Townsend snored gently in the rocker, her knitting resting on her generous lap . . .

"Here we are," Ursula said. "Thanks, Tony."

A young man had appeared beside me, clutching a makeshift tray of motley mugs and an old jam jar full of sugar. He released his load onto the side table and Ursula began distributing them. Ruth passed one to me.

"Mum, what is it?" She pulled out a handkerchief and reached for my face. "Are you unwell?"

I could feel then that my cheeks were moist.

It was the smell of the tea that did it. And being there, in that room, sitting on that chesterfield. The weight of distant memories. Of long-held secrets. The clash of past and present.

"Grace? Can I get you something?" This was Ursula. "Would you like the heating turned down?"

"I'm going to have to take her home." Ruth again. "I knew this wasn't a good idea. It's far too much for her."

Yes, I wanted to go home. To be home. I felt myself being hoisted up, my cane thrust into my hand. Voices swirled about me.

"I'm sorry," I said, to no one in particular. "I'm just so tired." So tired. So long ago.

My feet were aching: protesting their confinement. Someone—Ursula, perhaps—reached out to steady me. A cold wind slapped my damp cheeks.

I was in Ruth's car then, houses, trees and road signs rushing past.

"Don't worry, Mum, it's all over now," Ruth said. "I blame myself. I should never have agreed to take you."

I put my hand on her arm, felt her tense.

"I should have trusted my instincts," she said. "It was stupid of me."

I closed my eyes. Listened to the hum of the radiator, the pulse of the windscreen wipers, the drone of the traffic.

"That's it, you have a bit of a rest," Ruth said. "You're going home. You never have to go back again."

I smiled, felt myself drifting away.

It is too late, I am home. I am back.

The Nursery

✳

I T is mild this morning, a foretaste of spring, and I am sitting on the iron seat in the garden, beneath the elm. It's good for me to get a bit of fresh air (so says Sylvia), thus here I sit, playing peek-a-boo with the shy winter sun, my cheeks as cold and slack as a pair of peaches left too long in the fridge.

I have been thinking about the day I started at Riverton. I can see it clearly. The intervening years concertina and it is June 1914. I am fourteen again: naive, gauche, terrified, following Nancy up flight after flight of scrubbed elm stairs. Her skirt swishes efficiently with every step, each *swish* an indictment of my own inexperience. I am struggling behind, my suitcase handle cutting my fingers. I lose sight of Nancy as she turns to begin up yet another flight, rely on the swishing to lead the way . . .

When Nancy reached the very top she proceeded down a dark corridor with low ceilings, stopping finally, with a neat click of the heels, at a small door. She turned and frowned as I hobbled towards her, her pinched gaze as black as her hair.

"What's the matter with you?" she said, clipped English unable to disguise her Irish vowels. "I didn't know you were slow. Mrs. Townsend never said anything about it, I'm sure."

"I'm not slow. It's my suitcase. It's heavy."

"Well," she said. "I've never seen such a fuss. I don't know what kind of housemaid you're going to make if you can't carry a suitcase of clothing without lagging. You'd better hope Mr. Hamilton don't see you dragging the carpet sweeper around like a sack of flour."

She pushed open the door. The room was small and spare, and it smelled, unaccountably, like potatoes. But one half of it—an iron bed, chest of drawers and chair—was to be mine.

"There now. That's your side," she said, nodding towards the far edge of the bed. "I'm this side and I'd thank you not to touch anything." She walked her fingers along the top of her chest of drawers, past a crucifix, a Bible and a hairbrush. "Sticky fingers will not be abided here. Now get your things unpacked, get into uniform and come downstairs so you can start your duties. No dawdling, mind, and for heaven's sake, no leaving the servants' hall. Luncheon's at midday today on account of the Master's grandchildren arriving, and we're already behind with the rooms. Last thing I need is to have to go looking for you. You're not a dawdler, I hope."

"No, Nancy," I said, still smarting at the implication I might be a thief.

"Well," she said, "we'll see about that." She shook her head. "I don't know. I tell them I need a new girl and what do they send me? No experience, no references and, by the looks of you, a dawdler."

"I'm not—"

"Pish," she said, stamping a narrow foot. "Mrs. Townsend says your mother was quick and able, and that the apple don't fall far from the tree. All's I can say is you'd better hope it's so. The Mistress won't put up with dawdling from the likes of you, and neither will I." And with a final, disapproving toss of her head, she turned heel and left me alone in the tiny dim room at the top of the house. *Swish . . . Swish . . . Swish . . .*

I held my breath, listening.

Finally, alone with the sighing of the house, I tiptoed to the door and eased it shut, turning to take in my new home.

There was not much to see. I ran my hand over the foot of the bed, ducking my head where the ceiling slanted against the roof line. Across the end of the mattress was a gray blanket, one of its corners patched by a competent hand. A small, framed picture, the only hint of decoration in the room, hung on the wall: a primitive hunting scene, an impaled deer, blood leaking from its pierced flank. I looked away quickly from the dying animal.

Carefully, silently, I sat down, wary of wrinkling the smooth undersheet. The bed springs creaked in response and I jumped, chastened, my cheeks flooding with color.

A narrow window cast a shaft of dusty light into the room. I climbed up to kneel on the chair and peered outside.

The room was at the back of the house and very high. I could see all the way past the rose garden, over the trellises and to the south fountain. Beyond, I knew, lay the lake and, on the other side, the village and the cottage in which I had spent my first fourteen years. I pictured Mother, sitting by the kitchen window where the light was best, her back curled over the clothing she darned.

I wondered how she was managing alone. Mother had been worse lately. I'd heard her of a night, groaning in her bed as the bones of her back seized beneath her skin. Some mornings her fingers were so stiff I'd had to run them under warm water and rub them between my own before she could as much as pluck a reel of thread from her sewing basket. Mrs. Rodgers from the village had agreed to stop in daily, and the ragman passed by twice a week, but still, she'd be alone an awful lot. There was little chance she'd keep up the darning without me. What would she do for money? My meager salary would help, but surely I'd have been better to stay with her?

And yet it was she who had insisted I apply for the position. She'd refused to hear the arguments I made against the idea. Only shook her head and minded me that she knew best. She'd heard they were looking for a girl and was certain I'd be just what they were after. Not a word as to how she knew. Typical of Mother and her secrets.

"It's not far," she said. "You can come home and help me on your days off."

My face must have betrayed my qualms, for she reached out to touch my cheek. An unfamiliar gesture and one I wasn't expecting.

The surprise of her rough hands, her needle-pricked fingertips, made me flinch. "There, there, girl. You knew the time would come and you'd have to find yourself a position. It's for the best: a good opportunity. You'll see. There's not many places will take a girl so young. Lord Ashbury and Lady Violet, they're not bad people. And Mr. Hamilton might seem strict, but he's nothing if not fair. Mrs. Townsend, too. Work hard, do as you're told and you'll find no trouble." She squeezed my cheek hard then, fingers quivering. "And Gracie? Don't you go forgetting your place. There's too many young girls get themselves into trouble that way."

I had promised to do as she said, and the following Saturday trudged up the hill to the grand manor house, dressed in my Sunday clothes, to be interviewed by Lady Violet.

It was a small and quiet household, she told me, just her husband, Lord Ashbury, who was busy most of the time with the estate and his clubs, and herself. Their two sons, Major Jonathan and Mr. Frederick, were both grown up and lived in their own homes with their families, though they visited at times and I was sure to see them if I worked well and was kept on. With only the two of them living at Riverton they did without a housekeeper, she said, leaving the running of the household in Mr. Hamilton's capable hands, with Mrs. Townsend, the cook, in charge of the kitchen accounts. If the two of them were pleased with me, then that was recommendation enough to keep me on.

She had paused then and looked at me closely, in a way that made me feel trapped, like a mouse inside a glass jar. I had become instantly conscious of the edge of my hem, scarred with repeated attempts to match its length to my growing height, the small patch on my stockings that rubbed against my shoes and was becoming thin, my too-long neck and too-large ears.

Then she had blinked and smiled: a tight smile that turned her eyes into icy crescents. "Well, you look clean, and Mr. Hamilton tells me you can stitch." She had stood up as I nodded, and moved away from me towards the writing desk, trailing her hand lightly along the top of the chaise. "How is your mother?" she had asked, without turning. "Did you know she used to be in service here too?" To which I had told her I did know and that Mother was well, thank you for asking.

I must have said the right thing, because it was just after that she offered me fifteen pounds a year to start next day and rang the bell for Nancy to show me out.

I pulled my face from the window, wiped away the mark my breath had left and climbed back down.

My suitcase lay where I'd dropped it, by Nancy's side of the bed, and I dragged it around to the chest of drawers that was to be mine. I tried not to look at the bleeding deer, frozen in his moment of final horror, as I packed my clothes into the top drawer: two skirts, two blouses and a pair of black lisle stockings that Mother had bid me darn so they'd see me through the coming winter. Then, with a glance at the door and a speeding heart, I unloaded my secret haul.

There were three volumes in all. Dog-eared green covers with faded gold lettering. I stowed them at the back of the bottom drawer and covered them with my shawl, careful to fold it right around so they were completely concealed. Mr. Hamilton had been clear. The Holy Bible was acceptable, but any reading material beyond that was most likely injurious and must be presented for his approval or otherwise risk confiscation. I was not a rebel—indeed, back then I had a fierce sense of duty—but to live without Holmes and Watson was unthinkable.

I tucked the suitcase under the bed.

A uniform hung on the hook behind the door—black dress, white apron, frilly cap—and I put it on, feeling like a child who had discovered its mother's wardrobe. The dress was stiff beneath my fingers and the collar scratched my neck where long hours had molded it to someone else's wider frame. As I tied the apron, a tiny white moth fluttered away in search of a new hiding spot high up in the rafters, and I longed to join it.

The cap was white cotton, starched so that the front panel sat upright, and I used the mirror above Nancy's chest of drawers to make sure it was straight and to smooth my pale hair over my ears as Mother had shown me. The girl in the mirror caught my eye briefly, and I thought what a serious face she had. It is an uncanny feeling, that rare occasion when one catches a glimpse of oneself in repose. An unguarded moment, stripped of artifice, when one forgets to fool even oneself.

✹

SYLVIA has brought me a cup of steaming tea and a slice of lemon cake. She sits next to me on the iron bench and, with a glance towards the office, withdraws a pack of cigarettes. (Remarkable the way my apparent need for fresh air seems always to coincide with her need for a covert cigarette break.) She offers me one. I refuse, as I always do, and she says, as she always does: "Probably best at your age. Smoke yours for you, shall I?"

Sylvia looks good today—she has done something different with her hair—and I tell her so. She nods, blows a stream of smoke and tosses her head, a long ponytail appearing over one shoulder.

"I've had extensions," she says. "I've wanted them for ages and I just thought, girl, life's too short not to be glamorous. Looks real, doesn't it?"

I am late in my reply, which she takes for agreement.

"That's because it is. Real hair, the sort they use on celebrities. Here. Feel it."

"Goodness," I say, stroking the coarse ponytail, "real hair."

"They can do anything these days." She waves her cigarette and I notice the juicy purple ring her lips have left. "Of course, you have to pay for it. Luckily I had a bit put aside for a rainy day."

She smiles, glowing like a ripe plum, and I grasp the raison d'être for this reinvention. Sure enough, a photograph materializes from her blouse pocket.

"Anthony," she says, beaming.

I make a show of putting on my glasses, peering at the image of a gray-mustachioed man in late middle age. "He looks lovely."

"Oh, Grace," she says through a happy sigh. "He is. We've only been out for tea a few times, but I've got such a good feeling about this one. He's a real gentleman, you know? Not like some of them other layabouts that came before. He opens doors, brings me flowers, pulls my chair out for me when we go about together. A real old-fashioned gentleman."

The last sentence, I can tell, is added for my benefit. An assumption that the elderly cannot help but be impressed by the old-fashioned. "What does he do for a living?" I say.

"He's a teacher at the local comprehensive. History and English. He's awful clever. Community-minded too; does volunteer work for the local historical society. It's a hobby of his, he says, all those ladies and lords and dukes and duchesses. He knows all kinds of things about that family of yours, the one that used to live up in the grand house on the hill—" She breaks and squints towards the office, then rolls her eyes. "Oh, Gawd. It's Nurse Ratchet. I'm supposed to be doing tea rounds. No doubt Bertie Sinclair's complained again. You ask me, he'd be doing himself a favor to skip a biscuit now and then." She extinguishes her cigarette and pops the butt in the matchbox. "Ah well, no rest for the wicked. Anything I can get for you before I do the others, pet? You've hardly touched your tea."

I assure her I'm fine and she hurries across the green, hips and ponytail swinging in accord.

It is nice to be cared for, to have one's tea brought. I like to think I have earned this little luxury. Lord knows I have often enough been the bearer of tea. Sometimes I amuse myself imagining how Sylvia would have fared in service at Riverton. Not for her the silent, obedient deference of the domestic servant. She has too much bluff; has not been cowed by frequent assertions as to her "place," well-intentioned instructions to lower her expectations. No, Nancy would not have found Sylvia so compliant a pupil as I.

It is hardly a fair comparison, I know. People have changed too much. The century has left us bruised and battered. Even the young and privileged today wear their cynicism like a badge, their eyes blank and their minds full of things they never sought to know.

It is one of the reasons I have never spoken of the Hartfords and Robbie Hunter and what went on between them. For there have been times when I've considered telling it all, unburdening myself. To Ruth. Or more likely Marcus. But somehow I knew before beginning my tale that I would be unable to make them understand. How it ended the way it did. Why it ended the way it did. Make them see how much the world has changed.

Of course, the signs of progress were upon us even then. The first war—the Great War—changed everything, upstairs and down. How shocked we all were when the new staff began to trickle in (and out again, usually) after the war, full of agency ideas about minimum wages and days off. Before that, the world had seemed absolute somehow, the distinctions simple and intrinsic.

On my first morning at Riverton, Mr. Hamilton called me to his pantry, deep in the servants' hall, where he was bent over ironing *The Times*. He stood upright and straightened his fine round spectacle frames across the bridge of his long, beaked nose. So important was my induction into "the ways" that Mrs. Townsend had taken a rare break from preparing the luncheon galantine to bear witness. Mr. Hamilton inspected my uniform meticulously and then, apparently satisfied, began his lecture on the difference between us and them.

"Never forget," he said gravely, "you are fortunate indeed to be invited to serve in a great house such as this. And with good fortune comes responsibility. Your conduct in all matters reflects directly on the family and you must do them justice: keep their secrets and deserve their trust. Remember that the Master always knows best. Look to him, and his family, for example. Serve them silently . . . eagerly . . . gratefully. You will know your job is done well when it goes unnoticed, that *you* have succeeded when *you* are unnoticed." He lifted his gaze then and studied the space above my head, his ruddy skin flushed with emotion. "And Grace? Never forget the honor they do you, allowing you to serve in their home."

I can only imagine what Sylvia would have said to this. Certainly she wouldn't have received the address as I did; would not have felt her face constrict with gratitude and the vague, unnameable thrill of having been lifted up a step in the world.

I shift in my seat and notice she has left her photograph behind: this new man who woos her with talk of history, and who nurses a hobbyist's affection for the aristocracy. I know his type. They are the sort to keep scrapbooks of press clippings and photographs, to sketch elaborate family trees about families to which they have no entrée.

I sound contemptuous, but I am not. I am interested—intrigued even—by the way time erases real lives, leaving only vague imprints. Blood and spirit fade away so that only names and dates remain.

I close my eyes again. The sun has shifted and now my cheeks are warm.

The folk of Riverton have all been dead so long. While age has withered me, they remain eternally youthful, eternally beautiful.

There now. I am becoming maudlin and romantic. For they are neither young nor beautiful. They are dead. Buried. Nothing. Mere figments that flit within the memories of those they once knew.

But of course, those who live in memories are never really dead.

※

THE first time I saw Hannah and Emmeline and their brother David, they were debating the effects of leprosy on the human face. They had been at Riverton a week by then—their annual summer visit—but to that point I had caught only occasional wafts of laughter, tattoos of running feet amid the creaking bones of the old house.

Nancy had insisted I was too inexperienced to be trusted in polite society—juvenile though it might be—and had conferred on me only duties that distanced me from the visitors. While the other servants were preparing for the arrival of the adult guests a fortnight hence, I was responsible for the nursery.

They were too old, strictly, to need a nursery, said Nancy, and would probably never use it, but it was tradition, and thus the large second-floor room at the far end of the east wing was to be aired and cleaned, flowers replaced daily.

I can describe the room, but I fear any description will fail to capture the strange appeal it held for me. The room was large, rectangular and gloomy, and wore the pallor of decorous neglect. It gave the impression of desertion, of a spell in an ancient tale. It slept the sleep of a hundred-year curse. The air hung heavily, thick and cold and suspended; and in the doll's house by the fireplace the dining table was set for a party whose guests would never come.

The walls were covered in paper that might once have been blue and white stripe, but which time and moisture had turned murky gray, spotted and peeling in places. Faded scenes from Hans Christian Andersen hung along one side: the brave tin soldier atop his fire, the pretty girl in red shoes, the little mermaid weeping for her lost past. It smelled musty, of ghostly children and long-settled dust. Vaguely alive.

There was a sooty fireplace and a leather armchair at one end, huge arched windows on the adjacent wall. If I climbed up onto the dark timber window seat and peered down through the leadlight panes I could make out a courtyard where two bronze lions on weathered plinths stood guard, surveying the estate churchyard in the valley below.

A well-worn rocking horse rested by the window: a dignified dapple-gray with kind black eyes who seemed grateful for the dusting I gave him. And by his side, in silent communion, stood Raverley. The black and tan foxhound had been Lord Ashbury's when he was a boy; had died after getting his leg stuck in a trap. The embalmer had made a good attempt to patch the damage, but no amount of pretty dressing could hide what lurked beneath. I took to covering Raverley while I worked. With a dustsheet draped over him I could almost pretend he wasn't there, looking out at me with his dull glassy eyes, wound gaping beneath his patch.

But despite it all—Raverley, the smell of slow decay, the peeling paper—the nursery became my favorite room. Day after day, as predicted, I found it empty, the children engaged elsewhere on the estate. I took to rushing through my regular duties so that I might have a few spare minutes in which to linger, alone. Away from Nancy's constant corrections, from Mr. Hamilton's grim reproval, from the rowdy camaraderie of the other servants that made me feel I had so much still to learn. I stopped holding my breath, began to take the solitude for granted. To think of it as my room.

And then there were the books, so many books, more than I had ever seen in one place at one time: adventures, histories, fairytales, jostled together on huge shelves on either side of the fireplace. Once I dared pull one down, selected for no better reason than a particularly pretty spine. I ran my hand over the musty cover, opened it and read the carefully printed name: TIMOTHY HARTFORD. Then I turned the thick pages, breathed mildewed dust and was transported to another place and time.

I had learned to read at the village school and my teacher, Miss Ruby, pleased I expect to encounter such uncommon student interest, had started loaning me books from her own collection: *Jane Eyre*, *Frankenstein*, *The Castle of Otranto*. When I returned them we would discuss our favorite parts. It was Miss Ruby who suggested I might become a teacher myself. Mother had been none too pleased when I told her. She'd said it was all very well for Miss Ruby to go putting grand ideas in my head, but ideas didn't put bread and butter on the table. Not long afterwards she'd sent me up the hill to Riverton, to Nancy and Mr. Hamilton, and to the nursery . . .

And for a time the nursery was my room, the books my books.

But one day a fog blew in and it began to rain. As I hurried along the corridor with half a mind to look at an illustrated children's encyclopedia I'd discovered the day before, I stopped short. There were voices inside.

It was the wind, I told myself, carrying them from elsewhere in the house. An illusion. But when I cracked open the door and peeked inside: shock. There were people in there. Young people who fitted perfectly in that enchanting room.

And in that instant, with neither sign nor ceremony, it ceased to be mine. I stood, frozen by indecision, unsure whether it was proper to continue my duties or to return later. I peeked again, made timid by their laughter. Their confident, round voices. Their shiny hair and shinier hair bows.

It was the flowers that decided me. They were wilting in their vase atop the fire mantel. Petals had dropped in the night and now lay scattered like a rebuke. I couldn't risk Nancy seeing them; she had been clear on my duties. Had made certain I understood that Mother would learn if I were to run foul of my superiors.

Remembering Mr. Hamilton's instructions, I clutched my brush and broom to my chest and tiptoed to the fireside, concentrated on being invisible. I needn't have worried. They were used to sharing their homes with an army of the unseen. They ignored me while I pretended to ignore them.

Two girls and a boy: the youngest around ten, the eldest not yet seventeen. All three shared the distinctive Ashbury coloring—golden hair and eyes the fine, clear blue of Ceylonese sapphires—the legacy of Lord Ashbury's mother, a Dane who (so said Nancy) had married for love and been disowned, her dowry withdrawn. (She'd had the last laugh though, said Nancy, when her husband's brother passed away and she became Lady Ashbury of the British Empire.)

The taller girl stood in the center of the room, wielding a handful of papers as she described the niceties of leprous infections. The younger sat on the floor, legs crossed, watching her sister with widening blue eyes, her arm draped absently around Raverley's neck. I was surprised, and a little horrified, to see he had been dragged from his corner and was enjoying a rare moment of inclusion. The boy knelt on the window seat, gazing down through the fog towards the churchyard.

"And then you turn around to face the audience, Emmeline, and your face will be completely leprous," the taller girl said gleefully.

"I don't see why I have to be the one to get leprosy," Emmeline said.

"Take it up with God," Hannah said. "He wrote it."

"But why do I have to play Miriam? Can't I play a different part?"

"There are no other parts," Hannah said. "David has to be Aaron, because he's the tallest, and I'm playing God."

"Can't I be God?"

"Certainly not. I thought you wanted the main part."

"I did," Emmeline said. "I do."

"Well then. God doesn't even get to be onstage," Hannah said. "I have to do my lines from behind a curtain."

"I could play Moses," Emmeline said. "Raverley can be Miriam."

"You're not playing Moses," Hannah said. "We need a real Miriam. She's far more important than Moses. He only has one line. That's why Raverley's standing in. I can say his line from behind my curtain—I may even cut Moses altogether."

"Perhaps we could do another scene instead," Emmeline said hopefully. "One with Mary and the baby Jesus?"

Hannah huffed disgustedly.

They were rehearsing a play. Alfred the footman had told me there was to be a family recital on the bank-holiday weekend. It was a tradition: some family members sang, others recited poetry, the children always performed a scene from their grandmother's favorite book.

"We've chosen this scene because it's important," said Hannah.

"*You've* chosen it because it's important," said Emmeline.

"Exactly," said Hannah. "It's about a father having two sets of rules: one for his sons and one for his daughters."

"Sounds perfectly reasonable to me," said David ironically.

Hannah ignored him. "Both Miriam and Aaron are guilty of the same thing: discussing their brother's marriage—"

"What were they saying?" Emmeline said.

"It's not important, they were just—"

"Were they saying mean things?"

"No, and it's not the point. The important thing is that God decides Miriam should be punished with leprosy while Aaron gets no worse than a talking-to. Does that sound fair to you, Emme?"

"Didn't Moses marry an African woman?" Emmeline said.

Hannah shook her head, exasperated. She did that a lot, I noticed. A fierce energy infused her every long-limbed movement, led her easily to frustration. Emmeline, by contrast, had the calculated posture of a doll come to life. Their features, similar when considered individually—two neat noses, two pairs of intense blue eyes, two pretty mouths—manifested themselves uniquely on each girl's face. Where Hannah gave the impression of a fairy queen—passionate, mysterious, compelling—Emmeline's was a more accessible beauty. Though still a child, there was something in the way her lips parted in repose that reminded me of a glamour photograph I had once seen when it fell from the pedlar's pocket.

"Well? He did, didn't he?" Emmeline said.

"Yes, Emme," David said, laughing. "Moses married an Ethiopian. Hannah's just frustrated that we don't share her passion for women's suffrage."

"Hannah! He doesn't mean it. You're not a suffragette. Are you?"

"Of course I am," Hannah said. "And so are you."

Emmeline lowered her voice. "Does Pa know? He'll be ever so cross."

"Pooh," said Hannah. "Pa's a kitten."

"A lion, more like," said Emmeline, lips trembling. "Please don't make him cross, Hannah."

"I shouldn't worry, Emme," said David. "Suffrage is all the fashion amongst society women at the moment."

Emmeline looked doubtful. "Fanny never said anything."

"Anyone who's anyone will be wearing a dinner jacket for her debut this season," said David.

Emmeline's eyes widened.

I listened from the bookshelves, wondering what it all meant. I wasn't exactly sure what suffrage was, but had a vague idea it might be a sort of illness, the likes of which Mrs. Nammersmith in the village had caught when she took her corset off at the Easter parade, and her husband had to take her to the hospital in London.

"You're a wicked tease," Hannah said. "Just because Pa is too unfair to let Emmeline and me go to school doesn't mean you should try to make us look stupid at every opportunity."

"I don't have to try," David said, sitting on the toy box and flicking a lock of hair from his eyes. I drew breath: he was beautiful and golden like his sisters. "Anyway, you're not missing much. School's overrated."

"Oh?" Hannah raised a suspicious eyebrow. "Usually you're only too pleased to let me know exactly what I'm missing. Why the sudden change of heart?" Her eyes widened: two ice-blue moons. Excitement laced her voice. "Don't tell me you've done something dreadful to get yourself expelled?"

"Course not," David said quickly. "I just think there's more to life than book-learning. My friend Hunter says that life itself is the best education—"

"Hunter?"

"He only started at Eton this form. His father's some sort of scientist. Evidently he discovered something that turned out to be quite important and the King made him a marquess. He's a bit mad. Robert, too, if you believe the other lads, but I think he's topping."

"Well," Hannah said, "your mad Robert Hunter is fortunate to have the luxury of disdaining his education, but how am I supposed to become a respected playwright if Pa insists on keeping me ignorant?" Hannah sighed with frustration. "I wish I were a boy."

"I should hate to go to school," Emmeline said. "And I should hate to be a boy. No dresses, the most boring hats, having to talk about sports and politics all day."

"I'd love to talk politics," Hannah said. Vehemence shook strands loose from the careful confinement of her ringlets. "I'd start by making Herbert Asquith give women the vote. Even young ones."

David smiled. "You could be Great Britain's first play-writing prime minister."

"Yes," said Hannah.

"I thought you were going to be an archaeologist," Emmeline said. "Like Gertrude Bell."

"Politician, archaeologist. I could be both. This is the twentieth century." She scowled. "If only Pa would let me have a proper education."

"You know what Pa says about girls' education," said David. Emmeline chimed in with the well-worn phrase: " 'The slippery slope to women's suffrage.' "

"Anyway, Pa says Miss Prince is giving us all the education we need," said Emmeline.

"Pa would say that. He's hoping she'll turn us into boring wives for boring fellows, speaking passable French, playing passable piano and politely losing the odd game of bridge. We'll be less trouble that way."

"Pa says no one likes a woman who thinks too much," Emmeline said.

David rolled his eyes. "Like that Canadian woman who drove him home from the gold mines with her talk of politics. She did us all a disservice."

"I don't *want* everyone to like me," Hannah said, setting her chin stubbornly. "I should think less of myself if no one disliked me."

"Then cheer up," David said. "I have it on good authority that a *number* of our friends don't like you."

Hannah frowned, its impact weakened by the involuntary beginnings of a smile. "Well, I'm not going to do any of her stinking lessons today. I'm tired of reciting *The Lady of Shalott* while she snivels into her handkerchief."

"She's crying for her own lost love," Emmeline said with a sigh.

Hannah rolled her eyes.

"It's true!" Emmeline said. "I heard Grandmama tell Lady Clem. Before she came to us, Miss Prince was engaged to be married."

"Came to his senses, I suppose," Hannah said.

"He married her sister instead," Emmeline said.

This silenced Hannah, but only briefly. "She should have sued him for breach of promise."

"That's what Lady Clem said—and worse—but Grandmama said Miss Prince didn't want to cause him trouble."

"Then she's a fool," Hannah said. "She's better off without him."

"What a romantic," David said archly. "The poor lady's hopelessly in love with a man she can't have and you begrudge reading her the occasional piece of sad poetry. Cruelty, thy name is Hannah."

Hannah set her chin. "Not cruel, practical. Romance makes people forget themselves, do silly things."

David was smiling: the amused smile of an elder brother who believed that time would change her.

"It's true," Hannah said, stubbornly. "Miss Prince would be better to stop pining and start filling her mind—and ours—with interesting things. Like the building of the pyramids, the lost city of Atlantis, the adventures of the Vikings . . ."

Emmeline yawned and David held up his hands in an attitude of surrender.

"Anyway," Hannah said, frowning as she picked up her papers, "we're wasting time. We'll go from the bit where Miriam gets leprosy."

"We've done it a hundred times," Emmeline said. "Can't we do something else?"

"Like what?"

Emmeline shrugged uncertainly. "I don't know." She looked from Hannah to David. "Couldn't we play The Game?"

No. It wasn't The Game then. It was just the game. A game. Emmeline might have been referring to conkers, or jacks, or marbles, for all I knew that morning. It wasn't for some time that The Game took on capital letters in my mind. That I came to associate the term with secrets and fancies and adventures unimagined. On that dull, wet morning, as the rain pattered against the nursery windowpanes, I barely gave it a thought.

Hidden behind the armchair sweeping up the dried and scattered petals, I was imagining what it might be like to have siblings. I had always longed for one. I had told Mother once, asked her whether I might have a sister. Someone with whom to gossip and plot, whisper and dream. Mother had laughed, but not in a happy way, and said she wasn't given to making the same mistake twice.

What must it feel like, I wondered, to belong somewhere, to face the world a member of a tribe, with ready-made allies? I was pondering this, brushing absently at the armchair, when something moved beneath my duster. A blanket flapped and a female voice croaked: "What? What's all this? Hannah? David?"

She was as old as age itself. An ancient woman, recessed amongst the cushions, hidden from view. This, I knew, must be Nanny Brown. I had heard her spoken of in hushed and reverent tones, both upstairs and down: she had nursed Lord Ashbury himself when he was a lad and was as much a family institution as the house itself.

I froze where I stood, duster in hand, under the gaze of three sets of pale blue eyes.

The old woman spoke again. "Hannah? What's going on?"

"Nothing, Nanny Brown," Hannah said, finding her tongue. "We're just rehearsing for the recital. We'll be quieter from now on."

"You mind Raverley doesn't get too frisky, cooped up inside," Nanny Brown said.

"No, Nanny Brown," Hannah said, her voice revealing a sensitivity to match her fierceness. "We'll make sure he's nice and quiet." She came forward and tucked the blanket back around the old lady's tiny form. "There, there, Nanny Brown, dear, you rest now."

"Well," Nanny Brown said sleepily, "maybe just for a little while." Her eyes fluttered shut and after a moment her breathing grew deep and regular.

I held my own breath, waiting for one of the children to speak. They were still looking at me, eyes wide. A slow instant passed, during which I envisaged myself being hauled before Nancy, or worse, Mr. Hamilton; called to explain how I came to be dusting Nanny Brown; the displeasure on Mother's face as I returned home, released without references . . .

But they did not scold, or frown, or reprove. They did something far more unexpected. As if on cue, they started to laugh, raucously, easily, collapsing into one another so that they seemed somehow joined.

I stood, watching and waiting, their reaction more disquieting than the silence that preceded it. I could not help my lip from trembling.

Finally, the elder girl managed to speak. "I'm Hannah," she said, wiping her eyes. "Have we met?"

I exhaled, curtsied. My voice was tiny. "No m'lady. I'm Grace."

Emmeline giggled. "She's not your lady. She's just miss."

I curtsied again. Avoided her gaze. "I'm Grace, miss."

"You look familiar," Hannah said. "Are you sure you weren't here at Easter?"

"Yes, miss. I just started. Going on for a month now."

"You don't look old enough to be a maid," Emmeline said.

"I'm fourteen, miss."

"Snap," Hannah said. "So am I. And Emmeline is ten and David is practically ancient—sixteen."

David spoke then. "And do you always clean right over the top of sleeping persons, Grace?" At this, Emmeline started to laugh again.

"Oh, no. No, sir. Just this once, sir."

"Pity," David said. "It would be rather convenient never to have to bathe again."

I was stricken; my cheeks filled with heat. I had never met a real gentleman before. Not one my age, not the sort who made my heart flutter against my ribcage with his talk of bathing. Strange. I am an old woman now, yet as I think of David I find the echoes of those old feelings creeping back. I am not dead yet then.

"Don't mind him," Hannah said. "He thinks he's a riot."

"Yes, miss."

She looked at me quizzically, as if about to say something more. But before she could there came the noise of quick, light footsteps rounding the stairs and beginning down the corridor. Drawing closer. *Clip, clip, clip, clip* . . .

Emmeline ran to the door and peered through the keyhole.

"It's Miss Prince," she said, looking to Hannah. "Coming this way."

"Quick!" Hannah said in a determined whisper. "Or suffer death by Tennyson."

There was a scurry of footsteps and a flurry of skirts and, before I realized what was happening, all three had vanished. The door burst open and a gust of cold, damp air swept through. A prim figure stood across the doorway.

She surveyed the room, her gaze landing finally on me. "You," she said. "Have you seen the children? They're late for their lessons. I've been waiting in the library ten minutes."

I was not a liar, and I cannot say what made me do it. But in that instant, as Miss Prince stood peering over her glasses at me, I did not think twice.

"No, Miss Prince," I said. "Not for a time."

"Is that so?"

"Yes, miss."

She held my gaze. "I was sure I heard voices in here."

"Only my own, miss. I was singing."

"Singing?"

"Yes, miss."

The silence seemed to stretch forever, broken only when Miss Prince tapped her blackboard pointer three times against her open hand and stepped into the room; began to walk slowly around its perimeter. *Clip . . . Clip . . . Clip . . . Clip . . .*

She reached the doll's house and I noticed the tail of Emmeline's sash ribbon protruding from its stand. I swallowed. "I . . . I might have seen them earlier, miss, now I think of it. Through the window. In the old boathouse. Down by the lake."

"Down by the lake," Miss Prince said. She had reached the French windows and stood gazing out into the fog, white light on her pale face. " 'Where willows whiten, aspens quiver, little breezes dusk and shiver . . .' "

I was unfamiliar with Tennyson at that time, thought only that she produced a rather pretty description of the lake. "Yes, miss," I said.

After a moment she turned. "I shall have the gardener retrieve them. What's his name?"

"Dudley, miss."

"I shall have Dudley retrieve them. We must not forget that punctuality is a virtue without peer."

"No, miss," I said, curtsying.

And she clipped coldly across the floor, closing the door behind her.

The children emerged as if by magic from beneath dustcloths, under the doll's house, behind the curtains.

Hannah smiled at me, but I did not linger. I could not understand what I had done. Why I had done it. I was confused, ashamed, exhilarated.

I curtsied and hurried past, cheeks burning as I flew along the corridor, anxious to find myself once more in the safety of the servants' hall, away from these strange, exotic child-adults and the odd feelings they aroused in me.

WAITING FOR THE RECITAL

I COULD hear Nancy calling my name as I raced down the stairs into the shadowy servants' hall. I paused at the bottom, letting my eyes adapt to the dimness, then hurried into the kitchen. A copper pot simmered on the huge stove and the air was salty with the sweat of boiled ham. Katie, the scullery maid, stood by the sink scrubbing pans, staring blindly at the steamy hint of a window. Mrs. Townsend, I guessed, was having her afternoon lie-down before the Mistress rang for tea. I found Nancy at the table in the servants' dining room, surrounded by vases, candelabras, platters and goblets.

"There you are, then," she said, frowning so that her eyes became two dark slits. "I was beginning to think I'd have to come looking for you." She indicated the seat opposite. "Well, don't just stand there, girl. Get yourself a cloth and help me polish."

I sat down and selected a plump milk jug that hadn't seen the light of day since the previous summer. I rubbed at the flecked spots, but my mind lingered in the nursery upstairs. I could imagine them laughing together, teasing, playing. I felt as though I had opened the cover of a beautiful, glossy book and become lost in the magic of its story, only to be forced too soon to put the book aside. You see? Already I had fallen under the spell of the Hartford children.

"Steady on," Nancy said, wresting the cloth from my hand. "That's His Lordship's best silver. You'd better hope Mr. Hamilton don't see you scratching it like that." She held aloft the vase she was cleaning and began to rub it in deliberate circular motions. "There now. See as how I'm doing it? Gentle like? All in the one direction?"

I nodded and set about the jug again. I had so many questions about the Hartfords: questions I felt sure Nancy could answer. And yet I was reluctant to ask. It was in her power, I knew, and her nature, I suspected, to ensure my future duties took me far from the nursery, if she supposed I was gaining pleasure beyond the satisfaction of a job well done.

Yet just as a new lover imbues ordinary objects with special meaning, I was greedy for the least information concerning them. I thought about my books, tucked away in their attic hideaway; the way Sherlock Holmes could make people say the last thing they expected through artful questioning. I took a deep breath. "Nancy . . . ?"

"Mmm?"

"What is Lord Ashbury's son like?"

Her dark eyes flashed. "Major Jonathan? Oh, he's a fine—"

"No," I said, "not Major Jonathan." I already knew about Major Jonathan. One couldn't pass a day in Riverton without learning of Lord Ashbury's elder son, most recent in a long line of Hartford males to attend Eton and then Sandhurst. His portrait hung next to that of his father (and the string of fathers before him) at the top of the front staircase, surveying the hall below: head aloft, medals gleaming, blue eyes cold. He was the pride of Riverton, both upstairs and down. A Boer War hero. The next Lord Ashbury.

No. I meant Frederick, the "Pa" they spoke of in the nursery, who seemed to inspire in them a mix of affection and awe. Lord Ashbury's second son, whose mere mention caused Lady Violet's friends fondly to shake their heads and His Lordship to grumble into his sherry.

Nancy opened her mouth and closed it again, like one of the fish the storms washed up on the lake bank. "Ask no questions and I'll tell you no lies," she said finally, holding her vase up to the light for inspection.

I finished the jug and moved on to a platter. This was how it was with Nancy. She was capricious in her own way: unreservedly forthcoming at some times, absurdly secretive at others.

Sure enough, for no other reason than the clock on the wall had ticked away five minutes, she acquiesced. "I suppose you've heard one of the footmen talking, have you? Alfred, I'll warrant. Terrible gossips, footmen." She started on another vase. Eyed me suspiciously. "Your mother's never told you about the family, then?"

I shook my head and Nancy arched a thin eyebrow in disbelief, as if it were near impossible that people might find things to discuss that didn't concern the family at Riverton.

In fact, Mother had always been resolutely close-lipped about business at the house. When I was younger I had probed her, eager for stories about the grand old manor on the hill. There were enough tales about in the village as it was and I was hungry for my own tit-bits to trade with the other children. But she only ever shook her head and reminded me that curiosity killed the cat.

Finally, Nancy spoke. "Mr. Frederick . . . where to begin about Mr. Frederick?" She resumed polishing, speaking through a sigh. "He's not a bad sort of fellow. Not at all like his brother, mind, not one for heroics, but not a bad sort. Truth be told, most of us downstairs have a fondness for him. To hear Mrs. Townsend talk he was always a scamp of a lad, full of tall stories and funny ideas. Always very kindly to the servants."

"Is it true he was a gold miner?" It seemed a suitably exciting profession. It was right somehow that the Hartford children should have an interesting father. My own had always been a disappointment: a faceless figure who vanished into thin air before I was born, rematerializing only in hot whispered exchanges between Mother and her sister.

"For a time," Nancy said. "He's turned his hand to that many things I've all but lost count. Never been much of a one for settling, our Mr. Frederick. Never one to take to other folks. First there was the tea planting in Ceylon, then the gold prospecting in Canada. Then he decided he was going to make his fortune printing newspapers. Now it's motorcars, God love him."

"Does he sell motorcars?"

"He makes them, or those that work for him do. He's bought a factory over Ipswich way."

"Ipswich. Is that where he lives? Him and his family?" I said, nudging the conversation in the direction of the children.

She didn't take the bait: was concentrated on her own thoughts. "With any luck he'll make a go of this one. Heaven knows His Lordship would look gladly on a return for his investment."

I blinked, her meaning lost on me. Before I could ask what she meant, she had swept on. "Anyway, you'll see him soon enough. He arrives next Tuesday, along with the Major and Lady Jemima." A rare smile, approval rather than pleasure. "The family always come together for the midsummer dinner."

"But, Nancy," I said; it had been troubling me all week, "it's August. Not midsummer at all."

She looked at me as if I'd just declared that a boiled egg wasn't square. "Well, of course it's August. Are you daft, girl? And the midsummer dinner will be held on the bank holiday weekend as it always has been. Just you mind Mr. Hamilton don't hear you questioning your betters."

I shook my head quickly.

"The celebrations are a little smaller these days—there hasn't been a midsummer ball in some time—but there's not one of the family would dream of missing the dinner. It's a tradition, along with the other festivities."

"Like the recital," I said, daringly, avoiding her gaze.

"So," Nancy raised a brow, "someone's already blathered to you about the recital, have they?"

I ignored her peevish note. Nancy was unaccustomed to being pipped at the rumor post. "Alfred said the servants were invited to see the recital," I said.

"Footmen!" Nancy shook her head haughtily. "Never listen to a footman if you want to hear the truth, my girl. Invited, indeed! Servants are *permitted* to see the recital, and very kind of the Master it is, too. He knows how much the family mean to all of us downstairs, how we enjoy seeing the young ones growing up." She returned her attention momentarily to the vase in her lap and I held my breath, willing her to continue. After a moment that seemed an age, she did. "This'll be the fourth year they've put on theatricals. Ever since Miss Hannah was ten and took it into her head she wanted to be a theatre director." Nancy nodded. "Aye, she's a character is Miss Hannah. She and her father are as like as two eggs."

"How?" I asked.

Nancy paused, considering this. "There's something of the wanderlust in each of them," she said finally. "Both full of wit and new-fangled ideas, each as stubborn as the other." She spoke pointedly, accenting each description, a warning to me that such traits, while acceptable idiosyncrasies for them upstairs, would not be tolerated from the likes of me.

I'd had such lectures all my life from Mother. I nodded sagely as she continued. "They get on famously most of the time, but when they don't there's not a soul don't know it. There's no one can rile Mr. Frederick quite like Miss Hannah. Even as a wee girl she knew just how to set him off. She was a fierce little thing, full of tempers. One time, I remember, she was awful dark at him for one reason or another and took it into her head to give him a nasty fright."

"What did she do?"

"Now let me think . . . Master David was out having riding instruction. That's what started it all. Miss Hannah were none too happy to have been left out, so she bundled up Miss Emmeline and gave Nanny Brown the slip. Found their way to the far estates, they did, right the way down where the farmers were harvesting apples." She shook her head. "Convinced Miss Emmeline to hide away in the barn, did our Miss Hannah. Wasn't hard to do, I imagine; Miss Hannah can be very persuasive, and besides, Miss Emmeline was quite happy with all them fresh apples to feast on. Next minute, Miss Hannah arrived back at the house, puffing and panting like she'd run for her life, calling for Mr. Frederick. I was laying for luncheon in the dining room at the time, and I heard Miss Hannah tell him that a couple of foreign men with dark skin had found them in the orchards. Said they'd commented on how pretty Miss Emmeline was and promised to take her on a long journey across the seas. Miss Hannah said she couldn't be sure, but she believed them to be white slavers."

I gasped, shocked by Hannah's daring. "What happened then?"

Nancy, portentous with secrets, warmed to the telling. "Well, Mr. Frederick's always been wary of the white slavers, and his face went first white, then all red, and before you could count to three he scooped Miss Hannah into his arms and set off towards the orchards. Bertie Timmins, who was picking apples that day, said Mr. Frederick arrived in a terrible state. He started yelling orders to form a search party, that Miss Emmeline had been kidnapped by two dark-skinned men. They searched high and low, spreading out in all directions, but no one had seen two dark-skinned men and a golden-haired child."

"How did they find her?"

"They didn't. In the end she found them. After an hour or so, Miss Emmeline, bored with hiding and sick from apples, came strolling from the barn wondering about all the fuss. Why Miss Hannah hadn't come to get her . . ."

"Was Mr. Frederick very cross?"

"Oh yes," Nancy said matter-of-factly, polishing fiercely. "Though not for long: never could stay dark with her for long. They've a bond, those two. She'd have to do more'n that to set him against her." She held aloft the glistening vase, then placed it with the other polished items. Laid her cloth on the table and tilted her head, giving her thin neck a rub. "Anyways, as I hear it, Mr. Frederick was just getting a bit of his own medicine."

"Why?" I asked. "What did he do?"

Nancy glanced towards the kitchen, satisfying herself that Katie was out of earshot. There was a well-worn pecking order downstairs at Riverton, refined and ingrained by centuries of service. I may have been the lowest housemaid, subject to regular dressing-downs, worthy of only the lesser duties, but Katie, as scullery maid, was beneath contempt. I would like to be able to say this groundless inequity riled me; that I was, if not incensed, at least alert to its injustice. But to do so would be crediting my young self with empathy I did not possess. Rather, I relished what little privilege my place afforded me—Lord knows there were enough above me.

"Gave his parents quite a time when he was a lad, did our Mr. Frederick," she said through tight lips. "He was such a livewire Lord Ashbury sent him to Radley just so he couldn't give his brother a bad name at Eton. Wouldn't let him try for Sandhurst neither, when the time came, even though he was that set on joining the army."

I digested this information as Nancy continued. "Understandable, of course, with Major Jonathan doing so well in the forces. It doesn't take much to stain a family's good name. Wasn't worth the risk." She left off rubbing her neck and seized a tarnished salt dish. "Anyway. All's well that end's well. He's got his motorcars, and he's got himself three fine children. You'll see for yourself at the play."

"Will Major Jonathan's children be performing in the play with Mr. Frederick's?"

Nancy's expression darkened and her voice lowered. "Whatever can you be thinking, girl?"

The air bristled. I had said something wrong. Nancy glowered at me, forcing me to look away. The platter in my hands had been polished till it shone and in its surface I saw my cheeks growing redder.

Nancy hissed, "The Major doesn't have any children. Not any more." She snatched my cloth from me, long, thin fingers brushing mine. "Now, get on with you. I'm getting naught done with all your talk."

※

OVER the next couple of weeks I avoided Nancy as best one person can avoid another with whom they live and work. At night, as she

45

prepared for bed, I lay very still facing the wall, feigning sleep. It was a relief when she blew out the candle and the picture of the dying deer disappeared into the darkness. In the daytime, when we passed in the hall, Nancy would lift her nose disdainfully and I would study the floor, suitably chastened.

Blessedly, there was plenty to keep us occupied preparing to receive Lord Ashbury's adult guests. The east-wing guestrooms had to be opened and aired, the dustsheets removed and the furniture polished. The best linen had to be retrieved from enormous storage boxes in the attic, inspected for flaws, then laundered. The rain had set in and the clothes lines behind the house were of no use, so Nancy told me to drape the sheets over the clothes horses in the upstairs linen room.

And that is where I learned more of The Game. For as the rain held, and Miss Prince determined to educate them on the finer points of Tennyson, the Hartford children sought hiding spots deeper and deeper within the house's heart. The linen-room closet, tucked behind the chimney, was about as far from the library schoolroom as they could find. And there they took up quarters.

I never saw them play it, mind. Rule number one: The Game is secret. But I listened and, once or twice when temptation drove me and the coast was clear, I peeked inside the box. This is what I learned.

The Game was old. They'd been playing it for years. No, not playing. That is the wrong verb. Living; they had been living The Game for years. For The Game was more than its name suggested. It was a complex fantasy, an alternate world into which they escaped.

There were no costumes, no swords, no feathered headdresses. Nothing that would have marked it as a game. For that was its nature. It was secret. Its only accoutrement was the box. A black lacquered case brought back from China by one of their ancestors; one of the spoils from a spree of exploration and plunder. It was the size of a square hatbox—not too big and not too small—and its lid was inlaid with semiprecious gems to form a scene: a river with a bridge across it, a small temple on one bank, a willow weeping from the sloping shore. Three figures stood atop the bridge and above them a lone bird circled.

They guarded the box jealously, filled as it was with everything material to The Game. For although The Game demanded a good deal of running and hiding and wrestling, its real pleasure was enjoyed elsewhere. Rule number two: all journeys, adventures, explorations and sightings must be recorded. They would rush inside, flushed with danger, to record their recent adventures: maps and diagrams, codes and drawings, plays and books.

The books were miniature, bound with thread, writing so small and neat that one had to hold them close to decipher them. They had titles: *Escape from Koshchei the Deathless*; *Encounter with Balam and His Bear*; *Journey to the Land of White Slavers*. Some were written in code I couldn't understand, though the legend, had I had the time to look, would no doubt have been printed on parchment and filed within the box.

The Game itself was simple. It was Hannah and David's invention really, and as the oldest they were its chief instigators. They decided which location was ripe for exploration. The two of them had assembled a ministry of nine advisers—an eclectic group mingling eminent Victorians with ancient Egyptian kings. There were only ever nine advisers at any one time, and when history supplied a new figure too appealing to be denied inclusion, an original member would die or be deposed. (Death was always in the line of duty, reported solemnly in one of the tiny books kept inside the box.)

Alongside the advisers, each had their own character. Hannah was Nefertiti and David was Charles Darwin. Emmeline, only four when the governing laws were drawn up, had chosen Queen Victoria. A dull choice, Hannah and David agreed, understandable given Emmeline's limited years, but certainly not a suitable adventure mate. Victoria was nonetheless accommodated into The Game, most often cast as a kidnap victim whose capture was precipitant of a daring rescue. While the other two were writing up their accounts, Emmeline was allowed to decorate the diagrams and shade the maps: blue for the ocean, purple for the deep, green and yellow for land.

Occasionally, David wasn't available—the rain would subside for an hour and he would sneak out to play marbles with the other estate lads, or else he would occupy himself practising the piano. Then Hannah would realign her loyalties with Emmeline. The pair would hide away in the linen closet with a stash of sugar cubes from Mrs. Townsend's dry store, and would invent special names in secret languages to describe the traitorous absconder. But no matter how much they wanted to, they never played The Game without him. To do so would have been unthinkable.

Rule number three: only three may play. No more, no less. Three. A number favored as much by art as by science: primary colors, points required to locate an object in space, notes to form a musical chord. Three points of a triangle, the first geometrical figure. Incontrovertible fact: two straight lines cannot enclose a space. The points of a triangle may move, shift allegiance, the distance between two disappear as they draw away from the third, but together they always define a triangle. Self-contained, real, complete.

The Game's rules I learned because I read them. Written in neat but childish handwriting on yellowing paper, stuck beneath the lid of the box. I will remember them forever. To these rules, each had put their name. *By general agreement, this third day of April, 1908. David Hartford, Hannah Hartford*, and finally, in larger, more abstract print, the initials *E.H.* Rules are a serious business for children, and The Game required a sense of duty adults wouldn't understand. Unless of course they were servants, in which case duty was something they knew a lot about.

So there it is. It was just a children's game. And not the only one they played. Eventually they outgrew it, forgot it, left it behind. Or thought they did. By the time I met them it was already on its last legs. History was about to intervene: real adventure, real escape and adulthood were lurking, laughing, round the corner.

Just a children's game and yet . . . What happened in the end would surely not have come about without it?

※

T H E day of the guests' arrival dawned and I was given special permission, on condition my duties were complete, to watch from the first-floor balcony. As outside evening fell, I huddled by the banister, face pressed between two rails, eagerly awaiting the crunch of motorcar tires on the gravel out front.

First to arrive was Lady Clementine de Welton, a family friend with the grandeur and gloom of the late Queen, and her charge Miss Frances Dawkins (universally known as Fanny): a skinny, garrulous girl whose parents had gone down with the *Titanic* and who, at seventeen, was rumored to be in energetic pursuit of a husband. According to Nancy, it was Lady Violet's dearest wish that Fanny should make a match with the widowed Mr. Frederick, though the latter remained entirely unconvinced.

Mr. Hamilton led them to the drawing room, where Lord and Lady Ashbury were waiting, and announced their arrival with a flourish. I watched from behind as they disappeared into the room— Lady Clementine first, Fanny close behind—and was put in mind of Mr. Hamilton's salver of cocktail glasses on which the brandy balloons and champagne flutes jostled for space.

Mr. Hamilton returned to the entrance hall and was straightening his cuffs—a gesture that was a habit with him—when the Major and his wife arrived. She was a small, plump, brown-haired woman whose face, though kindly, bore the cruel etchings of grief. It is hindsight, of course, that makes me describe her thus, though even at the time I supposed her the victim of some misfortune. Nancy may not have been prepared to divulge the mystery of the Major's children, but my young imagination, fed as it was on Gothic novels, was a fertile place. Besides, the nuances of attraction between a man and a woman were foreign to me then and I reasoned that only tragedy could account for such a tall, handsome man as the Major being married to so plain a woman. She must once have been lovely, I supposed, until some fiendish hardship befell them and seized from her whatever youth or beauty she possessed.

The Major, even sterner than his portrait allowed, asked customarily after Mr. Hamilton's health, cast a proprietorial glance over the entrance hall and led Jemima to the drawing room. As they disappeared behind the door I saw that his hand rested tenderly at the base of her spine, a gesture that somehow belied his severe physical bearing, and which I have never quite forgotten.

My legs had grown stiff from crouching when finally Mr. Frederick's motorcar crunched along the gravel of the driveway. Mr. Hamilton glanced reprovingly at the hall clock, then pulled open the front door.

Mr. Frederick was shorter than I expected, certainly not so tall as his brother, and I could make out no more of his features than the rim of a pair of glasses. For even when his hat was taken he did not raise his head. Merely ran his hand tentatively over the top to smooth his fair hair.

Only when Mr. Hamilton opened the drawing-room door and announced his arrival did Mr. Frederick's attention flicker from his purpose. His gaze skittered about the room, taking in the marble, the portraits, the home of his youth, before alighting finally on my balcony. And in the brief moment before he was swallowed by the noisy room, his face paled as if he'd seen a ghost.

※

T H E week passed quickly. With so many extra people in the house, I was kept busy making up rooms, carrying tea trays, laying out luncheons. This pleased me well as I was not shy of hard work—Mother had made sure of that. Besides, I longed for the weekend to arrive and with it the bank-holiday play recital. For while the rest of the staff was focused on the late-summer dinner, all I could think of was the recital. I had barely seen the children since the adults arrived. The fog blew away as suddenly as it came, leaving in its place warm, clear skies too beautiful to waste indoors. Each day, as I rounded the corridor towards the nursery, I held my breath hopefully, but the fine weather was to hold and they were not to use the room again that year. They took their noise and their mischief and their Game outside.

And with them went the room's enchantment. Stillness became emptiness and the small flame of pleasure I had nurtured was extinguished. I hurried my duties now, straightened the bookshelves without so much as a glance at their contents, no longer caught the horse's eye; thought only of what they might be doing. And when I was finished I didn't linger, but moved on swiftly to complete my duties. Occasionally, when I was clearing the breakfast tray from a second-floor guestroom or disposing of the night-waters, a squeal of distant laughter would draw my eyes to the window and I would see them, far off in the distance, heading towards the lake, disappearing down the driveway, dueling with long straight sticks.

Downstairs, Mr. Hamilton had stirred the servants into a frenzy of activity. It was the test of a good staff, he said, not to mention the proof of a butler's mettle, to serve a household of guests. No request was to prove too much. We were to work as a finely oiled locomotive, rising to meet each challenge, exceeding the Master's every expectation. It was to be a week of small triumphs, culminating in the late-summer dinner.

Mr. Hamilton's fervor was infectious; even Nancy suffered an elevation of spirits and called a truce of sorts, offering, grudgingly, that I might help her clean the drawing room. It wasn't ordinarily my place, she reminded me, to be cleaning the main rooms, but with the Master's family visiting I was to be allowed the privilege—under strict observation—to practise these advanced duties. So it was that I added this dubious opportunity to my already inflated duty load and accompanied Nancy daily to the drawing room, where the adults sipped tea and discussed things that interested me little: weekend country parties, European politics and some unfortunate Austrian fellow who'd been shot in a faraway place.

The day of the recital (Sunday, 2 August 1914—I remember the date, though not for the recital as much as what came after) coincided with my afternoon off and my first visit to Mother since I'd started at Riverton. When I'd finished my morning duties I exchanged my uniform for regular clothes, strangely stiff and unfamiliar on my body. I brushed my hair out—pale and kinky where it had been twisted in its plait—then set about rebraiding, coiling a bun at the nape of my neck. Did I look any different, I wondered? Would Mother think so? It had only been five weeks and yet I felt inexplicably changed.

As I came down the servants' stairs and into the kitchen I was met by Mrs. Townsend who thrust a bundle into my hands. "Go on then, take it. Just a little something for your mother's tea," she said in a hushed voice. "Some of my lemon-curd tart and a couple of slices of Victoria sponge."

I glanced towards the staircase, dropped my own voice to a whisper. "But are you sure the Mistress—"

"You never mind about the Mistress. She and Lady Clementine won't be left wanting." She dusted down her apron, pulled her round shoulders to full height so that her chest seemed even more expansive than usual. "You just be sure an' tell your mother we're looking out for you up here." She shook her head. "Fine girl, your mother. Guilty of nothing that ain't been done a thousand times before."

Then she turned and bustled back to the kitchen as suddenly as she'd appeared. Leaving me alone in the darkened hallway, wondering what she'd meant.

I turned it over in my mind all the way to the village. It was not the first time Mrs. Townsend had perplexed me with an expression of fondness for my mother. My own puzzlement left me feeling disloyal, but there was little in her reminiscences of good humor that could be accorded with the Mother I knew. Mother with her moods and silences.

❦

SHE was waiting for me on the doorstep. Stood as she caught sight of me. "I was beginning to think you'd forgotten me."

"Sorry, Mother," I said. "I was caught up with my duties."

"Hope you made time for church this morning."

"Yes, Mother. The staff go to service at the Riverton church."

"I know that, my girl. I attended service at that church long before you came along." She nodded at my hands. "What's that you've got?"

I handed over the bundle. "From Mrs. Townsend. She was asking after you."

Mother peeked within the bundle, bit the inside of her cheek. "I'll be sure and have heartburn tonight." She rewrapped it, said grudgingly, "Still, it's good of her." She stood aside, pushed back the door. "Come on in, then. You can make me up a pot of tea and tell me what's been happening."

I cannot remember much of which we spoke, for I was an unconscientious conversationalist that afternoon. My mind was not with Mother in her tiny, cheerless kitchen, but up in the ballroom on the hill, where earlier I had helped Nancy arrange chairs into rows and hang gold curtains around the proscenium arch . . .

I was already late when we said our goodbyes. By the time I reached the Riverton gates the sun was low in the sky. I wove along the narrow road towards the house. Magnificent trees, the legacy of Lord Ashbury's distant ancestors, lined the way, their highest boughs arching to meet, outermost branches lacing so that the road became a dark, whispering tunnel.

As I burst into the light that afternoon, the sun had just slipped

53

behind the roofline and the house was in eclipse, the sky behind glowing mauve and orange. I cut across the grounds, past the Eros and Psyche fountain, through Lady Violet's garden of pink cabbage roses and down into the rear entrance. The servants' hall was empty and my shoes echoed as I broke Mr. Hamilton's golden rule and ran along the stone corridor. Through the kitchen I went, past Mrs. Townsend's workbench covered with a panoply of sweet breads and cakes, and up the stairs.

The house was eerily quiet, everyone already in attendance. When I reached the gilded ballroom door, I smoothed my hair, straightened my skirt and slipped inside the darkened room; I took my place on the side wall with the other servants.

ALL GOOD THINGS

I HADN'T realized the room would be so dark. It was the first recital I had ever attended, though I had once seen part of a Punch and Judy show when Mother took me to visit her sister, Dee, in Brighton. Black curtains had been draped across the windows and the room's only brightness came from four limelights retrieved from the attic. They glowed yellow along the front of the stage, casting light upwards and glazing the performers in a ghostly shimmer.

Fanny was onstage singing the final bars of "The Wedding Glide," batting her eyelids and trilling her notes. She hit the final G with a strident F and the audience broke into a round of polite applause. She smiled and curtsied coyly, her coquetry undermined somewhat by the curtain behind bulging excitedly with elbows and props belonging to the next act.

As Fanny exited stage right, Emmeline and David—draped in togas—entered stage left. They brought with them three long timber poles and a sheet, which were quickly arranged to form a serviceable, though lopsided, tent. They knelt beneath, holding their positions as a hush fell over the audience.

A voice came from beyond: "Ladies and gentlemen. A scene from the Book of Numbers."

A murmur of approval.

The voice: "Imagine if you will, in ancient times, a family camped on a mountainside. A sister and brother gather in private to discuss the recent marriage of their brother."

A round of light applause.

Then Emmeline spoke, voice buzzing with self-importance. "But, brother, what has Moses done?"

"He has taken a wife," said David, rather drolly.

"But she is not one of us," said Emmeline, eyeing the audience.

"No," said David. "You are right, sister. For she is an Ethiopian."

Emmeline shook her head, adopting an expression of exaggerated concern. "He has married outside the clan. Whatever will become of him?"

Suddenly a loud, clear voice from behind the curtain, amplified as if travelling through space (more likely a rolled-up piece of cardboard), "Aaron! Miriam!"

Emmeline gave her best performance of fearful attention.

"This is God. Your father. Come out ye two unto the tabernacle of the congregation."

Emmeline and David did as they were told, shuffling from beneath the teepee to the front of the stage. Flickering limelights threw an army of shadows onto the sheet behind.

My eyes had adjusted to the dark and I was able to identify certain members of the audience by their familiar shapes. In the front row of finely dressed ladies, Lady Clementine's tumbling jowls and Lady Violet's feathered hat. A couple of rows behind, the Major and his wife. Closer to me, Mr. Frederick, head high, legs crossed, eyes focused sharply ahead. I studied his profile. He looked different somehow. The flickering half-light gave his high cheekbones a cadaverous appearance and his eyes the look of glass. His eyes. He wasn't wearing glasses. I had never seen him without.

The Lord began to deliver his judgement, and I returned my attention to the stage. "Miriam and Aaron. Wherefore were ye not afraid to speak against my servant Moses?"

"We're sorry, Father," said Emmeline. "We were just—"

"Enough! My anger is kindled against thee!"

There was a burst of thunder (a drum, I think) and the audience jumped. A cloud of smoke plumed from behind the curtain, spilling over onto the stage.

Lady Violet exclaimed and David said, in a stage whisper, "It's all right, Grandmama. It's part of the show."

A ripple of amused laughter.

"My anger is kindled against thee!" Hannah's voice was fierce, bringing the audience to silence. "Daughter," she said, and Emmeline turned away from the audience to gaze into the dissipating cloud. "Thou! Art! Leprous!"

Emmeline's hands flew to her face. "No!" she cried. She held a dramatic pose before turning to the audience to reveal her condition.

A collective gasp; they had decided against using a mask, opting instead for a handful of strawberry jam and cream, smeared to gruesome effect.

"Those imps," came Mrs. Townsend's aggrieved whisper. "They told me they was needing jam for their scones!"

"Son," said Hannah after a suitably dramatic pause, "thou art guilty of the same sin, and yet I cannot bring myself to anger at you."

"Thank you, Father," said David.

"Wilt thou remember not to discuss your brother's wife again?"

"Yes, my Lord."

"Then you may go."

"Alas, my Lord," said David, hiding a smile as he extended his arm towards Emmeline. "I beseech thee, heal my sister now."

The audience was silent, awaiting the Lord's response. "No," it came, "I don't think I will. She will be shut out from camp for seven days. Only then will she be received again."

As Emmeline sank to her knees and David laid his hand on her shoulder, Hannah appeared from stage left. The audience drew breath as one. She was dressed immaculately in men's clothing: a suit, top hat, walking cane, fob watch and, on the bridge of her nose, Mr. Frederick's glasses. She walked to center stage, twirling her cane like a dandy. Her voice, when she spoke, was an excellent imitation of her father's. "My daughter will learn that there are some rules for girls and others for boys." She took a deep breath, straightened her hat. "To allow otherwise is to start down the slippery slope to women's suffrage."

The audience sat in electric silence, row on row, mouths agape.

My eyes sought Mr. Frederick. Still in his seat, he was rigid as a barge pole. As I watched, his shoulders began to twitch and I feared he was on the verge of one of the rages to which Nancy had alluded. Onstage, the children stood, frozen in a tableau like dolls in a doll's house, watching the audience while the audience watched them.

Hannah was a model of composure, innocence writ large across her face. For an instant it seemed she caught my eye, and I thought the glimmer of a smile crossed her lips. I could not help it, I smiled back, fearfully, only stopping when Nancy glanced sideways in the dark and gave my arm a pinch.

Hannah, glowing, joined hands with Emmeline and David, and the three stretched out across the stage and took a bow. As they did, a glob of jam-smeared cream dropped from Emmeline's nose and landed with a sizzle on a nearby limelight.

"Just so," came a high fluty voice from the audience—Lady Clementine. "A fellow I know knew a fellow with leprosy, out in India. His nose dropped off just like that in his shaving dish."

It was too much for Mr. Frederick. His eyes met Hannah's and he began to laugh. Such a laugh as I had never heard: infectious by virtue of its sheer sincerity. One by one, others joined him, though Lady Violet, I noticed, was not amongst them.

I couldn't help my own laughter, spontaneous ripples of relief, until Nancy hissed into my ear, "That's enough, miss. You can come and help me with supper."

I would miss the rest of the recital, but I had seen all I wanted to. As we left the room and made our way down the corridor, I was aware of the applause dying, the recital rolling on. And I felt infused by a strange energy.

❦

B Y the time we had carried Mrs. Townsend's supper and the trays of tea to the drawing room and given the armchair cushions a preparatory plump, the recital had ended and the guests had started to arrive, arm in arm in order of rank. First came Lady Violet and Major Jonathan, then Lord Ashbury and Lady Clementine, then Mr. Frederick with Jemima and Fanny. The Hartford children, I guessed, were still upstairs.

As they took their places, Nancy arranged the tea tray so Lady Violet could pour. While her guests chatted lightly around her, Lady Violet leaned towards Mr. Frederick's armchair and said, through a thin smile, "You indulge those children, Frederick."

Mr. Frederick's lips tightened. The criticism, I could tell, was not a new one.

Eyes on the tea she was pouring, Lady Violet said, "You may find their antics amusing now, but the day will come when you'll rue your leniency. You've let them grow wild. Hannah, especially. There's nothing spoils a young lady's loveliness so much as impertinence of intellect."

Her invective delivered, Lady Violet straightened, arranged her expression into one of cordial amiability and passed a cup to Lady Clementine.

Conversation had turned, predictably enough, to the strife in Europe and the likelihood of Great Britain going to war.

"There'll be war. There always is," Lady Clementine said, matter-of-factly, taking the proffered cup and wedging her buttocks deep into Lady Violet's favorite armchair. Her pitch rose. "And we'll all suffer. Men, women and children. The Germans aren't civilized like us. They'll pillage our countryside, murder our little ones in their beds and enslave good English women that we might propagate little

Huns for them. You mark my words, for I'm very rarely wrong. We'll be at war before the summer's out."

"Surely you exaggerate, Clementine," Lady Violet said. "The war—if it comes—couldn't be as bad as all that. These are modern times, after all."

"That's right," Lord Ashbury said. "It'll be twentieth-century warfare; a whole new game. Not to mention there's not a Hun could lift a torch to an Englishman."

"It might be improper to say," Fanny said, perching herself at one end of the chaise longue, curls shaking excitedly, "but I rather hope the war *does* come." She turned hastily to Lady Clementine. "Not all the pillaging and killing of course, Aunty, nor the propagating; I shouldn't like that. But I do so love seeing gentlemen dressed in uniform." She cast a furtive glance towards Major Jonathan, then returned her attention to the group. "I had a letter today from my friend Margery . . . You remember Margery, don't you, Aunty Clem?"

Lady Clementine quivered her heavy eyelids. "Regrettably. A foolish girl with provincial manners." She leaned towards Lady Violet. "Raised in Dublin, you know. Irish Catholic, no less."

I peeked at Nancy, offering sugar cubes, and noticed her back stiffen. She caught my glance and shot me a hot scowl.

"Well," Fanny continued, "Margery's holidaying with family by the seaside and she said when she met her mother at the station, the trains were absolutely packed with reservists rushing back to their headquarters. It's ever so exciting."

"Fanny darling," Lady Violet said, "I do think it's rather in poor taste to wish a war merely for excitement. Wouldn't you agree, Jonathan dear?"

The Major, standing by the unlit fire, straightened himself. "While I don't agree with Fanny's motivation, I must say I share her sentiment. I for one hope we do go to war. The whole continent's got itself into a *damnable* mess—excuse my strong language, Mother,

Lady Clem, but it has. They need good old Britannia to get in there and sort it out. Give those Huns a jolly good shake-up."

A general cheer went up around the room and Jemima clasped the Major's arm, gazed up adoringly, button eyes aglow.

Old Lord Ashbury puffed his pipe excitedly. "A bit of sport," he proclaimed, leaning back against his chair. "Nothing like a war to sort the men from the boys."

Mr. Frederick shifted in his seat, took the tea that Lady Violet offered and set about loading tobacco into his pipe.

"What about you, Frederick?" Fanny said coyly. "What will you do if war comes? You won't stop making motorcars, will you? It would be such a shame if there were no more lovely motorcars just because of a silly war. I shouldn't like to go back to using a carriage."

Mr. Frederick, embarrassed by Fanny's flirtation, plucked a stray piece of tobacco from his trouser leg. "I shouldn't worry. Motorcars are the way of the future." He tamped his pipe and murmured to himself, "God forbid a war should inconvenience senseless ladies with little to do."

At that moment the door opened and Hannah, Emmeline and David spilled into the room, faces still lit with exhilaration. The girls had changed from their costumes and were back in matching white dresses with sailor collars.

"Jolly good show," Lord Ashbury said. "Couldn't hear a word of it, but jolly good show."

"Well done, children," Lady Violet said. "Though perhaps you'll let Grandmama help with the selection next year?"

"And you, Pa?" said Hannah eagerly. "Did you enjoy the play?"

Mr. Frederick avoided his mother's gaze. "We'll discuss the more creative parts later, eh?"

"And what about you, David?" trilled Fanny above the others. "We were just talking of the war. Will you be joining up if Britain enters? I think you'd make a dashing officer."

David took a cup from Lady Violet and sat down. "I hadn't

thought about it." He wrinkled his nose. "I suppose I will. They say it's a fellow's one chance for a grand adventure." He eyed Hannah with a twinkle in his eye, perceiving the opportunity for a tease. "Strictly for lads I'm afraid, Hannah."

Fanny shrieked with laughter, causing Lady Clementine's eyelids to quiver. "Oh David, how silly. Hannah wouldn't want to go to war. How ridiculous."

"I certainly should," Hannah said fiercely.

"But my dear," Lady Violet said, flummoxed, "you wouldn't have any clothes to fight in."

"She could wear jodhpurs and riding boots," Fanny said.

"Or a costume," Emmeline said. "Like the one she wore in the play. Though maybe not the hat."

Mr. Frederick caught his mother's censorious look and cleared his throat. "While Hannah's sartorial dilemma makes for scintillating speculation, I must remind you it's not a moot point. Neither she nor David will be going to war. Girls do not fight and David has not yet finished his studies. He'll find some other way to serve King and country." He turned to David. "When you've completed Eton, been to Sandhurst, it'll be a different matter."

David's chin set. "*If* I complete Eton and *if* I go to Sandhurst."

The room quieted and someone cleared their throat. Mr. Frederick tapped his spoon against his cup. After a protracted pause he said, "David's teasing. Aren't you, boy?" The silence stretched on. "Eh?"

David blinked slowly and I noticed his jaw tremble, ever so slightly. "Yes," he said finally. "Of course I am. Just trying to lighten things up; all this talk of war. It just wasn't funny, I suppose. Apologies, Grandmama. Grandfather." He nodded to each of them, and I noticed Hannah give his hand a squeeze.

Lady Violet smiled. "I quite agree with you, David. Let's not talk of a war that may never come. Here, try some more of Mrs. Townsend's lovely tartlets." She nodded to Nancy, who once again offered the tray around.

They sat for a moment, nibbling tartlets, the ship's clock on the mantel marking time until someone could arrive at a subject as compelling as war. Finally, Lady Clementine said, "Never mind the fighting. The diseases are the real killers in wartime. It's the battlefields, of course—breeding grounds for all manner of foreign plagues. You'll see," she said dourly. "When the war comes, it'll bring the poxes with it."

"If the war comes," David said.

"But how will we know if it does?" Emmeline said, blue eyes wide. "Will someone from the government come and tell us?"

Lord Ashbury swallowed a tartlet whole. "One of the chaps at my club said there's to be an announcement any day."

"I feel just like a child on Christmas Eve," Fanny said, knotting her fingers. "Longing for the morning, anxious to wake up and open her presents."

"I shouldn't get too excited," the Major said. "If Britain enters the war it's likely to be over in a matter of months. Christmas at a stretch."

"Nonetheless," Lady Clementine said. "I'm writing to Lord Gifford first thing tomorrow to advise him of my preferred funeral arrangements. I'd suggest the rest of you do likewise. Before it's too late."

Hannah's eyes widened in mock offence. "You can't mean you don't trust us to make the best possible arrangements on your behalf, Lady Clementine?" She smiled sweetly and took the old lady's hand. "I for one would be honored to make sure you were given the send-off you deserve."

"Indeed," Lady Clementine puffed. "If you don't organize such occasions yourself, you never know into whose hands the task may fall." She looked pointedly at Fanny and sniffed so that her large nostrils flared. "Besides, I'm very particular about such events. I've been planning mine for years."

"Have you?" Lady Violet said, genuinely interested.

"Oh, yes," Lady Clementine said. "It's one of the most important public proceedings in a person's life and mine will be nothing short of spectacular."

"I look forward to it," said Hannah drily.

"As well you might," Lady Clementine said. "One can't afford to put on a bad show these days. People aren't as forgiving as they once were and one doesn't want a bad review."

"I didn't think you approved of newspaper reviews, Lady Clementine?" Hannah said, earning a warning frown from Pa.

"Not as a rule, I don't," Lady Clementine said. She pointed a jewel-laden finger at Hannah, then Emmeline, then Fanny. "Aside from her marriage, her obituary is the only time a lady's name should appear in the newspaper." She cast her eyes skyward. "And God help her if the funeral is savaged in the press, for she won't get a second chance the following season."

※

AFTER the theatrical triumph, only the late-summer dinner remained before the visit could be declared a resounding success. It was to be the climax of the week's activities. A final extravagance before the guests departed and stillness returned once more to Riverton. Dinner guests (including, Mrs. Townsend divulged, Lord Ponsonby, one of the King's cousins) were expected from as far away as London, and Nancy and I, under Mr. Hamilton's careful scrutiny, had spent all afternoon laying the table in the dining room.

We set for twenty, Nancy enunciating each item as she placed it: a spoon for soup, fish knife and fork, two knives, two large forks, four crystal wine glasses of varying proportions. Mr. Hamilton followed us around the table with his tape measure and cloth, ensuring each cover was the requisite foot apart from the next, and that his own distorted reflection gleamed back at him from every spoon. Down the center of the white linen cloth we trailed ivy and arranged red roses around crystal compotes of glistening fruit. These decorations pleased me; they were so pretty and matched perfectly Her La-

64

dyship's best dinner service—a wedding gift, Nancy said, from the Churchills, no less.

We positioned the place cards, lettered in Lady Violet's finest hand, according to her carefully sketched seating plan. The importance of placement, Nancy advised, could not be overestimated. Indeed, according to her, the success or failure of a dinner party hinged entirely on the seating arrangement. Evidently Lady Violet's reputation as a "perfect" hostess, rather than merely a "good" one, resulted from her ability to first invite the right people and then seat them prudently, peppering the witty and entertaining amongst the dull but important.

I am sorry to say I did not witness the late-summer dinner of 1914, for if cleaning the drawing room was a privilege, then serving at table was the highest honor, and certainly beyond my modest place. On this occasion, much to Nancy's chagrin, even she was to be denied the pleasure, by reason of Lord Ponsonby being known to abhor female servants at table. Nancy was soothed somewhat by Mr. Hamilton's decree that she should still serve upstairs, remaining hidden in the dining-room nook to receive the plates he and Alfred cleared, then feed them downstairs on the dumb waiter. This, Nancy reasoned, would at least grant her partial access to the dinner-party gossip. She would know what was said, if not by and to whom.

It was my duty, Mr. Hamilton said, to position myself downstairs next to the dumbwaiter. This I did, trying not to mind Alfred's jibes about the suitability of this partnership. He was always making jokes: they were well meant and the other staff seemed to know how to laugh, but I was inexperienced with such friendly teasing, was used to keeping to myself. I couldn't help shrinking when attention turned on me.

I watched with wonder as course after course of splendid fare disappeared up the chute—mock turtle soup, fish, sweetbreads, quail, asparagus, potatoes, apricot pies, blancmange—to be replaced with dirty plates and empty platters.

While upstairs the guests sparkled, deep beneath the dining room Mrs. Townsend had the kitchen steaming and whistling like one of the shiny new engines that had started to run through the village. She volleyed between workbenches, shifting her considerable heft at a furious pace, stoking the stove fire until beads of perspiration trickled down her flushed cheeks, clapping her hands and decrying, in a practised show of false modesty, the crisp golden pastry crusts on her pies. The only person who seemed immune to the contagious excitement was the wretched Katie, who wore her misery on her face: the first half of the evening spent peeling untold numbers of potatoes, the second scrubbing untold numbers of pans.

Finally, when the coffee pots, cream jugs and basins of crystallized sugar had been sent up on a silver salver, Mrs. Townsend untied her apron, a symbol to the rest of us that the evening's business was all but ended. She hung it on a hook by the stove and tucked the long gray hairs that had worked themselves loose back into the remarkable twist atop her head.

"Katie?" she called, wiping her warm forehead. "Katie?" She shook her head. "I don't know! That girl is always underfoot but never to be found." She tottered to the servants' table, eased herself into her seat and sighed.

Katie appeared at the doorway, clutching a dripping cloth. "Yes, Mrs. Townsend?"

"Oh, Katie," Mrs. Townsend scolded, pointing at the floor. "Whatever are you thinking, girl?"

"Nothing, Mrs. Townsend."

"Nothing's about right. You're wetting all over." Mrs. Townsend shook her head and sighed. "Get away with you now and find a towel to wipe that up. Mr. Hamilton will have your neck if he sees that mess."

"Yes, Mrs. Townsend."

"And when you're finished you can make us all a nice pot of hot cocoa."

Katie shuffled back towards the kitchen, almost colliding with Alfred as he bounded down the stairs, all arms, legs and exuberance. "Whoops, watch it, Katie, you're lucky I didn't topple you." He swung round the corner and grinned, his face as open and eager as a baby's. "Good evening, ladies."

Mrs. Townsend removed her glasses. "Well? Alfred?"

"Well, Mrs. Townsend?" he said, brown eyes wide.

"Well?" She flapped her fingers. "Don't leave us all in suspense."

I sat down at my place, easing off my shoes and stretching my toes. Alfred was twenty—tall, with lovely hands and a warm voice—and had been in service to Lord and Lady Ashbury all his working life. I believe Mrs. Townsend held a particular fondness for him, though certainly she never ventured so much herself and I would not then have dared to ask.

"Suspense?" Alfred said. "I don't know what you mean, Mrs. Townsend."

"Don't know what I mean, my foot." She shook her head. "How did it all go? Did they say anything that might interest me?"

"Oh, Mrs. Townsend," Alfred said, "I shouldn't say until Mr. Hamilton gets downstairs. It wouldn't be right, would it?"

"Now you listen here, my boy," Mrs. Townsend said. "Alls I'm asking is how Lord and Lady Ashbury's guests enjoyed their meals. Mr. Hamilton can hardly mind that now, can he?"

"I really couldn't say, Mrs. Townsend." Alfred winked at me, causing my cheeks to ripen. "Although I did happen to notice Lord Ponsonby having a second helping of your potatoes."

Mrs. Townsend smiled into her knotted hands and nodded to herself. "I heard it from Mrs. Davis, who cooks for Lord and Lady Bassingstoke, that Lord Ponsonby was special fond of potatoes à la crème."

"Fond? The others were lucky he left them any."

Mrs. Townsend gasped, but her eyes shone. "Alfred, you're wicked to say such things. If Mr. Hamilton heard . . ."

"If Mr. Hamilton heard what?" Nancy appeared at the door and took her seat, unpinning her cap.

"I was just telling Mrs. Townsend how well the ladies and gents enjoyed their dinner," said Alfred.

Nancy rolled her eyes. "I've never seen the plates come back so empty; Grace'll vouch for that." I nodded as she continued. "It's up to Mr. Hamilton, of course, but I'd say you've outdone yourself, Mrs. Townsend."

Mrs. Townsend smoothed her blouse over her bust. "Well, of course," she said smugly, "we all do our part." The jiggling of porcelain drew our attention to the door. Katie was inching around the corner, gripping tightly a tray of teacups. With each step, cocoa slopped over the cup rims and pooled on the saucers.

"Oh, Katie," Nancy said as the tray was jolted onto the table. "You've made a real mess of that. Look what she's done, Mrs. Townsend."

Mrs. Townsend cast her gaze upwards. "Sometimes I think I waste my time on that girl."

"Oh, Mrs. Townsend," Katie moaned. "I try my best, I really do. I didn't mean to—"

"Mean to what, Katie?" Mr. Hamilton said, clipping down the stairs and into the room. "Whatever have you done now?"

"Nothing, Mr. Hamilton, I only meant to bring the cocoa."

"And you've brought it, you silly girl," Mrs. Townsend said. "Now get back and finish those plates. You'll have let the water go cold now, you see if you haven't."

She shook her head as Katie disappeared up the hall, then turned to Mr. Hamilton and beamed. "Well, have they all gone then, Mr. Hamilton?"

"They have, Mrs. Townsend. I just saw the last guests, Lord and Lady Denys, to their motorcar."

"And the family?" she asked.

"The ladies have retired to bed. His Lordship, the Major and Mr.

Frederick are finishing their port in the drawing room and will see themselves up presently." Mr. Hamilton rested his hands on the back of his chair and paused for a moment, gazing into the distance the way he always did when he was about to impart important information. The rest of us took our seats and waited.

Mr. Hamilton cleared his throat. "You should all be most proud. The dinner was a great success and the Master and Mistress are well pleased." He smiled primly. "Indeed, the Master has given his very kind permission for us to open a bottle of champagne and share it amongst ourselves. A token of his appreciation, he said."

There was a flurry of excited applause while Mr. Hamilton fetched a bottle from the cellar and Nancy found some glasses. I sat very quietly, hoping I might be permitted a glass. All this was new to me: Mother and I had never had much cause for celebration.

When he reached the last flute, Mr. Hamilton peered over his glasses and down his long nose at me. "Yes," he said finally. "I think even you might be allowed a small glass tonight, young Grace. It isn't every night the Master entertains in such grand fashion."

I took the glass gratefully as Mr. Hamilton held his aloft. "A toast," he said. "To all who live and serve in this house. May we live long and graciously."

We clinked glasses and I leaned back against my chair, sipping champagne and savoring the tang of bubbles against my lips. Throughout my long life, whenever I have had occasion to drink champagne I have been reminded of that evening in the servants' hall at Riverton. It is a peculiar energy that accompanies a shared success, and Lord Ashbury's bubble of praise had burst over all of us, leaving our cheeks warm and our hearts glad. Alfred smiled at me over his glass and I smiled back shyly. I listened while the others replayed the night's events in vivid detail: Lady Denys's diamonds, Lord Harcourt's modern views on matrimony, Lord Ponsonby's penchant for potatoes à la crème.

A shrill ring jolted me from contemplation. Everyone else fell silent around the table. We looked at one another, puzzled, until Mr. Hamilton jumped from his seat. "Why. It's the telephone," he said, and hurried from the room.

Lord Ashbury had one of the first home telephone systems in England, a fact of which all who served in the house were immeasurably proud. The main receiver box was tucked away in Mr. Hamilton's pantry foyer so that he might, on such thrilling occasions as when it rang, access it directly and transfer the call upstairs. Despite this well-organized system, such occasions rarely arose, as regrettably few of Lord and Lady Ashbury's friends had telephones of their own. Nonetheless, the telephone was regarded with an almost religious awe, and visiting staff were always given reason to enter the foyer where they might observe at first hand the sacred object and, perforce, appreciate the superiority of the Riverton household.

It was little wonder then that the ringing of the phone rendered us all speechless. That the hour was so late turned astonishment into apprehension. We sat very still, ears strained, holding our collective breath.

"Hello?" Mr. Hamilton called down the line. "Lord Ashbury's residence."

Katie drifted into the room. "I just heard a funny noise. Ooh, you've all got champagne—"

"Sshhh," came the united response. Katie sat down and set about chewing her tatty fingernails.

From the pantry we heard Mr. Hamilton say, "Yes, this is the home of Lord Ashbury . . . Major Hartford? Why yes, Major Hartford is here visiting his parents . . . Yes, sir, right away. Who may I say is calling? . . . Just one moment, Captain Brown, while I connect you through."

Mrs. Townsend whispered loudly, knowingly, "Someone for the Major." And we all went back to listening. From where I sat I could just glimpse Mr. Hamilton's profile through the open door: neck stiff, mouth downturned.

"Hello, sir," Mr. Hamilton said into the receiver. "I'm most sorry to interrupt your evening, sir, but the Major is wanted on the telephone. It's Captain Brown, calling from London, sir."

Mr. Hamilton fell silent, but remained by the phone. It was his habit to hold on to the earpiece a moment, that he might ensure the call's recipient had picked up and the call was not cut off short.

As he waited, listening, I noticed his fingers tighten on the receiver. His body tensed and his breathing seemed to quicken.

He hung up quietly, carefully, and straightened his jacket. He returned slowly to his place at the head of the table and remained standing, his hands gripping the back of his chair. He gazed around the table, taking each of us in. Finally, gravely, he said:

"Our worst fears are realized. As of eleven o'clock this eve, Great Britain is at war. May God keep us all."

※

I AM crying. After all these years I have begun crying for them. Warm tears seep from my eyes, following the lines of my face until the air dries them, sticky and cool against my skin.

Sylvia is with me again. She has brought a tissue and uses it to mop cheerfully at my face. To her these tears are a simple matter of faulty plumbing. Yet another inevitable, innocuous sign of my great age.

She doesn't know I cry for the changing times. That just as I reread favorite books, some small part of me hoping for a different ending, I find myself hoping against hope that the war will never come. That this time, somehow, it will leave us be.

SAFFRON HIGH STREET

THE rain is on its way. My lower back is far more sensitive than any meteorologist's equipment and last night I lay awake, bone moaning to bone, whispering tales of long-ago litheness. I arched and bowed my stiff old frame: nuisance became frustration, frustration became boredom, and boredom became terror. Terror that the night would never end and I would be trapped forever in its long, lonely tunnel.

But enough. I refuse to ruminate further on my frailties. And I must eventually have slept, for this morning I woke, and as far as I can tell the one cannot be done without the other. I was still in bed, my nightie twisted about my middle, when a girl with rolled-up shirt sleeves and a long thin plait (though not as long as mine) bustled into my room and threw open the curtains, letting the light stream in. The girl was not Sylvia and thus I knew it must be Sunday.

The girl—Helen, read her name badge—bundled me into the shower, gripping my arm to steady me, mulberry fingernails burrowing into flaccid white skin. She flicked her plait over one shoulder and set about soaping my torso and limbs, scrubbing away the lingering film of night, humming a tune I do not know. When I was suitably sanitary she lowered me onto the plastic bath seat and left me alone to soak beneath the shower's warm course. I clutched the lower rail with both hands and eased forward, sighing as the water rained relief over my knotted back.

With Helen's assistance I was dried and dressed, thoroughly processed and seated in the morning room by seven-thirty. I managed a piece of rubbery toast and a cup of tea before Ruth arrived to take me to church.

I am not overly religious. Indeed there have been times when all faith has deserted me. But I made my peace with God a long time ago. Age is the great mellower. And besides, Ruth likes to go, and it's a small enough gesture for me to make.

It is Lent, the period of soul-searching and repentance that always precedes Easter, and this morning the church pulpit was draped in purple. The sermon was pleasant enough, its subject guilt and forgiveness. (Fitting when one considers the endeavor I have decided to undertake.) The minister read from John 14, beseeching the congregation to resist the scaremongers who preach millennial doom and to find instead an inner peace through Christ. "I am the way, the truth and the life," he read. "No man cometh unto the Father but by me." And then he bid us take our example from the faith of Christ's Apostles at the dawn of the first millennium. With the exception of Judas, of course.

It is our habit, after church, to walk the short distance to the High Street for morning tea at Maggie's. We always go to Maggie's, though Maggie herself left town with a suitcase and her best friend's husband many years ago.

We rested for a moment on the timber seat beneath the hundred-year elm whose mammoth trunk forms the junction of Church and Saffron High Streets. The wintry sun flickered through the lacework of naked branches, thawing my back. Strange these clear, bright days in winter's tail, when one can be hot and cold all at once.

When I was a girl, horses and carriages and hansom cabs rolled along these streets. Motorcars too, after the war: Austins and Tin Lizzies, with their goggle-eyed drivers and honking horns. The roads were dusty then, full of potholes and horse manure. Old ladies pushed spoke-wheeled perambulators and little boys with empty eyes sold newspapers out of boxes.

The salt seller always set up on the corner, where the petrol station is now. Vera Pipp: a wiry figure in a cloth cap, thin clay pipe permanently hanging off her lip. I used to hide behind Mother's skirt, watching bug-eyed as Mrs. Pipp used a big hook to heave slabs of salt onto her handcart, then a saw and knife to carve them into smaller pieces. She turned up in many a nightmare, with her clay pipe and shiny hook.

Ruth tapped my arm and hoisted me to my feet, and we set off again down Saffron High Street towards the faded red-and-white canvas awning of Maggie's. We ordered the usual—two cups of English breakfast tea and a scone to share—and sat at the table by the window.

We sipped in habitual silence until finally Ruth slid her plate across the table. "You have my half as well. You're looking thin."

I considered reminding her of Mrs. Simpson's advice, that a woman can never be too rich or too thin, but thought better of it. Her sense of humor, never abundant, had all but deserted her of late.

Ruth dabbed at her mouth, chasing an invisible crumb across her lips, then cleared her throat, folding the napkin in half and in half again, and tucking it under her knife. "I need a prescription dispensed at the chemist," she said. "Are you happy to sit?"

"A prescription?" I said. "Why? What's the matter?" She is in her sixties, the mother of a grown man, and still my heart skips.

"Nothing," she said. "Not really." She stood stiffly, then said in a low voice, "Just a little something to help me sleep."

I nod; we both know why she doesn't sleep. It sits between us, a shared sadness tied up neatly by our unspoken agreement not to discuss it. Or him.

Ruth rushed on, filling the silence. "You stay here while I dash across. It's warm with the heating on." She gathered her handbag and coat and stood, considering me for a second. "Don't you go wandering now, will you?"

I shook my head as she hurried to the door. It is Ruth's abiding fear that I will disappear if left alone. I wonder where it is she imagines I am so eager to go.

Through the window I watched until she vanished amid the people rushing past. All different shapes and sizes. And what clothes! What would Mrs. Townsend have said?

A pink-cheeked child wandered by, muffled up like a blimp, dragging behind a busy parent. The child—he or she, it was difficult to tell—regarded me with large round eyes, burdened by none of the social compulsion to smile that afflicts most adults. Memory flashed. I was that child once, long ago, lagging behind my own mother as she hurried along the street. The memory brightened. We had walked by this very shop, although it hadn't been a cafe then, but a butcher's. Ranks of cut meat on white marble slabs lined the window and beef carcasses swayed over the sawdust-strewn floor. Mr. Hobbins, the butcher, had waved at me, and I remembered wishing Mother would stop, that we would take home with us a lovely ham hock to turn into soup.

I lingered by the window, hoping, imagining the soup—ham, leek and potato—bubbling atop our wood stove, filling our tiny kitchen with its salty film of steam. So vivid was my imagining I could smell the broth so that it almost hurt.

But Mother didn't stop. She didn't even hesitate. As the *tip-tap* of her heels drew further and further away, I was seized by an overwhelming instinct to frighten her, to punish her because we were poor, to make her think I was lost.

I stayed where I was, certain she would soon realize I was missing and rush back. Maybe, just maybe, relief would overcome her and she'd decide gladly to purchase the hock . . .

All of a sudden I was wrenched about and dragged in the direction from which I'd come. It took me a moment to realize what was happening, that the button from my coat was caught in a well-dressed lady's string bag and I was being led spiritedly away. I remember vividly my little hand reaching out to tap her broad, bustling bottom, only to withdraw, overcome with timidity, as all the while my feet pedalled fiercely to keep up. The other lady crossed the street then, and I with her, and I began to cry. I was lost and becoming more so with each hurried step. I would never see Mother again. Would instead be at the mercy of this strange lady with her fancy clothes.

Suddenly, on the other side of the road, I glimpsed Mother striding ahead amongst the other shoppers. Relief! I wanted to call out, but was sobbing too much to catch my breath. I waved my arms, gasping, tears streaming.

Then Mother turned and saw. Her face froze, thin hand leaped to her flat chest, and within a moment she was at my side. The other lady, heretofore oblivious to the stowaway she dragged behind, was now alerted by the commotion. She turned and looked at us: my tall mother with her drawn face and faded skirt, and the tear-streaked urchin I must have seemed. She shook her bag, then clutched it to her chest, horrified. "Get away! Get away from me or I'll call for the constable."

A number of people had caught the whiff of impending excitement and started to form a circle around us. Mother apologized to the lady, who looked at her the way one might a rat in the larder. Mother tried to explain what had happened, but the lady continued to withdraw. I had little choice but to follow, which caused her to squeal louder. Finally, the constable appeared and demanded to know what all the ruckus was about.

"She's trying to steal my bag," the lady said, pointing a shaking finger at me.

"That so?" said the constable.

I shook my head, my voice still lost, certain I was to be arrested.

Then Mother explained what had happened, about my button and the string bag, and the constable nodded and the lady frowned doubtfully. Then they all looked down at the string bag and saw that my button was indeed caught, and the constable told Mother to help me free.

She untangled my button, thanked the constable, apologized

again to the lady, then stared at me. I waited to see whether she would laugh or cry. As it turned out, she did both, but not right then. She gripped my brown coat and led me away from the dispersing crowd, stopping only when we turned the corner of Railway Street. As the train bound for London pulled out of the station, she turned to me and hissed, "You wicked girl. I thought I'd lost you. You'll be the death of me, you hear? Do you want that? To kill your own mother?" Then she straightened my coat, shook her head and took my hand, holding it so tightly it almost hurt. "Sometimes I wish I'd made them take you at the Foundling Hospital after all, so help me God."

It was a common refrain when I was naughty and no doubt the threat contained more than a grain of true feeling. Certainly there were plenty would agree she'd have been better off to have left me at the Foundling. There was nothing so certain as pregnancy to lose a woman her place in service, and Mother's life since my arrival had been a litany of scraping by and making do.

I was told the story of my escape from the Foundling orphanage so many times I sometimes believed I was born knowing it. Mother's train journey to Russell Square in London, with me wrapped and tucked within her coat for warmth, had become for us a legend of sorts. The walk down Grenville Street and into Guilford Street, folks shaking their heads, knowing full well where she was headed with her tiny parcel. The way she'd recognized the Foundling building from far up the street by the crowd of other young women like herself who milled about outside, swaying dazedly with their mewling babes. Then, most important, the sudden voice, clear as day (God, said Mother; foolishness, said my Aunt Dee), telling her to turn around, that it was her duty to keep her wee baby. The moment, according to family lore, for which I should be eternally grateful.

On that morning, the day of the button and the string bag, Mother's mention of the Foundling Hospital moved me to silence. Though not, as she doubtless believed, because I was reflecting on my good fortune at having been spared its confinement. Rather, I was drifting along the well-trod paths of a favorite childhood fantasy. It cheered me no end to imagine myself at Coram's Foundling Hospital, singing away amongst the other children. I should have had lots of brothers and sisters with whom to play then, not just a tired and cranky mother whose face was lined with disappointments. One of which I feared was me.

A presence at my shoulder pulled me back down memory's long passage, back to the here and now. I turned to look at the young woman by my side. It was a moment before I recognized her as the waitress who had brought the tea. She was watching me expectantly.

I blinked, focusing. "I think my daughter has already paid the bill."

"Oh yes," said the young girl, her voice soft and Irish. "Yes, she has. Settled it when she ordered." But still she didn't move.

"Is there something else then?" I said.

She swallowed. "It's just that Sue in the kitchen says that you're the grandmother of . . . that is, she says that your grandson is . . . is Marcus McCourt, and I'm really, truly his biggest fan. I just love Inspector Adams. I've read every single one."

Marcus. The little moth of sorrow fluttered in my chest, the way it always does when someone speaks his name. I smiled at her. "That's very nice to hear. My grandson would be pleased."

"I was ever so sorry to read about his wife."

I nodded.

She hesitated, and I braced for the questions I knew were coming, that always came: was he still writing the next Inspector Adams? Would it be published soon? I was surprised when decency, or timidity, beat out curiosity. "Well . . . it was nice meeting you," she said. "I'd better get back to work or Sue'll go berserk." She made to leave, then turned back. "You will tell him, won't you? Tell him how much the books mean to me, to all his fans?"

I gave her my word, though I don't know when I will be able to

78

make good on it. Like most of his generation he is globetrotting. Unlike his peers, it is not adventure he craves, but distraction. He has disappeared inside a cloud of his own grief and I cannot guess his whereabouts. The last I heard was months ago. A postcard of the Statue of Liberty, postmarked California, dated last year. The message simply: *Happy Birthday, M.*

No, it is not so simple as grief. It is guilt that chases him. Misplaced guilt over Rebecca's death. He blames himself, believes that if he hadn't left her, things might have gone differently. I worry for him. I understand well the peculiar guilt of tragedy's survivors.

Through the window, I could see Ruth across the street; she'd got caught talking with the minister and his wife and hadn't yet reached the chemist. With great effort, I eased myself to the edge of my seat, hooked my handbag over my arm and clutched my cane. Legs trembling, I stood. I had an errand to run.

❀

THE haberdasher, Mr. Butler, has a tiny shopfront on the main street; little more than a hint of striped awning sandwiched between the bakery and a shop selling candles and incense. But beyond the red timber door, with its shiny brass knocker and silver bell, a trove of diverse items belies the modest entrance. Men's hats and ties, school bags and leather luggage, saucepans and hockey sticks all jostle for space in the deep, narrow store.

Mr. Butler is a short man of about forty-five, with a vanishing hairline and, I noticed, a vanishing waistline. I remember his father, and his father before him, though I don't ever say so. The young, I have learned, are embarrassed by tales of long ago. This morning he smiled over his glasses and told me how well I was looking. When I was younger, still in my eighties, vanity would have had me believe him. Now I recognize such comments as kindly expressions of surprise I'm still alive. I thanked him anyway—the comment was well meant—and asked whether he had a tape recorder.

"To listen to music?" said Mr. Butler.

"I wish to speak into it," I said. "Record my words."

He hesitated, probably wondering what I could possibly be meaning to tell the tape recorder, then pulled a small black object from his display. "This one ought to do you. It's called a Dictaphone."

"Yes," I said hopefully. "That looks the thing."

He must have sensed my inexperience, for he launched into an explanation. "It's easy. You press this one, then talk into here." He leaned forward and indicated a patch of metal gauze on the side of the machine. I could almost taste the camphor on his suit. "That there's the microphone."

Ruth was still not back from the chemist when I reached Maggie's. Rather than risk more of the waitress's questions, I pulled my coat around me and wilted onto the bus seat outside. The exertion had left me breathless.

A cold breeze brought with it a cluster of forgotten items: a confectionery wrapper, some dried leaves, a brown and green duck's feather. They danced along the reaches of the street, resting and then twirling in step with each gust. At one point, the feather reeled on ahead, embraced by a partner more vigorous than the last, which lifted it and sent it pirouetting up over the shop roofs and out of sight.

I thought of Marcus, dancing across the globe in the grip of some unruly tune from which he can't escape. Pressed, like an exhausted summer flower, between images of Hannah and Emmeline and Riverton: my grandson. Out of time and out of place. One moment a small boy with dewy skin and wide eyes, the next a grown man, hollowed by love and its loss.

I want to see his face again. Touch it. His lovely, familiar face, etched as all faces are by the efficient hands of history. Colored with ancestors and a past he knows little about.

He will return one day, of that I've little doubt, for home is a magnet that lures back even its most abstracted children. But whether tomorrow or years from now, I cannot guess. And I haven't time to wait. I find myself in time's cold waiting room, shivering as ancient ghosts and echoing voices recede.

That is why I've decided to make him a tape. Maybe more than one. I am going to tell him a secret, an old secret, long kept.

☘

O N the drive back to Heathview I watched out the window as street upon street of graystone cottages slipped past. In one of them, midway along, nestled quietly between two identical others, is the house in which I was born. I glanced at Ruth, but if she noticed she did not say. No reason she should, of course. We pass that way each Sunday.

As we wove along the narrow road and village became countryside, I held my breath—just a little—the way I always do.

Just beyond Bridge Road we turned a corner, and there it was. The entrance to Riverton. The lace-winged gates, as tall as lamp posts, doorway to the whispering tunnel of ancient trees. The gates have been painted white, no longer the gleaming silver of yesteryear. There is a sign affixed now alongside the cast-iron curls that spell "Riverton." It reads: *Open to the public. March–October. 10 a.m.–4 p.m. Admission: adults £4, children £2. No reentry.*

☘

T H E tape-recording took a little practice. Sylvia, thankfully, was on hand to help. She held the machine before my mouth and I spoke, at her behest, the first thing that came to mind. "Hello . . . hello. This is Grace Bradley speaking . . . Testing. One. Two. Three."

Sylvia examined the Dictaphone and grinned, "Very professional." She pressed a button and there came a whirring. "I'm just rewinding so we can hear it back."

There was a click as the tape returned to its start. She pressed "play" and we both waited.

It was the voice of age: faint, worn, almost invisible. A pale ribbon, frayed so that only brittle threads survive. Only the merest flecks of me, my real voice, the one I hear in my head and in my dreams.

Sylvia made to leave and I was beset, suddenly, with a sense of nervous expectation.

"Sylvia—"

She turned. "What is it, pet?"

"What will I say?"

"Well, I don't know, do I?" She laughed. "Pretend he's sitting here with you. Just tell him what's on your mind."

And that is what I did, Marcus. I imagined you on the end of my bed, stretched across my feet as you liked to lie when you were little, and I began to speak. I told you some of what I've been doing, about the film and Ursula. I trod cautiously around your mother, saying only that she misses you. That she longs to see you.

And I told you about the memories I've been having. Not all of them; I have a purpose and it isn't to bore you with tales from my past. Rather I told you about the curious sensation that they are becoming more real to me than my life. The way I slip away without warning, am disappointed when I open my eyes to see that I am back in 1999; the way the fabric of time is changing, and I am beginning to feel at home in the past and a visitor to this strange and blanched experience we agree to call the present.

A funny feeling, to sit, alone in one's room, and talk to a small black box. At first I whispered, concerned that the others would hear. That my voice and its secrets would drift down the corridor to the morning room, like a ship's horn floating forlornly into a foreign port. But when Matron popped in with my tablets, her look of surprise set my mind at ease.

She has gone now. The pills I have put on the windowsill beside me. I will take them later, but for now I need to be clear-headed.

I am watching the sun set over the heath. I like to follow its path as it slips silently behind the far-off band of trees. Today I blink and miss its last farewell. When my eyes open, the ultimate moment has passed and the shimmering crescent has disappeared, leaving the sky bereft: a clear, cold blue, lacerated by streaks of frosty white. The heath itself shivers in the sudden shadow, and in the distance a train sneaks through the valley fog, electric brakes moaning as it turns towards the village. I glance at my wall clock. It is the six o'clock train, filled with people returning from work in Chelmsford and Brentwood and even London.

I see the station in my mind. Not as it is, perhaps, but as it was. The big round station clock suspended over the platform, its steadfast face and diligent hands a stern reminder that time and the trains wait for no man. It has probably been replaced now with a blank, blinking digital device. I wouldn't know. It has been a long time since I visited the station.

I see it as it was the morning we waved Alfred off to war. Strings of paper triangles, red and blue, flirting with the breeze, children racing up and down, weaving in and out, blowing tin whistles and waving Union Jacks. Young men—such *young* men—starched and eager in their new uniforms and clean boots. And, snaked along the track, the glistening train, anxious to be on its way. To spirit its unsuspecting passengers to a hell of mud and death.

But enough of that. I jump too far ahead.

IN THE WEST

⁂

NINETEEN-FOURTEEN slipped towards 1915, and with each passing day went any chance that the war would end by Christmas. A gunshot in a faraway land had sent tremors across the plains of Europe and the sleeping giant of centuries-old rancor had awoken. Major Hartford was recalled to service, dusted off along with other heroes of long-forgotten campaigns, while Lord Ashbury moved into his London flat and joined the Bloomsbury Home Guard. Mr. Frederick, unfit for armed service on account of a bout of pneumonia in the winter of 1910, swapped motorcars for war planes and was issued a special government badge announcing his valuable contribution to a vital war industry. It was cold comfort, said Nancy, who knew about such things, it having always been a dream of Mr. Frederick's to serve with the military.

History tells that as 1915 unraveled, the war's true character began to emerge. But history is a faithless teller, for while in France young men battled fear undreamed of, at Riverton 1915 passed much as 1914 had before it. We were aware, of course, that the Western Front had reached a stalemate—Mr. Hamilton kept us well fed with his zealous recitations of the newspaper's grisly fare—and certainly there were enough minor inconveniences to keep folks shaking their heads and tut-tutting about the war, but these were tempered by the tremendous flurry of purpose the conflict gave those for whom daily life had become staid.

Lady Violet joined and formed countless committees: from the locating of suitable billets for suitable Belgian refugees, to the organizing of motorcar excursions for convalescing officers. All across Britain young women (and some of the younger boys too) did their bit for national defence, taking up knitting needles against a sea of troubles, producing a deluge of scarves and socks for the boys at the front. Fanny, unable to knit but anxious to impress Mr. Frederick with her patriotism, threw herself into the coordination of such enterprises, organizing for knitted goods to be boxed and mailed to France. Even Lady Clementine showed a rare community spirit, billeting one of Lady Violet's sanctioned Belgians—an elderly lady with poor English but fine enough manners to mask the fact—whom Lady Clementine proceeded to probe for all the most ghastly details of the invasion.

As December approached, Lady Jemima, Fanny and the Hartford children were summoned to Riverton, where Lady Violet was determined to celebrate a traditional Christmas season. Fanny would have preferred to stay in London—far more exciting—but was unable to refuse the summons of a woman whose son she hoped to marry. (Never mind that the son himself was firmly stationed elsewhere and firmly set against her.) She had little choice but to steel herself to long winter weeks in rural Essex. She managed to look bored as only the very young can and spent the time moving herself from room to room, striking pretty poses on the off-chance Mr. Frederick should make an unscheduled return home.

Jemima suffered by comparison, seemingly plumper and plainer than the year before. There was, however, one arena in which she outshone her counterpart: she was not only married, but married to a hero.

Meanwhile, upstairs, for Hannah and Emmeline time was dragging. They had already been at Riverton a fortnight, and with ghastly weather forcing them indoors and no lessons to distract them (Miss Prince being engaged in war work), they were running out of things to do. They'd played every game they knew—cat's cradle, jacks, gold miner (which, as far as I could figure, required one to scratch a spot on the other's arm until blood or boredom won out)—they'd helped Mrs. Townsend with the Christmas baking until they were ill from pilfered pastry dough, and they'd coerced Nanny Brown into unlocking the attic storeroom so they could climb amongst dusty, forgotten treasures. But it was The Game they longed to play. And for that they needed David, not due from Eton for another week.

※

DOWNSTAIRS, as ever, our lives were murky mirrors to those above.

One evening, when the household had all retired to bed, the staff gathered by the raging servants'-hall fire. Mr. Hamilton and Mrs. Townsend formed bookends on either side, while Nancy, Katie and I huddled between on dining chairs, squinting in the flickering firelight at the scarves we were dutifully knitting. A cold wind lashed against the windowpanes, and insurgent draughts set Mrs. Townsend's jars of dry goods to quivering on the kitchen shelf.

Mr. Hamilton shook his head and cast aside *The Times*. He removed his glasses and rubbed at his eyes.

"More bad news?" Mrs. Townsend looked up from the Christmas menu she was planning, cheeks red from the fire.

"The worst, Mrs. Townsend." He returned his glasses to the bridge of his nose. "More losses at Ypres." He rose from his seat and moved to the sideboard, where he had spread out a map of Europe, host to a score of miniature military figurines (David's old set, I think, retrieved from the attic) representing different armies and different campaigns. He removed the Duke of Wellington from a point in France and replaced him with two German Hussars. "I don't like this at all," he said to himself.

Mrs. Townsend sighed. "And I don't like *this* at all." She tapped her pen on the menu. "How am I supposed to prepare Christmas dinner for the family with no butter, or tea, or even turkey to speak of?"

"No turkey, Mrs. Townsend?" Katie gaped.

"Not so much as a wing."

"But whatever will you serve?"

Mrs. Townsend shook her head, "Don't go getting in a flap, now. I dare say I'll manage, my girl. I always do, don't I?"

"Yes, Mrs. Townsend," said Katie gravely. "I must say you do."

Mrs. Townsend peered down her nose, satisfied herself there was no irony intended and returned her attention to the menu.

I was trying to concentrate on my knitting, but when I dropped the third stitch in as many rows, I cast it aside, frustrated, and stood up. Something had been bothering me all evening. Something I had witnessed in the village that I didn't rightly understand.

I straightened my apron and approached Mr. Hamilton, who, it seemed to me, knew just about everything.

"Mr. Hamilton?" I said tentatively.

He turned towards me, peered over his glasses, the Duke of Wellington still pinched between two long, tapered fingertips. "What is it, Grace?"

I glanced back to where the others sat, engaged in animated discussion.

"Well, girl?" Mr. Hamilton said. "Cat got your tongue?"

I cleared my throat. "No, Mr. Hamilton," I said. "It's just . . . I wanted to ask you about something. Something I saw in the village today."

"Yes?" he said. "Speak up, my girl."

I glanced towards the door. "Where is Alfred, Mr. Hamilton?"

He frowned. "Upstairs, serving sherry. Why? What's Alfred got to do with all this?"

"It's just, I saw Alfred today, in the village—"

"Yes," Mr. Hamilton said. "He was running an errand for me."

"I know, Mr. Hamilton. I saw him. At McWhirter's. And I saw when he came out of the store." I pressed my lips together. Some unaccountable reticence made me loath to speak the rest. "He was given a white feather, Mr. Hamilton."

"A white feather?" Mr. Hamilton's eyes widened and the Duke of Wellington was released unceremoniously onto the table.

I nodded, remembering Alfred's shift in manner: the way he'd been stopped in his jaunty tracks. Had stood, dazed, feather in hand as passersby slowed to whisper knowingly at one another. Had dropped his gaze and hurried away, shoulders bent and head low.

"A white feather?" To my chagrin, Mr. Hamilton said this loudly enough to draw the attention of the others.

"What's that, Mr. Hamilton?" Mrs. Townsend peered over her glasses.

He brushed a hand down his cheek and across his lips. Shook his head in disbelief. "Alfred was given a white feather."

"No," Mrs. Townsend gasped, plump hand leaping to her chest. "He never was. Not a white feather. Not our Alfred."

"How do you know?" Nancy said.

"Grace saw it happen," Mr. Hamilton said. "This morning in the village."

I nodded, my heart beginning to race with the uneasy sense of having opened the Pandora's box of someone else's secret. Being unable now to close it.

"It's preposterous," Mr. Hamilton said, straightening his waistcoat. He returned to his seat and hooked his spectacles over his ears. "Alfred is not a coward. He's serving the war effort every day he helps keep this household running. He has an important position with an important family."

"But it's not the same as fighting, is it, Mr. Hamilton?" said Katie.

"It most certainly is," blustered Mr. Hamilton. "There's a role for each of us in this war, Katie. Even you. It's our duty to preserve the ways of this fine country of ours so that when the soldiers return victorious, the society they remember will be waiting for them."

"So even when I'm washing pots I'm helping the war effort?" said Katie in wonderment.

"Not the way you wash them," Mrs. Townsend said.

"Yes, Katie," Mr. Hamilton said. "By keeping up with your duties, and by knitting your scarves, you're doing your bit." He shot glances at Nancy and me. "We all are."

"It doesn't seem enough, if you ask me," Nancy said, her head bowed.

"What's that, Nancy?" Mr. Hamilton said.

Nancy stopped knitting and laid her bony hands in her lap. "Well," she said cautiously, "take Alfred, for example. He's a young, fit man. Surely he'd be of better use helping the other boys what are over there in France? Anyone can pour sherry."

"Anyone can pour . . . ?" Mr. Hamilton paled. "You of all people should know that domestic service is a skill to which not all are suited, Nancy."

Nancy flushed. "Of course, Mr. Hamilton. I never meant to suggest otherwise." She fidgeted with the marbles of her knuckles. "I . . . I suppose I've just been feeling a bit useless myself of late."

Mr. Hamilton was about to denounce such feelings when all of a sudden Alfred came clattering down the stairs and into the room. Mr. Hamilton's mouth dropped shut and we fell into a conspiracy of collective silence.

"Alfred," Mrs. Townsend said at last, "whatever's the matter, racing down them stairs like that?" She cast about and found me. "You scared poor Grace half to death. Poor girl nearly jumped out of her skin."

I smiled weakly at Alfred, for I hadn't been frightened at all. Merely surprised, like everyone else. And sorry. I should never have asked Mr. Hamilton about the feather. I was becoming fond of Alfred: he was kind-hearted and had often taken time to draw me from my shell. To discuss his embarrassment while his back was turned made a fool of him somehow.

"I'm sorry, Grace," Alfred said. "It's just, Master David has arrived."

"Yes," Mr. Hamilton said, looking at his watch, "as we expected. Dawkins was to collect him from the station off the ten o'clock train. Mrs. Townsend has his supper ready, if you'd care to take it up."

Alfred nodded, catching his breath. "I know that, Mr. Hamilton . . ." He swallowed. "It's just . . . Master David. He has someone with him. From Eton. I believe it's Lord Hunter's son."

※

I TAKE a breath. You once told me, Marcus, that there is a point in most stories from which there is no return. When all the central characters have made their way onstage and the scene is set for the drama to unfold. The storyteller relinquishes control and the characters begin to move of their own accord.

Robbie Hunter's entrance brings this story to the edge of the Rubicon. Am I going to cross it? Perhaps it is not yet too late to turn back. To fold them all away, gently, between layers of tissue paper in the boxes of my memory?

I smile, for I am no more able to stop this story than I am to halt the march of time. I am not romantic enough to imagine it wants to be told, but I am honest enough to acknowledge that I want to tell it.

※

EARLY next morning, Mr. Hamilton called me to his pantry, closed the door gently behind him and conferred on me a dubious honor. Every winter, each of the ten thousand books, journals and manuscripts housed in the Riverton library was removed, dusted and reshelved. This annual ritual had been an institution since 1846. It was Lord Ashbury's mother's rule originally. She was mad for dust, said Nancy, and she rightly had her reasons. For one night in the late autumn, Lord Ashbury's little brother, a month shy of his third year and favored by all who knew him, fell into a sleep from which he never awoke. Though she could find no doctor would support her claim, his mother was convinced that her youngest boy caught his death in the ancient dust that hung in the air. In particular she blamed the library, for that was where the two boys had spent the fateful day—playing make-believe amongst the maps and charts that described the voyages of long-ago forebears.

Lady Gytha Ashbury was not one to be trifled with. She put aside her grief to draw from the same well of courage and determination that saw her abandon her homeland, her family and her dowry for the sake of love. She declared immediate war; summoned her troops and commanded them to banish the insidious adversaries. They cleaned day and night for a week before she was finally satisfied that the last hint of dust was vanquished. Only then did she weep for her tiny boy.

Each year thereafter, as the final colored leaves fell from the trees outside, the ritual was scrupulously reenacted. Even after her death, the custom remained. And in the year 1915, it was I who was charged with satisfying the former Lady Ashbury's memory. (Partly, I'm sure, as penalty for having observed Alfred in town the day before. Mr. Hamilton gave me no thanks for bringing the specter of war shame home to Riverton.)

"You will be released early from your usual duties this week, Grace," he said, smiling thinly from behind his desk. "Each morning you will proceed directly to the library, where you will begin in the gallery and work your way down to the shelves on the ground level."

Then he bid me equip myself with a pair of cotton gloves, a damp cloth and an acquiescence befitting the awesome tedium of the chore.

"Remember, Grace," he said, hands pressed firmly on his desk, fingers wide apart, "Lord Ashbury is very serious about dust. You have been given a great responsibility and one for which you should be thankful—"

His homily was interrupted by a knock at the pantry door.

"Come in," he called, frowning down his long nose.

The door opened and Nancy burst through, thin frame nervous as a spider's. "Mr. Hamilton," she said. "Come quickly, there's something upstairs that needs your immediate attention."

He stood directly, slipped his black coat from a hanger on the back of the door and hurried up the stairs. Nancy and I followed close behind.

There, in the main entrance hall, stood Dudley the gardener, fumbling his woollen hat from one chapped hand to the other. Lying at his feet, still ripe with sap, was an enormous Norway spruce, freshly hewn.

"Mr. Dudley," Mr. Hamilton said. "What are you doing here?"

"I've brought the Christmas tree, Mr. Hamilton."

"I can see that. But what are you doing *here*?" He indicated the grand hall, dropping his gaze to take in the tree. "More importantly, what is *this* doing here? It's huge."

"Aye, she's a beauty," said Dudley gravely, looking upon the tree as another might a mistress. "I've had my eye on her for years, just biding my time, letting her reach her full glory. And this Christmas she's all growed up." He looked solemnly at Mr. Hamilton. "A little too growed up."

Mr. Hamilton turned to Nancy. "What in heaven's name is going on?"

Nancy's hands were clenched into fists by her side, her mouth drawn tight as a crosspatch. "It won't fit, Mr. Hamilton. He tried to stand it in the drawing room where it always goes, but it's a foot too tall."

"But didn't you measure it?" Mr. Hamilton said to the gardener.

"Oh yes, sir," said Dudley. "But I never was much of a one for arithmetic."

"Then take out your saw and remove a foot, man."

Mr. Dudley shook his head sadly. "I would, sir, but I'm afeared there's not a foot left to remove. The trunk's already short as can be, and I can't go taking none from the top now, can I?" He looked at us plainly. "Where would the pretty angel sit?"

We all stood, pondering this predicament, the seconds yawning across the marble hall. Each of us aware the family would soon appear for breakfast. Finally, Mr. Hamilton made a pronouncement. "I suppose there's nothing for it then. Short of lopping the top and leaving the angel with neither perch nor purpose, we'll have to stray from tradition—just this once—and erect it in the library."

"The library, Mr. Hamilton?" Nancy said.

"Yes. Beneath the glass dome." He looked witheringly at Dudley. "Where she'll be sure to achieve her full postural opportunity."

So it was, on the morning of 1 December 1915, as I perched high atop the library gallery at the furthest end of the furthest shelf, steeling myself to a week of dusting, that a precocious pine stood glorious in the library center, uppermost limbs pointing ecstatically to the heavens. I was level with her crown, and the fecund scent of pine was strong, impregnating the library's lazy atmosphere of warm dustiness.

The gallery of the Riverton library ran lengthways, high above the room itself, and it was hard not to be distracted. Reluctance to begin is quick to befriend procrastination, and the view of the room below was tremendous. It is a universal truth that no matter how well one knows a scene, to observe it from above is something of a revelation. I stood by the railings and peered over, beyond the tree.

The library—usually so vast and imposing—took on the appearance of a stage set. Ordinary items—the Steinway & Sons grand piano, the oak writing desk, Lord Ashbury's globe—were suddenly rendered smaller, ersatz versions of themselves, and gave the impression of having been arranged to suit a cast of players, yet to make its entrance.

The sitting area in particular bore a theatrical spirit of anticipation. The sofa at center stage; the armchairs on either side, pretty in William Morris skirts; the rectangle of winter sunlight that draped across the piano and onto the oriental rug. Props, all: patiently awaiting actors to take their marks. What kind of play would actors perform, I wondered, in such a setting as this?

Thus I could happily have procrastinated all day, but for the persistent voice inside my ear, Mr. Hamilton's voice, reminding me of Lord Ashbury's reputation for random dust inspections. And so, reluctantly, I abandoned such thoughts and withdrew the first book. Dusted it—front, back and spine—then replaced it and withdrew the second.

By mid-morning I had finished five of the ten gallery shelves and was poised to begin the next. A small mercy: having begun with the higher shelves, I had finally reached the lower and would be able to sit while I worked. After dusting hundreds of books my hands had become practised, performing their task automatically, which was just as well, for my mind had numbed to a halt.

I had just plucked the sixth spine from the sixth shelf when an impertinent piano note, sharp and sudden, trespassed on the room's winter stillness. I spun around involuntarily, peering down beyond the tree.

Standing at the piano, fingers brushing silently the ivory surface, was a young man I'd never seen before. I knew who he was, though; even then. It was Master David's friend from Eton. Lord Hunter's son who'd arrived in the night.

He was handsome. But who amongst the young is not? With him it was something more, the beauty of stillness. Alone in the room, his dark eyes grave beneath a line of dark brows, he gave the impression of sorrow past, deeply felt and poorly mended. He was tall and lean, though not so as to appear lanky, and his brown hair fell longer than was the fashion, some ends escaping others to brush against his collar, his cheekbone.

I watched him survey the library, slowly, deliberately, from where he stood. His gaze rested, finally, on a painting. Blue canvas etched in black to depict the crouching figure of a woman, her back turned to the artist. The painting hung furtively on the far wall, between two bulbous Chinese urns in blue and white.

He moved to inspect it closely, and there he remained. His utter absorption made him fascinating and my sense of propriety was no match for my curiosity. The books along the sixth shelf languished, spines dull with the year's dust, as I watched.

He leaned back, almost imperceptibly, then forwards again, his concentration absolute. His fingers, I noticed, fell long and silent at his side. Inert.

He was still standing, head tilted to the side, pondering the painting, when behind him the library door burst open and Hannah appeared, clutching the Chinese box.

"David! At last! We've had the best idea. This time we can go to—"

She stopped, startled, as Robbie turned and regarded her. A smile was slow to his lips, but when it came all hint of melancholy was swept away so completely I wondered if I'd imagined it. Without its serious demeanour, his face was boyish, smooth, almost pretty.

"Forgive me," she said, cheeks suffused with pink surprise, pale hair escaping from her bow. "I thought you were someone else." She rested the box on the corner of the sofa and, as an afterthought, straightened her white pinafore.

"You're forgiven." A smile, more fleeting than the first, and he returned his attention to the painting.

Hannah stared at his back, confusion plucking at her fingertips. She was waiting, as was I, for him to turn. To take her hand, to tell her his name, as was only polite.

"Imagine communicating so much with so little," was what he finally said.

Hannah looked towards the painting, but his back obscured it and she could offer no opinion. She took a deep breath, confounded.

"It's incredible," he continued. "Don't you think?"

His impertinence left her little choice but to accede and she joined him by the painting. "Grandfather's never liked it much." An attempt to sound breezy. "He thinks it miserable and indecent. That's why he hides it here."

"Do you find it miserable and indecent?"

She looked at the painting, as if for the first time. "Miserable perhaps. But not indecent."

Robbie nodded. "Nothing so honest could ever be indecent."

Hannah stole a glance at his profile and I wondered when she was going to ask him who he was, how he came to be admiring the paintings in her grandfather's library. She opened her mouth, but found no words forthcoming.

"Why does your grandfather hang it if he finds it indecent?" said Robbie.

"It was a gift," Hannah said, pleased to be asked a question she could answer. "From an important Spanish count who came for the hunt. It's Spanish, you know."

"Yes," he said. "Picasso. I've seen his work before."

Hannah raised an eyebrow and Robbie smiled. "In a book my mother showed me. She was born in Spain; had family there."

"Spain," said Hannah wondrously. "Have you been to Cuenca? Seville? Have you visited the Alcázar?"

"No," said Robbie. "But with all my mother's stories I feel I know the place. I always promised we'd go back together some day. Like birds, we'd escape the English winter."

"Not this winter?" Hannah said.

He looked at her, bemused. "I'm sorry, I presumed you knew. My mother's dead."

As my breath caught in my throat, the door opened and David strolled through. "I see you two have met," he said with a lazy grin.

David had grown taller since last I'd seen him, or had he? Perhaps it was nothing so obvious as that. Perhaps it was the way he walked, the way he held himself, that made him seem older, more adult, less familiar.

Hannah nodded, shifted uncomfortably to the side. She glanced at Robbie, but if she had plans to speak, to put things right between them, the moment was over too soon. The door flew open and Emmeline charged into the room.

"David!" she said. "At last. We've been so bored. We've been dying to play The Game. Hannah and I have already decided where—" She looked up, saw Robbie. "Oh. Hello. Who are you?"

"Robbie Hunter," David said. "You've already met Hannah; this is my baby sister, Emmeline. Robbie's come up from Eton."

"Are you staying the weekend?" Emmeline said, shooting a glance at Hannah.

"A bit longer, if you'll have me," said Robbie.

"Robbie didn't have plans for Christmas," said David. "I thought he might as well spend it here, with us."

"The *whole* Christmas vacation?" said Hannah.

David nodded. "We could do with some extra company, stuck all the way out here. We'll go mad otherwise."

I could feel Hannah's irritation from where I sat. Her hands had come to rest on the Chinese box. She was thinking of The Game— rule number three: only three may play. Imagined episodes, antici- pated adventures were slipping away. Hannah looked at David, her gaze a clear accusation he pretended not to see.

"Look at the size of that tree," he said with heightened cheer. "We'd better get decorating if we hope to finish by Christmas."

His sisters remained where they were.

"Come on, Emme," he said, lowering the box of decorations from the table to the floor, avoiding Hannah's eye. "Show Robbie how it's done."

Emmeline looked at Hannah. She was torn, I could tell. She shared her sister's disappointment, had been longing to play The Game herself. But she was also the youngest of three, had grown up playing third wheel to her two older siblings. And now David had singled her out. Had chosen her to join him. The opportunity to form a pair at the expense of the third was irresistible. David's affec- tion, his company, too precious to refuse.

She sneaked a glance at Hannah, then grinned at David, took the parcel he handed her and started to unwrap glass icicles, holding them up for Robbie's edification.

Hannah, meanwhile, knew when she was beaten. While Emmeline exclaimed over forgotten decorations, Hannah straightened her shoulders—dignity in defeat—and carried the Chinese box from the room. David watched her go, had the decency to look sheepish. When she returned, empty-handed, Emmeline looked up. "Hannah," she said, "you'll never believe it. Robbie says he's never even seen a Dresden cherub!"

Hannah walked stiffly to the carpet and knelt down; David sat at the piano, fanned his fingers an inch above the ivory. He lowered them slowly onto the keys, coaxing the instrument to life with gentle scales. Only when the piano and those of us listening were lulled and unsuspecting did he begin to play. A piece of music I believe to be amongst the most beautiful ever written. Chopin's waltz in C sharp minor.

Impossible as it now seems, that day in the library was the first music I had ever heard. Real music, I mean. I had vague recollections of Mother singing to me when I was very little, before her back got sore and the songs dried up, and Mr. Connelly from across the street had used to take out his flute and play maudlin Irish tunes when he had drunk too much at the public house of a Friday night. But it had never been like this.

I leaned the side of my face against the rails and closed my eyes, abandoned myself to the glorious, aching notes. I cannot truly say how well he played; with what would I compare it? But to me it was flawless, as all fine memories are.

While the final note still shimmered in the sunlit air, I heard Emmeline say, "Now let me play something, David; that's hardly Christmas music."

I opened my eyes as she started a proficient rendition of "O Come, All Ye Faithful." She played well enough, the music pretty, but a spell had been broken.

"Can you play?" Robbie said, looking towards Hannah who sat cross-legged on the floor, conspicuously quiet.

David laughed. "Hannah has many skills, but musicality is not amongst them." He grinned. "Although who knows, after all the secret lessons I hear you've been taking in the village . . ."

Hannah glanced at Emmeline, who shrugged contritely. "It just slipped out."

"I prefer words," Hannah said coolly. She unwrapped a bundle of tin soldiers and laid them in her lap. "They're more apt to do as I ask of them."

"Robbie writes too," David said. "He's a poet. A damn fine one. Had a few pieces published in the *College Chronicle* this year." He held up a glass ball, shooting splinters of prism light onto the carpet below. "What was the one I liked? The one about the decaying temple?"

The door opened then, stifling Robbie's answer, and Alfred appeared, carrying a tray laden with gingerbread men, sugarplums and paper cornucopias filled with nuts.

"Pardon me, miss," Alfred said, laying the tray atop the drinks table. "Mrs. Townsend sent these up for the tree."

"Ooh, lovely," Emmeline said, stopping mid-song and racing across to pick out a sugarplum.

As he was turning to leave, Alfred glanced surreptitiously towards the gallery and caught my prying eye. As the Hartfords turned their attention back to the tree, he slipped around behind and climbed the spiral staircase to meet me.

"How's it coming along?"

"Fine," I whispered, my voice odd to my own ears through lack of use. I glanced guiltily at the book in my lap, the empty place on the shelf, six books along.

He followed my gaze and raised his eyebrows. "Just as well I'm here to help you, then."

"But won't Mr. Hamilton—"

"He won't miss me for a half-hour or so." He smiled at me and pointed to the far end. "I'll start up that way and we can meet in the middle."

Alfred pulled a cloth from his coat pocket and a book from the shelf, and sat on the floor. I watched him, seemingly engrossed in his task, turning the book over methodically, ridding it of all dust, then returning it to the shelf and withdrawing the next. He looked like a child, turned by magic to a man's size, sitting there cross-legged, intent on his chore, brown hair, usually so tidy, flopping forward to swing in sympathy with the movement of his arm.

He glanced sideways, caught my eye just as I turned my head. His expression sparked a surprising frisson beneath my skin. I blushed despite myself. Would he think I had been looking at him? Was he still looking at me? I didn't dare check in case he mistook my attention. And yet? My skin prickled under his imagined gaze.

It had been like this for days. Something sat between us that I could not rightly name. The ease I had come to expect with him had evaporated, replaced by awkwardness, a confusing tendency towards wrong turns and misunderstandings. I wondered whether blame lay with the white-feather episode. Perhaps he'd seen me gawking in the street; worse, he'd learned it was I who'd blabbed to Mr. Hamilton and the others downstairs.

I made a show of polishing thoroughly the book in my lap and looked pointedly away, through the rails and onto the stage below. Perhaps if I ignored Alfred the discomfort would pass as blindly as the time.

Watching the Hartfords again, I felt detached: as a viewer who had dozed off during a performance, awoken to find the scenery had changed and the dialogue moved on. I focused on their voices, drifting up through the diaphanous winter light, foreign and remote.

Emmeline was showing Robbie Mrs. Townsend's sweets tray and the older siblings were discussing the war.

Hannah looked up from the silver star she was threading onto a fir frond, stunned. "But when do you leave?"

"Early next year," David said, excitement coloring his cheeks.

"But when did you . . . ? How long have you . . . ?"

He shrugged. "I've been thinking about it for ages. You know me, I love a good adventure."

Hannah looked at her brother; she had been disappointed by Robbie's unexpected presence, the inability to play The Game, but this new betrayal was much more deeply felt. Her voice was cold. "Does Pa know?"

"Not exactly," David said.

"He won't let you go." How relieved she sounded, how certain.

"He won't have a choice," said David. "He won't know I've gone until I'm safe and sound on French soil."

"What if he finds out?" Hannah said.

"He won't," David said, "because no one's going to tell him." He eyed her pointedly. "Anyway, he can make all the petty arguments he wants, but he can't stop me. I won't let him. I'm not going to miss out just because he did. I'm my own man, it's about time Pa realized that. Just because he's had a miserable life—"

"David," said Hannah sharply.

"It's true," said David, "even if you won't see it. He's been stuck under Grandmama's thumb all his life, he married a woman who couldn't stand him, he fails at every business he turns his hand to—"

"David!" said Hannah, and I felt her indignation. She glanced at Emmeline, satisfied herself that she was not within earshot. "You have no loyalty. You ought to be ashamed."

David met Hannah's eyes and lowered his voice. "I won't let him inflict his bitterness on me. It's pitiable."

"What are you two talking about?" This was Emmeline, returned with a handful of sugared nuts. Her brows knitted. "You're not rowing, are you?"

"Of course not," said David, managing a weak smile as Hannah glowered. "I was just telling Hannah I'm going to France. To war."

"How exciting! Are you going too, Robbie?"

Robbie nodded.

"I ought to have known," said Hannah.

David ignored her. "Someone's got to look after this fellow." He grinned at Robbie. "Can't let him have all the fun." I caught something in his glance as he spoke: admiration perhaps? Affection?

Hannah had seen it too. Her lips tightened. She had decided whom to blame for David's desertion.

"Robbie's going to war to escape his old man," said David.

"Why?" said Emmeline excitedly. "What did he do?"

Robbie shrugged. "The list is long and its keeper bitter."

"Give us a little hint," Emmeline said. "Please?" Her eyes widened. "I know! He's threatened to cut you from his will."

Robbie laughed, a dry, humourless laugh. "Hardly." He rolled a glass icicle between two fingers. "Quite the opposite."

Emmeline frowned. "He's threatened to put you *into* his will?"

"He'd like us to play happy families," Robbie said.

"You don't want to be happy?" Hannah said coolly.

"I don't want to be a family," Robbie said. "I prefer to be alone."

Emmeline's eyes widened. "I couldn't bear to be alone, without Hannah and David. And Pa, of course."

"It's different for people like you," Robbie said quietly. "Your family has done you no wrong."

"Yours has?" Hannah said.

There was a pause in which all eyes, including mine, focused on Robbie.

I held my breath. I already knew of Robbie's father. On the night of Robbie's unexpected arrival at Riverton, as Mr. Hamilton and Mrs. Townsend initiated a flurry of supper and accommodation arrangements, Nancy had leaned over and confided what she knew.

Robbie was son to the newly titled Lord Hasting Hunter, a scientist who had made his name and his fortune in the discovery of a new sort of glass that could be baked in the oven. He had bought a huge manor outside Cambridge, given a room over to his experiments, and he and his wife had proceeded to live the life of the landed gentry. This boy, said Nancy, was the result of an affair with his parlormaid. A Spanish girl with hardly a word of English. Lord Hunter had grown tired of her as her belly grew, but had agreed to keep her on and educate the boy in return for silence. But silence had driven her mad, driven her finally to take her own life.

It was a shame, Nancy had said, drawing breath and shaking her head, a serving maid mistreated, a boy grown up motherless. Who wouldn't have sympathy for the pair of them? All the same, she had looked at me knowingly, Her Ladyship wasn't going to appreciate this unexpected guest.

Her meaning had been clear: there were titles and there were titles, those that were of the blood and those that glistened shiny as a new motorcar. Robbie Hunter, son (illegitimate or not) of a newly titled lord, was not good enough for the likes of the Hartfords and thus not good enough for the likes of us.

"Well?" said Emmeline. "Do tell us! You must! What's your father done that's so terrible?"

"What is this," David said, smiling, "the Inquisition?" He turned to Robbie. "Apologies, Hunter. They're a snoopy pair. They don't receive much company."

Emmeline smiled and tossed a handful of paper at him. It fell far short of its mark and fluttered back upon the pile that had amassed beneath the tree.

"It's all right," Robbie said, straightening. He flicked a strand of hair from his eyes. "Since my mother's death my father has reclaimed me."

"Reclaimed you?" said Emmeline, frowning.

"After happily consigning me to a life of ignominy he now finds he needs an heir. It seems his wife can't provide one."

Emmeline looked from David to Hannah for translation.

"So Robbie's going to war," said David. "To be free."

"I'm sorry about your mother," Hannah said grudgingly.

"Oh, yes," Emmeline cut in, her childish face a model of practiced sympathy. "You must miss her terribly. I miss our own mother dreadfully and I didn't even know her; she died when I was born." She sighed. "And now you're going to war to escape your cruel father. It's like something in a novel."

"A melodrama," said Hannah.

"A romance," said Emmeline eagerly. She unrolled a parcel and a group of hand-dipped candles fell onto her lap, releasing the scent of cinnamon and hemlock. "Grandmama says it's every man's duty to go to war. She says those that stay home are shirkers."

Up in the gallery, my skin prickled. I glanced at Alfred, then looked away quickly when he met my gaze. His cheeks were blazing, eyes loud with self-reproach. Just as they had been that day in the village. He stood up abruptly, dropped his cleaning rag, but when I reached to return it to him he shook his head, refused to meet my eyes and murmured something about Mr. Hamilton wondering where he was. I watched helplessly as he hurried down the staircase and slipped from the library, unnoticed by the Hartford children. Then I cursed my lack of self-possession.

Turning from the tree, Emmeline glanced at Hannah, "Grandmama's disappointed in Pa. She thinks he's got it easy."

"She's got nothing to be disappointed about," Hannah said hotly. "And Pa's most certainly not got it easy. He'd be over there in an instant if he could."

A heavy silence fell upon the room and I was conscious of my own breath, grown fast in sympathy with Hannah.

"Don't be cross with me," Emmeline said sulkily. "It's Grandmama who said it, not me."

"Old witch," said Hannah fiercely. "Pa's doing what he's able for the war. That's all any of us can do."

"Hannah would like to be joining us at the front," David said to Robbie. "She and Pa just won't understand that war is no place for women and old men with bad chests."

"That's rubbish, David," said Hannah.

"What?" he said. "The bit about war not being for women and old men, or the bit about you wanting to join the fight?"

"You know I'd be just as much use as you. I've always been good at making strategic decisions, you said—"

"This is real, Hannah," said David abruptly. "It's a war: with real guns, real bullets and real enemies. It's not make-believe; it's not some children's game."

I drew breath; Hannah looked as if she'd been slapped.

"You can't live in a fantasy world all your life," David continued. "You can't spend the rest of your life inventing adventures, writing about things that never really happened, playing a made-up character—"

"David!" cried Emmeline. She glanced at Robbie, then back at David. Her bottom lip trembled as she said, "Rule number one: The Game is secret."

David looked at Emmeline and his face softened. "You're right. I'm sorry, Emme."

"It's secret," she whispered. "It's important."

"Course it is," said David. He tousled Emmeline's hair. "Come on, don't be upset." He leaned to peer into the decoration box. "Hey!" he said. "Look who I found. It's Mabel!" He held aloft a glass Nuremberg angel, with wings of spun glass, a crinkled gold skirt and a pious wax face. "She's your favorite, right? Should I put her up on top?"

"Can I do it this year?" Emmeline said, wiping at her eyes. Upset though she might have been, she wasn't going to let an opportunity pass.

David looked at Hannah pretending to inspect the palm of her hand. "What do you say, Hannah? Any objections?"

Hannah looked at him squarely, coldly.

"Please?" said Emmeline, jumping to her feet, a flurry of skirts and wrapping paper. "You two always put her up, I've never had a turn. I'm not a baby any more."

David made a show of deep consideration. "How old are you now?"

"Eleven," said Emmeline.

"Eleven . . ." repeated David. "Practically twelve."

Emmeline nodded eagerly.

"All right," he said finally. He nodded at Robbie, smiled. "Give me a hand?"

Between them they carried the decorating ladder to the tree, seated the base amongst the crumpled paper that was strewn across the floor.

"Ooh," Emmeline giggled, beginning to climb, the angel clutched in one hand. "I'm just like Jack climbing his beanstalk."

She continued until she reached the second-to-last rung. She stretched the hand that held the angel, reaching for the treetop, which remained tantalizingly aloof.

"Bully," she said under her breath. She glanced down at the three upturned faces. "Almost. Just one more."

"Careful," David said. "Is there something you can hold on to?"

She reached out with her free hand and clutched a flimsy bough of fir, then did the same with the other. Very slowly, she lifted her left foot and placed it carefully on the top rung.

I held my breath as she lifted her right. She was grinning triumphantly, reaching out to place Mabel on her throne, when all of a sudden our eyes locked. Her face, poking above the treetop, registered surprise, then panic as her foot slipped and she began to fall.

I opened my mouth to call out a warning, but it was too late. With a scream that made my skin prickle, she tumbled like a rag doll to the floor, a pile of white skirts amid the tissue paper.

The room seemed to expand. For just one moment, everything and everyone stood still, silent. Then, the inevitable contraction. Noise, movement, panic, heat.

David scooped Emmeline into his arms. "Emme? Are you all

right? Emme?" He glanced at the floor where the angel lay, glass wing red with blood. "Oh God, it's sliced right through."

Hannah was on her knees. "It's her wrist." She looked about for someone, found Robbie. "Fetch some help!"

I scrambled down the staircase, heart knocking against my ribcage. "I'll go, miss," I said, slipping out the door.

I ran along the corridor, unable to clear my mind of Emmeline's motionless body, every gasped breath an accusation. It was my fault she'd fallen. The last thing she had expected to see as she reached the treetop was my face.

I swung around the bottom of the stairs and bumped into Nancy.

"Watch it," she scowled.

"Nancy," I said between breaths. "Help. She's bleeding."

"I can't understand a word of your babble," said Nancy crossly. "Who's bleeding?"

"Miss Emmeline," I said. "She fell . . . in the library . . . from the ladder . . . Master David and Robert Hunter—"

"I might have known!" Nancy turned on her heel and hurried towards the servants' hall. "That boy! I had a feeling about him. Arriving unannounced as he did. It's just not done."

I tried to explain that Robbie had played no part in the accident, but Nancy would hear none of it. She clipped down the stairs, turned into the kitchen and pulled the medicine box from the sideboard. "In my experience, fellows as look like him are only ever bad news."

"But, Nancy, it wasn't his fault—"

"Wasn't his fault?" she said. "He's been here one night and look at what's happened."

I gave up my defence. I was still breathless from running and there was little I could ever say or do to change Nancy's mind once it was made up.

Nancy dug out disinfectant and bandage strips and hurried upstairs. I fell into step behind her thin, capable frame, hurrying to keep up as her black shoes beat a reproach down the dim, narrow hall. Nancy would make it better; she knew how to fix things.

But when we reached the library, it was too late.

Propped in the center of the sofa, a brave smile on her wan face, was Emmeline. Her siblings sat on either side, David stroking her healthy arm. Her wounded wrist had been bound tightly in a white strip of cloth—torn from her pinafore, I noted—and now lay across her lap. Robbie Hunter stood near, but apart.

"I'm all right," said Emmeline, looking up at us. "Mr. Hunter took care of everything." She looked at Robbie with eyes rimmed red. "I'm ever so grateful."

"We're all grateful," said Hannah, eyes still on Emmeline.

David nodded. "Mighty impressive, Hunter. You should become a doctor."

"Oh no," said Robbie quickly, "I'm not fond of blood."

David surveyed the red-stained cloths on the floor. "You did a good job pretending otherwise." He turned to Emmeline and stroked her hair. "Lucky you're not like the cousins, Emme; a nasty cut like that."

But if she heard, Emmeline made no sign. She was gazing at Robbie in much the same way Mr. Dudley had gazed at his tree. Forgotten, at her feet, the Christmas angel languished: face stoic, glass wings crushed, gold skirt red with blood.

Until We Meet Again

THAT night, high in the attic, Nancy and I curled up close in a desperate bid to stave off the icy air. The winter sun had long since set, and outside the angry wind shook the rooftop finials and crept, keening, through cracks in the wall.

"They say it's going to snow before year end," Nancy whispered, pulling the blanket up to meet her chin. "And I'd have to say as I believe them."

"The wind sounds like a baby crying," I said.

"No, it doesn't," Nancy said. "It sounds like many things, but never that."

And it was that night she told me the story of the Major and Jemima's children. The two little boys whose blood refused to clot, who had gone to their graves, one after the other, and now lay side by side in the cold hard ground of the Riverton graveyard.

The first, Timmy, had fallen from his horse, out riding with the Major on the Riverton estate.

He'd lasted four days and nights, Nancy said, before the crying finally stopped and the tiny soul found some rest. He was white as a sheet when he went, all the blood having raced to his swollen shoulder, eager for escape. I thought of the nursery book with its pretty spine, inscribed to Timothy Hartford.

"*His* cries were hard enough to listen to," Nancy said, shifting her foot so that a pocket of cold air escaped. "But they were nothing next to hers."

"Whose?" I whispered back.

"His mother's. Jemima's. Started when they carried the little one away and didn't stop for a week. If you'd only heard the sound. Grief to make your hair turn gray. Wouldn't eat, nor drink neither; faded away so as she was almost as pale as he, rest his soul."

I shivered; tried to accord this picture with the plain, plump woman who seemed far too ordinary to suffer so spectacularly. "You said 'children'? What happened to the others?"

"Other," Nancy said. "Adam. He made it older than Timmy, and we all thought he'd escaped the curse. Poor lad hadn't, though. He'd just been swaddled tighter than his brother. There wasn't much his mother would allow him to do more active than reading in the library. She wasn't planning on making the same mistake twice." Nancy sighed, pulled her knees up higher to her chest for warmth. "Ah, but there's not a mother alive who can stop her boy getting into mischief if mischief's on his mind."

"What mischief did he get up to? What was it killed him, Nancy?"

"In the end all it took was a trip up the stairs," Nancy said. "Happened at the Major's house in Buckinghamshire. I didn't see it myself, but Sarah, the housemaid there, saw it with her own two eyes, for she was dusting in the hall. She said he was running too fast, lost his footing and slipped. Nothing more. Mustn't have hurt too bad for he hopped himself up, right as rain, and kept on going. It was that evening, Sarah said, that his knee swelled up like a ripe melon—just like Timmy's shoulder before—and later in the night he started crying."

"Was it days?" I said. "Like the last time?"

"Not with Adam, no." Nancy lowered her voice. "Sarah said the poor lad screamed with agony most of the night, calling for his mother, begging her to take the pain away. There was no one in that house slept a wink that long night, not even Mr. Barker, the groom, who was all but deaf. They just lay in their beds, listening to the sound of that boy's pain. The Major stood outside the door all night, brave as anything, never shed a tear.

"Then, just before the dawn, according to Sarah, the crying stopped, sudden as you like, and the house fell to a dead silence. In the morning, when Sarah took the lad a breakfast tray, she found Jemima lying across his bed, and in her arms, face as peaceful as one of God's own angels, her boy, just as if asleep."

"Was she crying, like the time before?"

"Not this time," Nancy said. "Sarah said she looked almost as peaceful as him. Glad his suffering was over, I expect. The night was ended and she'd seen him off to a better place, where troubles and sorrows could find him no more."

I considered this. The sudden cessation of the boy's crying. His mother's relief. "Nancy," I said slowly, "you don't think—?"

"I think it was a mercy that boy went faster than his brother, is what I think," Nancy snapped.

There was silence then, and I thought for a minute she had fallen to sleep, though her breathing was still light, which made me think she had not and was just pretending. I pulled the blanket up around my neck and closed my eyes, tried not to picture screaming boys and desperate mothers.

I was just drifting off when Nancy's whisper cut through the cold air. "Now she's gone and expecting again, isn't she. Due next August." She turned pious then. "You're to pray extra hard, you hear? 'Specially now—He listens closer near Christmas. You're to pray she'll be delivered of a healthy babe this time." She rolled over and pulled the blanket with her. "One that won't go bleeding itself to an early grave."

※

CHRISTMAS came and went, Lord Ashbury's library was declared dust-free, and the morning after Boxing Day I defied the cold and headed into Saffron Green on an errand for Mrs. Townsend. Lady Violet was planning a New Year luncheon party with hopes of enlisting support for her Belgian refugee committee. She quite liked the idea, Nancy had heard her say, of expanding into French and Portuguese expatriates, should it become necessary.

According to Mrs. Townsend there was no surer way to impress at luncheon than with Mr. Georgias's genuine Greek pastries. Not that they were available to all and sundry, she added with an air of self-aggrandizement, particularly not in these testing times. No, indeed. I was to visit the grocery counter and ask for Mrs. Townsend of Riverton's special order.

Despite the glacial weather, I was glad to make the trip to town. It was a welcome change to get outside, to be alone, to spend a morning beyond the range of Nancy's endless scrutiny. For after months of relative peace, she had taken particular interest in my duties of late: watching, scolding, correcting. I had the uneasy sense of being groomed for a change I was yet to see coming.

Besides, I had my own secret reason for welcoming the village chore. The fourth of Arthur Conan Doyle's novels of Sherlock Holmes had been printed and I'd arranged with the pedlar to purchase a copy. It had taken me six months to save the money and it would be the first I had ever bought brand new. *The Valley of Fear.* The title alone made me thrill with anticipation.

The pedlar, I knew, lived with his wife and six children in a graystone back-to-back that stood at attention in a line of identical others. The street was part of a dreary housing pocket tucked behind the railway station, and the smell of burning coal hung heavy in the air. The cobblestones were black and a film of soot clung to the lamp posts. I knocked cautiously on the shabby door, then stood back to wait. A child of about three, with dusty shoes and a threadbare pullover, sat on the step beside me, drumming the downpipe with a stick. His bare knees were covered in scabs made blue by the cold.

I knocked again, harder this time. Finally the door opened to reveal a rake-thin woman with a pregnant belly tight beneath her apron and a red-eyed infant on her hip. She said nothing, looked through me with dead eyes while I found my tongue.

"Hello," I said in a voice I'd learned from Nancy. "Grace Reeves. I'm looking for Mr. Jones."

Still she said nothing.

"I'm a customer." My voice faltered slightly; an unwanted note of inquiry crept in. "I've come to buy a book?"

Her eyes flickered, an almost imperceptible sign of recognition. She hoisted the baby higher onto her bony hip and tilted her head towards a room behind. "He's out the back."

She shifted some and I squeezed past, heading in the only direction the tiny house afforded. Through the doorway was a kitchen, thick with the stench of rancid milk. Two little boys, grubby with poverty, sat at the table, rolling a pair of stones along the scratched pine surface.

The larger of the two rolled his stone into that of his brother, then looked up at me, his eyes full moons in his hollowed face. "Are you looking for my pappy?"

I nodded.

"He's outside, oiling the wagon."

I must have looked lost, for he pointed a stubby finger at a small timber door next to the stove.

I nodded again, tried to smile.

"I'll be starting working with him soon," the boy said, turning back to his stone, lining up another shot. "When I'm eight."

I made my way to the door and pushed it open.

Beneath a clothesline strung with yellow-stained sheets and shirts the pedlar was bent over inspecting the wheels of his cart. "Bloody bugger of a thing," he said under his breath.

I cleared my throat and he spun around, knocking his head on the cart handle.

"Bugger." He squinted up at me, a pipe hanging from his bottom lip.

I tried to recapture Nancy's spirit, failed, and settled for finding any voice at all. "I'm Grace. I've come about the book?" I waited. "Sir Arthur Conan Doyle?"

He leaned against the cart. "I know who you are." He exhaled and I breathed the sweet, burnt smell of tobacco. He wiped his oily hands on his trousers and regarded me. "Fixing my wagon so it's easy for the boy to manage."

"When are you going?" I said.

He gazed beyond the clothesline, heavy with its sallow ghosts, towards the sky. "Next month. With the Royal Marines." He brushed a dirty hand across his forehead. "Always wanted to see the ocean, ever since I was a boy." He looked at me and something in his expression, a sense of desolation, made me look away. Through the kitchen window I could see the woman, the infant, the two boys staring out at us. The dimpled glass, dull with soot, gave their faces the impression of reflections in a dirty pond.

The pedlar followed my gaze. "Fellow can make a good living in the forces," he said. "If he stays lucky." He threw down his cloth and headed for the house. "Come on then. Book's in here."

We made the transaction in the tiny front room, then he walked me to the door. I was careful not to glance sideways, careful not to glimpse the hungry little faces I knew would be watching. As I walked down the front steps I heard the eldest boy say, "What did the lady buy, Pappy? Did she buy soap? She smelled like soap. She was a nice lady, wasn't she, Pappy?"

I walked as quickly as my legs would carry me without breaking into a run. I wanted to be far away from that household and its children who thought that I, a common housemaid, was a lady of substance.

I was relieved finally to turn the corner into Railway Street and leave behind the oppressive stench of coal and poverty. I was no stranger to hardship—many times Mother and I had only thinly scraped by—but Riverton, I was learning, had changed me. Without realizing, I had grown accustomed to its warmth, and comfort, and plenty; had begun to expect such things. As I hurried on, crossing the street behind the horse and cart of Down's Dairies, my cheeks burning with bitter cold, I became determined not to lose them. Never to lose my place as Mother had done.

Just before the High Street intersection, I ducked beneath a canvas awning into a dim alcove and huddled by a shiny black door with a brass plaque. My breath hung white and cold in the air as I fumbled the purchase from my coat and removed my gloves.

I had barely glanced at the book in the pedlar's house save to ascertain it was the right title. Now I allowed myself to pore over its cover, to run my fingers across the leather binding and trace the cursive indentation of the letters that spelled along the spine, *The Valley of Fear*. I whispered the thrilling words to myself, then lifted the book to my nose and breathed the ink from its pages. The scent of possibilities.

I tucked the delicious, forbidden object inside my coat lining and hugged it to my chest. My first new book. My first new anything. I had now only to sneak it into my attic drawer without raising Mr. Hamilton's suspicions, or confirming Nancy's. I coerced my gloves back onto numb fingers, squinted into the frosty glare of the street and stepped out, colliding directly with a young lady walking briskly into the alcove.

"Oh, forgive me!" she said, surprised. "How clumsy I am."

I looked up and my cheeks flared. It was Hannah.

"Wait . . ." She puzzled a moment. "I know you. You work for Grandfather."

"Yes, miss. It's Grace, miss."

"Grace." My name was fluid on her lips.

I nodded. "Yes, miss." Beneath my coat, my heart drummed a guilty tattoo against my book.

She loosened a lapis-blue scarf, revealing a small patch of lily-white skin. "You once saved us from death by romantic poetry."

"Yes, miss."

She glanced at the street where icy winds were turning the air to sleet, shivered, involuntarily, into her coat. "It's an unforgiving morning to be out."

"Yes, miss," I said.

"I shouldn't have braved the weather," she added, turning back to me, her cheeks kissed by cold, "but for an extra music lesson I have scheduled."

"Me neither, miss," I said, "but for the order I'm collecting for Mrs. Townsend. Pastries. For the New Year luncheon."

She looked at my empty hands, then at the alcove from which I'd come. "An unusual place from which to purchase pastries."

I followed her gaze. The brass plaque on the black door read *Miss Dove's Secretarial School*. I cast about for a reply. Anything to explain my presence in such an alcove. Anything but the truth. I couldn't risk my purchase being discovered. Mr. Hamilton had made clear the rules concerning reading material. But what else should I say? If Hannah were to report to Lady Violet that I had been taking classes without permission, I risked losing my position.

Before I could think of an excuse, Hannah cleared her throat and fumbled with a brown paper package in her hands. "Well," she said, the word hanging in the air between us.

I waited, miserably, for the accusation to come.

Hannah shifted her position, straightened her neck and looked directly at me. She stayed that way for a moment, then finally she spoke. "Well, Grace," she said decisively. "It would appear we each have a secret."

So stunned was I that at first I didn't answer. I had been so nervous I hadn't realized she was equally so. I swallowed, clutched the rim of my hidden cargo. "Miss?"

She nodded, then confounded me, reaching forward to clasp one of my hands vehemently. "I congratulate you, Grace."

"You do, miss?"

"Yes," she said fervently. "For I know what it is you hide beneath your coat."

"Miss?"

"I know, because I've been doing the same." She indicated her package and bit back an excited smile. "These aren't music sheets, Grace."

"No, miss?"

"And I'm certainly not taking music classes." Her eyes widened. "Lessons for pleasure. At a time like this! Can you even imagine?"

I shook my head, mystified.

She leaned forward, conspiratorially. "Which is your favorite? Typing or shorthand?"

"I couldn't say, miss."

She nodded. "You're right of course: silly to talk of favorites. They're each as important as the other." She paused, smiled slightly. "Though I must admit a certain partiality to shorthand. There's something exciting about it. It's like . . ."

"Like a secret code?" I said, thinking of the Chinese box.

"Yes." Her eyes shone. "Yes, that's it exactly. A secret code. A mystery."

"Yes, miss."

She straightened then and nodded towards the door. "Well, I'd better get on. Miss Dove will be expecting me and I daren't keep her waiting. As you know, she's fierce about tardiness."

I curtsied and stepped out from under the awning.

"Grace?"

I turned back, blinking through the falling sleet. "Yes, miss?"

She lifted a finger to her lips. "We share a secret now."

I nodded, and we held each other's gaze in a moment of accord until, seemingly satisfied, she smiled and disappeared behind Miss Dove's black door.

⚘

O N 31 December, as the final moments of 1915 bled away, the staff gathered round the servants' hall dining table to usher in the New Year. Lord Ashbury had allowed us a bottle of champagne and two of beer, and Mrs. Townsend had conjured something of a feast from the ration-plundered pantry. We all hushed as the clock marched towards the ultimate moment, then cheered as it chimed in the New Year. When Mr. Hamilton had led us in a spirited verse of "Auld Lang Syne," conversation turned, as it always does, to plans and promises for the New Year. Katie had just informed us of her resolution never again to sneak cake from the larder, when Alfred made his announcement.

"I've joined up," he said, looking directly at Mr. Hamilton. "I'm going to the war."

I drew breath and everyone else fell silent, awaiting Mr. Hamilton's reaction. Finally, he spoke. "Well," he said, tightening his mouth into a grim smile. "That's a very worthy sentiment, Alfred, and I'll talk to the Master about it on your behalf, but I must say I don't imagine he'll be willing to part with you."

Alfred swallowed. "Thank you, Mr. Hamilton. But there's no need for that." He took a breath. "I've spoken to the Master myself. When he visited from London. He said I was doing the right thing, wished me luck."

Mr. Hamilton digested this. His eyes flickered at what he perceived as Alfred's perfidy. "Of course. The right thing."

"I'll be leaving in March," Alfred said tentatively. "They'll send me for training first."

"Then what?" Mrs. Townsend said, finally finding her voice. Her hands were firmly planted on her well-padded hips.

"Then . . ." an excited smile crept onto his lips. "Then France, I guess."

"Well," Mr. Hamilton said stiffly, collecting himself. "This deserves a toast." He stood and held his glass aloft, the rest of us tentatively following his lead. "To Alfred. May he be returned to us as happy and as healthy as he left us."

"You just be sure and take care of yourself, my boy," Mrs. Townsend said, her eyes glistening.

Alfred turned to me as the others refilled their glasses. "Doing my bit to defend the country, I am, Grace."

I nodded, wanting him to know that he had never been a coward. That I had never thought it of him.

"Write to me, will you, Gracie? Promise?"

I nodded again. "Course I will."

He smiled at me and I felt my cheeks warm.

"While we're celebrating," Nancy cut in, tapping her glass for quiet, "I have some news of my own."

Katie gasped. "You're never getting married, are you, Nancy?"

"Of course not," Nancy scowled.

"Then what?" Mrs. Townsend said. "Don't tell me you're leaving us too? I don't think I could take it."

"Not exactly," Nancy said. "I've signed on to become a railway-train guard. Down at the village station. I saw the advertisement when I was running errands last week." She turned to Mr. Hamilton. "The Mistress was ever so pleased with me. She said it reflected well on this house that the staff are all doing their bit."

"Indeed," Mr. Hamilton said through a sigh. "So long as the staff still manage to do their bit *inside* the house." He removed his glasses and wearily rubbed the bridge of his long nose. He replaced them and looked sternly at me. "It's you I feel sorry for, lass. There's going to be a lot of responsibility on your young shoulders with Alfred gone and Nancy working two jobs. I've no chance of finding anyone else to help. Not now. You'll need to be taking on a lot of the work upstairs until things return to normal. Do you understand?"

I nodded solemnly, "Yes, Mr. Hamilton." I also understood Nancy's recent investment in my proficiency. She had been grooming me to fill her shoes that she might more easily be granted permission to work outside.

Mr. Hamilton shook his head and rubbed his temples. "There'll be waiting at table, drawing-room duties, afternoon tea. And you'll have to help the young ladies, Miss Hannah and Miss Emmeline, with their dressing so long as they're here . . ."

His litany of chores continued, but I no longer listened. I was too excited about my new responsibilities to the Hartford sisters. After my accidental meeting with Hannah in the village, my fascination with the sisters, with Hannah in particular, had grown. To my mind, fed as it was on penny dreadfuls and mystery stories, she was a heroine: beautiful, clever and brave.

Though it would not then have occurred to me to think in such terms, I now perceive the nature of the attraction. We were two girls, the same age, living in the same house in the same country, and in Hannah I glimpsed the host of glistening possibilities that could never be mine.

✻

WITH Nancy's first railway shift scheduled for the following Friday, there was precious little time for her to brief me on my new duties. Night after night my sleep was broken by a sharp jab on the ankle, an elbow in the ribs and the impartation of a remembered instruction far too important to risk forgetting by morning.

I lay awake a good part of Thursday night, my mind racing fiercely away from sleep. By five o'clock, when I gingerly placed my bare feet on the cold timber floor, lit my candle and pulled on stockings, dress and apron, my stomach was swirling.

I fairly flew through my ordinary duties, then returned to the servants' hall and waited. I sat at the table, fingers too nervous to knit, and listened as the clock slowly ticked away the minutes.

By nine-thirty, when Mr. Hamilton checked his wristwatch against the wall clock and minded me it was time to be collecting the breakfast trays and helping the young ladies dress, I was almost bubbling over with anticipation.

Their rooms were upstairs, adjoining the nursery. I knocked

once, quickly and quietly—a mere formality, Nancy said—then pushed open the door to Hannah's bedroom. It was my first glimpse of the Shakespeare room. Nancy, reluctant to relinquish control, had insisted on delivering the breakfast trays herself before leaving for the station.

It was dark, an effect of discolored wallpaper and heavy furniture. The bedroom suite—bed, side table and duchesse—was carved mahogany, and a vermilion carpet reached almost to the walls. Above the bed hung three pictures from which the room drew its name; they were all heroines, said Nancy, from the finest English playwright that ever lived.

When I arrived, Hannah was already out of bed, sitting at the dressing table in a white cotton nightie, pale feet curled together on the vivid carpet as if in prayer, head bowed earnestly over a letter. It was as still as I'd ever seen her. Nancy had drawn the curtains and a ghost of weak sunlight crept through the sash window and up Hannah's back to play within her long flaxen braids. She didn't notice my entrance.

I cleared my throat and she looked up.

"Grace," she said matter-of-factly. "Nancy said you'd be taking over while she's at the station."

"Yes, miss," I said.

"It's not too much? Nancy's duties as well as your own?"

"Oh no, miss," I said. "Not too much at all."

Hannah leaned forward and lowered her voice, "You must be very busy—the lessons for Miss Dove on top of everything else?"

For a moment I was lost. Who was Miss Dove, and why might she be setting me lessons? Then I remembered. The secretarial school in the village. "I'm managing, miss." I swallowed, eager to change the subject. "Shall I start with your hair, miss?"

"Yes," said Hannah, nodding meaningfully. "Yes, of course. You're right not to speak of it, Grace. I should be more careful." She tried to suppress a smile, almost succeeded. Then laughed openly. "It's just . . . It's a relief having someone to share it with."

I nodded solemnly, while inside I thrilled. "Yes, miss."

With a final conspiratorial smile, she lifted a finger to her lips in a sign of silence and returned to the letter. By the address in the corner I could see it was from her father. She shifted in her seat and I looked away, fumbled with the ties at the base of her braids. I slipped them free, unravelled the long twists of hair and started to brush.

Hannah folded the letter in half and slipped it beneath a crystal bonbonnière on the dressing table. She regarded herself in the mirror, pressed her lips together and turned towards the window. "My brother is going to France," she said acrimoniously. "To fight the war."

"Is he, miss?" I said.

"He and his friend. Robert Hunter." The latter's name she said distastefully. She fingered the letter's edge. "Poor old Pa doesn't know. We're not supposed to tell him."

I brushed rhythmically, counting silently my strokes. (Nancy had said a hundred, that she'd know if I were to skip any.) Then Hannah said, "I wish I were going."

"To war, miss?"

"Yes," she said. "The world is changing, Grace, and I want to see it." She looked up at me in the mirror, blue eyes animated by sunlight, then she spoke as if reciting a line she'd learned by heart. "I want to know how it feels to be altered by life."

"Altered, miss?"

"Transformed, Grace. I don't want to go on forever reading and playing and pretending. I want to live." She looked at me again, her eyes shining. "Don't you ever feel that way? Don't you ever wish for more than life has given you?"

I stared at her an instant, warmed by the vague sense of having received a confidence; disconcerted that it seemed to require some sign of amity I was hopelessly underqualified to provide. The problem was, I simply didn't understand. The feelings she described were as a foreign language. Life had been good to me. How could I doubt it? Mr. Hamilton was always reminding me how fortunate I was to have my position, and if it wasn't him, Mother was always willing to pick up the argument. I could think of no way to respond, and yet Hannah was looking at me, waiting. I opened my mouth, my tongue pulled away from the roof with a promising click, but no words were forthcoming.

She sighed and shook her shoulders, her mouth settled into a faint smile of disappointment. "I'm sorry, Grace. I've unsettled you."

She looked away and I heard myself say, "I've sometimes thought I'd like to be a detective, miss."

"A detective?" Her eyes met mine in the mirror. "You mean like Mr. Bucket in *Bleak House*?"

"I don't know of Mr. Bucket, miss. I was thinking of Sherlock Holmes."

"Really? A detective?"

I nodded.

"Finding clues and solving crimes?"

I nodded.

"Well then," she said, disproportionately pleased. "I was wrong. You do know what I mean." And with that she looked again out of the window, smiling faintly.

I wasn't quite sure how it had happened, why my impulsive answer had pleased her so, and I didn't particularly care. All I knew was that I now basked in the warm glow of a connection having been made.

I slid the brush back onto the dressing table, wiped my hands on my apron. "Nancy said you would be wearing your walking costume today, miss."

I lifted the suit from the wardrobe and carried it to the dressing table. I held the skirt so that she might step inside.

Just then, a wallpapered door next to the bedhead swung open and Emmeline appeared. From where I knelt, holding Hannah's skirt, I watched her cross the room. Emmeline's was the type of beauty that belied her age. Something in her wide blue eyes, her full lips, even the way she yawned, gave the impression of lazy ripeness.

"How's your arm?" said Hannah, placing a hand on my shoulder for support and stepping into the skirt.

I kept my head down, hoping Emmeline's arm wasn't painful, hoping she wouldn't remember my part in her fall. But if she recognized me, it didn't show. She shrugged, rubbed absently her bandaged wrist. "It hardly hurts. I'm just leaving it bandaged for effect."

Hannah turned to face the wall and I lifted her nightie off, slipped the fitted bodice of the walking costume over her head. "You'll probably have a scar, you know," she teased.

"I know." Emmeline sat on the end of Hannah's bed. "At first I didn't want one, but Robbie said it would be a battle wound. That it would give me character."

"Did he?" said Hannah acerbically.

"He said all the best people have character."

I pulled Hannah's bodice tight, stretching the first button towards its eyelet.

"He's coming with us on our ride this morning," said Emmeline, drumming her feet against the bed. "He asked David if we could show him the lake."

"I'm sure you'll have a lovely time."

"But aren't you coming? It's the first fine day in weeks. You said you'd go mad if you had to spend much longer inside."

"I've changed my mind," said Hannah airily.

Emmeline was silent for a moment, then she said, "David was right."

As I continued to button, I was aware that Hannah's body had tensed. "What do you mean?"

"He told Robbie you were stubborn, that you'd lock yourself away all winter to avoid him if you decided on it."

Hannah pursed her lips. For a moment she was at a loss for words. "Well . . . you can tell David that he's wrong. I'm not avoiding

him at all. I have things to do inside. Important things. Things neither of you know about."

"Like sitting in the nursery, stewing, while you read through the
box again?"

"You little spy!" said Hannah indignantly. "Is it any wonder I'd
like some privacy?" She huffed. "You're wrong as it happens. I won't
be going through the box. The box is no longer here."

"What do you mean?"

"I've hidden it," said Hannah.

"Where?"

"I'll tell you next time we play."

"But we probably won't play all winter," Emmeline said. "We
can't. Not without telling Robbie."

"Then I'll tell you next summer," said Hannah. "You won't miss
it. You and David have plenty of other things to do now that Robert
Hunter is here."

"Why don't you like him?" said Emmeline.

There was an odd lull then, an unnatural pause in the conversation, during which I felt strangely conspicuous, aware of my own
heartbeat, my own breath.

"I don't know," Hannah said eventually. "Ever since he got here
things have been different. It feels like things are slipping away. Disappearing before I even know what they are." She held out her arm
while I straightened the lace cuff. "Why do you like him?"

Emmeline shrugged. "Because he's funny and clever. Because
David likes him so well. Because he saved my life."

"That's overstating it a bit," Hannah sniffed as I fastened the last
button on her bodice. She turned back to face Emmeline.

Emmeline's hand flew to her mouth and her eyes widened. She
started to laugh.

"What?" Hannah said, "What's so funny?" She stooped to take
in her reflection. "Oh," she said, frowning.

Emmeline, still laughing, collapsed sideways against Hannah's pillows. "You look like that simple boy from the village," she said. "The boy whose mother makes him wear clothes too small."

"That's cruel, Emme," Hannah said, but she laughed despite herself. She regarded her reflection, wriggled her shoulders back and forth, trying to stretch the bodice. "And quite untrue. That poor boy never looked anything like *this* ridiculous." She turned to view her reflection side-on. "I must've grown taller since last winter."

"Yes," Emmeline said, eyeing Hannah's bodice, tight across her breasts. "*Taller*. Lucky thing."

"Well," Hannah said. "I certainly can't wear this."

"If Pa would take as much interest in us as he does in his factory," Emmeline said, "he'd realize we need new clothing once in a while."

"He does his best."

"I'd hate to see his worst," Emmeline said. "We'll be making our debuts in sailor dresses if we're not careful."

Hannah shrugged. "I couldn't care less. Silly, outmoded pageant." She looked at her reflection again, tugged at the bodice. "Nonetheless, I'll have to write to Pa and ask whether we might have new clothing."

"Yes," Emmeline said. "And not pinafores. Proper dresses, like Fanny's."

"Well," Hannah said, "I'll have to wear a pinafore today. This won't do." She raised her eyebrows at me. "I wonder what Nancy will say when she finds out her rules have been broken."

"She won't be pleased, miss," I said, daring to smile back as I unbuttoned the walking suit.

Emmeline looked up; tilted her head and blinked at me. "Who's that?"

"This is Grace," Hannah said. "Remember? She saved us from Miss Prince last summer."

"Is Nancy unwell?"

"No, miss," I said. "She's down in the village, working at the station. On account of the war."

Hannah raised an eyebrow. "I pity the unsuspecting passenger who misplaces his ticket."

"Yes, miss," I said.

"Grace will be dressing us when Nancy's at the station," Hannah said to Emmeline. "Won't it be a nice change to have someone our own age?"

I curtsied and left the room, my heart singing. And a part of me hoped the war would never end.

※

I T was crisp, the March morning we saw Alfred off to war. The sky was clear and the air heady with the promise of excitement. I felt oddly infused with purpose as we walked to town from Riverton. While Mr. Hamilton and Mrs. Townsend kept the home fires burning, Nancy, Katie and I had been given special permission, on condition our duties were complete, to accompany Alfred to the station. It was our national duty, Mr. Hamilton said, to offer morale to Britain's fine young men as they dedicated themselves to their country.

Morale was to have its limits, however: under no circumstances were we to engage in conversation with any of the soldiers, for whom young ladies such as ourselves might represent easy prey.

How important I felt, striding down the High Street in my best dress, accompanied by one of the King's Army. I am certain I was not alone in feeling this rush of excitement. Nancy, I noticed, had made special efforts with her hair, her long black ponytail looped into a fancy chignon, much like the Mistress wore. Even Katie had made attempts to tame her wayward curls.

When we arrived, the station was brimming with other soldiers and their well-wishers. Sweethearts embraced, mothers straightened shiny new uniforms, and puffed-up fathers swallowed great lumps of pride. The Saffron Green recruiting depot, refusing to be outdone in such matters, had organized an enlisting drive the month before and posters of Lord Kitchener's pointed finger could still be found on every lamp post. They were to form a special battalion, Alfred said—the Saffron Lads—and would all be going in together. It was better that way, he said, to already know and like the fellows he'd be living with, fighting with.

The waiting train glistened, black and brass, punctuating the occasion from time to time with a great, impatient puff of self-important steam. Alfred carried his kit midway along the platform, then stopped. "Well, girls," he said, easing the kit to the floor and gazing about. "This looks as good a spot as any."

We nodded, drinking in the carnival atmosphere. Somewhere at the far end of the platform, up where the officers gathered, a band was playing. Nancy waved officially to a stern conductor, who nodded a curt reply.

"Alfred," said Katie coyly, "I've got something for you."

"Do you, Katie?" said Alfred. "That's mighty nice of you." He presented his cheek.

"Oh, Alfred," said Katie, blushing like a ripe tomato. "I never meant a *kiss*."

Alfred winked at Nancy and me. "Well now, that's a disappointment, Katie. Here I was, thinking you were going to leave me with a little something to remember home by when I'm far away across the sea."

"I am." Katie held out a crumpled tea towel. "Here."

Alfred raised an eyebrow. "A tea towel? Why, thank you, Katie. That'll certainly remind me of home."

"It's not a tea towel," said Katie. "Well, it is. But that's just the wrapping. Look inside."

Alfred peeled open the package to reveal three slices of Mrs. Townsend's Victoria sponge cake.

"There's no butter or cream, on account of the shortages," said Katie. "But it's not bad."

"And just how do you know that, Katie?" snapped Nancy. "Mrs. Townsend won't be happy you've been in her larder again."

Katie's bottom lip folded. "I just wanted to send something with Alfred."

"Yes," Nancy's expression softened. "Well, I suppose that's all right then. Just this once: for the sake of the war effort." She turned her attention to Alfred. "Grace and I have something for you, too, Alfred. Don't we, Grace? Grace?"

Up at the far end of the platform I had noticed a couple of familiar faces: Emmeline, standing near Dawkins, Lord Ashbury's chauffeur, amid a sea of young officers in smart new uniforms.

"Grace?" Nancy shook my arm. "I was telling Alfred about our gift."

"Oh. Yes." I reached into my bag and handed Alfred a small package wrapped in brown paper.

He unwrapped it carefully, smiling at its contents.

"I knitted the socks and Nancy the scarf," I said.

"Well," said Alfred, inspecting the items. "They look mighty fine." He closed his hand around the socks, looked at me. "I'll be sure to think of you—all three of you—when I'm snug as a bug and all the other boys are going cold. They'll envy me my three girls: the best in all of England."

He tucked the gifts into his kit, then folded the paper neatly and handed it back to me. "Here you are, Grace. Mrs. T will be on the warpath as it is, looking for the rest of her cake. Don't want her missing her baking paper too."

I nodded, pressed the paper into my bag; felt his eyes on me.

"You won't forget to write to me, will you, Gracie?"

I shook my head, met his gaze. "No, Alfred. I won't forget you."

"You'd better not," he said, smiling at me. "Or there'll be trouble when I'm back." He sobered. "I'm going to miss you." He looked then at Nancy and Katie. "All of you."

"Oh, Alfred," said Katie excitedly. "Look at the other fellows. Ever so smart in their new uniforms. Are they all Saffron Lads?"

As Alfred pointed out some of the other young men he'd met at the recruiting depot, I looked up the track again, watched as Emmeline waved to another group and ran off. Two of the young officers turned to watch her go and I saw their faces. David and Robbie Hunter. Where was Hannah? I craned to see. She had avoided David and Robbie as best she could over the winter, but surely she wouldn't miss seeing David off to war?

". . . and that's Rufus," said Alfred, pointing out a skinny soldier with long teeth. "His father's the ragman. Rufus used to help him, but he reckons he's more chance of a regular meal in the army."

"That may be," Nancy said. "If you're a ragman. But you can't say you don't do very well for yourself at Riverton."

"Oh no," said Alfred. "I've no complaints in that department. Mrs. Townsend, and the Master and Mistress, they keep us well fed." He smiled, then said, "I must say I get sick of being cooped up inside, though. I'm looking forward to living the open-air life for a bit."

An aeroplane droned overhead, a Blériot XI-2 said Alfred, and a cheer went up amongst the crowd. A wave of excitement rolled along the platform, collecting us all in its wash. The conductor, a distant speck of black and white, blew his whistle, then called for boarding through his megaphone.

"Well," said Alfred, a smile tugging at his lips. "Here I go then."

A figure appeared at the end of the station. Hannah. She scanned the platform, waved hesitantly when she saw David. She wove through the crowd, stopping only when she reached her brother. She stood for a moment, without speaking, then she pulled something from her bag and gave it to him. I already knew what it was. I had seen it on her duchesse that morning. *Journey Across the Rubicon*. It was one of the tiny books from The Game, one of their favorite adventures, carefully described, illustrated and bound with thread. She'd wrapped it in an envelope and tied it with string.

David looked at it, then at Hannah. He tucked it in his breast pocket, rubbed his hand over it, then reached out and squeezed both her hands; he looked as if he wanted to kiss her cheeks, hug her, but that was not the way it went with them. So he didn't. He leaned closer and said something to her. They both looked towards Emmeline, and Hannah nodded.

David turned then and said something to Robbie. He looked back at Hannah and she started searching through her bag again. She was looking for something to give him, I realized. David must have suggested that Robbie needed his own good-luck charm.

Alfred's voice, close to my ear, pulled my wandering attention back. "Bye-bye, Gracie," he said, his lips brushing hair near my neck. "Thanks ever so for the socks."

My hand leaped to my ear, still warm from his words, as Alfred threw his kit over his shoulder and headed for the train. As he reached the door he climbed onto the carriage step and turned, grinning at us over the heads of his fellow soldiers. "Wish me luck," he said, then disappeared, pushed through the door by the others eager to climb aboard.

I waved my arm. "Good luck," I called to the backs of strangers, sensing suddenly the hole that would be left at Riverton by his departure.

Up at first class, David and Robbie boarded with the other officers. Dawkins walked behind with David's bags. There were fewer officers than infantry, and they found seats easily, each appearing at a window while Alfred jostled for standing space in his carriage.

The train whistled again, and belched, filling the platform with steam. Long axles began to heave, gathering momentum, and the train drew slowly forward.

Hannah kept up alongside, still searching her bag, fruitlessly it seemed. Finally, as the train gained pace, she looked up, slipped the white satin bow from her hair, and held it up to Robbie's waiting hand.

PART TWO

THE TWELFTH OF JULY

❀

I AM to be in the film. Well, not me, but a young girl pretending to be me. Regardless how peripheral one's connection to calamity, it would appear that to live long enough is to be rendered an object of interest. I received the phone call two days ago: Ursula, the young filmmaker with the slim figure and the long ashen hair, wondering whether I would be willing to meet the actress with the dubious honor of playing the role of "Housemaid 1," now retitled "Grace."

They are coming here, to Heathview. It is not the most atmospheric place to rendezvous, but I have neither heart nor feet to journey far and can pretend otherwise for no one. So it is I am sitting in the chair in my room, waiting.

There comes a knock at the door. I look at the clock—half past nine. They are right on time. I realize I am holding my breath and wonder why.

Then they are in the room, my room. Sylvia and Ursula and the young girl charged with representing me.

"Good morning, Grace," Ursula says, smiling at me from beneath her wheat-colored fringe. She bends to brush a kiss on my cheek, utterly surprising me.

My voice sticks in my throat.

She sits on the blanket at the end of my bed—a presumptive action that I'm surprised to discover I don't mind—and takes my hand. "Grace," she says, "this is Keira Parker." She turns to smile at the girl behind me. "She'll be playing you in the film."

135

The girl, Keira, steps from the shadow. She is seventeen, if a day, and I am struck by her symmetrical prettiness. Blond hair to her shoulderblades pulled back in a ponytail. A round face, full lips coated in thick, shiny lip gloss, and blue eyes beneath a blank brow. A face made to sell chocolates.

I clear my throat, remember my manners. "Sit down, won't you?" And I point to the brown vinyl chair Sylvia brought in earlier from the morning room.

Keira sits daintily, wraps her thin denim-clad legs one around the other and glances surreptitiously to her left, my dressing table. Her jeans are tattered, loose threads hanging from the pockets. Rags are no longer a sign of poverty, Sylvia has informed me; they are an emblem of style. Keira smiles impassively, letting her gaze turn over my possessions. "Thanks for seeing me, Grace," she remembers to say.

Her use of my first name rankles. But I am being unreasonable and admonish myself. If she had addressed me by title or surname I would have insisted on the dispensation of such formality.

I am aware that Sylvia still lurks by the open door, wiping the dust from the jamb in a show of duty designed to disguise her curiosity. She is a great one for film actors and soccer stars. "Sylvia, dear," I say, "do you think we might have some tea?"

Sylvia looks up, her face a study in irreproachable devotion. "Tea?"

"Perhaps some biscuits," I say.

"Of course." Reluctantly, she pockets her cloth.

I nod towards Ursula.

"Yes, please," she says. "White and one."

Sylvia turns to Keira, "And you, Ms. Parker?" Her voice is nervous, her cheeks disappear beneath a creeping crimson, and I realize the young actress must be known to her.

Keira yawns. "Green tea and lemon."

"Green tea," Sylvia says slowly, as if she has just learned the answer to the origins of the universe. "Lemon." She remains unmoving in the doorjamb.

"Thank you, Sylvia," I say. "I'll have my usual."

"Yes." Sylvia blinks, a spell is broken, and she finally pulls herself away. The door closes behind her and I am left alone with my two guests.

Immediately I regret sending Sylvia away. I am overwhelmed by a sudden and irrational sense that her presence warded off the past's return.

But she is gone, and we remaining three share a moment's silence. I sneak another glance at Keira, study her face, try to recognize my young self in her pretty features. Suddenly a burst of music, muffled and tinny, breaks the silence.

"Sorry," says Ursula, fumbling in her bag. "I meant to turn the sound off." She withdraws a small black mobile phone and the volume crescendoes, stops mid-bar when she presses a button. She smiles, embarrassed. "I'm so sorry." She glances at the screen and a cloud of consternation colors her face. "Will you excuse me a moment?"

Keira and I both nod as Ursula leaves the room, phone to her ear.

The door sighs shut and I turn to my young visitor. "Well," I say, "I suppose we ought to begin."

She nods, almost imperceptibly, and pulls a folder from her tote bag. She opens it and withdraws a wad of paper held together with a bulldog clip. I can see from the layout that it is a script—bold words in capitals followed by longer portions of regular font.

She flicks past a few pages and stops, presses her shiny lips together. "I was wondering," she says, "about your relationship with the Hartford family. With the girls."

I nod. That much I had presumed.

"My part isn't one of the big ones," she says. "I haven't many lines, but I'm in a lot of the earlier shots." She looks at me. "You know. Serving drinks, that sort of thing."

I nod again.

"Anyway, Ursula thought it would be a good idea for me to talk to you about the girls: what you thought of them. That way I'll get some idea of my *motivation*." The final word she speaks pointedly, enunciating as if it were a foreign term with which I might not be familiar. She straightens her back and her expression takes on a varnish of fortification. "Mine isn't the starring role, but it's still important to give a strong performance. You never know who might be watching."

I nod and she continues.

"That's why I need you to tell me how you felt. About your job and about the girls." She leans forward, her eyes the cold blue of Venetian glass. "It gives me an advantage, you see, you still being . . . I mean, the fact that you're still . . ."

"Alive," I say. "Yes, I see." I almost admire her candor. "What exactly would you like to know?"

She smiles; relieved, I imagine, that her faux pas has been swallowed quickly by the current of our conversation. "Well," she says, scanning the piece of paper resting on her knees. "I'll get the dull questions out of the way first."

My heart quickens. I wonder what she's going to ask.

"Did you enjoy being a servant?" she says.

I exhale: more an escaped breath than a sigh. "Yes," I say, "for a time."

She looks doubtful. "Really? I can't imagine enjoying waiting on people all day every day. What did you like about it?"

"The others became like a family to me. I enjoyed the camaraderie."

"The others?" Her eyes widen hungrily. "You mean Emmeline and Hannah?"

"No. I mean the other staff."

"Oh." She is disappointed. No doubt she had glimpsed a larger role for herself, an amended script in which Grace the housemaid is no longer an outside observer, but a secret member of the Hartford sisters' coterie. She is young, of course, and from a different world. She doesn't conceive that certain lines should not be crossed. "That's nice," she says. "But I don't have scenes with the other actors playing servants, so it's not much use to me." She runs her pen down the list of questions. "Was there anything you *didn't* like about being a servant?"

Day after day of waking with the birds; the attic that was an oven in summer and an ice box in winter; hands red raw from laundering; a back that ached from cleaning; weariness that permeated to the center of my bones. "It was tiring. The days were long and full. There was not much time for oneself."

"Yes," she says, "that's how I've been playing it. I mostly don't even have to pretend. After a day of rehearsal my arms are agony from carrying the bloody tray around."

"It was my feet that hurt the most," I say. "But only in the beginning, and once when I turned sixteen and had my new shoes."

She writes something on the back of her script, in round cursive strokes, nods. "Good," she says. "I can use that." She continues to scribble, finishing with a flourish of the pen. "Now for the interesting stuff. I want to know about Emmeline. That is, how you felt about her."

I hesitate, wondering where to begin.

"It's just, we share a few scenes and I'm not sure what I should be thinking. Conveying."

"What kind of scenes?" I say, curious.

"Well, for instance, there's the one where she first meets R. S. Hunter, down near the lake, and she slips and almost drowns and I have to—"

"Near the lake?" I am confused. "But that's not where they met. It was the library, it was winter, they were—"

"The library?" she wrinkles her perfect nose. "No wonder the scriptwriters changed it. There's nothing dynamic about a room full of old books. It works really well this way, the lake being where he killed himself and all. Kind of like the end of the story is in the beginning. It's romantic."

I will have to take her word for it.

"Anyway, I have to run back to the house for help and when I get back he's already rescued her and revived her. The way the actress is playing it, she's too busy looking up at him to even notice that we've all come to help her." She pauses, looks at me wide-eyed, as if she has made her meaning clear. "Well, don't you think I should—Grace should—react a bit?"

I am slow to respond and she leaps ahead.

"Oh, not obviously. Just a subtle reaction. You know the sort of thing." She sniffs slightly, tilts her head so that her nose is in the air, and sighs. I do not realize that this is an impromptu performance for my benefit until she drops the expression and replaces it with a wide-eyed gaze in my direction. "See?"

I hesitate, choose my words judiciously. "It's up to you, of course, how you play your character. How you play Grace. But if it were me, and it was 1915 again, I can't imagine I would have reacted . . ." I wave my hand at her, unable to put words to her performance.

She stares at me as though I've missed some vital nuance. "But don't you think it's a bit thoughtless not even to thank Grace for running for help? I feel stupid running off and then coming back just to stand there again like a zombie."

I sigh. "Perhaps you're right, but that was the nature of service in those days. It would have been unusual had she not been that way. Do you see?"

She looks dubious.

"I didn't expect her to be any other way."

"But you must have *felt* something?"

"Of course." I am overcome with an unexpected distaste for discussing the dead. "I just didn't show it."

"Never?" She neither wants nor waits for an answer and I am

glad, for I don't want to give it. She pouts. "The whole servant-mistress thing just seems so ridiculous. One person doing the bidding of the other."

"It was a different time," I say simply.

"That's what Ursula says, too." She sighs. "It doesn't help me much, though, does it? I mean, acting's all about reacting. It's a bit hard to create an interesting character when the stage direction is 'don't react.' I feel like a cardboard cut-out, just 'yes, miss-ing,' 'no, miss-ing,' 'three bags full, miss-ing.' "

I nod. "Must be difficult."

"I tried out for the part of Emmeline originally," she says confidingly. "Now *that's* a dream role. Such an interesting character. And so glamorous, what with her being an actress and dying like she did in that car accident."

I can sense her disappointment and I do not blame her; I dare say there were many times I would have much preferred to be Emmeline rather than the housemaid.

"Anyway," she says discontentedly, "I'm playing Grace and I have to make the best of it. Besides, Ursula promised they'd interview me specially for the DVD release, seeing as I'm the only one who gets to meet my character in real life."

"I'm glad to be of some use."

"Yes," she says, my irony lost on her.

"Do you have any more questions?"

"I'll check." She turns a page, and something drops from its hiding spot, flutters to the ground like a mammoth gray moth, lands face down. When she reaches to pick it up I see that it is a photograph, a host of black and white figures with serious faces. Even from a distance the image is familiar to me. I remember it instantly, in the same way a film seen long ago, a dream, a painting, can be recalled through its merest shape.

"May I see?" I say, reaching out my hand.

She passes the photograph to me, lays it across my gnarled fingers. Our hands meet for an instant and she withdraws quickly, frightened she might catch something. Old age perhaps.

The photograph is a copy. Its surface smooth and cold and matt. I tilt the image towards the window so that it catches the light shining in off the heath. I squint through my glasses.

There we are. The Riverton household of summer 1916.

※

T H E R E was one like it for every year; Lady Violet used to insist on it. They were commissioned annually, a photographer brought in from a London studio, the auspicious day greeted with all due pomp and circumstance.

The resulting photograph, two rows of serious faces gazing unblinking at the black-hooded camera, would then be hand-delivered, displayed on the drawing-room mantel a while, then pasted in the appropriate page in the Hartford family scrapbook, along with invitations, menus and newspaper clippings.

Had it been the photograph from any other year, I might not have known its date. But this particular image is memorable for the events it immediately preceded.

Mr. Frederick sits front and center, his mother on one side, Jemima on the other. The latter is huddled, a black shawl draped about her shoulders to disguise her heavy pregnancy. Hannah and Emmeline sit at either end, parentheses—one taller than the other—in matching black dresses. New dresses, but not of the kind imagined by Emmeline.

Standing behind Mr. Frederick, center of a shadow row, is Mr. Hamilton, with Mrs. Townsend and Nancy beside. Katie and I stand behind the Hartford girls, with Mr. Dawkins, the chauffeur, and Mr. Dudley at the edges. The rows are distinct. Only Nanny Brown occupies a place between, dozing in a cane chair from the conservatory, neither in front nor behind.

I look at my serious face, my severe hairstyle giving my head the appearance of a pin, accentuating my too-large ears. I stand directly behind Hannah, her pale hair, brushed into ripples, stark against the edges of my black dress.

We all wear grave expressions, a custom of the time, but particularly appropriate to this photograph. The servants are in black as always, but so is the family. For that summer they had joined the mourning that was general across England and across the world.

It was the twelfth day of July 1916, the day after the joint funeral service for Lord Ashbury and the Major. The day Jemima's baby arrived, and the day the question on all our lips was answered.

❧

I T was awfully hot that summer, and on the morning of the photograph I woke earlier than usual. The sun topped the birch trees that lined the lake and pierced the attic window so that a stream of hot light pointed across the bed, stroked my face. I didn't mind. It was nice for a change to wake with the light rather than beginning work in the cold dark of the sleeping house. For a maid, the summer sun was a steadfast companion to the day's activities.

The photographer had been booked for nine-thirty, and by the time we assembled on the front lawn the air was tight with shimmering heat. The family of swallows who considered Riverton their own sought refuge beneath the attic eaves, watching us curiously and quietly, robbed of their spirit for singing. Even the trees that lined the driveway were silent. Their leafy tops sat motionless, as if to conserve energy, until coerced by some slight breeze to emit a disgruntled rustle.

The photographer, his face spotted with perspiration, arranged us, one by one, the family seated, the surplus standing at the back. There we remained, all in black, eyes on the camera box and thoughts in the churchyard valley.

Afterwards, in the comparative cool of the stone servants' hall, Mr. Hamilton had Katie pour lemonades while the rest of us sank listlessly onto chairs around the table.

"It's the end of an era, and that's a fact," Mrs. Townsend said, dabbing at her puffy eyes with a handkerchief. She had been crying for most of July, starting when news came of the Major's death in France, pausing only to gain momentum when Lord Ashbury suffered a fatal stroke the following week.

"The end of an era," Mr. Hamilton said, sitting opposite her. "That it is, Mrs. Townsend."

"When I think of His Lordship . . ." Her words tapered off and she shook her head, planted her elbows on the table and buried her swollen face in her hands.

"The stroke was sudden," Mr. Hamilton said.

"Stroke!" Mrs. Townsend said, lifting her face. "That may be what they're calling it, but he died of a broken heart. You mark my words. Couldn't bear losing his son like that."

"I dare say you're right, Mrs. Townsend," Nancy said, tying her guard's scarf around her neck. "They were tight, he and the Major."

"The Major!" Mrs. Townsend's eyes brimmed anew and her bottom lip trembled. "That dear boy. To think of him going like that. On some God-awful mudflat in France."

"The Somme," I said, tasting the roundness of the word, its hum of foreboding. I thought of Alfred's most recent letter, thin sheets of grubby paper that smelled of far away. It had arrived for me two days earlier, posted from France the week before. The letter had presented a light enough veneer, but there was something in its tone, the things that were not said, that left me uneasy. "Is that where Alfred is, Mr. Hamilton? The Somme?"

"I should say so, my girl. From what I've heard in the village, I'd say that's where they've sent the Saffron Lads."

Katie, who had arrived with a tray of lemonades, gasped. "Mr. Hamilton, what if Alfred—"

"Katie!" Nancy cut in sharply, glancing at me as Mrs. Townsend's hand leaped to her mouth. "Just you mind where you put that tray and keep your trap shut."

Mr. Hamilton's lips pursed. "Now don't you girls worry about Alfred. He's in good spirits and good hands. Those in command will do what's best. They wouldn't send Alfred and his lads into battle if they weren't confident of their abilities to defend King and country."

"That doesn't mean he won't get shot," Katie said, sulking. "The Major did, and he's a hero."

"Katie!" Mr. Hamilton's face turned the color of stewed rhubarb as Mrs. Townsend gasped. "Show some respect." He dropped his voice to a quivering whisper. "After all the family has had to endure these last weeks." He shook his head, straightened his glasses. "I can't even look at you, girl. Get into the scullery and . . ." He turned to Mrs. Townsend for help.

Mrs. Townsend lifted her puffy face from the table and said, between sobs, "And clean out every one of my baking pots and pans. Even the old ones left out for the pot man."

We remained in silence as Katie crept off to the scullery. Silly Katie, with her talk of dying. Alfred knew how to take care of himself. He was always saying so in his letters, telling me not to get too used to his duties because he'd be back in no time to take them up again. Telling me to keep his place warm for him. I thought then of something else Alfred had said. Something that had me worried about all our places.

"Mr. Hamilton," I said quietly. "I don't mean any disrespect by it, but I've been wondering what it all means for us? Who will be in charge now that Lord Ashbury . . . ?"

"Surely it will be Mr. Frederick?" said Nancy. "He's Lord Ashbury's only other son."

"No," Mrs. Townsend said, looking to Mr. Hamilton. "It will be the Major's son, won't it? When he's born. He's next in line for the title."

"I'd say it all depends," Mr. Hamilton said gravely.

"On what?" Nancy said.

Mr. Hamilton surveyed us all. "On whether it's a son or a daughter Lady Jemima's carrying."

Mention of her name was enough to start Mrs. Townsend crying again. "That poor lamb," she said. "To lose her husband. And she about to have a wee baby. It just isn't right."

"I imagine there's others like her right across England," Nancy said, shaking her head.

"But it's not the same, is it?" Mrs. Townsend said. "Not the same as when it happens to one of your own."

The third bell along the bracket near the stairs rang and Mrs. Townsend jumped. "Oh my," she said, hand fluttering to her ample bosom.

"Front door." Mr. Hamilton stood and pushed his chair neatly beneath the table. "Lord Gifford, no doubt. Here to read the will." He slipped his arms into his jacket coat and straightened the collar, looked at me over his glasses before he started up the stairs. "Lady Ashbury will ring for tea any minute, Grace. When you've done that, be sure and take a carafe of lemonade outside to Miss Hannah and Miss Emmeline."

As he disappeared up the stairs, Mrs. Townsend patted one hand rapidly across her heart. "My nerves aren't what they were," she said sadly.

"Not helped by this heat," Nancy said. She glanced at the wall clock. "Look here, it's only just now gone half ten. Lady Violet won't ring for luncheon for another two hours. Why don't you take your rest early today? Grace can manage the tea."

I nodded, glad for something to do that would take my mind off the household's grief.

※

I CARRIED the tray up the darkened servants' hall stairs and into the main hall. Was enveloped immediately by light and heat. While every curtain in the house had been drawn in accordance with Lady Ashbury's insistence on strict Victorian mourning, there were none to cover the elliptical glass panel above the front door, and sunlight was left to penetrate without restraint. It made me think of the camera. The room was a flash of light and life in the center of a shrouded black box.

I crossed to the drawing room and pushed open the door. The room was heavy with warm, stale air that had drifted in with summer's start and become trapped by the house's grief. The huge French doors remained closed and both the heavy brocade curtains and the silk undercurtains had been drawn, hanging in an attitude of lethargy. I hesitated by the door. There was something about the room that made me loath to proceed, some difference that had nothing to do with the dark or the heat.

As my eyes readjusted, the room's somber tableau began to materialize. Lord Gifford, a man of later years and florid complexion, sat in the late Lord Ashbury's armchair, a black leather folder open across his generous lap. He was reading aloud, enjoying his voice's resonance in the dim room. On the table next to him, an elegant brass lamp with a floral shade cast a neat ring of soft light.

On the leather sofa opposite, Jemima sat beside Lady Violet. Widows both. The latter seemed to have diminished in size and stature even since the morning: a tiny figure in a black crêpe dress, face obscured by a veil of dark lace. Jemima was also in black, her face an ashen contrast. Her hands, usually fleshy, now seemed small and frail as they caressed absently her swollen belly. Lady Clementine had retired to her bedroom, but Fanny, still in ardent pursuit of Mr. Frederick's hand in marriage, had been permitted attendance and sat self-importantly on Lady Violet's other side, a practised expression of sorrow on her face.

Atop the nearby table, flowers I had picked from the estate garden only that morning, blooms of pink rhododendrons, creamy clematis and sprigs of jasmine, now wept from their vase in sad despondency. The fragrance of jasmine filled the closed room with a pungency that threatened suffocation.

On the other side of the table, Mr. Frederick stood with his hand resting on the mantelpiece, his coat stiff on his tall frame. In the half-light his face was as still as a wax mannequin's, his eyes unblinking, his expression stony. The lamp's feeble glow threw a shadow across one eye. The other was dark, fixed, intent on its prey. As I watched him, I realized he was watching me.

He beckoned with the fingertips of the hand that braced the mantelpiece: a subtle gesture that I would have missed had not the rest of his body been so still. He wished me to bring the tray to him. I glanced towards Lady Violet, unsettled as much by this change in convention as I was by Mr. Frederick's unnerving attention. She did not look my way so I did as he proposed, careful to avoid his gaze. When I slid the tray onto the table he nodded again at the teapot, commanding me to pour, then returned his attention to Lord Gifford.

I had never poured tea before, not in the drawing room, not for the Mistress. I hesitated, unsure how to proceed, then picked up the milk jug, glad of the dark, as Lord Gifford continued to speak.

". . . in effect, aside from the exceptions already specified, Lord Ashbury's entire estate, along with his title, was to pass to his eldest son and heir, Major Jonathan Hartford . . ."

Here he paused. Jemima stifled a sob, all the more wretched for its suffocation.

Above me, Frederick made a clicking sound in his throat. Impatience, I decided, sneaking a glance as I poured milk into the final cup. His chin was stiffly set, jutting out from his neck in an attitude of stern authority. He exhaled: a long and measured breath. His fingers drummed a quick tattoo on the mantelpiece and he said, "Go on, Lord Gifford."

Lord Gifford shifted in Lord Ashbury's seat and the leather sighed, grieving for its departed master. He cleared his throat, raised his voice.

". . . given that no new arrangements were made after news of Major Hartford's death, the estate will pass, in line with the ancient laws of primogeniture, to Major Hartford's eldest male child." He looked over the rim of his glasses at Jemima's belly and continued. "Should Major Hartford have no surviving male children, the estate and title pass instead to Lord Ashbury's second son, Mr. Frederick Hartford."

Lord Gifford looked up and the lamplight reflected in the glass of his spectacles. "It would appear we have a waiting game ahead."

He paused and I took the opportunity to hand tea to the ladies. Jemima took hers automatically, without looking at me, and lowered it to her lap. Lady Violet waved me away. Only Fanny took the proffered cup and saucer with any appetite.

"Lord Gifford," Mr. Frederick said in a calm voice, "how do you take your tea?"

"Milk but no sugar," Lord Gifford said, running his fingers along his collar, separating the cotton from his sticky neck.

I lifted the teapot carefully and began to pour, mindful of the steaming spout. I handed him the cup and saucer, which he took without seeing me. "Business is well, Frederick?" he said, rubbing his pillowy lips together before sipping his tea.

From the corner of my eye I saw Mr. Frederick nod. "Well enough, Lord Gifford," he said. "My men have made the transition from motorcar to aeroplane production and there's another contract with the war ministry up for tender."

Lord Gifford raised a brow. "Better hope that American company doesn't submit a quote. One hears they've made enough planes for every man, woman and child in Britain!"

"I won't argue they've produced a lot of planes, Lord Gifford, but you wouldn't catch me flying in one."

"No?"

"Mass production," said Mr. Frederick, by way of explanation. "People working too quickly, trying to keep up with conveyor belts, no time to make sure things are done properly."

"The ministry doesn't seem to mind."

"The ministry can't see past the bottom line," said Mr. Frederick. "But they will. Once they see the quality we're producing, they won't sign up for any more of those tin cans." And then he laughed rather too loudly.

I glanced up, despite myself. It seemed to me that for a man who had lost his father and only brother within a matter of days, he was coping remarkably well. Too well, I thought, and I began to doubt Nancy's fond description of him, Hannah's devotion, tallying him more with David's characterization of a petty and embittered man.

"Any word from young David?" Lord Gifford said.

A sharp intake of breath from Jemima drew all eyes in synchronicity. She straightened, clutched at her side, walked flat hands across her tight belly.

"What is it?" Lady Violet said from beneath her lace veil.

Jemima did not respond, engaged, or so it seemed, in silent communication with her babe. She stared, unseeing, directly ahead, still prodding her belly.

"Jemima?" This was Lady Violet again, concern icing a voice already chilled by loss.

Jemima inclined her head as if to listen. She said, barely a whisper, "He stopped moving." Her breaths had become rapid. "He's been active all the way through, but he's stopped."

"You must go and rest," Lady Violet said. "It's this blessed heat." She swallowed. "This blessed heat." She looked about, seeking corroboration. "That, and . . ." She shook her head, tightened her lips, unwilling, unable perhaps, to speak the final clause. "That's all it is." She drew up all her courage, straightened and said firmly, "You must rest."

"No," Jemima said, bottom lip trembling. "I want to be here. For Jonathan. And for you."

Lady Violet took Jemima's hands, withdrew them gently from her stomach and cradled them within her own. "I know you do." She reached out, stroked tentatively Jemima's mousy brown hair. It was a simple gesture, but in its enactment I was reminded that Lady Violet was herself a mother. Without moving, she said, "Grace. Help Mrs. Hartford upstairs so that she may rest."

"Yes, my Lady." I curtsied and came to Jemima's side. I reached down and helped her stand, glad for the opportunity to leave the room and its misery.

On my way out, Jemima beside me, I realized what was different about the room, aside from the dark and the heat. The mantel clock, which usually marked each passing second with detached consistency, was silent. Its slender black hands frozen in arabesque, observing Lady Ashbury's instructions to stop all the upstairs clocks at ten minutes before five, the moment of her husband's passing.

THE FALL OF ICARUS

WITH Jemima settled in her room, I returned to the servants' hall, where Mr. Hamilton was inspecting the pots and pans Katie had been scrubbing. He looked up from Mrs. Townsend's favorite sauté pan only to tell me that the Hartford sisters were down by the old boathouse and I was to take them refreshments. I fetched a jug of lemonade from the ice room, loaded it onto a tray with two tall glasses and a platter of Mrs. Townsend's ribbon sandwiches, and left via the servants' hall door.

I stood on the top step, blinking into the shimmering glare while my eyes adjusted. In a month without rain, color had been bleached from the estate. The sun was midway across the sky and its direct light provided a final wash, giving the garden the hazy look of one of the watercolors that hung in Lady Violet's boudoir. Although I wore my cap, the line down the center of my head where I parted my hair remained exposed and was instantly scorched.

I crossed the Theatre Lawn, freshly mown and rich with the soporific scent of dry grass. Dudley crouched nearby, clipping the border hedges. The blades of his shears were smeared with green sap, patches of bare metal glistened.

He must have sensed me nearby because he turned and squinted. "She's a hot one," he said, hand shielding his eyes.

"Hot enough to cook eggs on the railway," I said, quoting Nancy, wondering whether there was truth in the expression.

At the lawn's edge, a grand set of graystone stairs led into Lady

Ashbury's rose garden. Pink blooms hugged the trellises, alive with the warm drone of diligent bees hovering about their yellow hearts.

I passed beneath the arbor, unlatched the kissing gate and started down the Long Walk: a stretch of gray cobblestones set amongst a carpet of white alyssum. Halfway along, tall hornbeam hedges gave way to the miniature yew that bordered the Egeskov Garden. I blinked as a couple of topiaries came to life, then smiled at myself and the pair of indignant ducks that had wandered up from the lake and now stood regarding me with shiny black eyes.

At the end of the Egeskov Garden was the second kissing gate, the forgotten sister (for there is always a forgotten sister), victim of the wiry jasmine tendrils. On the other side lay the Icarus fountain, and beyond, at the lake's edge, the boathouse.

The gate's clasp was beginning to rust and I had to lay down my load that I might unlatch it. I nestled the tray on a flat spot amongst a cluster of strawberry plants and used my fingers to prise open the latch. I pushed open the gate, picked up the lemonade and continued, through a cloud of jasmine perfume, towards the fountain.

Though Eros and Psyche sat vast and magnificent in the front lawn, a prologue to the grand house itself, there was something wonderful—a mysterious and melancholic aspect—about the smaller fountain, hidden within its sunny clearing at the bottom of the south garden.

The circular pool of stacked stone stood two feet high and twenty feet across at its widest point. It was lined with tiny glass tiles, azure blue like the necklace of sapphires Lord Ashbury had brought back for Lady Violet after serving in the Far East. From the center emerged a huge craggy block of russet marble, the height of two men, thick at the base but tapering to a peak. Midway up, creamy marble against the brown, the lifesize figure of Icarus had been carved in a position of recline. His wings, pale marble etched to give the impression of feathers, were strapped to his outspread arms and fell behind, weeping over the rock. Rising from the pool to tend the fallen figure were three mermaids, long hair looped and coiled about angelic faces: one held a small harp, one wore a coronet of woven ivy leaves, and one reached beneath Icarus's torso, white hands on creamy skin, to pull him from the deep.

On that summer's day a pair of purple martins, oblivious to the statue's beauty, swooped overhead, alighting atop the marble rock, only to take flight again, skim the pond surface and fill their beaks with water. As I watched them, I was overcome with heat and a desire, strong and sudden, to plunge my hand into the cool water. I glanced back towards the distant house, far too intent upon its grief to notice if a housemaid, all the way at the bottom of the south park, paused a moment to cool herself.

I rested the tray on the rim of the pool and placed one tentative knee on the tiles, warm through my black stockings. I leaned forward, held out my hand, withdrew it again at the first touch of sun-kissed water. I rolled up my sleeve, reached out again, ready to submerge my arm.

There came a laugh, tinkling music in the summer stillness.

I froze, listened, inclined my head and peered beyond the statue.

I saw them then, Hannah and Emmeline, not at the boathouse after all, but perched along the rim on the other side of the fountain. My shock was compounded: they had removed their black mourning dresses and wore only petticoats, corset covers and lace-trimmed drawers. Their boots, too, lay discarded on the white stone path that rounded the pool. Their long hair glistened in complicity with the sun. I glanced back to the house, wondering at their daring. Wondering whether my presence implicated me somehow. Wondering whether I feared—or hoped—it did.

Emmeline lay on her back: feet together, legs bent, knees, as white as her petticoat, saluting the clear blue sky. Her outer arm was arranged so that her head rested on her hand. The other arm—soft, pale skin, a stranger to the sun—was extended straight over the pool, her wrist dancing a lazy figure of eight so that alternate fingers pricked the pool's surface. Tiny ripples lapped one another keenly.

Hannah sat beside, one leg curled beneath her, the other bent so her chin rested on her knee, her toes flirting carelessly with the water. Her arms were wrapped around her raised leg and from one hand dangled a piece of paper so thin as to be almost transparent beneath the sun's glare.

I withdrew my arm, rolled down my sleeve, collected myself. With one last longing glance at the sparkling pool, I picked up the tray.

As I drew closer, I could hear them talking.

". . . I think he's being awfully pig-headed," Emmeline said. They had accumulated a pile of strawberries between them and she popped one in her mouth, tossed the stalk into the garden.

Hannah shrugged. "Pa's always been stubborn."

"All the same," Emmeline said. "To flat out refuse is just silly. If David can be bothered to write to us all the way from France, the least Pa could do is read the thing."

Hannah gazed towards the statue, inclined her head so that the pool's reflected ripples shimmered, in ribbons, across her face. "David made a fool of Pa. He went behind his back, did the very thing Pa told him not to."

"Pooh. It's been over a year."

"Pa doesn't forgive easily. David knows that."

"But it's such a *funny* letter. Read again the bit about the mess hall, the pudding."

"I'm *not* going to read it again. I shouldn't have read it the first three times. It's far too coarse for your young ears." She held out the letter. It cast a shadow across Emmeline's face. "Here. Read it yourself. There's an enlightening illustration on the second page." There was a warm breath of wind then and the paper fluttered so that I could see the black lines of a sketch in the top corner.

My footsteps crunched the white stones of the path and Emmeline looked up, saw me standing behind Hannah. "Ooh, lemonade," she said, withdrawing her arm from the pool, letter forgotten. "Good. I'm dying of thirst."

Hannah turned, tucked the letter into her waistband. "Grace," she said, smiling.

"We're hiding from Old Grope-ford," Emmeline said, swinging to sit upright, her back to the fountain. "Ooh, that sun's delicious. It's gone straight to my head."

"And your cheeks," Hannah said.

Emmeline raised her face to the sun, closed her eyes. "I don't mind. I wish it could be summer all year round."

"Has Lord Gifford been and gone, Grace?" Hannah said.

"I couldn't say for sure, miss." I rested the tray on the fountain edge. "I should think so. He was in the drawing room when I served tea and Her Ladyship didn't mention he was staying."

"I hope not," Hannah said. "There's enough that's unpleasant at the moment without him making excuses to look down my dress all afternoon."

A small wrought-iron garden table was nestled by a cluster of pink and yellow honeysuckle and I carried it over to hold the refreshments. I planted its curled feet amongst the stones of the path and set the tray on top; started to pour the lemonades.

Between thumb and index finger, Hannah twirled a strawberry by its stalk. "You didn't happen to hear any of what Lord Gifford was saying, did you, Grace?"

I hesitated. I wasn't supposed to be listening when I served the tea.

"About Grandfather's estate," she pressed. "About Riverton." Her eyes wouldn't meet mine, and I suspected she felt as uncomfortable asking as I did answering.

I swallowed, set down the jug. "I . . . I'm not sure, miss . . ."

"She did!" Emmeline exclaimed. "I can tell—she's blushing. You did, didn't you?" She leaned forward, eyes wide. "Well then, tell us. What's to happen? Is it to go to Pa? Are we to stay?"

"I don't know, miss," I said, shrinking, as I always did, when faced with Emmeline's imperious attention. "Nobody knows."

Emmeline took a glass of lemonade. "Someone must know," she said haughtily. "Lord Gifford, I'd have thought. Why else was he here today if not to talk over Grandfather's will?"

"What I mean, miss, is it depends."

"On what?"

Hannah spoke then. "On Aunt Jemima's baby." Her eyes met mine. "That's it, isn't it, Grace?"

"Yes, miss," I said quietly. "At least I think that's what they were saying."

Emmeline said, "On Aunt Jemima's baby?"

"If it's a boy," Hannah said thoughtfully, "then everything is rightly his. If not, Pa becomes Lord Ashbury."

Emmeline, who had just popped a strawberry in her mouth, clapped her hand to her lips and laughed. "Imagine. Pa, lord of the manor. It's *too* silly." The peach ribbon that threaded around the waistline of her petticoat had snagged on the pool rim and started to unravel. A long thread zig-zagged down her leg. I would have to remember to mend it later. "Do you think he would want us to live here?"

Oh, yes, I thought hopefully. Riverton had been so quiet the year past. Naught to do but redust empty rooms and try not to worry too much about those still fighting.

"I don't know," Hannah said. "I certainly hope not. It's bad enough being trapped here over the summer. The days are twice as long in the country and there's only half as much with which to fill them."

"I'll bet he would."

"No," Hannah said resolutely. "Pa couldn't bear the separation from his factory."

"I don't know," Emmeline said. "If there's one thing Pa loves better than his silly motors, it's Riverton. It's his favorite place in the whole world." She cast her eyes skyward. "Though why anyone would want to be stuck in the middle of nowhere with no one to talk to—" She broke off, gasped. "Oh, Hannah, do you know what I've just thought of? If Pa becomes a lord, then that makes us Honorable, doesn't it?"

"I suppose it does," Hannah said. "For what that's worth."

Emmeline jumped up, rolled her eyes. "It's worth a lot." She put her glass back on the table and climbed onto the rim of the pool. "The Honorable Emmeline Hartford of Riverton Manor. It has a nice ring to it, don't you think?" She turned and curtsied to her reflection, batted her eyelids and presented her hand. "Pleased to meet you, handsome sir. I'm the Honorable Emmeline Hartford." She laughed, delighted by her own skit, and began to skip along the tiled edge, arms out to the sides for balance, repeating the titled introduction between bursts of renewed laughter.

Hannah watched her for a moment, bemused. "Have you any sisters, Grace?"

"No, miss," I said. "Nor brothers neither."

"Really?" she said, as if existence without siblings was something she hadn't considered.

"I was not so lucky, miss. It's just Mother and me."

She looked at me, squinted into the sun. "Your mother. She was in service here."

It was a statement rather than a question. "Yes, miss. Until I was born, miss."

"You're very like her. To look at, I mean."

I was taken aback. "Miss?"

"I saw her picture. In Grandmama's family scrapbook. One of the household photographs from last century." She must have felt my confusion, for she rushed on, "Not that I was looking for it; you mustn't think that, Grace. I was trying to find a certain picture of my own mother when I came across it. The resemblance to you was striking. The same pretty face, same kind eyes."

I had never seen a photograph of Mother—not from when she was younger—and Hannah's description was so at odds with the Mother I knew that I was seized by a sudden and irrepressible longing to see it for myself. I knew where Lady Ashbury kept her scrapbook—the left-hand drawer of her writing desk. And there were times, many times now Nancy was away, that I was left alone to clean the drawing room. If I made sure the household was busy elsewhere, and if I were very quick, it wouldn't be difficult, surely, to glimpse it for myself?

"Why did she not come back to Riverton?" Hannah was saying. "After you were born, I mean?"

"It wasn't possible, miss. Not with a babe."

"I'm sure Grandmama's had families on the staff before." She smiled. "Just imagine: we might have known each other when we were children if she had." Hannah looked out over the water, frowned slightly. "Perhaps she was unhappy here, didn't want to return?"

"I don't know, miss," I said, inexplicably discomfited to be discussing Mother with Hannah. "She doesn't much talk about it."

"Is she in service somewhere else?"

"She takes in stitching now, miss. In the village."

"She works for herself?"

"Yes, miss." I had never thought of it in those terms.

Hannah nodded. "There must be some satisfaction in that."

I looked at her, unsure whether she was teasing. Her face was serious, though. Thoughtful.

"I don't know, miss," I said, faltering. "I . . . I'm seeing her this afternoon. I could ask if you like?"

Her eyes had a cloudy look about them, as if her thoughts were far away. She glanced at me and the shadows fled. "No. It's not important." She fingered the edge of David's letter, still tucked into her petticoat. "Have you had news of Alfred?"

"Yes, miss," I said, glad of the change of subject. Alfred was safer territory. He was a part of this world. "I had a letter this week past. He'll be home on leave in September."

"September," she said. "That's not so long. You'll be glad to see him."

"Oh yes, miss, I certainly will."

Hannah smiled knowingly and I blushed. "What I mean, miss, is we'll all be glad to see him downstairs."

"Of course you will, Grace. Alfred is a lovely fellow."

My cheeks were tingling red. For Hannah had guessed correctly. While letters from Alfred still arrived for the collective staff, increasingly they were addressed solely to me. Their content was changing too. Talk of battle was being replaced with talk of home and other secret things. How much he missed me, cared for me. The future . . . I blinked. "And Master David, miss?" I said. "Will he be home soon?"

"December, he thinks." She ran her fingers over the etched surface of her locket, glanced at Emmeline and lowered her voice. "You know, I've the strongest feeling it will be the last time he comes home to us."

"Miss?"

"Now that he's escaped, Grace, seen the world . . . Well, he has a new life, doesn't he? A real life. The war will end, he'll remain in London and study the piano and become a grand musician. Lead a life rich with excitement and adventure, just like the games we used to play . . ." She looked beyond me in the direction of the house and her smile faded. She sighed then. A long, steady exhalation that made her shoulders deflate. "Sometimes . . ."

The word hung between us: languorous, heavy, full, and I waited for a conclusion that did not come. I could think of nothing to say, so I did what I did best. Remained silent and poured the last of the lemonade into her glass.

She looked up at me then. Held out her glass. "Here, Grace. You have this one."

"Oh no, miss. Thank you, miss. I'm all right."

"Nonsense," Hannah said. "Your cheeks are almost as red as Emmeline's. Here." She thrust the glass towards me.

I glanced at Emmeline, setting honeysuckle flowers to float on the other side of the pool. "Really, miss, I—"

"Grace," she said, mock sternly. "It's hot and I insist."

I sighed, took the glass. It was cool in my hand, tantalizingly cool. I lifted it to my lips, perhaps just a tiny sip . . .

An excited whoop from behind made Hannah swing around. I lifted my gaze, squinted into the light. The sun had begun its slide to the west and the air was hazy.

Emmeline was crouched midway up the statue on the ledge near Icarus. Her pale hair was loose and wavy, and she had threaded a cluster of white clematis behind one ear. The wet hem of her petticoat clung to her legs.

In the warm, white light she looked to be part of the statue. A fourth mermaid, come to life. She waved at us. At Hannah. "Come up here. You can see all the way to the lake."

"I've seen it," Hannah called back. "I showed you, remember?"

There was a drone, high in the sky, as a plane flew overhead. I wasn't sure what kind it was. Alfred would have known.

Hannah watched it go, not looking away until it disappeared, a tiny speck, into the sun's glare. Then suddenly she stood, resolutely, and hurried to the garden seat that held their clothing. As she pulled on her black dress, I set down the lemonade and made to help her.

"What are you doing?" Emmeline asked her.

"I'm getting dressed."

"Why?"

"I have something to do at the house." Hannah paused as I straightened her bodice. "Some French verbs for Miss Prince."

"Since when?" Emmeline wrinkled her nose suspiciously. "It's the holidays."

"I asked for extra."

"You did not."

"I did."

"Well, I'm coming too," Emmeline said, without moving.

"Fine," Hannah said coolly. "And if you get bored, perhaps Lord Gifford will still be at the house to keep you company." She sat on the garden seat and started lacing up her boots.

"Come on," Emmeline said, pouting. "Tell me what you're doing. You know I can keep secrets."

"Thank goodness," Hannah said, looking at her with wide eyes. "I wouldn't want anyone to find out I was doing extra French verbs."

Emmeline sat for a moment, watching Hannah and drumming her legs against a marble wing. She inclined her head. "Do you *promise* that's all you're doing?"

"I *promise*," Hannah said. "I'm going to the house to do some translations." She sneaked a glance at me then, and I realized the precise nature of her half-truth. She was going to work on translations, but they were in shorthand and not French. I lowered my eyes, disproportionately pleased at my casting as conspirator.

Emmeline shook her head slowly, narrowed her eyes. "It's a mortal sin to lie, you know." She was clutching at straws.

"Yes, O pious one," Hannah said, laughing.

Emmeline crossed her arms. "Fine. Keep your silly secrets. I'm sure I don't mind."

"Good," Hannah said. "Everybody's happy." She smiled at me and I smiled back. "Thank you for the lemonade, Grace." And then she disappeared, through the kissing gate and into the Long Walk.

※

MY visit to Mother that afternoon was brief and would not have been notable, had it not been for one thing.

Usually when I visited, Mother and I sat in the kitchen where the light was best for stitching and where we had spent most of our time together before I started at Riverton. That day, however, when she met me at the door she led me to the tiny sitting room that opened off the kitchen. I was surprised, and wondered who else Mother was expecting, for the room was rarely used, had always been reserved for the visits of important folk like Dr. Arthur or the church minister. I sat on a chair by the window and waited while she fetched tea.

Mother had made an effort to present the room at its best. I recognized the signs. A favored vase that had once belonged to her own mother, white porcelain with tulips painted on the front, stood on the side table, clutching proudly a handful of tired daisies. And the cushion she usually rolled up and propped against her back when she worked had been beaten smooth and arranged in the middle of the sofa. It was a sly impostor, sitting there squarely, looking for all the world as if it served no other function than decoration.

Mother brought the tea and sat opposite me. I watched as she poured. There were only two cups. It was to be just the two of us, after all. The room, the flowers, the cushion were for me.

Mother cupped her tea in two hands and I saw that the fingers of each hand had plaited stiffly, one over another. There was no way she'd be able to stitch in that condition. I wondered how long they'd been that bad, how she was affording to live. I had been forwarding her a portion of my own earnings each week, but surely it wasn't enough. Warily, I broached the subject.

"That's none of your business," she said. "I'm managing."

"But Mother, you should have told me. I could have sent you more. I've nothing to spend it on."

Her gaunt face vacillated between defensiveness and defeat. Finally, she sighed. "You're a good girl, Grace. You're doing your share. Your mother's bad fortune's not yours to worry about."

"Of course it is, Mother."

"You just be sure an' don't make the same mistakes."

I steeled myself, dared to ask gently, "What mistakes, Mother?"

She looked away and I waited, heart beating quickly, as she chewed on her dry bottom lip. Wondering whether at last I was to be trusted with the secrets that had sat between us as long as I could remember . . .

"Pish," she said finally, turning back to face me. And with that the subject's door was slammed closed. She lifted her chin and asked about the house, the family, as she always did.

What had I expected? A sudden, magnificently uncharacteristic break from habit? An outpouring of past grievances that explained away my mother's acrimony, enabled us to reach an understanding that had thus far eluded us?

You know, I think perhaps I had. I was young, and that is my only excuse.

But this is a history, not a fiction, thus it will not surprise you that such was not forthcoming. Instead, I swallowed the sour lump of disappointment and told her about the deaths, unable to prevent a guilty note of importance from creeping in as I recounted the family's recent misfortune. First the Major—Mr. Hamilton's somber receipt of the black-rimmed telegraph, Jemima's fingers shaking so that she was unable at first to open it—and then Lord Ashbury, only days after.

She shook her head slowly, an action that accentuated her long, thin neck, and set down her tea. "I'd heard as much. I didn't know how much to put down to gossip. You know as well as I how bad this village is for tittle-tattle."

I nodded.

"What was it took Lord Ashbury, then?" she said.

"Mr. Hamilton said it was a mix. Partly a stroke and partly the heat."

Mother continued to nod, chewing the inside of her cheek. "And what did Mrs. Townsend say?"

"She said it was none of those things. She said it was grief that killed him, plain and simple." I lowered my voice, adopting the same reverent tone that Mrs. Townsend had used. "She said the Major's death broke His Lordship's heart. That when the Major was shot, all his father's hopes and dreams bled with him into the soil of France."

Mother smiled, but it was not a happy smile. She shook her head slowly, looked at the wall before her with its pictures of the distant sea. "Poor, poor Frederick," she said. This surprised me and at first I thought I must have misheard, or that she had made a mistake, uttered the wrong name accidentally, for it made little sense. Poor Lord Ashbury. Poor Lady Violet. Poor Jemima. But Frederick?

"You needn't worry about him," I said. "He's as like to inherit the house."

"There's more to happiness than riches, girl."

I didn't like it when Mother spoke of happiness. The sentiment was hollowed by its speaker. Mother, with her pinched eyes and her empty house, was the last person fit to offer such advice. I felt chastened somehow. Reprimanded for an offence I couldn't name. I answered sulkily, "Try telling that to Fanny."

Mother frowned, and I realized the name was unknown to her.

"Oh," I said, inexplicably cheered. "I forgot. You wouldn't know her. She's Lady Clementine's charge. She hopes to marry Mr. Frederick."

Mother looked at me, disbelieving. "Marry? Frederick?"

I nodded. "Fanny's been working on him all year."

"He's not asked her, though?"

"No," I said. "But it's only a matter of time."

"Who told you so? Mrs. Townsend?"

I shook my head. "Nancy."

Mother recovered somewhat, managed a thin smile. "She's mistaken then, this Nancy of yours. Frederick wouldn't marry again. Not after Penelope."

"Nancy doesn't make mistakes."

Mother crossed her arms. "On this, she's wrong."

Her certainty grated on me, as if she would know better than I the goings-on up at the house. "Even Mrs. Townsend agrees," I said. "She says Lady Violet approves the match and that, though Mr. Frederick mightn't appear to mind what his mother says, he's never gone against her when it counted."

"No," said Mother, her smile flickering, then fading. "No, I don't suppose he has." She turned to stare through the open window. The graystone wall of the house next door. "I never thought he would remarry."

Her voice had lost all resolution and I felt badly. Ashamed of my desire to put her in her place. Mother had been fond of this Penelope, of Hannah and Emmeline's mother. She must've been. What else explained her reluctance to see Mr. Frederick replace his late wife? Or her dejection when I insisted it was true? I put my hand on hers. "You're right, Mother. I was speaking out of turn. We don't know anything for sure."

She didn't answer.

I leaned close. "And certainly there's none could accuse Mr. Frederick of genuine feeling for Fanny. He looks more lovingly at his riding crop."

My joke was an attempt to cajole her, and I was pleased when she turned to face me. I was surprised, too, for in that moment, as the afternoon sunlight brushed her cheek and teased green from her brown eyes, Mother almost looked pretty.

I thought of Hannah's words, her talk of Mother's photograph, and I was even more resolved to see it for myself. To glimpse the type of person Mother might have been. The girl Hannah called pretty and Mrs. Townsend remembered so fondly.

"He was always a great one for riding," she said, setting her teacup on the window ledge. She surprised me then, took my hand between hers and stroked the hard patches on my palm. "Tell me about your new duties. Looks of these, they've been keeping you awful busy up there."

"It's not so bad," I said, moved by her rare affection. "There's not much to recommend the cleaning and the laundering, but there's other duties I don't mind so much."

"Oh?" She inclined her head.

"Nancy's been so busy at the station that I've been doing a lot more of the upstairs work."

"You like that do you, my girl?" Her voice was quiet. "Being upstairs in the grand house?"

I nodded.

"And what do you like about it?"

Being amongst fine rooms with delicate porcelains and paintings and tapestries. Listening to Hannah and Emmeline joke and tease and dream. I remembered Mother's earlier sentiment and suddenly knew a way to please her. "It makes me happy," I said. And I confessed something then that I hadn't even owned myself. "One day I hope to become a proper lady's maid."

She looked at me, the tremors of a frown plucking at her brow. "There's future enough as a lady's maid, my girl," she said, voice strained thin. "But happiness . . . happiness grows at our own firesides," she said. "It is not to be picked in strangers' gardens."

❧

I WAS still turning over Mother's comment as I walked home to Riverton late that afternoon. She was telling me not to forget my place, of course; I'd received that lecture more than once before. She wanted me to remember that my happiness would only be found in the coals of the servants' hall fireplace, not in the delicate pearls of a lady's boudoir. But the Hartfords were not strangers. And if I took some happiness from working near them, listening to their conversations, minding their beautiful dresses, then what harm was there in that?

It struck me then that she was jealous. She envied me my place at the grand house. She had cared for Penelope, for the girls' mother, she must have: that's why she was so put out by my talk of Mr. Frederick remarrying. And now, seeing me in the position she once enjoyed reminded her of the world she'd been forced to give away. And yet she hadn't been forced, had she? Hannah said that Lady Violet had employed families before. And if Mother were jealous that I had taken her place, why had she been so insistent I go into service at Riverton?

I emerged from the tree-lined drive, pausing for a moment to observe the house. The sun had shifted and Riverton was in shadow. A huge black beetle on the hill, hunkering down against the heat and its own sorrow. And yet, as I stood there, I was filled with a warm sense of certitude. For the first time in my life I felt solid; somewhere between the village and Riverton I had lost the sense that if I didn't hold on tightly I would be blown away.

I entered the dark servants' hall and headed down the dim corridor. My footsteps echoed on the cool stone floor. When I reached the kitchen, all was still. The lingering smell of beef stew clung to the walls, but there was no one else about. Behind me, in the dining room, the clock ticked loudly. I peered around the door. That room was also empty. One lone teacup sat on its saucer on the table, but its drinker was nowhere to be seen. I removed my hat, draped it over a hook on the wall and smoothed my skirt. I sighed and the noise lapped against the silent walls. I smiled slightly. I had never had the downstairs all to myself before.

I glanced at the clock. There was still a half-hour until I was expected back. I would have a cup of tea. The one at Mother's house had left a bitter taste in my mouth.

The teapot on the kitchen bench was still warm, shrouded in its woollen cosy. I was laying out a teacup when Nancy fairly flew around the corner, her eyes widening when she saw me.

"It's Jemima," she said. "The baby's coming."

"But it's not due till September," I said.

"Well, it doesn't know that, does it?" she said, throwing a small square towel at me. "Here, take that and a bowl of warm water upstairs. I can't find any of the others, and someone has to call for the doctor."

"But I'm not in uniform—"

"I don't think mother or child is going to mind," said Nancy, disappearing into Mr. Hamilton's pantry to use the telephone.

"But what will I say?" This I directed to the empty room, to myself, to the cloth in my hand. "What will I do?"

Nancy's head appeared around the door. "Well, I don't know, do I? You'll think of something." She waved an arm in the air. "Just tell her everything's all right. God willing, it will be."

I draped the towel over my shoulder, filled a bowl and started upstairs as Nancy had said to. My hands were shaking a little and some of the water slopped over onto the corridor carpet runner, leaving dark vermilion spots.

When I reached Jemima's room I hesitated. From behind the solid door came a muffled groan. I took a deep breath, knocked and went inside.

The room was dark, with the exception of a single bold sliver where the curtains coyly parted. The ribbon of dusky light was flecked with listless dust. The maple four-poster bed was a shadowy mass in the center of the room. Jemima lay very still, her breathing labored.

I crept to the bed and crouched tentatively beside it. I put the bowl on the small reading table.

Jemima moaned and I bit my lip, unsure how to proceed. "There now," I said softly, the way Mother had tended me when I was sick with scarlet fever. "There now."

She shuddered, made three quick gasps for air. She clenched her eyes shut.

"Everything's all right," I said. I soaked the towel in the water and folded it in four, draping it across her forehead.

"Jonathan . . ." she said. "Jonathan . . ." His name on her lips was beautiful.

There was naught I could say to that and so I remained in silence.

There came more groans, more whimpers. She writhed, moaning into the pillow. Her fingers chased elusive comfort across the empty sheet beside her.

Then the still returned. Her breathing slowed.

I lifted the cloth from her forehead. It had warmed against her skin and I dipped it again in the bowl of water. I wrung it out, folded it and reached to lay it back across her head.

Her eyes opened, blinked, searched my face in the dim. "Hannah," she said through a sigh. I was startled by her mistake. And pleased beyond measure. I opened my mouth to correct her, but stopped when she reached out and took my hand. "I'm so glad it's you." She squeezed my fingers together. "I'm so frightened," she whispered. "I can't feel anything."

"It's all right," I said. "The baby's resting."

This seemed to calm her a little. "Yes," she said. "It's always so, right before they come. I just didn't . . . It's too soon." She turned her head away. When she spoke again, her voice was so low I had to strain to hear. "Everybody wants a boy for me, but I can't. I can't lose another one."

"You won't," I said, hoping it was so.

"There's a curse upon my family," she said, face still hidden. "My mother told me so, but I didn't believe her."

She has lost her sense, I thought. Grief has overtaken her and she has given in to superstition. "There's no such thing as curses," I said softly.

She made a noise, a cross between a laugh and a sob. "Oh yes. It's the same that robbed our dear late Queen of her son. The bleeders' curse." She went quiet, then ran her hand over her stomach and shifted so that she faced me. Her voice was little more than a whisper. "But girls . . . it passes girls over."

The door flew open and Nancy was there. Behind her was a thin man of middle years and a permanently censorious expression who I took to be the doctor, though he wasn't Dr. Arthur from the village. Pillows were plumped, Jemima was positioned and a lamp was lit. At some point I realized my hand was once more my own, and I was pushed aside, ferried from the room.

As afternoon became evening, evening became night, I waited and wondered and hoped. Time lagged even though there were plenty of chores with which to fill it. There was dinner to serve, beds to be turned down, laundry to be gathered for the next day, yet all the while my mind remained with Jemima.

Finally, as through the kitchen window the last shimmer of the sun's corona slipped behind the west heath, Nancy clattered down the stairs, bowl and cloth in hand.

We had just finished our dinner and were still seated around the table.

"Well?" Mrs. Townsend said, handkerchief clutched anxiously to her heart.

"Well," Nancy said. "Mother was delivered of her baby at twenty-six minutes after eight. Small but healthy."

I waited nervously.

"Can't help but feel a little sorry for her, though," Nancy said, raising her eyebrows. "It's a girl."

※

I T was ten o'clock when I returned from collecting Jemima's supper tray. She had fallen asleep, little Gytha swaddled and in her arms. Before I switched off the bedside lamp, I paused a moment to gaze at the tiny girl: puckered lips, a scrap of strawberry-blond hair, eyes screwed tightly shut. Not an heir, then, but a baby, who would live and grow and love.

I tiptoed from the room, tray in hand. My lamp cast the only light in the dark corridor, throwing my shadow across the row of portraits hanging along the wall. While the newest family member slept soundly behind the closed door, a line of Hartfords past carried on a timeless vigil, gazing silently across the entrance hall they once possessed.

When I reached the main hall I noticed a thin strip of soft light seeping beneath the drawing-room door. In all the evening's drama,

Mr. Hamilton had forgotten to turn off the lamp. I thanked God I had been the one to see. Despite the blessing of a new grandchild, Lady Violet would have been furious to discover her mourning conditions flouted.

I pushed open the door and stopped dead.

There, in his father's seat, sat Mr. Frederick. The new Lord Ashbury.

His long legs were crossed one over the other, his head bowed onto one hand so that his face was concealed.

Hanging from his left hand, recognizable for its distinguishing black sketch, was the letter from David. The letter Hannah had read by the fountain, which had made Emmeline giggle so.

Mr. Frederick's back was shaking and at first I thought he was laughing too.

Then came the sound I have never forgotten. A gasp. Guttural, involuntary, hollow. Wretched with regret.

I stood for a moment longer, unable to move, then backed away. Pulled the door behind me so I was no longer a hidden party to his sorrow.

A KNOCK at the door and I am returned. It is 1999 and I am in my room at Heathview, the photograph, our grave unknowing faces, still in my fingers. The young actress sits in the brown chair, scrutinizing the ends of her long hair. How long have I been away? I glance at my clock. It is a little after ten. Is it possible? Is it possible the floors of memory have dissolved, ancient scenes and ghosts have come to life, and yet no time has passed at all?

The door is open and Ursula is back in the room, Sylvia directly behind balancing three teacups on a silver tray. Rather more fancy than the usual plastic one.

"I'm so sorry," Ursula says, resuming her position on the end of my bed. "I don't usually do that. It was urgent."

I am unsure at first as to what she means; then I see the mobile phone in her hand.

Sylvia passes me a cup of tea, walks around my chair to present a steaming cup to Keira.

"I hope you started the interview without me," Ursula says.

Keira smiles, shrugs. "We've pretty much finished."

"Really?" Ursula says, eyes wide beneath her heavy fringe. "I can't believe I missed the entire interview. I was so looking forward to hearing Grace's memories."

Sylvia places a hand across my forehead. "You're looking a little peaky. Do you need some analgesic?"

"I'm perfectly fine," I say, my voice croaky.

Sylvia raises an eyebrow.

"I'm fine," I say with all the firmness I can muster.

Sylvia humphs. Then she shakes her head and I know she is washing her hands of me. For now. Have it your way, I can see her thinking. I can deny it all I like, but there's no doubt in her mind I'll be ringing for pain relief before my guests reach the Heathview car park. She's probably right.

Keira takes a sip of green tea, then rests the cup and saucer on my dressing table. "Is there a loo?"

I can feel Sylvia's eyes burning holes in me. "Sylvia," I say. "Would you show Keira the washroom in the hall?"

Sylvia is barely able to contain herself. "Certainly," she says, and although I cannot see her, I know that she is preening. "It's this way, Ms. Parker."

Ursula smiles at me as the door closes. "I appreciate you seeing Keira," she says. "She's the daughter of one of the producer's friends, so I'm obliged to take a special interest." She looks to the door and lowers her voice, chooses her words carefully. "She's not a bad kid, but she can be a little . . . tactless."

"I hadn't noticed."

Ursula laughs. "It comes of having industry parents," she says.

"These kids see their parents receiving accolades for being rich, famous and beautiful—who can blame them for wanting the same?"

"It's quite all right."

"Still," says Ursula. "I meant to be here. To play chaperone . . ."

"If you don't stop apologizing, you're going to convince me you've done something wrong," I say. "You remind me of my grandson." She looks abashed and I realize there is something new within those dark eyes. A shadow I hadn't noticed earlier. "Did you sort out your problems?" I say. "On the telephone?"

She sighs, nods. "Yes."

She pauses and I remain silent, wait for her to continue. I learned long ago that silence invites all manner of confidences.

"I have a son," she says. "Finn." The name leaves a sad-happy smile on her lips. "He was three last Saturday." Her gaze leaves my face for an instant, alights on the rim of her teacup, with which she fidgets. "His father . . . he and I were never . . ." She taps her nail twice against her cup, looks at me again. "It's just Finn and me. That was my mother on the phone. She's minding Finn while the film's shooting. He had a fall."

"Is he all right?"

"Yes. He sprained his wrist. The doctor wrapped it for him. He's fine." She is smiling, but her eyes fill with tears. "I'm sorry . . . goodness me . . . he's fine, I don't know why I'm crying."

"You're worried," I say, watching her. "And relieved."

"Yes," she says, suddenly very young and fragile. "And guilty."

"Guilty?"

"Yes," she says, but doesn't elaborate. She takes a tissue from her bag and wipes her eyes. "You're easy to talk to. You remind me of my grandmother."

"She sounds a lovely woman."

Ursula laughs. "Yes." She sniffs into a tissue. "Goodness, look at me. I'm sorry for off-loading all this on you, Grace."

"You're apologizing again. I insist you stop."

There are footsteps in the hall. Ursula glances at the door, blows her nose. "Then at least let me thank you. For seeing us. For talking to Keira. Listening to me."

"I've enjoyed it," I say, and surprise myself by meaning it. "I don't have many callers these days."

The door opens and she stands. Leans over and kisses my cheek. "I'll come again soon," she says, gently squeezing my wrist.

And I am unaccountably glad.

THE PHOTOGRAPH

✺

I T is a beautiful March morning. The pink gillyflowers beneath my window are in bloom, filling the room with their sweet and heady scent. If I lean close to the windowsill and peer down at the garden bed, I can see the outermost petals, bright with sun. The peach blossom will be next, then the jasmine. Each year it is the same; will continue to be the same for years to come. Long after I am here to enjoy them. Eternally fresh, eternally hopeful, always ingenuous.

I have been thinking about Mother. About the photograph in Lady Violet's scrapbook. For I saw it, you know. A few months after Hannah first mentioned it, that summer's day by the fountain.

It was September of 1916. Mr. Frederick had inherited his father's estate, Lady Violet (in an impeccable show of etiquette, said Nancy) had vacated Riverton and taken up residence in the London townhouse, and the Hartford girls had been dispatched indefinitely to help her settle.

We were a tiny staff at that time—Nancy was busier than ever in the village, and Alfred, whose leave I'd so anticipated, had been unable at the last to return. It confused us at the time: he was in Britain, sure enough, his letters assured us he wasn't injured, yet he was to spend his leave at a military hospital. Even Mr. Hamilton was unsure what to make of this. He thought long and hard, sat in his pantry pondering Alfred's letter, until eventually he emerged, rubbed his eyes beneath his glasses and made his announcement. The only explanation was Alfred's involvement in a secret war mission of

176

which he was unable to speak. It seemed a reasonable suggestion, for what else explained the hospital accommodation of a man with no injuries?

And so the matter was closed. Little more was said about it, and in the early autumn of 1916, as leaves dropped and the ground outside began to harden, steeling itself for the freeze to come, I found myself alone in the Riverton drawing room.

I had cleaned and reset the fire and was finishing up dusting. I ran the cloth across the top of the writing desk, traced its rim, then started on the drawer handles, bringing the brass to a gleam. It was a regular duty, performed each second morning as sure as day followed night, and I cannot say what set that day apart. Why that morning as my fingers reached the left-hand drawer they slowed, stopped, refused to recommence their cleaning. As if they glimpsed before I did the furtive purpose that fluttered on the edges of my thoughts.

I sat a moment, perplexed, unable to move. And I became aware of the sounds around me. The wind outside, leaves hitting the windowpanes. The mantel clock ticking insistently, counting away the seconds. My breath, grown quick with expectation.

Fingers trembling, I began to slide it open. Slowly, carefully, acting and observing myself in equal measure. The drawer reached halfway and tilted on its tracks, the contents sliding to the front.

I paused. Listened. Satisfied myself I was still alone. Then I peered inside.

There beneath a pen set and a pair of gloves: Lady Violet's scrapbook.

No time for hesitation, the incriminating drawer already open, heartbeat pulsing against the bones of my inner ears, I slid the book from the drawer and laid it on the floor.

Flicked through the pages—photographs, invitations, menus, diary entries—scanning for dates: 1896, 1897, 1898 . . .

There it was: the household photograph of 1899, its shape familiar but its proportions different. Two long rows of straight-faced servants complementing the front line of family. Lord and Lady Ashbury, the Major in his uniform, Mr. Frederick—all so much younger and less tattered—Jemima and an unknown woman I took to be Penelope, Mr. Frederick's late wife, both with swollen stomachs. One of those bulges was Hannah, I realized; the other, an ill-fated boy whose blood would one day fail him. A lone child stood at the end of the row near Nanny Brown (ancient even then). A small blond boy: David. Full of life and light; blissfully unaware of all the future had in store.

I let my gaze shift from his face and onto the rows of staff behind. Mr. Hamilton, Mrs. Townsend, Dudley . . .

My breath caught. I stared into the gaze of a young serving maid. There was no mistaking her. Not because she resembled Mother—far from it. Rather, she resembled me. The hair and eyes were darker, but the likeness was uncanny. The same long neck, chin tapered to a dimpled point, brows curved to give a permanent impression of deliberation.

Most surprising of all, though, far more so than our resemblance: Mother was smiling. Oh, not so as you'd realize unless you knew her well. It wasn't a smile of mirth or social greeting. It was slight, little more than a muscular tremor, easily excused as a trick of the light by those who didn't know her. But I could see. Mother was smiling to herself. Smiling like someone with a secret—

※

—I APOLOGIZE, Marcus, for the interruption, but I have had an unexpected caller. I was sitting here, admiring the gillyflowers, telling you of Mother, when a knock came at the door. I expected Sylvia, come to tell me about her male friend or complain about one of the other residents, but it wasn't. Rather it was Ursula, the film-maker. I've mentioned her before, surely?

"I hope I'm not disturbing you," she said.

"No," I said, setting aside my Dictaphone.

"I won't stay long. I was in the neighborhood and it seemed silly to head back to London without popping in."

"You've been at the house."

She nodded. "We were shooting a scene in the gardens. The light was just perfect."

I asked her about the scene, curious as to which part of their story had been reconstructed today.

"It was a scene of courtship," she said, "a romantic scene. It's actually one of my favorites." She blushed, shook her head so that her fringe swung like a curtain. "It's silly. I wrote the lines, I knew them when they were mere black marks on white paper—scratched them out and rewrote them a hundred times—yet I was still so moved to hear them spoken today."

"You're a romantic," I said.

"I suppose I am." She tilted her head to the side. "Ridiculous, isn't it? I didn't know the real Robbie Hunter at all; I've created a version of him from his poetry, from what other people wrote about him. Yet I find . . ." She paused, raised her eyebrows self-deprecatingly. "I fear I'm in love with a figure of my own creation."

"And what is your Robbie like?"

"He's passionate. Creative. Devoted." She leaned her chin on her hand as she considered. "But I think what I admire most about him is his hope. Such brittle hope. People say he was a poet of disillusionment, but I'm not so sure. I've always found something positive in his poems. The way he found possibility amid the horrors he experienced." She shook her head, empathy narrowed her eyes. "It must have been unspeakably difficult. A sensitive young man thrust into such a devastating conflict. It's a wonder any of them were ever able to resume their lives, pick up where they left off. Love again."

"I was once loved by a young man like that," I said. "He went to war and we exchanged letters. It was through those letters I realized how I felt about him. And he about me."

"Was he changed when he came back?"

"Oh yes," I said softly. "There were none that came back un-changed."

Her voice was gentle. "When did you lose him? Your husband?"

It took me a moment to realize what she meant. "Oh no," I said. "He wasn't my husband. Alfred and I were never married."

"Oh, I'm sorry, I thought . . ." She motioned towards the wed-ding picture on my dressing table.

I shook my head. "That's not Alfred, that's John: Ruth's father. He and I were married sure enough. Lord knows we shouldn't have been."

She raised her eyebrows in query.

"John was a terrific waltzer and a terrific lover, but not much of a husband. I dare say I wasn't much of a wife, either. I'd never in-tended to marry, you see. I wasn't at all prepared."

Ursula stood, picked up the photograph. Traced her thumb ab-sently along the top. "He was handsome."

"Yes," I said. "That was the attraction, I expect."

"Was he an archaeologist too?"

"Heavens, no. John was a public servant."

"Oh," she set the photograph down. Turned to me. "I thought you might have met through work. Or at university."

I shook my head. In 1938, when John and I met, I'd have called a doctor for anyone who suggested I might some day attend univer-sity. Become an archaeologist. I was working in a restaurant—the Lyons' Corner House in the Strand—serving unending fried fish to the unending dining public. Mrs. Havers, who ran the place, liked the idea of someone who'd been in service. She was fond of telling anyone who'd listen there was none knew how to polish cutlery quite like the girls from service.

"John and I met by accident," I said. "At a dance club."

I had agreed, grudgingly, to meet a girl from work. Another waitress. Patty Everidge: a name I've never forgotten. Strange. She was nothing to me. Someone I worked with, avoided where I could, though that was easier said than done. She was one of those women who couldn't let well enough alone. A busybody, I suppose. Had to know everyone else's business. Was only too ready to interfere. Patty must've taken it into her head I didn't socialize enough, didn't join in with the other girls on Monday mornings when they cackled about the weekend, for she started on at me about coming dancing, wouldn't let up until I'd agreed to meet her at Marshall's Club on Friday night.

I sighed. "The girl I was supposed to meet didn't show up."

"But John did?" Ursula said.

"Yes," I said, remembering the smoky air, the stool in the corner where I perched uncomfortably, scanning the crowd for Patty. Oh, she was full of excuses and apologies when I saw her next, but it was too late then. What was done was done. "I met John instead."

"And you fell in love?"

"I fell pregnant."

Ursula's mouth formed an *o* of realization.

"I realized it four months after we met. We were married a month later. That's the way things were done back then." I shifted so that my lower back was resting on a pillow. "Lucky for us war intervened and we were spared the charade."

"He went to war?"

"We both did. John enlisted and I went to work in a field hospital in France."

She looked confused. "What about Ruth?"

"She was evacuated to an elderly Anglican minister and his wife. Spent the war years there."

"All of them?" Ursula said, shocked. "How did you bear it?"

"Oh, I visited on leave, and I received regular letters: gossip from the village and bosh from the pulpit; rather grim descriptions of the local children."

She was shaking her head, brows drawn together in dismay. "I can't imagine . . . Four years away from your child."

I was unsure how to answer, how to explain. How does one begin to confess that mothering didn't come naturally? That from the first Ruth had seemed a stranger? That the fond feeling of inevitable connectedness, of which books are written and myths are fashioned, was never mine?

My empathy had been used up, I suppose. On Hannah, and the others at Riverton. Oh, I was fine with strangers, was able to tend them, reassure them, even ease them into death. I just found it difficult to let myself get close again. I preferred casual acquaintances. Was hopelessly underprepared for the emotional demands of parenthood.

Ursula saved me from having to answer. "I suppose there was a war on," she said sadly. "Sacrifices had to be made." She reached out to squeeze my hand.

I smiled, tried not to feel false. Wondered what she would think if she knew that far from regretting my decision to send Ruth away, I'd relished the escape. That after a decade of drifting through tedious jobs and hollow relationships, unable to put the events of Riverton behind me, in war I'd found my thread of purpose.

"So it was after the war you decided to become an archaeologist?"

"Yes," I said, my voice hoarse. "After the war."

"Why archaeology?"

The answer to that question is so complicated I could only say simply: "I had an epiphany."

She was delighted. "Really? During the war?"

"There was so much death. So much destruction. Things became clearer somehow."

"Yes," she said, "I can imagine that."

"I found myself wondering at the impermanence of things. One day, I thought, people will have forgotten any of this happened. This war, these deaths, this demolition. Oh, not for some time, but eventually it will fade. Take its place amongst the layers of the past. Its savagery and horrors replaced in popular imagination by others still to come."

Ursula shook her head. "Hard to imagine."

"But certain to happen. The Punic Wars at Carthage, the Peloponnesian War, the Battle of Artemisium. All reduced to chapters in history books." I paused. Vehemence had tired me, robbed me of breath. I am not used to speaking so many words in quick succession. My voice when I spoke was reedy. "I became obsessed with discovering the past. Facing the past."

Ursula smiled, her dark eyes shining. "I know exactly what you mean. That's why I make historical films. You uncover the past, and I try to re-create it."

"Yes," I said. I hadn't thought of it like that.

Ursula shook her head. "I admire you, Grace. You've done so much with your life."

"Temporal illusion," I said, shrugging. "Give someone more time and they'll appear to have done more with it."

She laughed. "You're being modest. It can't have been easy. A woman in the fifties—a mother—trying to get a tertiary education. Was your husband supportive?"

"I was on my own by then."

Her eyes widened. "But how did you manage?"

"I studied part time for a long time. Ruth was at school in the days and I had a very good neighbor, Mrs. Finbar, who used to sit with her some evenings when I worked." I hesitated. "I was just fortunate the educational expenses were taken care of."

"A scholarship?"

"In a sense. I'd come into some money, unexpectedly."

"Your husband," said Ursula, brows knitting in sympathy. "He was killed in the war?"

"No," I said, "No, he wasn't. But our marriage was."

Her gaze drifted once more to my wedding photo.

"We divorced when he returned to London. Times had changed by then. Everyone had seen and done so much. It seemed rather pointless to remain joined to a spouse one didn't care for. He moved to America and married the sister of a GI he'd met in France. Poor fellow; he was killed soon after in a road accident."

She shook her head. "I'm sorry . . ."

"Don't be. Not on my account. It was so long ago. I barely remember him, you know. Odd snatches of memory, more like dreams. It's Ruth who misses him. She's never forgiven me."

"She wishes you'd stayed together."

I nodded. Lord knows my failure to provide her with a father figure is one of the old grievances that color our relationship.

Ursula sighed. "I wonder whether Finn will feel that way one day."

"You and his father . . . ?"

She shook her head. "It wouldn't have worked." She said it so firmly I knew better than to probe. "Finn and I are better this way."

"Where is he today?" I said. "Finn?"

"My mother's minding him again. They were at the park for ice cream last I heard." She rolled her watch around her wrist to read the time. "Goodness! I hadn't realized it was getting so late. I'd better be going, give her some relief."

"I'm sure she doesn't need relieving. It's special, grandparents and grandchildren. So much simpler."

Is it always so, I wonder? I think perhaps it is. While one's child takes a part of one's heart to use and misuse as they please, a grandchild is different. Gone are the bonds of guilt and responsibility that burden the maternal relationship. The way to love is free.

When you were born, Marcus, I was knocked sideways. What a wonderful surprise those feelings were. Parts of me that had shut down decades before, that I'd grown used to doing without, were suddenly awakened. I treasured you. Recognized you. Loved you with a power almost painful.

As you grew, you became my little friend. Followed me about my house, claimed your own space in my study and set about exploring the maps and drawings I'd collected on my travels. Questions, so many questions, that I never tired of answering. Indeed, it is a conceit I allow myself that I am responsible, in some part, for the fine, accomplished man you have become . . .

"They must be in here somewhere," said Ursula, searching her bag for car keys, preparing to leave.

I was beset by a sudden impulse to make her stay. "I have a grandson, you know. Marcus. He's a writer of mysteries."

"I know," she said, smiling as she stopped rummaging. "I've read his books."

"Have you?" Pleased, as I always am.

"Yes," she said. "They're very good."

"Can you keep a secret?" I said.

She nodded eagerly, leaned close.

"I haven't read them," I whispered. "Not right the way through."

She laughed. "I promise not to tell."

"I'm so proud of him, and I've tried, I really have. I begin each with strong resolve, but no matter how much I'm enjoying them, I only ever get halfway. I adore a good mystery—Agatha Christie and the like—but I'm afraid I'm rather weak-stomached. I'm not one for all that bloody description they go on with these days."

"And you worked in a field hospital!"

"Yes, perhaps that's why; war is one thing, murder quite another."

"Maybe his next book . . ."

"Perhaps," I said. "Though I don't know when that will be."

"He's not writing?"

"He suffered a loss recently."

"I read about his wife," Ursula said. "I'm very sorry. An aneurism, wasn't it?"

"Yes. Terribly sudden."

Ursula nodded. "My father died the same way. I was fourteen. Away at school camp." She exhaled. "They didn't tell me until I got back to school. I fought with him before I left. Something ridiculous. I can't even remember now. I slammed the door of the car and didn't look back."

"You were young. All the young are like that."

"I still think of him every day." She pressed her eyes shut, then opened them again. Shook the memories away. "How about Marcus? How is he?"

"He took it badly," I said. "He blames himself."

She nodded, didn't look surprised. Seemed to understand guilt and its peculiarities.

"I don't know where he is," I said then.

Ursula looked at me. "What do you mean?"

"He's missing. Neither Ruth nor I know where he is. He's been gone the better part of a year."

She was perplexed. "But . . . is he okay? You've heard from him?" Her eyes were trying to read mine. "A phone call? A letter?"

"Postcards," I said. "He's sent a few postcards. But no return address. I fear he doesn't want to be found."

"Oh, Grace," she said, kind eyes meeting mine. "I'm so sorry."

"So am I," I said. And it was then I told her about the tapes. About how much I need to find you. That it's all I can think to do.

"It's the perfect thing to do," she said emphatically. "Where do you send them?"

"I have an address in California. A friend of his from years ago. I send them there, but as for whether he receives them . . ."

"I bet he does," she said.

They were mere words, well-meant assurances, yet I needed to hear more. "Do you think so?" I said.

"Yes," she said firmly, full of youthful certainty. "I do. And I know he'll come back. He just needs space and time to realize it wasn't his fault. That there was nothing he could have done to change it." She stood up and leaned across my bed. Picked up my Dictaphone and placed it gently on my lap. "Keep talking to him,

186

Grace," she said, and then she leaned towards me and kissed my cheek. "He'll come home. You'll see."

※

THERE now. I have forgotten my purpose. Have been telling you things you already know. Sheer self-indulgence on my part: Lord knows I don't have time for such distraction. War was consuming the fields of Flanders, the Major and Lord Ashbury were yet warm in their graves, and two long years of slaughter were still to come. So much devastation. Young men from the furthest reaches of the earth choreographed in a bloody waltz of death. The Major, then, in October 1917 at Passchendaele, David . . .

※

NO. I have neither stomach nor inclination to relive them. It is enough to say that they occurred. Instead, we will return to Riverton. January 1919. The war is over and Hannah and Emmeline, who have spent the last two years in London at Lady Violet's townhouse, have just arrived to take up residence with their father. But they are changed: they have grown since last we spoke. Hannah is eighteen, about to make her society debut. Emmeline, fourteen, teeters on the edge of an adult world she is impatient to embrace. Gone are the games of yesteryear. Gone, since David's death, is The Game. (Rule number three: only three may play. No more, no less.)

One of the first things Hannah does on returning to Riverton is recover the Chinese box from the attic. I see her do it, though she does not know it. I follow her as she puts it carefully into a fabric bag and takes it with her to the lake.

I hide where the path between the Icarus fountain and the lake narrows and watch as she takes her bag across the lake bank to the old boathouse. She stands for a moment, looks around, and I duck lower behind the bushes so she doesn't see me.

She goes to the edge of the escarpment, stands with her back to

187

its ridge, then lines up her feet so the heel of one boot touches the toe of the other. She proceeds towards the lake, counting three steps before stopping.

She repeats this three times, then kneels on the ground and opens her bag. Pulls from it a small spade.

Hannah digs. It is difficult at first, due to the pebbles that coat the lake bank, but in time she reaches the dirt beneath and is able to scoop more at a time. She doesn't stop until the pile beside her is a foot high.

She removes the Chinese box from her bag then, and lays it deep within the hole. She is about to scoop the dirt on top when she hesitates. She retrieves the box, opens it, takes one of the tiny books from inside. She opens the locket around her neck and conceals it within, then returns the box to the hole and resumes burying it.

I leave her then, alone on the lake bank; Mr. Hamilton will miss me if I'm away much longer and he is not in any mood to be trifled with. Downstairs, the Riverton kitchen is abuzz with excitement. Preparations are under way for the first dinner party since war broke out, and Mr. Hamilton has impressed upon us that tonight's guests are very important to the Family's Future.

And they were. Just how important, we could never have imagined.

BANKERS

✻

"BANKERS," Mrs. Townsend said knowingly, looking from Nancy to Mr. Hamilton to me. She was leaning against the pine table, using her marble rolling pin to quash resistance from a knot of sweaty dough. She stopped and wiped her forehead, leaving a trail of flour clinging to her eyebrows. "Americans at that," she said, to no one in particular.

"Now, Mrs. Townsend," Mr. Hamilton said, scrutinizing the silver salt and pepper dishes for tarnish. "While it's true Mrs. Luxton is one of the New York Stevensons, I think you'll find Mr. Luxton is as English as you or I. He hails from the north, according to *The Times*." Mr. Hamilton peered over his half-rimmed glasses. "A self-made man, you know."

Mrs. Townsend snorted. "Self-made man indeed. Can't have hurt marrying *her* family's fortune."

"Mr. Luxton may have married into a wealthy family," Mr. Hamilton said primly, "but he's certainly done his bit to increase the fortune. Banking's a complicated business: knowing who to lend to and who not. I'm not arguing that they don't like a fair dollop of cream off the top, but that's what the business is about."

Mrs. Townsend humphed.

"Let's just hope they see fit to lend the Master what he needs," Nancy said. "A bit of money would make a welcome change around here, if you ask me."

Mr. Hamilton straightened and shot me a stern look, though I had not been the one to speak. As the war had progressed and Nancy had spent more time working on the outside, she had changed. In her duties she remained efficient as ever, but when we sat around the servants' table and spoke of the world, she was more comfortable in voicing opposition, more likely to question the way things were done. I, on the other hand, had not yet been corrupted by external forces and, like a shepherd who decides 'tis better to forsake one lost sheep than risk the flock through inattention, Mr. Hamilton had determined to keep both eyes on me. "I'm surprised at you, Nancy," he said, looking at me. "You know the Master's business affairs are not ours to query."

"I'm sorry, Mr. Hamilton," Nancy said, in a voice without contrition. "But all I know is that ever since Mr. Frederick came to Riverton, he's been closing rooms faster than I can say. Not to mention the furniture that's been sold from the west wing. The mahogany writing bureau, Lady Ashbury's Danish four-poster." She eyed me over her polishing cloth. "Dudley says most of the horses are going too."

"His Lordship is simply being prudent," Mr. Hamilton said, turning to Nancy to better argue his case. "The west rooms were closed because, with your railway work and Alfred being away, there was far too much cleaning for young Grace to manage on her own. As for the stables, what need does His Lordship have for so many horses with all his fine motorcars?"

The question, once launched, he let linger in the cool winter's air. He removed his glasses, huffed on their lenses and wiped them clean with a triumphant theatricality.

"If you must know," he said, stage business complete, glasses restored to his nose's end, "the stables are to be converted into a brand-new garage. The largest in all the county."

Nancy was nonplussed. "All the same," she said, lowering her voice, "I've heard whispers in the village—"

"Nonsense," Mr. Hamilton said.

"What kind of whispers?" Mrs. Townsend said, bosom heaving with each roll of her pin. "News about the Master's business?"

At the stairs, the shadows shifted and a slim woman of middle years stepped into the light.

"Miss Starling . . ." Mr. Hamilton faltered. "I didn't see you there. Come on in and Grace will make you a cup of tea." He turned to me, mouth tight as the top of a coin purse. "Go on then, Grace," he said, motioning towards the stove. "A cup of tea for Miss Starling."

Miss Starling cleared her throat before stepping away from the stairwell. She tiptoed towards the nearest chair, little leather satchel clamped beneath a freckled arm.

Lucy Starling was Mr. Frederick's secretary, employed, originally, for the factory in Ipswich. When the war ended and the family moved permanently to Riverton, she started coming from the village, twice a week, to work in Mr. Frederick's study.

She had lost her fiancé on the Ypres Salient and wore her mourning, like her clothing, with enduring plainness, her grief too reasonable ever to excite great sympathy. Nancy, who knew such things, said it was a great shame she had gone and lost a man prepared to marry her, for lightning did not strike twice and with her looks and at her age she would almost certainly end up an old maid. What's more, Nancy added sagely, we were as well to pay particular attention that nothing go missing from upstairs, as Miss Starling was as likely as not to be looking towards her old age.

Nancy's were not the only suspicions aroused by Miss Starling. The arrival of this quiet, unassuming and, by all accounts, conscientious woman created a stir downstairs that now seems unimaginable.

It was her place that caused such uncertainty. It wasn't right, Mrs. Townsend said, for a young lady of the middle class to be taking liberties in the main house, seating herself in the Master's study, gadding about with airs and graces out of step with her position. And, though it was doubtful that Miss Starling with her sensible mouse-brown hair, home-stitched clothing and cautious smile could ever be accused of airs and graces, I understood Mrs. Townsend's bother. The lines between upstairs and down had once been clearly and comfortably drawn, but with Miss Starling's arrival old certainties had begun to shift.

For while she was not one of Them, neither was she one of Us.

Her presence downstairs that afternoon brought a cerise glow to Mr. Hamilton's cheeks and a nervous animation to his fingertips, which now hovered busily about his lapel. The curious matter of station perplexed Mr. Hamilton specially, for in the poor, unsuspecting woman he perceived an adversary. Though as butler he was the senior servant, responsible for overseeing the house's management, as personal secretary she was privy to the shimmering secrets of the family's business affairs.

Mr. Hamilton plucked his gold fob watch from his pocket and made a show of comparing its time with that on the wall clock. The watch had been a gift from the former Lord Ashbury and of it Mr. Hamilton was immeasurably proud. It never failed to deliver him stillness, to help retain authority in instances of stress or bother. He ran a pale, steady thumb across its face. "Where is Alfred?" he said, finally.

"Laying the table, Mr. Hamilton," I said, relieved that the taut balloon of silence had finally been pricked.

"Still?" Mr. Hamilton snapped the watch closed, his agitation finding welcome focus. "It's been almost a quarter-hour since I sent him with the brandy balloons. Honestly. That boy. I'd like to know what they've been teaching him in the military. Ever since he got back he's been flighty as a feather."

I flinched as if the criticism had been leveled at me.

Miss Starling cleared her throat and said, in a voice leavened with careful elocution, "They're calling it shell shock, I believe." She looked about timidly as the room fell silent. "At least, that's what I've read. Many of the men are struck by it. It doesn't do to be too hard on Alfred."

In the kitchen my hand slipped and black tea leaves rained over the pine table.

Mrs. Townsend lay down her rolling pin and pushed her floury sleeves up over her elbows. Blood had rushed to her cheeks. "Now just you listen here," she said, with an unqualified authority usually the preserve of policemen and mothers. "I will not hear talk of that in my kitchen. There's nothing wrong with Alfred that a few of my dinners won't fix."

"Of course not, Mrs. Townsend," I said, eyeing Miss Starling. "Alfred will be right as rain once he's had some of your good home cooking."

"They're not a patch on my old dinners, of course, what with the U-boats and now the shortages." Mrs. Townsend looked at Miss Starling and her voice caught a waver. "But I do know what young Alfred likes."

"Of course," Miss Starling said, traitorous freckles materializing as her cheeks paled. "I didn't mean to suggest . . ." Her mouth continued to move around the words she couldn't find to say. Her lips straightened into a wan smile. "You know Alfred best, of course."

⁂

WHEN the war ended and Mr. Frederick and the girls took up permanent residence at Riverton, Hannah and Emmeline had chosen new bedrooms in the east wing. They were residents now rather than guests, and it was only fitting, said Nancy, that they take new rooms to demonstrate the point. Emmeline's room overlooked Eros and Psyche on the front lawn, while Hannah preferred the smaller one with a view to the rose garden and the lake beyond. The two bedrooms were adjoined by a small sitting area, which was always referred to as the burgundy room, though I never could think why as the walls were a pale shade of duck-egg blue and the curtains a Liberty floral in blues and pinks.

The burgundy room bore little evidence of its recent reoccupation, retaining the hallmarks of whichever erstwhile inhabitant had overseen its original decoration. It was comfortably appointed, with a pink chaise longue beneath one window and a burr walnut writing desk beneath the other. An armchair sat stately by the door to the hall. Atop a small mahogany table, gleaming splendidly, proclaiming its newness, was a gramophone. Its very novelty seemed to bring a blush to the prudent old furnishings.

As I made my way along the dim corridor, wistful strains of a familiar song seeped beneath the closed door, mingling with the cold, stale air that hugged the skirting boards. *If you were the only girl in the world, And I were the only boy . . .*

It was Emmeline's current favorite, on permanent rotation since they'd arrived from London. We were all singing it in the servants' hall. Even Mr. Hamilton had been heard whistling to himself in his pantry.

I knocked once and entered, crossed the once-proud carpet and busied myself sorting the mound of silks and satins that smothered the armchair. I was glad for the occupation. Though I had longed since they left for the girls' return, in the intervening two years the familiarity I'd felt when last I served them had evaporated. A quiet revolution had taken place and the two girls with pinafores and plaits had been replaced by young women. I felt shy of them again.

And there was something else, something vague and unnerving. They were two now where they had been three. David's death had dismantled the triangle, and an enclosed space was now open. Two points are unreliable; with nothing to anchor them, there is nothing to stop them drifting in opposite directions. If it is string that binds, it will eventually snap and the points will separate; if elastic, they will continue to part, further and further, until the strain reaches its limit and they are pulled back with such speed that they cannot help but collide with devastating force.

Hannah was lying on the chaise, book in hand, a faint frown of focus on her brow. Her free hand was pressed against one ear in a vain attempt to block the record's crackly fervency.

The book was the new James Joyce: *A Portrait of the Artist as a Young Man.* I could tell by its spine, though I hardly had to look. It had kept her in its thrall since they'd arrived.

Emmeline stood in the middle of the room before a full-length mirror dragged in from one of the bedrooms. Against her middle she hugged a dress that I had not yet seen: pink taffeta with ruffles along the hemline. Another of Grandmama's gifts, I guessed, purchased with dour conviction that the current shortage of marriageable men would render all but the most attractive prospects superfluous.

The final shimmer of wintry sun reached through the French window and hovered winsomely before turning Emmeline's long ringlets to gold, and landing, exhausted, in a series of pale squares at her feet. Emmeline, on whom such subtleties were wasted, swayed back and forth, pink taffeta rustling, as she hummed along with the record in a pretty voice colored by its owner's longing for romance. When the final note dissolved with the sun's last light, the record continued to spin and bump beneath its needle. Emmeline tossed the dress onto the empty armchair and twirled across the floor. She drew back the needle arm and set about realigning it on the record's rim.

Hannah looked up from her book. Her long hair had disappeared in London—along with any lingering trace of childhood—and was now brushing her shoulder blades in soft, golden waves. "Not again, Emmeline," she said, frowning. "Play something else. *Anything* else."

"But it's my favorite."

"This week," Hannah said.

Emmeline pouted theatrically. "How do you think poor Stephen would feel if he knew you wouldn't listen to his record? It was a gift. The least you could do is enjoy it."

"We've enjoyed it quite enough," Hannah said. She noticed me then. "Don't you agree, Grace?"

I curtsied and felt my face flush, unsure how to answer. I avoided having to by lighting the gas lamp.

"If I had an admirer like Stephen Hardcastle," Emmeline said dreamily, "I should listen to his record a hundred times each day."

"Stephen Hardcastle is not an admirer," Hannah said, the very suggestion seeming to appal her. "We've known him forever. He's a chum. He's Lady Clem's godson."

"Godson or not, I don't think he called at Kensington Place every day when he was on leave out of a ghoulish desire to hear of Lady Clem's latest ailment. Do you?"

Hannah bristled slightly. "How should I know? They're very close."

"Oh, Hannah," Emmeline said. "For all your reading you can be so dense. Even *Fanny* could see." She wound the gramophone handle and dropped the needle arm so that the record started once more to spin. As the music began its sentimental swell she turned and said, "Stephen was hoping you'd make him a *promise*."

Hannah folded down the corner of her current page, then unfolded it again, running her finger along the crease.

"You know," Emmeline said eagerly. "A promise of marriage."

I held my breath; it was the first I'd learned of Hannah receiving a proposal.

"I'm not an idiot," Hannah said, eyes still on the triangular ear beneath her finger. "I know what he wanted."

"Then why didn't you—?"

"I wasn't going to make a promise I couldn't keep," Hannah said quickly.

"You can be such a stick-in-the-mud. What harm would there have been in laughing at his jokes, letting him whisper silly sweet things in your ear? You were the one always droning on about helping the war effort. If you weren't so mulish you could have given him a lovely memory to take with him to the front."

Hannah draped a fabric bookmark across the page of her book and placed it beside her on the chaise. "And what would I have done when he returned? Told him I didn't really mean it?"

Emmeline's conviction slipped momentarily, then resurrected itself. "But that's the point," she said. "Stephen Hardcastle hasn't returned."

"He still might."

It was Emmeline's turn to shrug. "Anything's possible, I suppose. But if he does I imagine he'll be too busy counting his lucky stars to worry about you."

A stubborn silence settled between them. The room itself seemed to take sides: the walls and curtains retreating into Hannah's corner, the gramophone offering obsequious support to Emmeline.

Emmeline pulled her long ringleted ponytail over one shoulder and fingered the ends. She picked up her hairbrush from the floor beneath the mirror and dragged it through in long, even strokes. The bristles whooshed conspicuously. She was observed for a moment by Hannah, whose face clouded with an expression I couldn't read—exasperation perhaps, or incredulity—before returning its attention to Joyce.

I picked up the pink taffeta dress from the chair. "Is this the one you'll be wearing tonight, miss?" I said softly.

Emmeline jumped. "Oh! You mustn't sneak up like that. You frightened me half to death."

"Sorry, miss." I could feel my cheeks growing hot and tingly. I shot a glance at Hannah, who appeared not to have heard. "Is this the dress you'd like, miss?"

"Yes. That's it." Emmeline chewed gently on her bottom lip. "At least, I think so." She pondered the dress, reached out and flicked the ruffled trim. "Hannah, which do you think? Blue or pink?"

"Blue."

"Really?" Emmeline turned to Hannah, surprised. "I thought pink."

"Pink then."

"You're not even looking."

Hannah looked up reluctantly. "Either. Neither." A frustrated sigh. "They're both fine."

Emmeline sighed peevishly. "You'd better fetch the blue dress. I'll need to have another look."

I curtsied and disappeared around the corner into the bedroom. As I reached the wardrobe, I heard Emmeline say, "It's important, Hannah. Tonight is my first proper dinner party and I want to look sophisticated. You should too. The Luxtons are American."

"So?"

"You don't want them thinking us unrefined."

"I don't much care what they think."

"You should. They're very important to Pa's business." Emmeline lowered her voice and I had to stand very still, cheek pressed close against the dresses, to make out what she was saying. "I overheard Pa talking with Grandmama—"

"Eavesdropped, more like," Hannah said. "And Grandmama thinks I'm the wicked one!"

"Fine then," said Emmeline, and in her voice I heard the careless shrug of her shoulders. "I'll keep it to myself."

"You couldn't if you tried. I can see it in your face, you're bursting to tell me what you heard."

Emmeline paused a moment to savour her ill-gotten gains. "Oh . . . all right," she said eagerly, "I'll tell you if you insist." She cleared her throat importantly. "It all started because Grandmama was saying what a tragedy the war had been for this family. That the Germans had robbed the Ashbury line of its future and that Grandfather would turn in his grave if he knew the state of things. Pa tried to tell her that it wasn't as desperate as all that, but Grandmama was having none of it. She said she was old enough to see clearly and how else could the situation be described but desperate, when Pa was last in line with no heirs to follow? Grandmama said it was a shame that Pa hadn't done the right thing and married Fanny when he had the chance!

"Pa turned snippy then and said that while he had lost his heir, he still had his factory, and Grandmama could stop worrying for he would take care of things. Grandmama didn't stop worrying, though. She said the bank was starting to ask questions.

"Then Pa was quiet for a little while and *I* began to worry, thinking that he had stood up and was on his way to the door and I was to be discovered. I almost laughed with relief when he spoke again and I could hear that he was still in his chair."

"Yes, yes, and what did he say?"

Emmeline continued, in the cautiously optimistic manner of an actor nearing the end of a complicated passage. "Pa said that while it was true things had been tight during the war, he'd given up the aeroplanes and was back making motorcars now. The *damned* bank— his words, not mine—the *damned* bank was going to get its money. He said he met a man at his club. A finance man. The fellow, Mr. Simion Luxton, has connections, Pa said, in business *and* in the government." Emmeline sighed triumphantly, monologue successfully delivered. "And that was the end of it, or near enough. Pa sounded ever so embarrassed when Grandmama mentioned the bank. I decided then and there that I'd do anything I could to help make a good impression with Mr. Luxton, to help Pa keep his business."

"I didn't know you took such keen interest."

"Of course I do," Emmeline said primly. "And you needn't be angry with me just because I know more about it than you this time."

A pause, then Hannah: "I don't suppose your sudden, ardent devotion to Pa's business has anything to do with that fellow, the son, whose photo Fanny was mooning over in the newspaper?"

"*Theodore* Luxton? Is he going to be at dinner? I had no idea," Emmeline said, but a smile had crept into her voice.

"You're far too young. He's at least thirty."

"I'm almost fifteen and everyone says I look mature for my age." Hannah rolled her eyes.

"I'm not too young to be in love, you know," Emmeline said. "Juliet was only fourteen."

"And look what happened to her."

"That was just a misunderstanding. If she and Romeo had been allowed to marry properly and their silly old parents had stopped giving them such trouble, I'm sure they'd have lived happily ever after." She sighed. "I can't wait to be married."

"Marriage isn't just about having a handsome man to dance with," said Hannah. "There's a lot more to it."

The gramophone song had stopped playing, but the record continued to spin beneath the needle.

"Like what?"

Against the cold silk of Emmeline's dresses, my cheeks grew warm.

"Private things," Hannah said. *"Intimacies."*

"Oh," Emmeline said, almost inaudible. *"Intimacies.* Poor Fanny."

There was a silence in which we all pondered Poor Fanny's misfortune. Newly married and trapped, on honeymoon, with a Strange Man.

"Hannah," Emmeline said. "What *are* intimacies, exactly?"

"I . . . well . . . They're expressions of love," Hannah said breezily. "Quite pleasant, I believe, with a man with whom you're passionately in love; unthinkably distasteful with anyone else."

"Yes, yes. But what are they? *Exactly?"*

Another silence.

"You don't know, either," Emmeline said. "I can tell by your face."

"Well, not exactly—"

"I'll ask Fanny when she gets back," Emmeline said. "She ought to know by then."

I ran my fingertips along the row of pretty fabrics in Emmeline's wardrobe, looking for the blue dress, wondered whether what Hannah said was true. I thought about the few times Alfred had stood very near me in the servants' hall, the strange but not unwelcome feeling that had overcome me . . .

"Anyway, I didn't say I wanted to marry *immediately.*" This was Emmeline. "All I meant is that Theodore Luxton is very handsome."

"Very wealthy, you mean," Hannah said.

"Same thing, really."

"You're just lucky that Pa's decided to let you dine downstairs at all," Hannah said. "I should never have been allowed when I was fourteen."

"Almost fifteen."

"I suppose he had to make up numbers somehow."

"Yes. Thank goodness Fanny agreed to marry that terrible bore, and thank goodness he decided they should honeymoon in Italy. If they'd been home, I'm sure I'd have been left to dine with Nanny Brown in the nursery instead."

"I should prefer Nanny Brown's company to that of Pa's Americans any day."

"Rubbish," Emmeline said.

"I should be just as happy to read my book."

"Liar," Emmeline said. "You've set your ivory satin dress aside, the one Fanny was so determined you shouldn't wear when we met her old bore. You wouldn't wear that one unless you were as excited as I am."

There was a silence.

"Ha!" Emmeline said. "I'm right! You're smiling!"

"All right, I am looking forward to it," Hannah said. "But not," she added quickly, "because I want the good opinion of some rich Americans I've never met."

"Oh no?"

"No."

The floorboards creaked as one of the girls trod across the room, and the spent gramophone record, still spinning drunkenly, was halted.

"Well?" This was Emmeline. "It certainly can't be Mrs. Townsend's ration menu that's got you excited."

There was a pause, during which I held very still, waiting, listening. Hannah's voice, when finally she spoke, was calm, but a slim thread of excitement ran through it. "Tonight," she said, "I'm going to ask Pa whether I might return to London."

Deep within the closet, I gasped. They had only just arrived; that Hannah might leave again so soon was unthinkable.

"To Grandmama?" said Emmeline.

"No. To live by myself. In a flat."

"A *flat*? Why on earth would you want to live in a flat?"

"You'll laugh . . . I want to take work in an office."

Emmeline did not laugh. "What sort of work?"

"Office work. Typing, filing, shorthand."

"But you don't know how to do short—" Emmeline broke off, sighed with realization. "You *do* know shorthand. Those papers I found the other week: they weren't really Egyptian hieroglyph—"

"No."

"You've been learning shorthand. In secret." Emmeline's voice took on a note of indignation. "From Miss Prince?"

"Lord, no. Miss Prince teach something so useful? Never."

"Then where?"

"The secretarial school in the village."

"When?"

"I started ages ago, just after the war began. I felt so useless and it seemed as good a way as any to help with the war effort. I thought when we went to stay with Grandmama I'd be able to get work—there are so many offices in London—but . . . it didn't work out like that. When I finally got away from Grandmama long enough to inquire, they wouldn't take me. Said I was too young. But now that I'm eighteen I should walk into a job. I've done so much practice and I'm really very quick."

"Who else knows?"

"No one. Except you."

Veiled amongst the dresses, as Hannah continued to extol the virtues of her training, I lost something. A small confidence, long cherished, was released. I felt it slip away, float down amid the silks and satins, until it landed amongst the flecks of silent dust on the dark wardrobe floor and I could see it no more.

"Well?" Hannah was saying. "Don't you think it's exciting?"

Emmeline huffed. "I think it's sneaky. That's what I think. And silly. And so will Pa. War work is one thing, but this . . . It's *ridiculous*, and you may as well get it out of your mind. Pa will never allow it."

"That's why I'm going to tell him at dinner. It's the perfect opportunity. He'll have to say yes if there are other people around. Especially Americans with all their modern ideas."

"I can't believe even you would do this." Emmeline's voice was gathering fury.

"I don't know why you're so upset."

"Because . . . it isn't . . . it doesn't . . ." Emmeline cast about for adequate defence. "Because you're supposed to be the hostess tonight and instead of making sure things run smoothly, you're going to embarrass Pa. You're going to create a scene in front of the Luxtons."

"I'm not going to create a scene."

"You always say that and then you always do. Why can't you just be—"

"Normal?"

"You've gone completely mad. Who would want to work in an office?"

"I want to see the world. Travel."

"To London?"

"It's a first step," Hannah said. "I want to be independent. To meet interesting people."

"More interesting than me, you mean."

"Don't be silly," Hannah said. "I just mean new people with clever things to say. Things I've never heard before. I want to be free, Emme. Open to whatever adventure comes along and sweeps me off my feet."

I glanced at the clock on Emmeline's wall. Four o'clock. Mr. Hamilton would be on the warpath if I wasn't downstairs soon. And yet I had to hear more, to learn the precise nature of these adventures Hannah was so intent upon. Torn between the two, I compromised. Closed the wardrobe, draped the blue dress over my arm and hesitated by the doorway.

Emmeline was still sitting on the floor, brush in hand. "Why don't you go and stay with friends of Pa's somewhere? I could come too," she said. "The Rothermeres, up in Edinburgh—"

"And have Lady Rothermere inquire after my every move? Or worse, saddle me with those ghastly daughters of hers?" Hannah's face was a study in disdain. "That's hardly independence."

"Neither is working in an office."

"Perhaps not, but I'm going to need money from somewhere. I'm not going to beg or steal, and I can't think of anyone from whom I could borrow."

"What about Pa?"

"You heard Grandmama. Some people may have made money from the war, but Pa was not amongst them."

"Well, I think it's a terrible idea," Emmeline said. "It . . . it just isn't proper. Pa would never allow it . . . and Grandmama . . ." Emmeline drew breath. Exhaled deeply so that her shoulders deflated. When she spoke again her voice was young and pale. "I don't want you to leave me." Her gaze sought Hannah's. "First David, and now you."

Her brother's name was a physical blow for Hannah. It was no secret that she had mourned his death especially. The family had still been in London when the dreaded black-rimmed letter arrived, but news traveled surely across the servants' halls of England in those days, and we had all learned of Miss Hannah's alarming loss of spirits. Her refusal to eat was the cause of much concern, and had Mrs. Townsend intent upon baking raspberry tartlets, Hannah's favorite since a girl, to send to London.

Whether oblivious to the effect her invocation of David had caused, or entirely aware, Emmeline continued. "What will I do, all alone in this great big house?"

"You won't be alone," Hannah said quietly. "Pa will be here for company."

"That's little comfort. You know Pa doesn't care for me."

"Pa cares a great deal for you, Emme," said Hannah firmly. "For all of us."

Emmeline glanced over her shoulder and I pressed myself against the doorframe. "But he doesn't really *like* me," she said. "Not as a person. Not as he does you."

Hannah opened her mouth to argue, but Emmeline hurried on.

"You don't have to pretend. I've seen the way he looks at me when he thinks I can't see. Like he's puzzled, like he's not sure exactly who I am." Her eyes glazed, but she did not cry. Her voice was a whisper. "It's because he blames me for Mother."

"That's not true." Hannah's cheeks had turned pink. "Don't even say such things. No one blames you for Mother."

"Pa does."

"He doesn't."

"I heard Grandmama tell Lady Clem that Pa was never the same after the dreadful business with Mother." Emmeline spoke then with a firmness that surprised me. "I don't want you to leave me." She rose from the floor and sat by Hannah, clasped her hand. An uncharacteristic gesture, which seemed to shock Hannah as much as it did me. "Please." And then she began to cry.

The two sat side by side upon the chaise, Emmeline sobbing, her final word between them. Hannah's expression bore the stubborn set that was so singularly hers, but behind the strong cheekbones, the wilful mouth, I noticed something else. A new aspect, not so easily articulated as the natural consequence of reaching adulthood . . .

And then I realized. She was the eldest now and had inherited the vague, relentless, unsolicited responsibility such familial rank demanded.

Hannah turned to Emmeline and gave an appearance of brightness. "Cheer up," she said, patting Emmeline's hand. "You don't want red eyes at dinner."

I glanced at the clock again. Quarter past four. Mr. Hamilton would be fuming. There was nothing for it . . .

I re-entered the room, blue dress draped over one arm. "Your dress, miss?" I said to Emmeline.

She did not respond. I pretended not to notice that her cheeks were wet with tears. Focused on the dress instead, brushed flat a piece of lace trim.

"Wear the pink one, Emme," Hannah said gently. "It suits you best."

Emmeline remained unmoved.

I looked at Hannah for clarification. She nodded. "The pink."

"And you, miss?" I said.

She chose the ivory satin, just as Emmeline had said she would.

"Will you be there tonight, Grace?" Hannah said as I fetched the beautiful satin gown and corset from her wardrobe.

"I shouldn't think so, miss," I said. "Alfred has been demobilized. He'll be helping Mr. Hamilton and Nancy at table."

"Oh," Hannah said. "Yes." She picked up her book, opened it, closed it, ran her fingers lightly along the spine. Her voice, when she spoke, was cautious. "I've been meaning to ask, Grace. How is Alfred?"

"He's well, miss. He had a small cold when he returned, but Mrs. Townsend fixed him up with some lemon and barley and he's been right since then."

"She doesn't mean how is he *physically*," Emmeline said unexpectedly. "She means how is he in the head."

"In the head, miss?" I looked at Hannah, who was frowning faintly at Emmeline.

"Well, you did." Emmeline turned to me, her eyes red-rimmed. "When he served tea yesterday afternoon he behaved most peculiarly. He was offering the tray of sweets, just as usual, when suddenly the tray started quivering back and forth." She laughed: a hollow, unnatural sound. "His whole arm was shaking, and I waited for him to steady it so I could take a lemon tart, but it was as if he *couldn't* make it stop. Then, sure enough, the tray slipped and sent an avalanche of Victoria sponges all over my prettiest dress. At first I was quite cross—it was really too careless; the dress could have been ruined—but then, as he continued to stand there with the strangest look on his face, I became frightened. I was sure he'd gone quite mad." She shrugged. "He snapped out of it eventually and cleaned the mess. But still, the damage was done. He was just lucky that I was the one to suffer. Pa wouldn't have been so forgiving. He'd be ever so dark if it happened again tonight." She looked directly at me, blue eyes cold. "You don't think it's likely, do you?"

"I couldn't say, miss." I was taken aback. This was the first I'd heard of the event. "I mean, I shouldn't think so, miss. I'm sure Alfred is all right."

"Of course he is," Hannah said quickly. "It was an accident, nothing more. Returning home must take some adjustment after being away so long. And those salvers look awfully heavy, especially the way Mrs. Townsend loads them. I'm sure she's on a quest to fatten us all up." She smiled, but the echo of a frown still creased her brow.

"Yes, miss," I said.

Hannah nodded, the matter closed. "Now let's get these dresses on so we can play dutiful daughters for Pa's Americans and be done with it."

THE DINNER

A L L along the corridor and down the stairs I replayed Emmeline's reportage. But no matter which way I twisted it, I arrived at the same conclusion. Something was amiss. It was not like Alfred to be clumsy.

And yet, the episode was surely not a fabrication—what reason, after all, had Emmeline to invent such a thing? No, it must have occurred, and the reason must be as Hannah suggested. An accident: a moment of distraction as the dying sun caught the windowpane, a slight cramp of the wrist, a slippery tray. No one was immune to such occurrences, particularly, as Hannah pointed out, someone who had been away some years and was out of practice.

But though I wished to believe this simple explanation, I could not. For in a small pocket of my mind a collection of motley incidents—no, not so much as that—a collection of motley observations was forming. Misinterpretations of benign queries after his health, overreactions to perceived criticisms, frowns where once he would have laughed. Indeed, a general air of confused irritability applied itself to everything he did.

If I were honest, I had perceived it from the evening of his return. We had planned a little party: Mrs. Townsend had baked a special supper and Mr. Hamilton had received permission to open a bottle of the Master's wine. We had spent much of the afternoon laying out the servants' hall table, laughing as we arranged and rearranged items so that they might best please Alfred. We were all a little drunk, I think, on gladness that evening, though none more so than I.

When the expected hour arrived we positioned ourselves in a tableau of poorly pretended casualness. Expectant glances met one another as we continued to wait, ears registering every noise outside. Finally, the crunch of gravel, low voices, a car door closing. Footsteps drawing near. Mr. Hamilton stood, smoothed his jacket and took up position by the door. A moment of eager silence as we awaited Alfred's knock, and then the door was open and we were upon him.

It was nothing dramatic: Alfred didn't rant or rave or cower. He let me take his hat and then he stood, uncomfortably, in the doorjamb as if afraid to enter. Schooled his lips into a smile. Mrs. Townsend threw her arms around him, dragging him across the threshold as one might a resistant roll of carpet. She led him to his seat, guest of honor to Mr. Hamilton's right, and we all spoke at once, laughing, exclaiming, recounting events of the past two years. All except Alfred, that is. Oh, he made a stab at it. Nodded when required, provided answers to questions, even managed another strangled smile or two. But they were the responses of an outsider, of one of Lady Violet's Belgians, contriving to please an audience set on including them.

I was not the only one to notice. I saw the tremors of unease pulling at Mr. Hamilton's brow, an unwelcome knowledge arranging itself on Nancy's. But we never spoke of it, never came closer than the day the Luxtons came to dinner, the day Miss Starling offered her ill-received opinions. That evening, and the other observations I had made since his arrival, were left to lie dormant. We all picked up the slack and remained complicit in an unspoken pact not to notice things had changed. Times had changed and Alfred had changed.

※

I N the absence of a suitable hostess, Hannah, much to her amused vexation, had been given the duty of assigning places. Her plan was hastily sketched on a sheet of lined notepaper, jagged along the edge where it had been torn from a book of similar sheets.

The place cards themselves were lettered plainly: black on white, the Ashbury crest embossed on the upper left corner. They lacked the flair of the Dowager Lady Ashbury's cards, but would serve the purpose well enough, matching the comparatively austere table setting favored by Mr. Frederick. Indeed, to Mr. Hamilton's eternal chagrin, Mr. Frederick had elected to dine en famille (rather than in the formal à la Russe style to which we were accustomed) and would be carving the pheasant himself. Though Mrs. Townsend was aghast, Nancy, fresh from her stint outside the house, quietly approved the choice, noting that the Master's decision was surely calculated to suit the tastes of his American guests.

It was not my place to say, but I preferred the table in its more modern manner. Without the tree-like epergnes, pregnant with their overloaded salvers of sweetmeats and elaborate fruit displays, the table had a simple refinement that pleased me. The stark white of the cloth, starched at each corner, the silver lines of cutlery and sparkling clusters of stemware.

I peered closer. A large thumbprint blotted the rim of Mr. Frederick's champagne flute. I puffed a hot breath onto the offending mark and rubbed at it quickly with a bunched corner of my apron.

So intent was I on the task that I jumped when the door from the hall swung forcefully inwards.

"Alfred!" I said. "You frightened me! I almost dropped a glass!"

"You shouldn't be touching them," Alfred said, a familiar frown settled on his forehead. "Glasses are my duty."

"There was a print," I said. "You know what Mr. Hamilton's like. He'd have your guts for garters if he saw. And Mr. Hamilton in garters is something I hope never to see!"

An attempt at humor destined for failure before it was made. Somewhere in the trenches of France Alfred's laughter had died, and he could only grimace. "I was going to polish them later."

"Well," I said, "now you won't have to."

"You needn't keep doing that." His tone was measured.

"Doing what?"

"Checking up on me. Following me around like a second shadow."

"I'm not. I was just laying the place cards and I saw a fingerprint."

"And I told you, I was going to do it later."

"All right," I said quietly, setting the glass back in place. "I'll leave it."

Alfred grunted his gruff satisfaction and pulled a cloth from his pocket.

I fiddled with the place cards though they were already straight, and pretended not to watch him.

His shoulders were hunched, the right raised stiffly so that his body turned from me. It was an entreaty for solitude, yet the cursed bells of good intentions rang loudly in my ears. Maybe if I drew him out, learned what was bothering him, I could help? Who better than me? For surely I had not imagined the closeness that had grown between us while he was away? I knew I had not: he had said as much in his letters. I cleared my throat to speak, proceeded softly to say: "I know what happened yesterday."

He gave no appearance of having heard, remained focused on the glass he was polishing.

A little louder: "I know what happened yesterday. In the drawing room."

He stopped, glass in hand. Stood very still. The offending words hung like fog between us and I was struck by an overwhelming wish to retract the utterance.

His voice was deathly quiet. "Little miss been telling tales, has she?"

"No—"

"Bet she had a good laugh about it."

"Oh no," I said quickly. "It wasn't like that. She was worried about you." I swallowed, dared to say: "*I'm* worried about you."

He looked up sharply from beneath the lock of hair that his glass-shuffling had worked loose. His mouth was etched with tiny angry lines. "Worried about me?"

His strange, brittle tone made me wary, yet I was seized by an uncontrollable urge to make things right. "It's just, it's not like you to drop a tray, and then you didn't mention it . . . I thought you might be frightened of Mr. Hamilton finding out. But he wouldn't be angry, Alfred. I'm sure of it. Everyone makes mistakes sometimes in their duties."

He looked at me, and for a moment I thought he might laugh. Instead, his features were contorted by a sneer. "You silly little girl," he said. "You think I care about a few cakes ending up on the floor?"

"Alfred—"

"You think I don't know about duty? After where I've been?"

"I didn't say that—"

"It's what you're thinking, though, isn't it? I can feel you all looking at me, watching me, waiting for me to make a mistake. Well, you can stop waiting and you can keep your worrying. There's nothing wrong with me, you hear? Nothing!"

My eyes were smarting, his bitter tone made my skin prickle. I whispered, "I just wanted to help—"

"To help?" He laughed bitterly. "And what makes you think you can help me?"

"Why, Alfred," I said tentatively, wondering what he could possibly mean. "You and I . . . we're . . . It's like you said . . . in your letters—"

"Forget what I said."

"But Alfred—"

"Stay away from me, Grace," he said coldly, returning his attention to the glasses. "I never asked for your help. I don't need it and I don't want it. Go on, get out of here and let me get on with my work."

My cheeks burned: with disillusionment, with the feverish afterglow of confrontation, but most hotly with embarrassment. I had

perceived a closeness where none existed. God help me, in my most
private moments I had even begun to imagine a future for Alfred and
me. Courtship, marriage, maybe even a family of our own. And now,
to realize I had mistaken absence for greater feeling . . .

I spent the early evening downstairs. If Mrs. Townsend wondered where my sudden dedication to the finer points of pheasant
roasting came from, she knew better than to ask. I basted and boned,
and even helped with stuffing. Anything to avoid being sent back upstairs where Alfred was serving.

My course of avoidance was on good track until Mr. Hamilton
thrust a cocktail salver into my hands.

"But Mr. Hamilton," I said disconsolately. "I'm helping Mrs.
Townsend with the meals."

Mr. Hamilton, eyeballs glistening behind his glasses at the perceived challenge, replied, "And I am telling you to take the cocktails."

"But Alfred—"

"Alfred is busy fixing the dining room," Mr. Hamilton said.
"Quickly now, girl. Don't keep the Master waiting."

❧

I T was a small party, six in all, and yet the room gave the impression
of being overfull. Thick with loud voices and inordinate heat. Mr.
Frederick, eager to make a good impression, had insisted on extra
heating and Mr. Hamilton had risen to the challenge, hiring two oil
stoves. A particularly strident female perfume had flourished in the
hothouse conditions and now threatened to overwhelm the room
and its occupants.

I saw Mr. Frederick first, dressed in his black dinner suit, looking almost as fine as the Major had once done, though thinner and
somehow less starched. He stood by the mahogany bureau, talking to
a puffy man with salt-and-pepper hair that perched like a wreath
around his shiny pate.

The puffy man pointed towards a porcelain vase on the bureau. "I saw one of those at Sotheby's," he said in an accent of gentrified northern English mixed with something else. "Identical." He leaned closer. "It's worth a pretty penny, old boy."

Mr. Frederick replied vaguely. "I wouldn't know, Great-grandfather brought that back from the Far East. It's sat there ever since."

"You hear that, Estella?" Simion Luxton called across the room to his doughy wife, seated between Emmeline and Hannah on the sofa. "Frederick said it's been in the family for generations. He's been using it as a paperweight."

Estella Luxton smiled tolerantly at her husband and between them passed a type of unspoken communication born of years of joint existence. In that moment's glance I perceived their marriage as one of practical endurance. A symbiotic relationship whose usefulness had long outlived its passion.

Duty to her husband fulfilled, Estella returned her attention to Emmeline, in whom she had discovered a fellow high-society enthusiast. What her husband lacked in hair, Estella more than made up for. Hers, the color of pewter, was wound into a sleek and impressive chignon, curiously American in its construction. It reminded me of a photograph Mr. Hamilton had pinned on the noticeboard downstairs, a New York skyscraper covered in scaffolding: complex and impressive without ever being properly attractive. She smiled at something Emmeline said and I was stunned by her unusually white teeth.

I skirted the room, laid the cocktail tray on the dumbwaiter beneath the window and curtsied routinely. The young Mr. Luxton was seated in the armchair, half listening as Emmeline and Estella discussed the upcoming country season in rapturous tones.

Theodore—Teddy as we came to think of him—was handsome in the way all wealthy men were handsome in those days. Basic good looks enhanced with confidence created a facade of wit and charm, put a knowing gleam in the eyes.

He had dark hair, almost as black as his Savile Row dinner

jacket, and he wore a distinguished moustache, which made him look like a screen actor. Like Douglas Fairbanks, I thought suddenly, and felt my cheeks flush. When he smiled it was broad and free, his teeth whiter even than his mother's.

As Estella commenced a detailed description of Lady Belmont's most recent ball, in a metallic accent I had never heard before, Teddy's gaze began to wander the room. Noticing his guest's lack of occupation, Mr. Frederick motioned tensely to Hannah, who cleared her throat and said, half-heartedly, "Your crossing was pleasant, I trust?"

"Very pleasant," he said with an easy smile. "Though Mother and Father would answer differently, I'm sure. Neither have sea legs. Each was as sick as the other from the moment we left New York until we reached Bristol."

Hannah took a sip from her cocktail, then submitted another stiff sample of polite conversation. "How long will you be staying in England?"

"Just a short visit for me, I'm afraid. I'm off to the Continent next week. Egypt."

"Egypt," Hannah said, eyes widening.

Teddy laughed. "Yes. I have business there."

"You're going to see the pyramids of Egypt?"

"Not this time, I'm afraid. Just a few days in Cairo and then on to Florence."

"God-awful place," Simion said loudly from his seat in the second armchair. "Full of pigeons and wogs. Give me good old England any day."

Mr. Hamilton motioned towards Simion's glass, nearly empty despite having recently been filled. I took my cocktail bottle to his side.

I could feel Simion's eyes on me as I topped up his glass. "There are certain pleasures," he said, "unique to this country." He leaned slightly and his warm arm brushed my thigh. "Try as I might, I haven't found them anywhere else."

I had to concentrate to keep a blank expression on my face, and not to pour too quickly. An eternity passed before the glass was finally full and I could leave his side. As I rounded the sofa, I saw Hannah frowning at the place where I had been.

"My husband does love England," Estella said rather pointlessly.

"Hunting, shooting and golf," Simion said. "No one does them better than the British." He took a swig of his cocktail and leaned back in the armchair. "Best thing of all, though, is the English mindset," Simion said. "There are two types of people in England. Those born to give orders." His gaze found mine across the room. "And those born to take them."

Hannah's frown deepened.

"It keeps things running well," Simion continued. "Not so in America, I'm afraid. The fellow who shines your shoes on the street corner is as like as not to be dreaming of owning his own company. There's little to make a man so damnably nervous as an entire population of laborers puffed up with unreasonable . . ." he rolled the distasteful word around his mouth a moment and spat it out, *"ambitions."*

"Imagine," Hannah said, "a working man who expects more from life than the stench of other men's feet."

"Abominable!" Simion said, blind to Hannah's irony.

"One would think they'd realize," she said, voice rising a semitone, "that only the fortunate have a right to concern themselves with ambition."

Mr. Frederick shot her a warning glance.

"They'd save us all a lot of bother if they did," Simion said with a nod. "You only have to look at the Bolsheviks to realize how dangerous these people can be when they get ideas above their station."

"A man shouldn't seek to improve himself?" Hannah said.

The younger Mr. Luxton, Teddy, continued to look at Hannah, a slight smile making his lips twitch beneath his moustache. "Oh, Father approves of self-improvement, don't you, Father? As a boy I heard of little else."

"My grandfather pulled himself out of the mines with sheer determination," Simion said. "Now look at the Luxton family."

"An admirable transformation." Hannah smiled. "Just not to be attempted by everyone, Mr. Luxton?"

"Just so," he said. "Just so."

Mr. Frederick, eager to leave precarious waters, cleared his throat impatiently and looked towards Mr. Hamilton.

Mr. Hamilton nodded imperceptibly and leaned near to Hannah. "Dinner is served, miss." He looked at me and signaled that I should return downstairs.

"Well," Hannah said as I slipped from the room. "Shall we dine?"

🪶

FISH followed green pea soup, pheasant followed fish and by all accounts things were going well. Nancy made occasional appearances downstairs, providing welcome reports of the evening's progress. Though working at a frantic pace, Mrs. Townsend was never too busy for an update on Hannah's performance as hostess. She nodded when Nancy announced that though Miss Hannah was doing well, her manner was not yet so charming as her grandmother's.

"Of course not," Mrs. Townsend said, sweat beading at her hairline. "It's *natural* with Lady Violet. She couldn't host a party that wasn't perfect if she tried. Miss Hannah will improve with practice. She may never be a *perfect* hostess, but she'll certainly be a good one. It's in the blood."

"You're probably right, Mrs. Townsend," Nancy said.

"Of course I am. That girl'll turn out just fine, so long as she doesn't get swept up with . . . *modern notions.*"

"What sort of modern notions?" I said.

"She always was an intelligent child," Mrs. Townsend said with a sigh. "And all those books are bound to put ideas in a girl's head."

"What sort of modern notions?"

"Marriage will cure her, though. You mark my words," Mrs. Townsend said to Nancy.

"I'm sure you're right, Mrs. Townsend."

"What sort of modern notions?" I said impatiently.

"There's some young ladies just don't know what they need until they find themselves a suitable husband," Mrs. Townsend said.

I could stand it no longer. "Miss Hannah's not going to get married," I said. "Never. I heard her say so herself. She's going to travel the world and live a life of adventure."

Nancy gasped and Mrs. Townsend stared at me. "What are you talking about, you silly girl?" Mrs. Townsend said, pressing a hand firmly against my forehead. "You've gone mad, talking nonsense like that. You sound like Katie. Of course Miss Hannah's going to get married. It's every debutante's wish: to be married briskly and brilliantly. What's more, it's her duty now that poor Master David—"

"Nancy," Mr. Hamilton said, hurrying down the stairs. "Where is that champagne?"

"I've got it, Mr. Hamilton." Katie's voice preceded her loping form. She emerged from the ice room, bottles clutched awkwardly under both arms, smiling broadly. "The others were too busy arguing, but I've got it."

"Well, hurry up then, girl," Mr. Hamilton said. "The Master's guests will be going thirsty." He turned towards the kitchen and peered down his nose. "I must say it's not like you to dawdle over your duties, Nancy."

"Here you are, Mr. Hamilton," said Katie.

"Up you go, Nancy," he said disparagingly. "Now that I'm here I might as well bring them myself."

Nancy glared at me and disappeared up the stairs.

Katie released the bottles onto the kitchen table.

Mr. Hamilton, reminded of the task at hand, began to open the first bottle. Despite his expertise, the cork was stubborn, refusing to emerge until its handler least expected and—

Bang!

It shot from the bottle, exploded a lamp globe into a hundred pieces, and landed in Mrs. Townsend's pot of butterscotch sauce. The liberated champagne showered Mr. Hamilton's face and hair with triumphant effervescence.

"Katie, you silly girl!" Mrs. Townsend exclaimed. "You've gone and shaken the bottles!"

"I'm sorry, Mrs. Townsend," Katie said, beginning to giggle as she was wont to do in moments of bother. "I was just trying to hurry, like Mr. Hamilton said."

"More haste, less speed, Katie," Mr. Hamilton said, the slick of champagne on his face detracting from the seriousness of his admonition.

"Here, Mr. Hamilton." Mrs. Townsend clutched the corner of her apron to wipe his shiny nose. "Let me get you cleaned up."

"Oh, Mrs. Townsend," Katie giggled. "You've gone and put flour all over his face!"

"Katie!" Mr. Hamilton snapped, swiping at his face with a handkerchief that had materialized amid the confusion. "You are a *silly* girl. Not an ounce of sense to show for any of your years here. Sometimes I really do wonder why we keep you . . ."

I heard Alfred before I saw him.

Over the din of Mr. Hamilton's scolding, Mrs. Townsend's fussing and Katie's protestations, the rasping rise and fall of breath.

He later told me he had come downstairs to find out what was keeping Mr. Hamilton, but now he stood at the bottom, so still and so pale, a marble statue of himself, or else a ghost . . .

As my eyes found his, a spell was broken and he turned on his heel, disappeared down the corridor, footsteps echoing on stone, through the back door and into the dark.

Everyone watched, silent. Mr. Hamilton's body twitched as if he thought to follow, but duty was ever his master. He ran his handkerchief across his face one last time and turned to us, lips pressed together so they sketched one pale line of dutiful resignation.

"Grace," he said as I prepared to chase Alfred. "Put on your good apron. You're needed upstairs."

✳

IN the dining room I took my place between the chiffonier and the Louis XIV chair. On the opposite wall Nancy raised her eyebrows. Powerless to convey all that had happened downstairs, unsure what such an explanation would contain, I lifted my shoulders slightly and looked away. Wondered where Alfred was and whether he would ever be himself again.

They were finishing the pheasant course and the air quivered with the polite tinkle of cutlery on fine china.

"Well," Estella said, "that was—" slight pause "—just lovely." She cleared a valley between the leftover mounds of solidifying pheasant and laid down her cutlery. She kissed cherry splotches onto a white linen napkin I would have to scrub later, then smiled at Mr. Frederick. "It must be difficult with the shortages."

Nancy raised her eyebrows. For a guest to comment directly on the meal was almost unheard of. We would have to be cautious when recounting to Mrs. Townsend.

Mr. Frederick, as astonished as we, launched an uneasy oratory on Mrs. Townsend's unparalleled skill as a ration cook, under which veil Estella took the opportunity to peruse the room. Her gaze alighted first on the ornate plaster cornices marrying wall to ceiling, slid south to the William Morris frieze on the dado rail, before resting, finally, on the wall-mounted Ashbury crest. All the while her tongue darted methodically beneath her cheek, working some stubborn and distasteful morsel from between her gleaming teeth.

Small sociable chat was not Mr. Frederick's metier in life, and his narration, once started, became a desolate conversational island from which there seemed no escape. He began to flounder. He cast

220

about with his eyes, but Estella, Simion, Teddy and Emmeline had all found discreet occupation elsewhere. Finally, in Hannah, he found an ally. They exchanged a glance, and while he allowed his desultory description of Mrs. Townsend's butterless scones to wilt, she cleared her throat.

"You mentioned a daughter, Mrs. Luxton," Hannah said. "She isn't with you on this trip?"

"No," Estella said quickly, her attention returned to her tablemates. "No, she isn't."

Simion looked up from his pheasant and grunted. "Deborah hasn't accompanied us in some time," he said. "She has commitments at home. *Work* commitments," he said ominously.

Hannah showed a resurrection of genuine interest. "She works?"

"Something in publishing." Simion swallowed a forkful of pheasant. "Don't know the details."

"Deborah is the fashion columnist for *Women's Style*," Estella said. "She writes a little report each month."

"Ridiculous—" Simion's body shook, capturing a hiccough before it became a burp, "—tripe about shoes and dresses and other extravagances."

"Now, Father," Teddy said with a slow smile. "Deb's column is very popular. She's been influential in shaping the way New York's society ladies dress."

"Guff! You're fortunate your daughters don't put you through such things, Frederick." Simion pushed his gravy-smeared plate aside. "Work indeed. You British girls are much more sensible."

It was the perfect opportunity and Hannah knew it. I held my breath, wondering whether her desire for adventure would win out. Hoping it wouldn't. That she would honor Emmeline's entreaty and stay here at Riverton. With Alfred as he was, I couldn't bear to think that Hannah might also disappear.

She and Emmeline exchanged a glance, and before Hannah had a chance to speak, Emmeline said quickly, in the clear musical voice young ladies were advised to cultivate for use in company, "I certainly never would. Working is hardly respectable, is it, Pa?"

"I'd sooner tear out my own heart than see either of my daughters working," Mr. Frederick said matter-of-factly.

Hannah's lips tightened.

"Damn near broke my heart," Simion said. He looked at Emmeline. "If only my Deborah had your sense."

Emmeline smiled, her face blooming with a precocious ripeness of beauty I was almost embarrassed to observe.

"Now, Simion," Estella placated. "You know Deborah wouldn't have accepted the position if you hadn't granted your permission." She smiled, too broadly, at the others. "He never could say no to her."

Simion humphed, but did not disagree.

"Mother's right, Father," Teddy said. "Taking a little job is quite the thing amongst the New York smart set. Deborah is young and she's not yet married. She'll settle down when the time comes."

"I've always preferred correctness to smartness," Simion said. "But that's modern society for you. They all want to be considered smart. I blame the war." He tucked his thumbs beneath the tight rim of his trousers, concealed from all but my view, and provided his stomach with some welcome breathing space. "My only consolation is that she earns good money." Reminded of his favorite topic, he cheered somewhat. "I say, Frederick. What do you think of the penalties they're talking of imposing on poor old Germany?"

As the conversation swept along, Emmeline looked sideways beneath her eyelids at Hannah. Hannah kept her chin up, eyes following the conversation, face a model of calm, and I wondered whether she had been going to ask at all. Perhaps Emmeline's earlier appeal had changed her mind. Perhaps I imagined her light shudder as the opportunity disappeared in a sudden draught up the chimney.

"One does feel rather sorry for the Germans," Simion said. "There's a lot to be admired in their people. Excellent employees, eh, Frederick?"

"I don't employ Germans in my factory," Frederick said.

"There's your first mistake. You won't find a more diligent race. Humorless, I'll grant you, but meticulous."

"I'm quite happy with my local men."

"Your nationalism is admirable, Frederick. But not, surely, at the expense of business?"

"My son was killed by a German bullet," Mr. Frederick said, fingers spread, light but taut, on the table rim.

The remark was a vacuum into which all bonhomie was drawn. Mr. Hamilton caught my gaze and motioned Nancy and me to create a diversion by collecting the main plates. We were halfway around the table when Teddy cleared his throat and said, "Our deepest sympathies, Lord Ashbury. We had heard about your son. About David. Word at White's, he was a good man."

"Boy."

"What's that?"

"My son was a boy."

"Yes," Teddy corrected himself. "A fine boy."

Estella reached a plump hand across the table, rested it limply on Mr. Frederick's wrist. "I don't know how you bear it, Frederick. I can't think what I'd do if I lost my Teddy. I thank God every day he decided to fight the war from home. He and his political friends."

Her helpless gaze flitted to her husband, who had the decency to look at least a little discomfited. "We're in their debt," he said. "Young men like your David made the ultimate sacrifice. It's up to us to prove they didn't die in vain. To thrive in business and return this great land to her rightful standing."

Mr. Frederick's pale eyes fixed on Simion and for the first time I perceived a flicker of distaste. "Indeed."

I loaded the plates into the dumbwaiter and pulled the rope to send them down, then leaned into the cavity, listening to hear whether Alfred's voice was amongst the distant strains below. Hoping he was back from wherever it was he'd run to in such a hurry.

Through the shaft came the distant jiggling of removal, the drone of Katie and reprimand of Mrs. Townsend. Finally, with a jerk, the ropes began to move and the dumbwaiter returned, loaded with fruit, blancmange and butterscotch sauce, sans cork.

"Business today," Simion said, straightening authoritatively, "is all about economies of scale. The more you produce, the more you can afford to produce."

Mr. Frederick nodded. "I've got some fine workers. Indeed, they're fine men. If we train the others—"

"Waste of time. Waste of money." Simion thumped an open hand on the table with a vehemence that made me jump, almost spilling the butterscotch sauce I was ladling into his bowl. "Mechanization! That's the way of the future."

"Assembly lines?"

Simion winked. "Speed up the slow men, slow down the fast."

"I'm afraid I don't sell enough to warrant assembly lines," Mr. Frederick said. "There are only so many people in Britain can afford my cars."

"Precisely my point," Simion said. Enthusiasm and liquor had combined to bring a crimson sheen to his face. "Assembly lines lower prices. You'll sell more."

"Assembly lines won't lower the price of parts," Mr. Frederick said.

"Use different parts."

"I use the best."

Mr. Luxton erupted into a fit of laughter from which it seemed he wouldn't emerge. "I like you, Frederick," he said finally. "You're an idealist. A *perfectionist*." The latter was spoken with the exultant self-gratification of a foreigner who had correctly plucked an unfamiliar word from memory. "But, Frederick," he leaned forward seriously, elbows on the table, and pointed a fat finger at his host, "do you want to make cars, or do you want to make money?"

Mr. Frederick blinked. "I'm not sure I—"

"I believe my father is suggesting you have a choice," came Teddy's measured interruption. He had heretofore been following the exchange with reserved interest, but now said, almost apologetically, "There are two markets for your automobiles. The discerning few who can afford the best—"

"Or the seething sprawl of aspirational middle-class consumers out there," Simion broke in. "Your factory; your decision. But from the banker's point of view . . ." He leaned back, loosened a button on his dinner jacket, exhaled gladly. "I know which I'd be aiming for."

"The middle class," Mr. Frederick said, frowning faintly, as if realizing for the first time that such a group existed outside doctrines of social theory.

"The middle class," Simion said. "They're untapped, and God help us, their ranks are growing. If we don't find ways to take their money from them, they'll find ways to take ours from us." He shook his head. "As if the workers weren't problem enough."

Frederick frowned, unsure.

"Unions," Simion said with a snarl. "Murderers of business. They won't rest until they've seized the means of production and put men like you out of action."

"Father paints a vivid picture," Teddy said with a diffident smile.

"I call things as I see them," Simion said.

"And you?" Frederick said to Teddy. "You don't see unions as a threat?"

"I believe they can be accommodated."

"Rubbish." Simion rolled a swig of dessert wine round his mouth, swallowed. "Teddy's a moderate," he said dismissively.

"Father, please, I'm a Tory—"

"With funny ideas."

"I merely propose we listen to all sides—"

"He'll learn in time," said Simion, shaking his head at Mr. Frederick. "Once he's had his fingers bitten by those he's fool enough to feed."

He set down his glass and resumed the lecture. "I don't think you realize how vulnerable you are, Frederick. If something unforeseen should happen. I was talking with Ford the other day, Henry Ford—" He broke off, whether for ethical or oratorical reasons, I couldn't tell, and motioned me to bring an ashtray. "Let's just say, in this economic climate you need to steer your business into profitable waters. And fast." His eyes flickered. "If things should go the way of Russia—and there are certain indications—only a healthy profit margin will keep you in good odor with your banker. Friendly as he may be, the bottom line needs to be black." He took a cigar from the silver box offered to him by Mr. Hamilton. "And you've got to have yourself protected, haven't you? You and your lovely girls. If you don't look after them, who will?" He smiled at Hannah and Emmeline, then added, as if an afterthought, "Not to mention this grand house of yours. How long did you say it had been in the family?"

"I didn't," Mr. Frederick said, and if his voice contained a note of misgiving, he managed quickly to dissolve it. "Three hundred years."

"Well," Estella purred on cue, "isn't that something? I *adore* the history in England. You old families are so intriguing. It's one of my favorite pastimes, reading about you all."

Simion exhaled impatiently, eager to get back to business.

Estella, practised after so many years of marriage, took her cue. "I wonder if we girls might retire to the drawing room while the men continue their talk," she said. "You can tell me all about the history of the Ashbury line."

Hannah coached her expression into one of polite acquiescence, but not before I saw her impatience. She was at the mercy of her warring selves, longing to stay and hear more, yet recognizing her duty as hostess to retire the ladies to the drawing room and await the men.

"Yes," she said, "of course. Though I'm afraid there's not much we can tell that you won't find in *Debrett*."

The men stood. Simion took Hannah's hand as Mr. Frederick as-

sisted Estella. Simion registered Hannah's youthful figure, his face
unable to conceal its coarse approval. He kissed the top of her hand
with wet lips. To her credit she concealed her distaste. She followed
Estella and Emmeline and, as she neared the door, her gaze swept
sideways and met mine. In an instant, her grown-up facade dissolved
as she poked her tongue out at me and rolled her eyes, before disappearing from the room.

As the men retook their seats and resumed their talk of business, Mr. Hamilton appeared at my shoulder.

"You may go now, Grace," he whispered. "Nancy and I will finish up here." He looked at me. "And do find Alfred. We can't have
one of the Master's guests look out of the window and see a servant
roaming the grounds."

✤

STANDING on the stone platform at the top of the rear stairs, I
scanned the dark beyond. The moon cast a white glow, painting the
grass silver and making skeletons of the briars that clung to the
arbor. The scattered rosebushes, glorious by day, revealed themselves
by night an awkward collection of lonely, bony old ladies.

Finally, on the far stone staircase I saw a dark shape that
couldn't be accounted for by any of the garden's vegetation.

I steeled myself and slipped into the night.

With each step, the wind blew colder, meaner.

I reached the top step and stood for a moment beside him, but
Alfred gave no sign that he was aware of my presence.

"Mr. Hamilton sent me," I said cautiously. "You needn't think
I'm following you."

There was no answer.

"And you needn't ignore me. If you don't want to come in, just
tell me and I'll go."

He continued to gaze into the tall trees of the Long Walk.

"Alfred!" My voice cracked with the cold.

227

"You all think I'm the same Alfred as left for France," he said softly. "Folks seem to recognize me, so I must look close enough to the same, but I'm a different fellow, Gracie."

I was taken aback. I had been prepared for another attack, angry entreaties to leave him alone. His voice dropped to a whisper and I had to crouch right by to hear. His bottom lip trembled, whether from the cold or something other, I wasn't sure. "I see them, Grace. Not so bad in the day, but all the night, I see them and I hear them. In the drawing room, the kitchen, the village street. They call my name. But when I turn around . . . they're not . . . they're all . . ."

I sat down. The frosty night had turned the graystone steps to ice and through my skirt and drawers my legs grew numb.

"It's so cold," I said. "Come inside and I'll make you a cup of cocoa."

He gave no acknowledgement, continued to stare into the darkness.

"Alfred?" My fingertips brushed his hand and on impulse I spread my fingers over his.

"Don't." He recoiled as if struck and I knotted my hands together on my lap. My cold cheeks burned as if they'd been slapped.

"Don't," he whispered.

His eyes were clenched shut and I watched his face, wondered what it was he saw on his blackened eyeballs that made them race so frantically beneath his moon-bleached lids.

Then he turned to face me and I drew breath. It was a trick of the night, surely, but his eyes were as none I had ever looked into. Deep, dark holes that were somehow empty. He stared at me with his unseeing eyes and it seemed that he looked for something. An answer to a question he had not asked. His voice was low. "I thought that once I got back . . ." His words floated into the night unfinished. "I so wanted to see you . . . The doctors said if I kept busy . . ." There was a tight sound in his throat. A click.

The armor of his face collapsed, crumbled like a paper bag, and he began to cry. Both hands leaped to his face in a futile attempt at obfuscation. "No, oh no . . . Don't look . . . please, Gracie, please . . ." He cried into his hands. "I'm such a coward—"

"You're not a coward," I said firmly.

"Why can't I get it out of my head? I just want it out of my head." He hit his palms against his temples with a ferocity that alarmed me.

"Alfred! Stop it." I tried to grab his hands, but he wouldn't let them leave his face. I waited, watching as his body shook, cursing my ineptitude. Finally, he seemed to calm some. "Tell me what it is you see," I said.

He turned to me, but he did not speak, and I glimpsed for a moment how I must appear to him. The yawning gulf between his experience and mine. And I knew then that there would be no telling me what he saw. I understood somehow that certain images, certain sounds, could not be shared and could not be lost.

So I didn't ask again. I laid my hand on the far side of his face and gently guided his head to my shoulder. Sat very still as his body shuddered next to mine.

And like that, together, we sat on the stair.

A SUITABLE HUSBAND

✻

HANNAH and Teddy were married on the first Saturday of May 1919. It was a pretty wedding at the little church on the Riverton estate. The Luxtons would have preferred London so that more of the very important people they knew could have come, but Mr. Frederick was insistent, and he'd suffered so many blows in the months preceding that no one had much spirit for arguing. So it was. She married in the small church in the valley, just as her grandparents and her parents had done before her.

It rained—many children, said Mrs. Townsend; weeping past lovers, whispered Nancy—and the wedding photographs were stained with black umbrellas. Later, when Hannah and Teddy were living in the townhouse in Grosvenor Square, a photograph sat upon the morning-room writing desk. The six of them in a line: Hannah and Teddy at the center, Simion and Estella beaming on one side, Mr. Frederick and Emmeline blank-faced on the other.

You are surprised. For how could such a thing have come to pass? Hannah was so set against marriage, so full of other ambitions. And Teddy: sensible, kindly even, but certainly not the man to sweep a young woman like Hannah off her feet . . .

But it was not so complicated really. Such things rarely are. It was a simple case of stars aligning; those that didn't being nudged into place.

✻

T H E morning after the dinner party, the Luxtons left for London. They had business engagements, and we all presumed—if indeed we gave it any thought at all—that it was the last we would ever see of them.

Our focus, you see, had shifted already to the next grand event. For over the coming week, a cluster of indomitable women descended upon Riverton, charged with the weighty duty of overseeing Hannah's entrance into society. January was the zenith of country balls, and the mortification of leaving things too late, being forced to share the date with another, larger ball, was unthinkable. Thus, the date had been picked—20 January—and invitations long since sent.

One morning in the early new year I served tea to Lady Clementine and the Dowager Lady Ashbury. They were in the drawing room, side by side on the sofa, diaries open on their laps.

"Fifty ought to do well," Lady Violet said. "There's nothing worse than a thin dance."

"Except a crowded one," Lady Clementine said with distaste. "Not that it's a problem these days."

Lady Violet surveyed her guest list, a thread of dissatisfaction pulling her lips to pout. "My dear," she said, "whatever are we to do about the shortages?"

"Mrs. Townsend will rise to the occasion," Lady Clementine said. "She always does."

"Not the food, Clem, the men. Wherever shall we find more men?"

Lady Clementine leaned to observe the guest list. She shook her head crossly. "It's an absolute crime. That's what it is. A dreadful inconvenience. England's best seed left to rot on godforsaken French fields, while her young ladies are left high and dry, nary a dance partner between them. It's a plot, I tell you. A *German* plot." Her eyes widened at the possibility. "To prevent England's elite from breeding!"

"But surely you know someone we could ask, Clem? You've proved yourself quite the matchmaker."

"I counted myself lucky to find that fool of Fanny's," Lady Clementine said, rubbing the powdery rolls of neck beneath her chin. "It's a great shame Frederick never took an interest. Things would have been a lot simpler. Instead, I had to scrape the barrel's bottom."

"My granddaughter is not to have a husband from the barrel's bottom," Lady Violet said. "This family's future depends upon her match." She gave a distressed sigh, which became a cough, shuddering through her thin frame.

"Hannah will do better than poor simple Fanny," Lady Clementine said assuredly. "Unlike my charge, your granddaughter is blessed with wit, beauty and charm."

"And no inclination to use them," Lady Violet said. "Frederick has indulged those children. They've known too much freedom and not enough instruction. Hannah in particular. That girl is full of outrageous notions of independence."

"Independence . . ." Lady Clementine said with distaste.

"Oh, she's in no hurry to be married. Told me as much when she was in London."

"Indeed."

"Looked me straight in the eyes, maddeningly courteous, and told me she didn't mind a bit if it was too much trouble to launch her into society."

"Impudence!"

"She said a ball would likely be wasted on her as she had no intention of going into society even when she was of an age. She said she finds society . . ." Lady Violet closed her eyes. "She finds society dull and pointless."

Lady Clementine gasped. "She didn't."

"She did."

"But what does she propose to do instead? Stay here in her father's home and become an old maid?"

That there could be another option was beyond their ability to conceive. Lady Violet shook her head, despair bringing a sag to her shoulders.

Lady Clementine, perceiving that some amelioration of spirits was called for, straightened and patted Violet's hand. "There, there," she said. "Your granddaughter is still young, Violet dear. There's plenty of time for her to change her mind." She tilted her head to the side. "I seem to remember you had a touch of the free spirit at her age. You grew out of it. Hannah will too."

"She must," Lady Violet said gravely.

Lady Clementine caught the whiff of desperation. "There's no *particular* reason she need make a match so soon . . ." She narrowed her eyes. "Is there?"

Lady Violet sighed.

"There is!" Lady Clementine said, eyes widening.

"It's Frederick. His confounded motorcars. The bank sent me a letter this week. He's missed more payments."

"And this was the first you knew?" Lady Clementine said hungrily. "Dear, dear."

"I dare say he feared telling me," Lady Violet said. "He knows how I feel. He's mortgaged all our futures for the sake of his factory. He's even sold the estate in Yorkshire to pay the death duties on his inheritance."

Lady Clementine tut-tutted.

"Would that he'd sold that factory instead. It's not as if he hasn't had offers, you know."

"Recently?"

"Regrettably not." Lady Violet sighed. "Frederick is a wonderful son, but a businessman he is not. Now I gather he's pinning all his hopes on receiving a loan from some syndicate that Mr. Luxton is involved with." She shook her head. "He lurches from disaster to disaster, Clem. Not a thought for the duties of his position." She rested her fingertips on her temples, sighed again. "I can hardly blame him. The position was never meant to be his." Then came the familiar lament. "If only Jonathan were here."

"Now, now," Lady Clem said. "Frederick's sure to make a success of it. Motorcars are quite the thing these days. Every man and his dog are out driving them. I was almost flattened the other day as I crossed the road outside Kensington Place."

"Clem—! Were you injured?"

"Not *this* time," Lady Clementine said matter-of-factly. "I'm sure I won't be so fortunate the next." She raised one eyebrow. "A most gruesome death, I can assure you. I spoke to Dr. Carmichael at great length regarding the types of injuries one might sustain."

"Terrible," Lady Violet said, shaking her head distractedly. She sighed. "I wouldn't mind so much about Hannah if Frederick would only marry again."

"Is it likely?" Lady Clementine said.

"Hardly. As you know, he's shown little interest in taking another wife. He didn't show nearly enough interest in his first wife, if you ask me. He was far too busy with—" She glanced at me and I busied myself straightening the tea cloth. "With that other despicable business." She shook her head and tightened her lips. "No. There'll be no more sons and it's no use hoping otherwise."

"Which leaves us with Hannah." Lady Clementine took a sip of tea.

"Yes." Lady Violet sighed irritably and smoothed the lime satin of her skirt. "I'm sorry, Clem. It's this cold I've got. It's put me in quite a mood." She shook her head. "I just can't seem to shake the ill feeling I've been carrying of late. I'm not a superstitious person—you know that—but I've the oddest sense . . ." She glanced at Lady Clementine. "You'll laugh, but I've the oddest sense of impending doom."

"Oh?" It was Lady Clementine's favorite subject.

"It's nothing specific. Just a feeling." She gathered her shawl about her shoulders and I noticed how frail she had become. "Nonetheless, I will not sit back and watch this family disintegrate. I will see Hannah engaged—and engaged well—if it's the last thing I do. Preferably *before* I accompany Jemima to America."

"New York. I'd forgotten you were going. Good of Jemima's brother to take them."

"Yes," Lady Violet said. "Though I shall miss them. Little Gytha is so like Jonathan."

"I've never been much for babies," Lady Clementine sniffed. "All that mewling and puking." She shuddered so that her second and third chins quivered, then smoothed her diary page and tapped a pen on its blank surface. "How long does that leave us then, to find a suitable husband?"

"One month. We sail on the fourth of February."

Lady Clementine wrote the date on her journal page, then sat up with a start. "Oh . . . ! Oh, Violet. I've had rather a good idea," she said. "You say Hannah's determined to be independent?"

The word itself brought a flutter to Lady Violet's eyelids. "Yes."

"So if someone were to give her a little kindly instruction . . . ? Make her see marriage as the way to independence . . . ?"

"She's as stubborn as her father," Lady Violet said. "I'm afraid she wouldn't listen."

"Not to you or me, perhaps. But I know someone to whom she might." She pursed her lips. "Yes . . . With a little coaching even *she* should be able to manage this."

✺

S O M E days later, her husband happily ensconced in a tour of Mr. Frederick's garage, Fanny joined Hannah and Emmeline in the burgundy room. Emmeline, swept up in the excitement of the upcoming ball, had persuaded Fanny to help her practice dancing. A waltz was playing on the gramophone and the two were triple-stepping about the room, laughing and teasing as they went. I had to be careful to avoid them while I dusted and made up the rooms.

Hannah sat at the writing desk scribbling in her notebook, oblivious to the merriment behind her. After dinner with the Luxtons, when it had become clear that her dreams of finding work were contingent on paternal permission that wouldn't be forthcoming, she had entered a state of quiet preoccupation. While the currents of ball preparation swirled excitedly about her, she remained outside its flow.

After a week of brooding, she entered an opposing phase. She returned to her shorthand practice, translating furiously from whichever book was close to hand, obscuring her work cagily if someone should come close enough to notice. These periods of occupation, too fierce to be sustained, were always followed by a relapse into apathy. She would toss her pen aside, push her books away with a sigh, and sit inert, waiting until such time as a meal might be served, a letter arrive, or it was time again to dress.

Of course, her mind, as she sat, was not immobile. She looked as though she were trying to solve the conundrum of her life. She longed for independence and adventure, yet she was a prisoner—a comfortable, well-tended prisoner, but a prisoner nonetheless. Independence required money. Her father hadn't money to give her and she wasn't permitted to work.

That morning, in the burgundy room, she sat at the writing desk, back turned to Fanny and Emmeline, translating the *Encyclopaedia Britannica* into shorthand. So concentrated was she on the task that she didn't so much as flinch when Fanny shrieked, "Ow! You elephant!"

Fanny limped to the armchair as Emmeline collapsed with laughter onto the chaise. She slipped off her shoe and leaned to inspect her stockinged toe. "I dare say it's going to swell," she said petulantly.

Emmeline continued to laugh.

"I probably won't be able to fit into any of my prettiest shoes for the ball!"

Each protest only served to plunge Emmeline into deeper glee.

"Well," Fanny said indignantly. "You've ruined my toe. The least you could do is apologize."

Emmeline tried to arrest her amusement. "I . . . I'm sorry," she said. She bit her lip, laughter threatening again. "But it's hardly my fault that you continue to put your feet in the way of mine. Perhaps if they weren't so big . . ." And she collapsed again.

"I'll have you know," Fanny said, chin trembling with pique, "that Mr. Collier at Harrods says I have beautiful feet."

"He would. He probably charges twice as much to make your shoes as he does for other ladies."

"Oh . . . ! You ungrateful little—"

"Come on, Fanny," Emmeline said, sobering. "I'm only joking. Of course I'm sorry to have stepped on your toe."

Fanny humphed.

"Let's try the waltz again. I promise to pay better attention this time."

"I don't think so," Fanny said, pouting. "I need to rest my toe. I wouldn't be surprised if it's broken."

"Surely it's not as serious as that. I barely trod on it. Here. Let me take a look."

Fanny curled her leg beneath her on the sofa, obscuring the foot from Emmeline's view. "I think you've done more than enough already."

Emmeline drummed her fingers on the chair's arm. "Well, how am I to practise my dance steps?"

"You needn't bother; Great Uncle Bernard's too blind to notice, and second-cousin Jeremy will be too busy boring you with interminable talk of war to care."

"Pooh. I don't intend to dance with the great-uncles," Emmeline said.

"I'm afraid you'll have little choice," said Fanny.

Emmeline raised her eyebrows smugly. "We'll see."

"Why?" Fanny said, eyebrows narrowing. "What do you mean?"

Emmeline smiled broadly. "Grandmama's convinced Pa to invite the Luxtons—"

"Theodore Luxton?" Fanny flushed.

"Isn't it thrilling?" Emmeline clutched Fanny's hands. "Pa didn't think it was proper to invite business acquaintances to Hannah's ball, but Grandmama insisted."

"My," said Fanny, pink and flustered. "That is exciting. Some sophisticated company for a change." She giggled, patted each warm cheek in turn. "Theodore Luxton, indeed."

"Now you see why I have to learn to dance."

"You should have thought of that before you crushed my foot."

Emmeline frowned. "If only Pa had let us take *proper* lessons at the Vacani school. No one will dance with me if I can't do the right steps."

Fanny's lips thinned into an almost-smile. "You're certainly not blessed as a dancer, Emmeline," she said. "But you needn't worry. You won't want for partners at the ball."

"Oh?" Emmeline said, with the ersatz artlessness of one accustomed to compliments.

Fanny rubbed her stockinged toe. "*All* the gentlemen present are expected to ask the daughters of the house to dance. Even the elephants."

Emmeline scowled.

Buoyed by her small victory, Fanny continued. "I remember my coming-out dance as if it was yesterday," she said, with the fond nostalgia of a woman twice her age.

"I suppose with your grace and charm," Emmeline said, rolling her eyes, "you had more than your fair share of handsome young gentlemen lined up to dance with you."

"Hardly. I'd never seen so many old men waiting to step on my toes so they could return to their old wives and catch some sleep. I was ever so disappointed. All the best men were busy with the war. Thank goodness Godfrey's bronchitis kept him out or else we might never have met."

"Was it love at first sight?"

Fanny screwed up her nose. "Certainly not! Godfrey became violently ill and spent most of the night in the bathroom. We only danced once that I remember. It was the quadrille; he became greener and greener with each turn until midway through he took his leave and disappeared. I was really rather cross at the time. I was completely stranded and very embarrassed. I didn't see him again for months. Even then it took us a year before we were married." She sighed and shook her head. "The longest year of my life."

"Why?"

Fanny considered this. "Somehow I imagined that after my coming-out dance life would be different."

"Wasn't it?" Emmeline said.

"Yes, but not the way I thought. It was dreadful. Officially I was grown up, yet I was still unable to go anywhere or do anything without Lady Clementine or some other dusty old lady minding my business. I was never so happy in all my life as when Godfrey proposed. It was the answer to my prayers."

Emmeline, having difficulty figuring Godfrey Vickers—bloated, balding and habitually unwell—as the answer to anybody's prayers, wrinkled her nose. "Really?"

Fanny looked pointedly at Hannah's back. "People treat one differently when one's married. I only have to be introduced as 'Mrs.' Vickers and people realize I'm not a silly girl, but a married woman capable of adult considerations."

Hannah, apparently unmoved, continued her fierce translation.

"Have I told you about my honeymoon?" Fanny said, returning her attention to Emmeline.

"Only a thousand times."

Fanny was undeterred. "Florence is the most romantic foreign city I've ever seen."

"It's the only foreign city you've seen."

"Every evening, after we dined, Godfrey and I strolled along the River Arno. He bought me the most beautiful necklace at a quaint little shop on the Ponte Vecchio. I felt quite a different person in Italy. Transformed. One day we climbed the Forte di Belvedere and looked out all over Tuscany. It was so beautiful, I could have wept. And the art galleries! There was simply *too* much to see. Godfrey's promised to take me back again as soon as we can go." Her eyes flickered towards the desk, where Hannah continued to write. "And the *people* one meets when traveling; quite fascinating really. One fellow on the train over was en route to Cairo. You'll never guess what he was going to do there. Dig for buried treasures! I couldn't quite believe it when he told us. Apparently the ancients used to be buried with their jewels. I can't think why. Seems an awful waste. Dr. Humphreys said it was something to do with religion. He told us the most exciting stories, even invited us to visit the dig if we found ourselves out that way!" Hannah had stopped writing. Fanny stifled a small smile of accomplishment. "Godfrey was a little suspicious— thought the fellow was pulling our legs—but I found him awfully interesting."

"Was he handsome?" Emmeline said.

"Oh yes," Fanny gushed, "he . . ." She stopped, remembered herself and returned to the script. "I've had more excitement in the two months I've been married than in the rest of my life." She eyed Hannah beneath her eyelashes and delivered the trump card. "It's funny. Before I was married, I used to imagine that, having a husband, one would lose oneself. Now I find it's quite the opposite. I've never felt so . . . so independent. One is attributed with so much more sense. No one blinks if I determine to take myself out for a walk. Indeed, I'll probably be asked to chaperone you and Hannah until such time as you are married yourselves." She sniffed imperiously. "You're lucky to have someone like me, instead of being saddled with someone old and dull."

Emmeline raised her eyebrows, but Fanny did not see. She was watching Hannah, whose pen now lay by her book.

Fanny's eyes flickered with self-satisfaction. "Well," she said, easing her shoe over her injured toe, "much as I've enjoyed your spirited company, I'll take my leave. My husband will be back from his walk by now and I find myself thirsting for some . . . *adult* conversation."

She smiled sweetly and left the room, head high. The posture was undermined somewhat by a slight limp.

While Emmeline started another record and triple-stepped herself around the room, Hannah remained at the desk, back still turned. Her hands were clasped, forming a bridge on which her chin rested, and she was staring out of the windows across the neverending fields. As I dusted the cornice behind her, I could see by the glass's faint reflection that she was in deep thought.

❦

THE following week the house party arrived. As was customary, its members set about immediately enjoying the activities their hosts had undertaken to provide. Some rambled across the estate, others played bridge in the library, and the more energetic took to fencing in the gymnasium.

After her herculean effort of organization, Lady Violet's health took a sudden turn for the worse and she was confined to bed. Lady Clementine sought company elsewhere. Lured by the glinting and grating blades, she took up bulky occupation in a leather armchair in view of the fencing. When I served tea she was engaged in a cozy tête-à-tête with Simion Luxton.

"Your son fences well," Lady Clementine said, indicating one of the masked swordsmen. "For an American."

"He may talk like an American, Lady Clementine, but I assure you, he's an Englishman through and through."

"Indeed," Lady Clementine said.

"He fences like an Englishman," Simion said vociferously. "Deceptively simple. Same style that'll see him into Parliament in the coming elections."

"I did hear of his nomination," Lady Clementine said. "You must be very pleased."

Simion was even more puffed up than usual. "My son has an excellent future."

"Certainly he represents almost everything we Conservatives look for in a parliamentarian. At my most recent Conservative Women's tea, we were discussing the lack of good, solid men to manage the likes of Lloyd George." Her gaze of appraisal returned to Teddy. "Your son may be just the thing, and I'll be more than happy to endorse him if I find him so." She took a sip of tea. "Of course, there is the small matter of his wife."

"No matter there," Simion said dismissively. "Teddy doesn't have a wife."

"Precisely my point, Mr. Luxton."

Simion frowned.

"Some of the other ladies are not so liberal as I," Lady Clementine said. "They see it as a mark of weak character. Family values are so important to us. A man of certain years without a wife . . . people start to wonder."

"He just hasn't met the right girl."

"Of course, Mr. Luxton. You and I both know that. But the other ladies . . . They look at your son and see a fine good-looking fellow with so much to offer, yet left wanting a wife. You can't blame them that they start to wonder why." She raised her eyebrows pointedly.

Simion's cheeks turned red. "My son is not . . . No Luxton man has ever been accused of . . ."

"Of course not, Mr. Luxton," Lady Clementine said smoothly, "and these are not my opinions, you understand. I'm just passing on the thoughts of some of our ladies. They like to know a man is a man. Not an aesthete." She smiled thinly and repositioned her spectacles. "Whatever the case, it's a small matter and there's plenty of time. He's still young. Twenty-five, is he?"

"Thirty-one," Simion said.

"Oh," she said. "Not so young then." Lady Clementine knew when to let silence speak for her. She returned her attention to the jousting.

"You may rest assured, Lady Clementine. There's nothing wrong with Teddy," said Simion. "He's very popular with the ladies. He'll have his pick of brides when he's ready."

"Glad to hear it, Mr. Luxton." Lady Clementine continued to watch the fencing. She took a sip of tea. "I just hope for his sake that time comes soon. And that he chooses the right *sort* of girl."

Simion raised a querying brow.

"We English are a nationalistic lot. Your son has much to recommend him, but some people, particularly in the Conservative Party, may think him a little *new*. I do hope when he takes a wife she brings more to the marriage than her honorable self."

"What could be more important than a bride's honor, Lady Clementine?"

"Her name, her family, her breeding." Lady Clementine looked on as Teddy's opponent landed a strike and won the match. "Overlooked as they may be in the New World, here in England these things are very important."

"Alongside the girl's purity, of course," said Simion.

"Of course."

"And deference."

"Certainly," said Lady Clementine with less conviction.

"None of these modern women for my son, Lady Clementine," said Simion, licking his lips. "We Luxton men like our ladies to know who's boss."

"I understand, Mr. Luxton," said Lady Clementine.

Simion applauded the close of game. "If only one knew where to find such a suitable young lady."

Lady Clementine kept her eyes on the court. "Don't you find, Mr. Luxton, that often the very things one seeks can be found right under one's own nose?"

"I do, Lady Clementine," said Simion with a close-lipped smile. "I most certainly do."

※

I WASN'T required at dinner and saw neither Teddy nor his father for the rest of Friday. Nancy reported that the two were engaged in earnest discussion in the upstairs corridor late on Friday night, but of what they spoke I could not say. On Saturday morning, when I came to check on the drawing-room fire, Teddy was his usual amiable self. He was sitting in the armchair reading the morning newspaper, concealing his amusement as Lady Clementine bemoaned the floral arrangements. They had just arrived from Braintree, resplendent with roses where Lady Clementine had been promised dahlias. She was not happy.

"You," she said to me, flicking a rose stem, "find Miss Hartford. She'll need to see them for herself."

"I believe Miss Hartford is preparing to take her horse out this morning, Lady Clementine," I said.

"I don't care if she's planning on riding in the Grand National. The arrangements need her attention."

Thus, while the other young ladies ate breakfast in bed, pondering the night ahead, Hannah was summoned to the drawing room. I had helped her into her riding costume half an hour earlier, and she had the look of a cornered fox, anxious to escape. While Lady Clementine raged, Hannah, with little opinion as to whether dahlias were preferable to roses, could only nod and sneak occasional, longing glances at the ship's clock.

"But whatever will we do?" Lady Clementine reached her argument's end. "It's too late to order more."

Hannah rubbed her lips together, blinked herself back into the moment. "I suppose we shall have to make do with what we have," she said with mock fortitude.

"But can you bear it?"

Hannah feigned resignation. "If I must, I shall." She waited a requisite few seconds and said, brightly, "Now, if that's all—"

"Come on upstairs," Lady Clementine interrupted. "I'll show you how dreadful they look in the ballroom. You won't believe . . ."

As Lady Clementine continued to deride the rose arrangements, Teddy cleared his throat. He folded the paper and placed it on the table beside him. "It's such a lovely winter's day," he said to nobody in particular. "I've a good mind to take a ride. See more of the estate."

Lady Clementine drew breath mid-sentence and the light of higher purpose seemed to flicker in her eyes. "A ride," she said, without missing a beat. "What a lovely idea, Mr. Luxton. Hannah, isn't that a lovely idea?"

Hannah looked up with surprise as Teddy smiled conspiratorially at her. "You're welcome to join me."

Before she could answer, Lady Clementine said, "Yes . . . splendid. We'd be happy to join you, Mr. Luxton. If you don't mind of course?"

"I'd count myself lucky to have two such lovely tour guides."

Lady Clementine turned to me, her expression one of trepidation. "You, girl, have Mrs. Townsend send up a packed tea." She turned back to Teddy and said, through a thin-lipped smile, "I do so love to ride."

They made an odd procession as they set off for the stables— even odder, Dudley said, once all were on horseback. He had fallen about laughing, he said, watching as they disappeared across the west glade, Lady Clementine paired with Mr. Frederick's ancient mare whose girth exceeded even her rider's.

They were gone two hours, and when they returned for lunch Teddy was soaking wet, Hannah was awfully quiet and Lady Clementine as smug as a cat with a bowl of cream. What happened on their ride, Hannah told me herself, though not for many months.

☙

T H E Y rode for some time in silence: Hannah up front, Teddy close behind, Lady Clementine bringing up the rear. Wintry twigs snapped beneath the horses" hooves and the river tripped coldly on its way to join the Thames.

Finally, Teddy brought his horse up beside Hannah and said, in a jolly voice, "It's certainly a pleasure to be here, Miss Hartford. I must thank you for your kind invitation."

Hannah, who had been enjoying the silence, said, "It's my grandmother you'll have to thank, Mr. Luxton. For I had little to do with the whole affair."

"Ah . . ." Teddy said. "I see. I shall have to remember to thank her."

Pitying Teddy, who, after all, had just been making conversation, Hannah said, "What is it you do for a living, Mr. Luxton?"

He was quick to answer, relieved perhaps. "I'm a collector."

"What do you collect?"

"Objects of beauty."

"I thought perhaps you worked with your father."

Teddy shrugged away a birch leaf that had fallen onto his shoulder. "My father and I do not see eye to eye on matters of business, Miss Hartford," he said. "He sees little of worth in anything not directly related to the creation of wealth."

"And you, Mr. Luxton?"

"I seek wealth of a different sort. A wealth of new experiences. The century is young and so am I. There are too many things to see and do to become bogged down in business."

Hannah looked at him. "Pa said that you were entering politics. Surely that will curtail your plans?"

He shook his head. "Politics gives me more reason to broaden my horizons. The best leaders are those who bring perspective to their position, wouldn't you say?"

They rode on, all the way to the back meadows, stopping every so often that the stragglers might catch up. When finally they reached the shelter of an old marble folly, both Lady Clementine and her mare were equally relieved to rest their beaten flanks. Teddy helped her inside while Hannah arranged the spoils from Mrs. Townsend's picnic hamper.

When they had finished the thermos of hot tea and slices of boiled fruitcake, Hannah said, "I think I shall take a walk to the bridge."

"Bridge?" Teddy said.

"Over there beyond the trees," Hannah said, standing, "where the lake thins and joins the stream."

"Would you mind company?" Teddy said.

"Not at all," Hannah said, but she did.

Lady Clementine, torn between her duty as chaperone and her duty to her aching buttocks, said finally, "I'll stay here and mind the horses. Don't be too long, now. I shall start to worry. There are many dangers in the woods, you know."

Hannah smiled slightly at Teddy and headed off in the direction of the bridge. Teddy followed, caught her up and walked beside at a polite distance.

"I am sorry, Mr. Luxton, that Lady Clementine has forced our company on you this morning."

"Not at all," Teddy said. "I've enjoyed the company." He glanced at her. "Some more than others."

Hannah continued to look directly ahead. "When I was younger," she said quickly, "my brother and sister and I would come down to the lake to play. In the boathouse and on the bridge." She sneaked a sidelong glance at him. "It's a magical bridge, you know."

"A magical bridge?" Teddy raised an eyebrow.

"You'll understand when you see it," Hannah said.

"And what did you used to play on this magical bridge of yours?"

"We used to take turns running across." She looked at him. "Sounds simple enough, I know. But this isn't any ordinary magical bridge. This one's governed by a particularly nasty and vengeful lake demon."

"Indeed," said Teddy, smiling.

"Most times we would make it across all right, but every so often one of us would wake him."

"What would happen then?"

"Why then there'd be a duel to the death." She smiled. "His death, of course. We were all excellent swordsmen. Luckily he was immortal or there wouldn't have been much of a game in it."

They turned the corner and the rickety bridge was before them, perched astride a narrow reach of the stream. Though the month was cold, the water had not yet frozen.

"There," said Hannah breathlessly.

The bridge, which had long ago fallen into disuse, usurped by a larger one closer to town that motorcars could cross, had lost all but a few flakes of paint and was grown over with moss. The reedy river banks sloped gently towards the water's edge where wild flowers bloomed in summer.

"I wonder if the lake demon's in today?" said Teddy.

Hannah smiled. "Don't worry. If he shows up, I have his measure."

"You've waged your share of battles?"

"Waged and won," said Hannah. "We used to play down here whenever we could. We didn't *always* fight the lake demon, though. Sometimes we used to write letters. Make them into boats and throw them over."

"Why?"

"So they would take our wishes to London."

"Of course." Teddy smiled. "To whom did you write?"

Hannah smoothed the grass with her foot. "You'll think it silly."

"Try me."

She looked up at him, bit back a smile. "I wrote to Jane Digby. Every time."

Teddy frowned.

"You know," Hannah said. "Lady Jane, who ran away to Arabia, lived a life of exploration and conquest."

"Ah," Teddy said, memory dawning. "The infamous absconder. Whatever did you have to say to her?"

"I used to ask her to come and rescue me. I offered her my services as a devoted slave on condition that she took me on her next adventure."

"But surely, when you were young, she was already—"

"Dead? Yes. Of course, she was. Long dead. I didn't know that then." Hannah looked sideways at him. "Of course, if she'd been alive, the plan would have been foolproof."

"Undoubtedly," he said with arch seriousness. "She'd have come right down and taken you with her to Arabia."

"Disguised as a Bedouin sheikh, I always thought."

"Your father wouldn't have minded a bit."

Hannah laughed. "I'm afraid he would. And did."

Teddy raised an eyebrow. "Did?"

"One of the tenant farmers found a letter once and returned it to Pa. The farmer couldn't read it himself, but I'd drawn the family crest and he thought it must have been important. I dare say he expected a reward for his efforts."

"I'm guessing he didn't get one."

"He certainly did not. Pa was livid. I was never sure whether it was my desire to join such scandalous company or the impertinence of my letter that he objected to more. I suspect his main concern was that Grandmama might find out. She always thought me an impudent child."

"What some would call impudent," Teddy said, "others might call spirited." He looked at her seriously. With intent, Hannah thought, though of what kind she wasn't sure. She felt herself blush and turned away. Her fingers sought animation in the clump of long, thin reeds that grew about the river bank. She pulled one from its shaft and, seized suddenly by a strange energy, ran onto the bridge. She tossed the reed over one side, into the rushing river below, then hurried to the other side to witness its reemergence.

"Take my wishes to London," she called after it as it disappeared around the bend.

"What did you wish for?" Teddy asked.

She smiled at him and leaned forward, and in that moment fate intervened. The clasp of her locket, weak with wear, relinquished its hold on her chain, slipped around her pale neck and dropped below. Hannah felt the loss of weight, but realized its cause too late. The next she saw of it, the locket was little more than a glimmer disappearing beneath the water's surface.

She gasped, ran back across the bridge and clambered through the reeds to the river's edge.

"What is it?" Teddy said, bewildered.

"My locket," Hannah said. "It slipped . . ." She began to unlace her shoes. "My brother . . ."

"Did you see where it went?"

"Right out in the middle," Hannah said. She began treading through the slippery moss to the water's edge, the hem of her skirt becoming wet with mud.

"Wait," Teddy said, shaking off his jacket, tossing it onto the river's bank and pulling off his boots. Though narrow at that point, the river was deep and he was soon up to his thighs.

Hannah, deaf with panic, ran back atop the bridge, desperately seeking a glimpse of the locket so that she could guide Teddy to it.

He rose and dived, and rose and dived as she scanned the water, and just as she was giving up hope he reappeared, the locket glimmering between his clenched fingers.

Such a fine heroic deed. So unlike Teddy, a man given more to prudence than gallantry, despite his best intentions. Over the years, as the story of their engagement was deployed at social gatherings, it took on a mythical quality, even in Teddy's accounts. As if he, as much as his smiling guests, was unable quite to believe that it really happened. But happen it did. And at the precise moment, and before the precise person, upon whom it would have the fateful effect.

When she told me of it, Hannah said that as he stood before her, dripping wet, shivering, clutching her locket in his large hand, she was suddenly and overwhelmingly conscious of his physicality. His wet skin, the way his shirt clung to his arms, his dark eyes focused triumphantly on hers. She had never felt such a thing before—how could she have, and for whom? She longed for him to grab hold of her, as tightly as he held the locket.

Of course he did nothing of the sort; rather, smiled quite proudly, then handed her the locket. She took it gratefully and turned away as he began the ungraceful task of layering dry clothes over wet.

But by then the seed was sown.

THE BALL AND AFTER

HANNAH'S ball went off splendidly. The musicians and champagne arrived as ordered, and Dudley plundered the estate hothouse to augment the unsatisfactory floral arrangements. The fires were stoked at each end of the room, making good on the promise of winter warmth.

The room itself was all brilliance and dazzle. Crystal chandeliers glistened, black and white tiles shone, guests sparkled. Clustered in the center were twenty-five giggling young ladies, self-conscious in their delicate dresses and white kid gloves, self-important in their family's ancient and elaborate jewels. At their center was Emmeline. Though at fifteen she was younger than most of the attendees, Lady Clementine had granted her special dispensation to attend, with the understanding she wasn't to monopolize the marriageable men and ruin the chances of the older girls. A battalion of fur-draped chaperones lined the walls, perched on gold chairs with hot-water bottles under their lap rugs. Veterans were recognizable for the reading and knitting they had sensibly brought to while away the wee hours.

The men were a rather more motley collection, a home guard of dependable sorts, answering diligently the call to service. The handful who could rightly be labelled "young" comprised a set of rather ruddy Welsh brothers, recruited to the ranks by Lady Violet's second cousin, and a local lord's prematurely balding son. Beside this assembly of ham-fisted provincial gentry, Teddy, with his black hair, filmstar's moustache and American suit, seemed immeasurably suave.

As the smell of crackling fires filled the room and Irish air gave way to Viennese waltz, the old men got down to business squiring the young girls around the room. Some with grace, others with gusto, most with neither. With Lady Violet confined to her bed, fever raging, Lady Clementine took up the mantle of chaperonage and looked on as one of the young men with spotty cheeks rushed to request Hannah's hand.

Teddy, who had also been making his approach, turned his broad, white smile to Emmeline. Her face was radiant as she accepted. Ignoring Lady Clementine's reproving scowl, she curtsied, letting her eyelids flicker closed momentarily, before opening them widely—too widely—as she rose to full height. Dance she could not, but the tuition money Mr. Frederick had been induced to pay for private curtsy lessons had been well spent. As they took the floor, I noticed the way she held Teddy very close, hung on every word he spoke, laughed too broadly when he joked.

The night swirled on, and dance by dance the room grew hotter. The faint tang of perspiration blended with smoke from a green log, and by the time Mrs. Townsend sent me up with the cups of consommé, elegant hairstyles had begun to crumble and cheeks were uniformly flushed. By all accounts, the guests were enjoying themselves, with the notable exception of Fanny's husband for whom the festivity had been too much, and who had retired to bed citing migraine.

When Nancy bid me tell Dudley we'd need more logs, it was a welcome relief to escape the ballroom's nauseating heat. Along the hall and down the stairs small groups of girls giggled together, whispering over their cups of soup. I took the back door and was halfway along the garden walk when I noticed a lone figure standing in the dark.

It was Hannah, still as a statue, gazing up towards the night sky. Her bare shoulders, pale and fine beneath the moonlight, were indistinguishable from the white slipper satin of her gown, the silk of her

253

draping stole. Her blond hair, almost silver in that instant, crowned her head, curls escaping to hug the nape of her neck. Her hands, encased by white kid gloves, were by her side.

But surely she was cold, standing out in the middle of the wintry night with only a silk stole for warmth? She needed a jacket—at the very least a cup of soup. I resolved to fetch her both, but before I could move, another figure appeared from the dark. At first I thought it was Mr. Frederick, but when he emerged from the shadow I saw that it was Teddy. He reached her side and said something I could not hear. She turned. Moonlight stroked her face, caressed lips that were parted in repose.

She shivered lightly and for a moment I thought that Teddy would take off his jacket and drape it around her shoulders the way heroes did in the romantic novels Emmeline liked to read. He did not; rather, said something else, something that caused her to look again towards the sky. He reached gently for her hand, hanging lightly by her side, and she stiffened slightly as his fingers grazed her own. He turned her hand so that he could gaze upon her pale forearm, then lifted it, ever so slowly, towards his own mouth, bending his head so that his lips met the cool band of skin between her glove and stole.

She watched his dark head bow to deliver its kiss, but she did not pull her arm away. I could see her chest, rising and falling as her breath quickened.

I shivered then, wondering whether his lips were warm, his moustache prickly.

After a long moment, he stood and looked at her, still holding her hand. He said something to which she nodded slightly.

And then he walked away.

※

I N the wee hours of the morning, the ball officially over, I prepared Hannah for bed. Emmeline was already asleep, dreaming of silk and satin and swirling dancers, but Hannah sat silently before the vanity as I removed her gloves, button by button. As I reached the pearls at her wrist, she pulled away her hand and said, "I want to tell you something, Grace."

"Yes, miss?"

"I haven't told anybody else." She hesitated, glanced towards the closed door and lowered her voice. "You have to promise not to tell. Not Nancy, nor Alfred, nor anyone."

"I can keep a secret, miss."

"Of course you can. You have kept my secrets before." She took a deep breath. "Mr. Luxton has asked me to marry him." She glanced at me uncertainly. "He says that he's in love with me."

I was unsure how to answer. To feign surprise felt disingenuous. Again, I took her hand in mine. This time there was no resistance and I resumed my task. "Very good, miss."

"Yes," she said, chewing the inside of her cheek. "I suppose it is."

Her eyes met mine and I had the distinct feeling I had failed some sort of test. I looked away, slipped the first glove off her hand like a discarded second skin and began on the other. Silently, she watched my fingers. A nerve flickered beneath the skin of her wrist. "I haven't given him an answer yet."

※

As Hannah sat at her dressing table, musing on this strange and unexpected new turn of events, downstairs in the study Mr. Frederick was facing shock of a different kind. In a show of breathtakingly insensitive timing, Simion Luxton had delivered his blow. (The wheels of business couldn't be stopped just so young ladies could make their debuts, now could they?)

While the dance had been swirling in the ballroom, he'd told Mr. Frederick that the syndicate had declined to refinance his ailing factory. They did not consider it a good risk. It was still a valuable piece of land, Simion reassured him, and one for which he'd be able to find a buyer quickly and advantageously should Frederick wish to save himself the embarrassment of the bank's foreclosing. (Why, just off the top of his head, he knew of an American friend seeking land in that area to build a copy of the garden of Versailles. Something for his new wife.)

It was Simion's valet, after one too many brandies in the servants' hall, who relayed the news to us downstairs. But despite being surprised and worried, we could do little else but carry on as usual. The house was full of guests who had come a long way in the middle of winter and were determined to have a good time. Thus, we continued our duties, serving tea, making up rooms and delivering meals.

Mr. Frederick, however, felt no such compunction to carry on as normal and, while his guests made themselves at home, eating his food, reading his books and enjoying his largesse, he remained sequestered in his study. Only when the last car pulled away did he emerge and begin the roaming that was to be a habit with him until his last days: noiseless, ghost-like, his facial nerves tightening and knotting with the sums and scenarios that must have tormented him.

Lord Gifford began to make regular visits and Miss Starling was called from the village to locate official letters from the filing system. Day in, day out, she was required in Mr. Frederick's study, emerging hours later, clothes somber, face wan, to lunch downstairs with us. We were impressed and annoyed in equal measure by the way she kept to herself, never divulging so much as a word of what went on behind the closed door.

Lady Violet, still sick in bed, was to be spared the news. The doctor said there was nothing he could do for her now and if we valued our lives we were to keep away. For it was no ordinary head cold that had her in its grip, but a particularly virulent influenza, said to have come all the way from Spain. It was God's cruel show of attrition, the doctor mused, that for millions of good people who survived four years of war, death was to be a caller at the dawn of peace.

Faced with the dire state of her friend, Lady Clementine's

ghoulish taste for disaster and death was tempered somewhat, as was her fear. She ignored the doctor's warning, arranging herself in an armchair next to Lady Violet and chatting blithely of life outside the warm, dark bedroom. She spoke of the ball's success, the hideous dress worn by Lady Pamela Wroth, and then she declared that she had every reason to believe Hannah would soon be engaged to Mr. Theodore Luxton, heir to his family's massive fortune.

Whether Lady Clementine knew more than she let on, or merely plied her friend with hope in her hour of need, she showed a gift for prophecy. For next morning, the engagement was announced. And when Lady Violet succumbed to her flu, she drifted into death's arms a happy woman.

※

O N E morning in February, when I was helping Hannah look for her mother's wedding dress, Emmeline appeared at the linen-room door. Wordlessly, she came to stand by Hannah, watching as we unfolded the white tissue paper to reveal the satin and lace dress within.

"Old-fashioned," said Emmeline. "Wouldn't catch me wearing something like that."

"Just as well you don't need to then," said Hannah, smiling side-long at me.

Emmeline humphed.

"Look, Grace," said Hannah, "I think that's the veil at the back there." She leaned into the large cedar armoire. "Can you see? Right at the very back?"

"Yes, miss," I said, reaching to retrieve it.

Hannah took hold of one side and we unfurled it. "Just like mother to have the longest and heaviest veil."

It was beautiful: fine Brussels lace with tiny seed pearls en-crusted around the edges. I held it up, the better to admire it.

"You'll be lucky to make it down the aisle without tripping," said Emmeline. "You won't be able to see for all those pearls."

"I'm sure I'll manage," Hannah said, reaching out to squeeze Emmeline's wrist. "With you as my bridesmaid."

The sting was taken from Emmeline's tail. She sighed. "I wish you weren't doing this. Everything's going to be different."

"I know," said Hannah. "You'll be able to play whichever song you like on the gramophone with no one to tell you not to."

"Don't make a joke." Emmeline pouted. "You promised you wouldn't leave."

I placed the veil on Hannah's head, careful not to pull her hair.

"I said I wouldn't get a job and I didn't," Hannah said. "I never said I wouldn't get married."

"Yes, you did."

"When?"

"Always, you always said you wouldn't get married."

"That was before."

"Before what?"

Hannah didn't answer. "Emme," she said, "would you mind taking my locket. I don't want the clasp to catch the lace."

Emmeline undid the locket. "Why Teddy?" she said. "Why do you have to marry Teddy?"

"I don't *have* to marry Teddy, I *want* to marry Teddy."

"You don't love him," said Emmeline.

The hesitation was slight, the answer offhand. "Of course I do."

"Like Romeo and Juliet?"

"No, but—"

"Then you shouldn't be marrying him. You should leave him for someone who does love him like that."

"No one loves like Romeo and Juliet," Hannah said. "They're made-up characters."

Emmeline ran her fingertip over the locket's etched surface. "I would," she said.

"Then I pity you," Hannah said, trying to make light. "Look what happened to them!"

I stepped aside so that I could arrange the veil's headpiece. "It looks beautiful, miss," I said.

"David wouldn't approve," Emmeline said suddenly, swinging the locket like a pendulum. "I don't think he'd like Teddy."

Hannah stiffened at the mention of her brother's name. "Don't be such a child, Emmeline." She reached for the locket, missed. "And stop being so rough; you'll break it."

"You're running away." Emmeline's voice had taken on a sharp edge.

"I am not."

"David would think so. He'd say you were abandoning me."

Hannah's voice was low. "And he'd be a fine one to talk." Standing close, rearranging the lace across her face, I could see that her eyes had glazed.

Emmeline didn't say anything, continued to swing the locket in sulky figures of eight.

There was a taut silence during which I straightened the sides of the veil, noticed a tiny catch that would need mending.

"You're right," Hannah said finally. "I am running away. Just like you will as soon as you can. Sometimes when I walk across the estate, I can almost feel the roots growing from my feet, tying me here. If I don't get away soon, my life will be over and I'll be just another name on the family headstone." The sentiments were unusually Gothic for Hannah and thus I realized the depth of her malaise. "Teddy is my opportunity," she continued. "To see the world, to travel, to meet interesting people."

Emmeline's eyes brimmed with tears. "I knew you didn't love him."

"But I do like him; I will love him."

"*Like* him?"

"It's enough," said Hannah, "for me. I'm different from you, Emme. I'm not good at laughing and smiling with people I don't enjoy. I find most society people tedious. If I don't marry, my life will be one of two things: an eternity of lonely days in Pa's house, or a relentless succession of boring parties with boring chaperones until I'm old enough to be one of the chaperones myself. It's like Fanny said—"

"Fanny makes things up."

"Not this." Hannah was firm. "Marriage will be the beginning of my adventure."

Emmeline had dropped her gaze, was idly dangling Hannah's locket. She began to prise it open.

Hannah reached for it at the moment its treasure was spilled. We all froze as the tiny book, its spine hand-stitched, its cover faded, fell from inside, tumbled onto the floor. *Battle with the Jacobites*.

There was silence. Then Emmeline's voice. Almost a whisper. "You said they were all gone."

She tossed the locket onto the ground and ran from the room, slamming the door behind her. Hannah, still wearing her mother's veil, picked it up. She took the tiny book, turned it over and smoothed its surface. Then she placed it back into the hollow of the locket's chest and pressed it carefully closed. But it wouldn't clasp. The hinge was broken.

⚜

EMMELINE was not the only Hartford for whom the engagement didn't bring unrivaled joy. As wedding preparations got under way in earnest, the household swept up in dress-fittings, decorations and baking, Mr. Frederick remained very quiet, sitting by himself in his study, a permanent expression of trouble clouding his face. He seemed thinner too. The loss of his factory and his mother had taken their toll. So had Hannah's decision to marry Teddy.

The night before the wedding, while I was collecting Hannah's supper tray, he came to her room. He sat in the chair by her dressing table, then stood and, almost immediately, paced towards the window, looked out over the back lawn. Hannah was in bed, her nightie white and crisp, her hair hanging, like silk. She watched her father and her face grew serious as she took in his bony frame, his hunched shoulders, the way his hair had gone from golden to silver in the space of a few months.

"Wouldn't be surprised if it rains tomorrow," he said finally, still looking out of the window.

"I've always liked the rain."

Mr. Frederick did not answer.

I finished loading the supper tray. "Will that be all, miss?"

She had forgotten I was there. She turned to me. "Yes. Thank you, Grace." With a sudden movement, she reached out and took my hand. "I'll miss you, Grace, when I go."

"Yes, miss." I curtsied, my cheeks flushed with sentiment. "I'll miss you too." I curtsied to Mr. Frederick's turned back. "Goodnight, m'Lord."

He appeared not to have heard.

I wondered what it was that brought him to Hannah's room. What it was he had to say on the eve of her wedding that could not have been said at dinner, or afterwards in the drawing room. I left the room, pulled the door behind me, and then, I am ashamed to say, I laid the tray on the corridor floor and leaned in close.

There was a long silence and I began to fear the doors were too thick, Mr. Frederick's voice too quiet. Then I heard him clear his throat.

He spoke quickly, his tone low. "Emmeline I expected to lose as soon as she was of an age, but you?"

"You're not losing me, Pa."

"I am," he said, volume rising sharply. "David, my factory, now you. All my dearest . . ." He checked himself and when he spoke again his voice was so tight it threatened to buckle. "I'm not blind to my part in all this."

"Pa?"

There was a pause and the bed springs squeaked. Mr. Frederick's voice, when he spoke, had shifted position and I imagined he now sat on the foot of Hannah's bed. "You are not to do this," he said quickly.

Squeak. He was on his feet again. "The very idea of you living amongst those people. They sold my factory out from under me—"

"Pa, there were no other buyers. The ones Simion found paid a good price. Imagine the humiliation if the bank had foreclosed. They saved you from that."

"Saved me? They robbed me blind. They could've helped me. I could've been in business still. And now you're joining them. It makes my blood . . . No, it's out of the question. I should have put my foot down earlier, before any of this business got out of hand."

"Pa—"

"I didn't stop David in time, but I'll be damned if I'm going to make the same mistake twice."

"Pa—"

"I won't let you—"

"Pa," Hannah said, and in her voice was a firmness that had not been there before. "I've made my decision."

"Change it," he roared.

"No."

I was frightened for her. Mr. Frederick's tempers were legendary at Riverton. He had refused all contact with David when he dared deceive him. What would he do now, faced with Hannah's outright defiance?

His voice quivered, white with rage. "You would answer no to your father?"

"If I thought him wrong."

"You're a stubborn fool."

"I'm like you."

"To your folly, my girl," he said. "Your strength of will has always inclined me to leniency, but this I will not tolerate."

"It's not your decision, Pa."

"You are my child and you'll do as I say." He paused and an unwanted note of desperation colored his anger. "I order you not to marry him."

"Pa . . ."

"Marry him," his volume leaped, "and you won't be welcome here."

On the other side of the door, I was horrified. For though I understood Mr. Frederick's sentiment, shared his desire to keep Hannah at Riverton, I also knew threats were never a way to make her change her mind.

Sure enough, her voice when she spoke was steely with resolve. "Goodnight, Pa."

"Fool," he said in the bewildered tone of one who couldn't yet believe the game had been played and lost. "Stubborn fool of a child."

His footsteps drew near and I hurried to pick up my tray. Was withdrawing from the door when Hannah said: "I'll be taking my maid with me when I go." My heart leaped as she continued. "Nancy will look after Emmeline."

I was so surprised, so pleased, I barely heard Mr. Frederick's reply. "You're welcome to her. Lord knows I don't need her here."

※

W H Y did Hannah marry Teddy? Not because she loved him, but because she was prepared to love him. She was young and inexperienced— to what would she compare her feelings?

They were married on a rainy Saturday in May 1919, and a week later we left for London. Hannah and Teddy in the car up front, while I shared the second car with Teddy's valet and Hannah's trunks.

Mr. Frederick stood on the stairs, stiff and pale. From where I sat, unseen in the second car, I was able, for the first time, to look properly upon his face. It was a beautiful, patrician face, though suffering had robbed it of expression.

To his left was the line of staff, in descending order of rank. Even Nanny Brown had been exhumed from the nursery, and stood at half Mr. Hamilton's height, leaking silent tears into a white handkerchief.

Only Emmeline was absent, having refused to watch them leave. I saw her, though, right before we left. Her pale face framed behind one of the etched Gothic panes of the nursery window. Or I thought I did. It may have been a trick of the light. One of the little boy ghosts who spent their eternity in the nursery.

I had already said my goodbyes. To the staff, and to Alfred. Since the night on the garden stairs we'd made tentative amends. We were circumspect these days, Alfred treating me with a polite caution almost as alienating as his irritation. Nonetheless, I'd promised to write. Extracted from him an undertaking to do likewise.

And I'd seen Mother the weekend before the wedding. She'd given me a little package of things: a shawl she had knitted years before, and a jar of needles and threads so that I might keep up my stitching. When I'd thanked her she'd shrugged and said they were no use to her; she wouldn't be likely to use them now her fingers were locked and as good as useless. On that last visit she'd asked me questions about the wedding and Mr. Frederick's factory and Lady Violet's death. She surprised me, taking her former mistress's death easily. I'd come lately to realize that Mother had enjoyed her years of service, yet when I spoke of Lady Violet's final days she offered no condolences, no fond remembrances. She merely nodded slowly and let her face relax into an expression of remarkable dispassion.

But I did not think to query it then, for my mind was full of London.

※

THE dull thump of faraway drums. Do you hear them, I wonder, or is it just me?

You have been patient. And there is not much longer to wait. For into Hannah's world Robbie Hunter is about to make his return. You knew he would, of course, for he has his part to play. This is not a fairy tale, nor a romance. The wedding does not mark the happy ending of this story. It is simply another beginning, the ushering in of a new chapter.

In a far gray corner of London, Robbie Hunter wakes. Shrugs off his nightmares and pulls a small parcel from his pocket. A parcel, nursed in his breast pocket since the final days of war, its safe delivery promised to a dying friend.

PART THREE

CATCHING BUTTERFLIES

✻

THEY have brought us to the spring fair by minibus. Eight in all: six residents, Sylvia and a nurse whose name I can't remember—a young girl with a wispy plait snaking down her back to sweep her belt. I expect they think the day out does us good. Though what can be gained from exchanging comfortable surroundings for a muddy oval of tents selling cakes and toys and soaps, I do not know.

A makeshift stage has been erected behind the town hall, as it is each year, and rows of white plastic chairs assembled before it, but I prefer it here on the little iron seat by the memorial. I feel strange today. It is the heat, I'm sure. When I woke my pillow was damp, and I've been unable to shake this odd foggy sensation all morning. My thoughts are skimming. Coming quickly, fully formed, then slipping away before I can properly grasp them. Like catching a butterfly. It is unsettling, leaves me irritable.

A cup of tea will see me right.

Where has Sylvia gone? Did she tell me? She was here only a moment ago, about to smoke a cigarette. Talking again about her man-friend and their plans to cohabit.

The exposed skin on the top of my feet is cooking. I consider slipping them into the shade, but an irresistible sense of masochistic ennui bids me leave them where they are. Sylvia will see the red patches later, will realize how long she has left me.

From where I sit I see the cemetery. The eastern side with its line of poplars, new leaves quivering at the suggestion of a breeze.

269

Beyond the poplars, on the other side of the ridge, are the gravestones, amongst them my mother's.

It's been an age since we buried her. A wintry day in 1922 when the earth was frozen solid and my skirts blew icy against my stockinged legs, and a figure, a man, stood on the hill, barely recognizable. She took her secrets with her, into the cold, hard earth, but I learned them in the end. I know a lot about secrets; I have made them my life.

I am hot. It is far too hot for April. No doubt global warming is to blame. Global warming, melting the polar ice caps, the ozone hole, genetically modified food. Some other disease of the 1990s. The world has become a hostile place. Even the rainwater is not safe these days.

That's what's eating the war monument. One side of the soldier's stone face has been ravaged, the cheek pockmarked, the nose devoured by time. Like a piece of fruit left too long in a ditch, gnawed by scavengers.

He knows about duty. Despite his wounds he stands at attention atop the cenotaph, as he has for eighty years, surveying the plains beyond the town, hollow gaze cast over Bridge Street towards the car park of the new shopping center; a land fit for heroes. He is almost as old as I am. Is he as tired?

He and his pillar have become mossy; microscopic plants thrive in the etched names of the dead. David's is on there, at the top with the other officers; and Rufus Smith the ragman's son, suffocated in Belgium by a collapsed trench. Further down, Raymond Jones, the village pedlar when I was a girl. Those little boys of his would be men now. Old men, though younger than I. It is possible they are dead.

No wonder he is crumbling. It is a lot to ask of one man, to bear the strain of countless tragedies, bear witness to countless echoes of death.

But he is not alone: there is one like him in every English town.

They are the nation's scars; a rash of gallant scabs spread across the land in 1919, a spate of determined healing. Such extravagant faith we had then: in the League of Nations, the possibility of a civilized world. Against such determined hope the poets of disillusionment were lost. For every T. S. Eliot, for every R. S. Hunter, there were fifty bright young men espousing Tennyson's dreams of the parliament of man, the federation of the world.

It didn't last of course. It couldn't. Disillusionment was inevitable; after the twenties came the depression thirties and then another war. And things were different after that one. No new memorials emerged triumphantly, defiantly, hopefully out of the mushroom cloud of World War Two. Hope perished in the gas chambers of Poland. A new generation of the battle-damaged were blown home and a second set of names chiselled onto the bases of existing statues; sons below fathers. And in everybody's mind, the weary knowledge that some day young men would once again be falling.

Wars make history seem deceptively simple. They provide clear turning points, easy distinctions: before and after, winner and loser, right and wrong. True history, the past, is not like that. It isn't flat or linear. It has no outline. It is slippery, like liquid; infinite and unknowable, like space. And it is changeable: just when you think you see a pattern, perspective shifts, an alternative version is proffered, a long-forgotten memory resurfaces.

I have been trying to fix upon the turning points in Hannah and Teddy's story; all thoughts, these days, lead to Hannah. Looking back, it seems clear: there were certain events in the first year of their marriage that laid the foundation of what was to come. I couldn't see them at the time. In real life turning points are sneaky. They pass by unlabeled and unheeded. Opportunities are missed, catastrophes unwittingly celebrated. Turning points are only uncovered later, by historians who seek to bring order to a lifetime of tangled moments.

I wonder how their marriage will be handled in the film. What will Ursula decide led them to unhappiness? Was it Deborah's arrival from New York? Teddy's election loss? The absence of an heir? Will she agree that the signs were there as early as the honeymoon—the future fissures visible even by the dusky light of Paris, like faint flaws in the diaphanous fabrics of the twenties: beautiful, trivial fabrics so flimsy they could not hope to last?

✻

I N the summer of 1919 Paris basked in the warm optimism of the Versailles Peace Conference. In the evenings I helped Hannah undress, peeled off yet another new gossamer gown in pale green, or pink, or white (Teddy was a man who liked his brandy straight and his women pure), while she told me of the places they had visited, the things she had seen. They climbed the Eiffel Tower, strolled the Champs-Elysées, dined in famous restaurants. But it was something more, and less, that appealed to Hannah.

"The sketches, Grace," she said one night as I unwrapped her. "Who'd have thought I so adored sketches?"

Sketches, artefacts, people, smells. She was hungry for every new experience. She had years to make up for, years she considered had been wasted, marking time, waiting for her life to begin. There were so many people to speak to: wealthy folk they met in restaurants, politicians fresh from devising the treaty, buskers she encountered on the street.

Teddy was not blind to her reactions, her tendency to exaggerate, her inclination towards wild enthusiasm, but he put her high spirits down to youth. It was a condition, enchanting and bewildering in equal parts, which she would outgrow in good time. Not that he wished her to, not then; at that stage he was still enamored. He promised her a trip to Italy the following year to see Pompeii, the Uffizi, the Colosseum; there was little then he wouldn't promise. For she was a mirror in which he saw himself no longer the son of his father—solid, conventional, dull—but the husband of a charming, unpredictable woman.

272

For her part, Hannah did not speak much of Teddy. He was an adjunct. An accessory whose attendance made possible the adventure she was on. Oh, she liked him well enough. She found him amusing at times (though often when he least intended), well meaning and not unpleasant company. His interests were rather less varied than her own, his intellect less keen, but she learned to stroke his ego when required and seek intellectual stimulation elsewhere. And if she wasn't in love, what did it matter? She didn't notice the absence, not then. Who needed love when there was so much else in the offing?

One morning, towards the end of the honeymoon, Teddy woke with a migraine. He would have others in the time I knew him; they did not come often, but were severe when they did, the legacy of a childhood illness. He could do little but lie very still in a darkened, silent room and drink small amounts of water. Hannah was unsettled that first time; she had been shielded, for the most part, from the unpleasantness of illness.

She made an uncertain offer to sit with him, but Teddy was a sensible man not given to extracting comfort from the discomfort of others. He told her there was nothing she could do, that it was a crime not to enjoy her last days in Paris.

I was required as companion; Teddy considered it unseemly that a lady be seen alone in the street, no matter that she was married. Hannah had no wish to shop and had grown tired of being indoors. She wanted to explore, to unearth her very own Paris. We went outside and began to walk. She used no map, just turned in any direction that took her fancy.

"Come on, Grace," she said, time and again. "Let's see what's down this one."

Eventually we reached an alleyway, darker and thinner than those that had come before. A narrow path between two rows of buildings that leaned together, the tops embracing to enclose those below. Music drifted along the pathway, threading out into the square. There was a smell, vaguely familiar, of something edible, or perhaps something dead. And there was movement. People. Voices. Hannah stood at the entrance, deciding, then started down the alley. I had little choice but to follow.

A man sitting on gold and red cushions played a clarinet, though I didn't know its name then, the long black stick with shiny rings and keys. In my mind I called it the snake. It made music as the man's fingers pressed all over it: music I couldn't place, that made me feel vaguely uncomfortable, seemed somehow to describe intimate things, dangerous things. It was jazz, as it turned out, and I was to hear much more of it before the decade was out.

There were tables along the alley, and men sat reading, or talking, or arguing. They drank coffee and mysterious colored drinks—liquor, I was sure—from strange bottles. They looked up as we passed, interested, uninterested, it was hard to tell. I tried not to meet their eyes; silently willed Hannah to change her mind, turn around and lead us back into light and safety. But while my nostrils were filling with unwelcome foreign smoke, my ears with foreign music, Hannah seemed to float. Her attention was elsewhere. Along the alley walls pictures were strung, but not like those at Riverton. These were charcoal. Human faces, limbs, eyes, staring out at us from between the bricks.

Hannah stopped before a picture. It was large, and was the only one to include a whole person. It was a woman sitting on a chair. Not an armchair, or a chaise longue, or an artist's couch. A plain, wooden chair with heavy legs. Her knees were apart and she sat facing directly ahead. She was naked and she was black, luminous in charcoal. Her face stared from the painting. Wide eyes, sharp cheeks, pleated lips. Her hair was wrapped into a knot behind her head. Like a warrior queen.

I was shocked by the drawing, expected Hannah to react similarly. But she felt something different. She reached out and touched it; stroked the curved line of the woman's cheek. She inclined her head.

A man was somehow beside her. "You like?" he said, heavy accent, heavier lids. I didn't like the way he looked at Hannah. He knew she had money. He could tell by her clothing.

Hannah blinked, as if released from a spell. "Oh yes," she said softly.

"You want to buy perhaps?"

Hannah pressed her lips together and I knew what she was thinking. Despite his professed love of art, Teddy would not approve. And she was right. There was something about the woman, the painting, that was dangerous. Subversive. And yet Hannah wanted it. It reminded her, of course, of the past. Of The Game. Nefertiti. A role she had played with the unencumbered vigor of childhood. She nodded. Oh yes, she wanted it.

Misgivings prickled beneath my skin. The man's face remained expressionless. He called someone. When there was no answer he gestured for Hannah to follow. They seemed to have forgotten my presence, but I stayed close to her as she followed him to a small red door. He pushed it open. It was an artist's studio, little more than a dark hole in the wall. The walls were faded green, wallpaper peeling in long strips. The floor—what I could see of it beneath the hundreds of loose paper sheets scarred with charcoal—was stone. There was a mattress in the corner, covered with faded cushions and a quilt; empty liquor bottles were strewn around its edges.

Inside was the woman from the painting. To my horror she was naked. She looked at us with interest that was quickly extinguished, but didn't say anything. She stood up, taller than us, taller than the man, and walked to the table. There was something in her movement, a freedom, a disregard for the fact that we were watching her, could see her breasts, one larger than the other, that unnerved me. These weren't people like us. Like me. She lit a cigarette and smoked it as we waited. I looked away. Hannah didn't.

"Madame wants to buy your portrait," said the man in stilted English.

The black woman stared at Hannah, then said something in a language I didn't speak. Not French. Something far more foreign.

The man laughed and said to Hannah, "It's not for sale." He reached out then and grabbed her chin. Alarm pulsed loudly in my ears. Even Hannah flinched as he held her firmly, turned her head from side to side, then let her go. "Trade only."

"Trade?" said Hannah.

"Your own image," said the man in his heavy accent. He shrugged. "You take hers, you leave your own."

The very thought! A portrait of Hannah—in Lord knew what state of undress—left hanging here in this dismal French alley for all who cared to see! It was unthinkable.

"We have to go, ma'am," I said with a firmness that surprised me. "Mr. Luxton. He'll be expecting us."

My tone must have surprised Hannah too, for to my relief she nodded. "Yes. You're right, Grace."

She walked with me to the door, but as I waited for her to pass through she turned back to the charcoal man. "Tomorrow," she said faintly. "I'll come back tomorrow."

We did not speak on the way back. Hannah walked quickly, her face set. That night I lay awake, anxious and afraid, wondering how to stop her, certain that I must. There was something in the sketch that unsettled me; something I saw in Hannah's reflection when she looked at it. A flicker reignited.

Lying in my bed that night, sounds of the street took on a malevolence they hadn't had before. Foreign voices, foreign music, a woman's laughter in a nearby apartment. I longed to return to England, to a place where the rules were clear and everybody knew their place. It didn't exist, of course, this England, but the night times have a way of encouraging extremes.

As it happens, things next morning took care of themselves. When I went to dress Hannah, Teddy was already awake and sitting in the armchair. His head was still aching, he said, but what kind of a husband would he be if he left his pretty wife alone on the final day of their honeymoon? He suggested they go shopping. "It's our last day. I'd like to take you out to pick some souvenirs. Something to remind you of Paris."

When they returned, I noted, the sketch was not amongst the things Hannah had me pack for England. I am not sure whether Teddy refused and she acceded, or whether she knew better than to ask, but I was glad. Teddy had bought her a fur wrap instead: mink, with brittle little paws and dull black eyes.

And so we returned to England.

✻

W E arrived in London on 19 July 1919, the day of the Peace Procession. The driver steered us through cars and omnibuses and horse-drawn carriages, along crowd-lined streets where people had crammed together to wave flags and streamers. The ink was still wet on the treaty, sanctions that would lead to the bitterness and division responsible for the next world war, but folk back home knew none of that. Not then. They were just glad that the south wind no longer dragged the sound of gunfire across the Channel. That there'd be no more boys dying at the hands of other boys on the plains of France.

The car dropped me off with the bags at the London town house and then continued on. Simion and Estella were expecting the newlyweds to join them for tea. Hannah would have preferred to go straight home, but Teddy was insistent. He hid a smile. He had something up his sleeve.

A footman emerged from the front entrance, took a suitcase in each hand, then disappeared back into the house. Hannah's personal bag he left at my feet. I was surprised. I hadn't expected other servants, not yet, and wondered vaguely who'd engaged him.

I stood, breathing in the atmosphere of the square. Petrol mingled with the sweet tang of warm manure. I craned my neck to take in all six stories of the grand house. It was brown brick with white columns on either side of the front entrance, and it stood at attention in a line of identical others. One of the white columns bore the black number: 17. Number seventeen, Grosvenor Square. My new home where I was to be a real lady's maid.

The servants' entrance was a flight of stairs that ran parallel to the street, from pavement to basement, and was bordered by a black cast-iron railing. I picked up Hannah's bag of particulars and started down.

The door was closed, but muffled voices, unmistakably angry, seeped from inside. Through the basement window I saw the back of a girl whose bearing ("saucy," Mrs. Townsend would have said), along with the flock of bouncy red curls escaping from beneath her hat, gave the impression of youthfulness. She was arguing with a short, fat man whose neck was disappearing beneath a red stain of indignation.

She punctuated a final, triumphant statement by swinging a bag over her shoulder and striding towards the door. Before I could move, she had pushed it open and we were face to startled face, warped reflections in a sideshow mirror. She reacted first: hearty laughter that sprayed saliva on my neck. "And I thought housemaids was hard to come by!" she said. "Well, you're welcome to it. Fat chance I'm going to scrounge around in other people's dirty houses for minimum wage!"

She pushed past and dragged her suitcase up the stairs. At the top she turned and shouted, "Say goodbye, Izzy Batterfield. Bonjour, Mademoiselle Isabella!" And with a final ripple of laughter, a theatrical flounce of her skirt, she was gone. Before I could respond. Explain that I was a lady's maid. Not a housemaid at all.

I knocked on the door, still ajar. There was no answer and I took myself inside. The house had the unmistakable smell of beeswax (though not Stubbins & Co.) and potatoes, but there was something else, something underlying it, which, though not unpleasant, rendered everything unfamiliar.

The man was at the table, a skinny woman standing behind, hands draped over his shoulders, gnarled hands, skin red and torn around the fingernails. They turned to me as one. The woman had a large black mole beneath her left eye.

"Good afternoon," I said. "I—"

"Good, is it?" said the man. "I've just lost my third housemaid in as many weeks, we've a party scheduled for two hours hence, and you want me to believe it's a good afternoon?"

"There now," said the woman, pursing her lips. "She was a tarty one, that Izzy. Career as a fortune-teller, indeed. If she's got the gift, I'm the Queen of Sheba. She'll meet her end at the hands of an unhappy customer. You see if I'm wrong!"

There was something in the way she said it, a cruel smile that played about her lips, a glimmer of repressed glee in her voice, that made me shudder. I was overcome by a desire to turn and leave the way I'd come, but I remembered Mr. Hamilton's advice that I was to start as I meant to continue. I cleared my throat and said, with all the poise I could muster, "My name is Grace Reeves."

They looked at me with shared confusion.

"The Mistress's lady's maid?"

The woman drew herself to full height, narrowed her eyes and said, "The Mistress never mentioned a new lady's maid."

I was taken aback. "Did she not?" I stammered despite myself. "I . . . I'm certain she wrote with instructions from Paris. I posted the letter myself."

"Paris?" They looked at one another.

Then the man seemed to remember something. He nodded several times quickly and shook the woman's hands from his shoulders.

"Of course," he said. "We were expecting you. I'm Mr. Boyle, butler here at number seventeen, and this is Mrs. Tibbit."

I nodded, still confused. "Glad to make your acquaintances." Both continued to stare at me in a way that made me wonder if they were one as simple as the other. "I'm rather tired from the journey," I said, enunciating slowly. "Perhaps you would be so kind as to call a housemaid to show me to my room?"

Mrs. Tibbit sniffed, so that the skin around her mole quivered and then drew taut. "There are no more housemaids," she said. "Not yet. The Mistress . . . that is, Mrs. *Estella* Luxton, hasn't been able to find one as will stay put."

"Aye," Mr. Boyle said, lips tight, white as his face. "And we've a party scheduled this evening. It'll have to be all hands on deck. Miss Deborah won't stand for imperfection."

Miss Deborah? Who was Miss Deborah? I frowned. "*My* mistress, the *new* Mrs. Luxton, didn't mention a party."

"No," Mrs. Tibbit said, "she wouldn't, would she? It's a surprise, to welcome Mr. and Mrs. Luxton home from their honeymoon. Miss Deborah and her mother have been planning it for weeks."

※

T H E party was in full swing by the time Teddy and Hannah's car arrived. Mr. Boyle had given instructions that I was to meet them at the door and show them to the ballroom. It would usually be the butler's duty, he said, but Miss Deborah had given him orders that necessitated his presence elsewhere.

I opened the door and they stepped inside, Teddy beaming, Hannah weary, as might be expected after a visit with Simion and Estella. "I'd kill for a cup of tea," she said.

"Not so soon, darling," said Teddy. He handed me his coat and gave Hannah a rushed kiss on the cheek. She flinched slightly, as she always did. "I've a little surprise first," he said, hurrying away, smiling and rubbing his hands together. Hannah watched him go, then lifted her gaze to take in the entrance hall: its freshly painted yellow walls, the rather ugly modern chandelier that hung above the stairs, the potted palm trees bent over beneath strings of fairy lights. "Grace," she said, eyebrow cocked, "what on earth is going on?"

I shrugged apologetically, was about to explain when Teddy

reappeared and took her arm. "This way, darling," he said, leading her in the direction of the ballroom.

The door opened and Hannah's eyes widened when she saw it was full of people she didn't know. Then a burst of light, and as my gaze swept up towards the glowing chandelier I sensed movement on the staircase behind. There were appreciative gasps; halfway down the stairs stood a slim woman with dark hair curled about her tight, bony face. It was not a pretty face, but there was something striking about it; an illusion of beauty I would learn to recognize as a mark of the chronically chic. She was tall and thin and standing in a way I had not yet seen: hunched forward so that her silk dress seemed almost to fall from her shoulders, drip down her curved spine. The posture was at once masterful and effortless, nonchalant and contrived. Draped across her arms was a pale fur I took at first for a warmer, until it yapped and I realized she held a tiny fluffy dog, as white as Mrs. Townsend's best apron.

I didn't recognize the woman, but I knew at once who she must be. She paused momentarily before gliding down the final stairs and across the floor, the sea of guests parting as if by choreography.

"Deb!" Teddy said when she was near, a broad smile dimpling his easy, handsome face. He took her hands, leaned forward to kiss a proffered cheek.

The woman stretched her lips into a smile. "Welcome home, Tiddles." Her words were breezy, her New York accent flat and loud. She had a way of speaking that eschewed intonation. It was a leveler, making the ordinary seem extraordinary and vice versa. "What a fabulous house! And I've assembled some of London's brightest young things to help you warm it." She waved her long fingers at a well-dressed woman whose eye she caught over Hannah's shoulder.

"Are you surprised, darling?" Teddy said, turning to Hannah. "Mother and I cooked it up between us, and darling Deb just lives to organize parties."

"Surprised," said Hannah, her eyes briefly finding mine. "That doesn't begin to describe it."

Deborah smiled, that wolfish smile, so particularly hers, and laid a hand on Hannah's wrist. A long, pale hand that gave the impression of wax gone cold. "We meet at last," she said. "I just know we're going to be the best of friends."

※

NINETEEN-TWENTY started badly; Teddy had lost the election. It was not his fault, the timing was wrong. The situation was misread, mishandled. It was the fault of the working classes and their nasty little newspaper presses. Filthy campaigns waged against their betters. They were trumped up after the war; they expected too much. They would become like the Irish if they were not careful, or the Russians. Never matter. There would be another opportunity; they'd find him a safer seat. This time next year, Simion promised, if he dropped the foolish ideas that confused Conservative voters, Teddy would be in Parliament.

Estella thought Hannah should have a baby. It would be good for Teddy. Good for his future constituents to see him as a family man. They were married, she was fond of saying, and there came a time in every marriage when a man deserved an heir.

Teddy went to work with his father. Everybody agreed it was for the best. After the election defeat, he had taken on the look of someone who'd survived a trauma, a shock; like Alfred used to look, back in the days straight after the war.

Men like Teddy were not used to losing, but it wasn't the Luxton way to mope; Teddy's parents began spending a lot of time at number seventeen, where Simion told frequent stories about his own father, the journey to the top not being one for weaklings and failures. Teddy and Hannah's trip to Italy was postponed; it didn't look good for Teddy to be fleeing the country, Simion said. The impression of success breeds success. Besides, Pompeii wasn't going anywhere.

Meanwhile, I was doing my best to settle into London life. My new duties I learned quickly. Mr. Hamilton had given me countless briefings before I left Riverton—from straightforward responsibilities like maintaining Hannah's wardrobe to the more particular, like maintaining her good character—and in these, I felt assured. In my new domestic sphere, however, I was at sea. Cast adrift on a lonely sea of unfamiliarity. For if they weren't exactly perfidious, Mrs. Tibbit and Mr. Boyle were certainly not straightforward. They had a way of being together, an intense and apparent pleasure in each other's company, that was utterly exclusive. Moreover, Mrs. Tibbit in particular seemed to derive great comfort from such exclusion. Hers was a happiness fed by the discontent of others, and when such was not forthcoming she felt no compunction in manufacturing misfortune for some unwitting soul. I learned quickly that the way to survive at number seventeen was to keep myself to myself and to watch my own back.

It was a drizzly morning when I found Hannah standing alone in the drawing room. Teddy had just left for his office in the City and she was watching the street. Motorcars, bicycles, busy people walking back and forth, here and there.

"Would you like to take your tea, ma'am?" I said.

No answer.

"Or perhaps I could have the chauffeur bring the car around?"

I came closer and I realized Hannah had not heard. She was in company with her own thoughts and I could guess at them without much trouble. She was bored, wore an expression I recognized from the long days at Riverton when she would stand at the nursery window, Chinese box in hand, waiting for David to arrive, desperate to play The Game.

I cleared my throat and she looked up. When she saw me, she cheered somewhat. "Hello, Grace," she said.

I repeated my question then, about where she'd like her tea.

"I'm going to read, Grace," she said. "I've a book with me." And she held up her well-worn copy of *Jane Eyre*.

"Again, ma'am?"

She shrugged, smiled. "Again."

I don't know why that troubled me so, but it did. It rang some small bell of warning that I didn't know how to heed.

※

TEDDY worked hard and Hannah made an effort. She attended his parties, made chitchat with the wives of business associates and the mothers of politicians. The talk amongst the men was always the same—of money, business, the threat of the underclasses. Simion, like all men of his type, was profoundly suspicious of those he termed "bohemians." Teddy, despite his best intentions, was falling into line.

Hannah would have preferred to talk real politics with the men. Sometimes, when she and Teddy had retired for the night to their adjoining suites and I was brushing out her hair, Hannah would ask him what so-and-so had said about the declaration of martial law in Ireland, and Teddy would look at her with weary amusement and tell her not to worry her pretty head. That's what he was for.

"But I want to know," Hannah would say. "I'm interested."

And Teddy would shake his head. "Politics is a man's game."

"Let me play," Hannah would say.

"You are playing," he would answer. "We're on a team, you and I. It's your job to look after the wives."

"But it's boring. They're boring. I want to talk about important things. I don't see why I can't."

"Oh, darling," Teddy would say simply. "Because it's the rules. I didn't make them, but I have to stick to them." He would smile then and chip her shoulder. "It's not all bad, eh? At least you've got Mother to help, and Deb. She's a sport, isn't she?"

Hannah had little choice then but to nod grudgingly. It was true: Deborah was always on hand to help. Would continue to be, now she'd decided not to return to New York. A London magazine had offered her a position writing society fashion pages and how could she resist? A whole new city of ladies to decorate and dominate? She would be staying with Hannah and Teddy until she found a suitable place of her own. After all, as Estella had pointed out, there was no reason to hurry. Number seventeen was a large home with plenty of rooms to spare. Especially while there were no children.

※

IN November of that year, Emmeline came to London for her sixteenth birthday. It was her first visit since Hannah and Teddy's marriage, and Hannah had been looking forward to it. She spent the morning waiting in the drawing room, hurrying to the window whenever a motorcar slowed outside, only to return, disappointed, to the sofa when it proved a false alarm.

In the end, she had grown so despondent she missed it. She didn't realize Emmeline had arrived until Boyle knocked on the door and made his announcement.

"Miss Emmeline to see you, ma'am."

Hannah squealed and jumped to her feet as Boyle showed Emmeline into the room. "Finally!" she said, hugging her sister tightly. "I thought you'd never get here." She stepped back and turned to me. "Look, Grace, doesn't she look beautiful?"

Emmeline gave a half-smile, then quickly schooled her mouth back into a sulky pout. Despite her expression, or perhaps because of it, she was beautiful. She'd grown taller and thinner and her face had gained new angles that drew attention to her full lips and large round eyes. She had mastered the attitude of tired disdain that suited so perfectly her age and era.

"Come, sit down," Hannah said, leading Emmeline to the sofa. "I'll call for tea."

Emmeline slumped into the corner of the sofa and, when Hannah turned away, smoothed her skirt. It was a plain dress of a season ago; someone had attempted to refashion it into the newer, looser style, but it still wore the telltale marks of its original architecture.

When Hannah turned back from the service bell, Emmeline stopped fussing and cast an exaggeratedly nonchalant gaze around the room.

Hannah laughed. "Oh, it's the latest thing; Elsie de Wolfe chose everything. It's hideous, isn't it?"

Emmeline raised her eyebrows and nodded slowly.

Hannah sat next to Emmeline. "It's so good to see you," she said. "We can do anything you like this week. Tea and walnut cake at Gunter's, we can see a show."

Emmeline shrugged, but her fingers, I could see, were working again at her skirt.

"We could visit the museum," said Hannah. "Or take a look at Selfridge's—" She hesitated. Emmeline was nodding half-heartedly. Hannah laughed uncertainly. "Listen to me, going on," she said. "You've only just got here and I'm already planning the week. I've hardly let you get a word in. Haven't even asked you how you are."

Emmeline looked at Hannah. "I like your dress," she said finally, then tightened her lips as if she'd broken some resolution.

It was Hannah's turn to shrug. "Oh, I've a wardrobe full of them," she said. "Teddy brings them home when he's been abroad. He believes a new dress makes up for missing the trip itself. Why would a woman go abroad except to buy dresses? So I've a wardrobe full and nowhere to—" She caught herself, realizing, and bit back a smile. "Far too many dresses for me ever to wear." She eyed Emmeline casually. "I don't suppose you'd like to take a look? See if there's anything you'd like? You'd be doing me a favor, helping me to clear some space."

Emmeline looked up quickly, unable to mask her excitement. "I suppose I could. If it would be a help."

Hannah let Emmeline add ten Parisian dresses to her luggage, and I was set to making better alterations to the clothing she had brought with her. I suffered a wave of homesickness for Riverton as I unpicked Nancy's perfunctory stitches. I hoped she wouldn't take my revisions as personal affronts.

Things between the sisters improved after that: Emmeline's

slump of disaffection vanished, and by the end of the week things were much as they'd always been. They'd relaxed back into an easy friendship, each as relieved as the other by the return to the status quo. I was relieved as well: Hannah had been entirely too glum of late. I hoped the elevation of spirits would outlast the visit.

On Emmeline's final day, she and Hannah sat at either end of the morning-room sofa, waiting for the car from Riverton. Deborah, on her way to an editorial meeting, was at the writing desk, back turned, sketching a hurried note of condolence for a bereaved friend.

Emmeline reclined luxuriously and gave a wistful little sigh. "I could take tea at Gunter's every day and never grow tired of walnut cake."

"You would once you lost that slim little waist," said Deborah, dragging her scratchy pen nib across the writing paper. "A minute on the lips and all that."

Emmeline fluttered her eyelids at Hannah who tried not to laugh.

"Are you sure you don't want me to stay?" said Emmeline. "It really would be no trouble."

"I doubt Pa would agree."

"Pooh," said Emmeline. "He wouldn't care a whit." She inclined her head. "I could live quite comfortably in the coat closet, you know. You wouldn't even know I was here."

Hannah appeared to give this due consideration.

"You'll be quite bored without me, you know," said Emmeline.

"I know," said Hannah, swooning. "How will I ever find things to sustain me?"

Emmeline laughed and tossed a cushion at Hannah.

Hannah caught it and sat straightening the tassels for a moment. Eyes still on the cushion, she said, "About Pa, Emme . . . Is he . . . ? *How* is he?"

Her strained relations with Mr. Frederick, I knew, were a constant source of regret for Hannah. On more than one occasion I had found the beginnings of a letter in her escritoire, but none was ever posted.

"He's Pa," said Emmeline, shrugging. "Same as always."

"Oh," said Hannah disconsolately. "Good. I hadn't heard from him."

"No," said Emmeline, yawning. "Well, you know what Pa's like once he sets his mind."

"Yes," said Hannah. "Still, I rather thought . . ." Her voice tapered off and for a moment there was silence between them. Though Deborah's back was turned, I could see her ears had pricked, with Alsatian hunger, at the hint of gossip. Hannah must have seen too, for she straightened and changed the subject with forced brightness. "I don't know whether I mentioned, Emme—I'd thought to take some work when you've gone."

"Work?" said Emmeline. "In a dress shop?"

Now Deborah laughed. She sealed her envelope and swung around on her chair. She stopped laughing when she saw Hannah's face. "You're serious?"

"Oh, Hannah's usually serious," said Emmeline.

"When we were on Oxford Street the other day," said Hannah to Emmeline, "and you were having your hair done, I saw a small press, Blaxland's, with a sign in the window. They were looking for editors." She raised her shoulders. "I love to read, I'm interested in politics, my grammar and spelling are better than average—"

"But don't be ridiculous, darling," said Deborah, handing her letter to me. "See it makes this morning's mail." She turned to Hannah. "They'd never take you."

"They already have," said Hannah. "I applied on the spot. The owner said he needed somebody urgently."

Deborah inhaled sharply, schooled her lips into a dilute smile. "But surely you must see it's out of the question."

"What question?" said Emmeline, feigning earnestness.

"The question of rightness," said Deborah.

"I didn't realize there was a question of rightness," said Emmeline. She started to laugh. "What's the answer?"

Deborah inhaled, her nostrils sucking together. "Blaxland's?" she said thinly to Hannah. "Aren't they the publishers responsible for all those nasty little red pamphlets the soldiers are handing out on street corners?" Her eyes narrowed. "My brother would have a fit."

"I don't think so," said Hannah. "Teddy's often expressed sympathy for the unemployed."

Deborah's eyes flashed wider: the surprise of a predator interested briefly by its prey. "You've misheard, darling," she said. "Tiddles knows better than to alienate his future constituents. Besides . . ." She stood triumphantly before the hearth mirror, stabbed a pin into her hat, ". . . sympathy or not, I don't imagine he'd be too pleased to learn you'd joined forces with the very people who printed those filthy articles that lost him the election."

Hannah's face fell—she hadn't realized. She glanced at Emmeline who shrugged her shoulders sympathetically. Deborah, observing their reactions in the mirror, swallowed a smile and turned to face Hannah, tut-tutting disappointedly. "Darling, how dreadfully disloyal! It'll kill poor old Tiddles when he finds out. Kill him."

"Then don't tell him," said Hannah.

"You know me, *I'm* the soul of discretion," she said. "But you're forgetting the hundreds of other people without my scruples. They'll be only too happy to report back when they see your name, *his* name, on that propaganda."

"I'll tell them I can't take the position," said Hannah quietly. She set the cushion aside. "But I intend to look for something else. Something more suitable."

"Dearest child," said Deborah, laughing. "Put it out of your mind. There are no suitable jobs for you. I mean, how would it look? Teddy's wife working? What would people say?"

"You work," said Emmeline, slyly lowering her eyelids.

"Oh, but that's different, darling," said Deborah, without skipping a beat. "I haven't met my Teddy yet. I'd give it all up in a flash for the right man."

"I need to do something," said Hannah. "Something other than sitting around here all day waiting to see if anyone calls."

"Well, of course," said Deborah, scooping her handbag from the writing desk. "No one likes to be idle." She arched an eyebrow. "Though I'd have thought there was a′lot more to do around here than sit and wait. A household doesn't run itself, you know."

"No," said Hannah. "And I would happily take over some of the running—"

"Best stick to things you do well," said Deborah, slinking towards the door. "That's what I always say." She paused, holding the door open, then turned, a slow smile spreading across her face. "I know," she said. "It's a wonder I didn't think of it earlier." She pursed her lips. "I'll have a word with Mother. You can join her Conservative Women's group. They've been looking for volunteers for the upcoming gala. You can help write place cards and paint decorations— explore your artistic side."

Hannah and Emmeline exchanged a glance as Boyle came to the door.

"The car is here for Miss Emmeline," he said. "Can I call you a taxi, Miss Deborah?"

"Don't bother yourself, Boyle," said Deborah chirpily. "I feel like some fresh air."

Boyle nodded and left to supervise the stowing of Emmeline's bags in the motorcar.

"What a stroke of genius!" Deborah said, smiling broadly at Hannah. "Teddy will be so pleased, you and Mother spending all that time together!" She inclined her head and lowered her voice. "And this way, he'll never need know about that other unfortunate business."

DOWN THE RABBIT HOLE

※

I WON'T wait for Sylvia. I am done waiting. I will find my own cup of tea. A loud, tinny, thumping music comes from the speakers on the makeshift stage, and a group of six young girls are dancing. They are dressed in black and red Lycra—little more than swimsuits—and black boots that come all the way to their knees. The heels are high and I wonder how they manage to dance in them at all, then I remember the dancers of my youth. The Hammersmith Palais, the Original Dixieland Jazz Band, Emmeline doing the Charleston.

I claw my fingers around the armrest, lean so that my elbow digs into my ribs and push myself upwards, hugging the rail. I hover for a moment, then transfer my weight to my cane, wait for the landscape to stand still. Blessed heat. I poke my cane gingerly at the ground. The recent rain has left it soft and I am wary of becoming bogged. I use the indentations made by other people's footsteps. It is a slow process, but I go surely . . .

"Hear your future . . . Read your palm . . ."

I cannot abide fortune-tellers. I was once told I had a short life line; did not properly shake the vague sense of foreboding until I was midway through my sixties.

I pick my way onwards, will not look. I am resigned to my future. It is the past that troubles.

※

HANNAH saw the fortune-teller in early 1921. It was a Wednesday morning; Hannah's "at-homes" were always Wednesday mornings. Deborah was meeting Lady Lucy Duff-Gordon at the Savoy Grill and Teddy was at work with his father. Teddy had lost his air of trauma by then; he looked like someone who had woken from a strange dream relieved to realize he was still who he used to be. He had been surprised, he told Hannah one night at dinner, at how much opportunity the world of banking offered. Not just for the acquisition of wealth, he was quick to specify, rather for the nourishment of a man's cultural interests. Soon, he promised, when the time was right, he was going to ask his father whether he might head up a foundation to nurture young painters. Or sculptors. Or some other sort of artist. Hannah said that sounded wonderful and turned her attention back to her meal while he spoke of his new manufacturing client. She was becoming used to the chasm between Teddy's intentions and his actions.

A parade of fashionably dressed women had been leaving number seventeen for the past five minutes when I started to clear the tea items. (We had just lost our fifth housemaid and no replacement had yet been found.) Only Hannah, Fanny and Lady Clementine remained sitting on the sofas, finishing their tea. Hannah was tapping her spoon lightly, distractedly, against her saucer. She was anxious for them to go, though I did not yet know why.

"Really dear," Lady Clementine said, eyeing Hannah over her empty teacup, "*you* should think about starting a family." She exchanged a glance with Fanny, who repositioned proudly her own sizeable heft. She was expecting her second. "Children are good for a marriage. Aren't they, Fanny?"

Fanny nodded, but was unable to speak as her mouth was full with sponge cake.

"A woman married too long without children," Lady Clementine said dourly. "People start to talk."

"I'm sure you're right," said Hannah. "But there's really nothing

292

to talk about." She said it so breezily I shivered. One would have been hard-pressed to detect the hint of strife beneath the veneer. The bitter arguments Hannah's failure to fall was causing.

Lady Clementine exchanged another glance with Fanny, who raised her eyebrows. "There's nothing wrong, is there? Downstairs?"

My first thought was that she referred to our lack of housemaids; I realized her true meaning only when Fanny swallowed her cake and added eagerly, "There's doctors you could see. *Ladies'* doctors."

There was really very little Hannah could say to that. Well, there was, of course. She could have told them to mind their own business, and once she probably would have, but time had been rubbing at her edges. So she said nothing. She just smiled and silently willed them to leave.

When they had gone, she collapsed back into the sofa. "Finally," she said. "I thought they'd never go." She watched me loading the last of the cups onto my tray. "I'm sorry you have to do that, Grace."

"It's all right, ma'am," I said. "I'm sure it won't be for long."

"All the same," said Hannah. "You're a lady's maid. I'll speak to Boyle about finding a replacement."

I continued arranging the teaspoons.

Hannah was still watching me. "Can you keep a secret, Grace?"

"You know I can, ma'am."

She withdrew something, a folded piece of newspaper, from beneath her skirt waist and smoothed it open. "I found this in the back of one of Boyle's newspapers." She handed it to me.

Fortune-teller, it read. *Renowned spiritualist. Communicate with the dead. Learn your future.*

I couldn't hand it back quickly enough, wiped my hands on my apron afterwards. I had heard talk downstairs about such things. It was the newest craze, born of the grief and suffering that were general all over England. The world.

"I have an appointment this afternoon," Hannah said.

I couldn't think what to say. I wished she hadn't told me. I exhaled. "If you don't mind me saying, ma'am, I don't hold with seances and the like."

"Really, Grace," Hannah said, surprised, "of all people I'd have thought you'd be more open-minded. Sir Arthur Conan Doyle is a believer, you know. He communicates regularly with his son Kingsley. He even has séances at his home."

She wasn't to know I was no longer devoted to Sherlock Holmes; that in London I had discovered Agatha Christie.

"It's not that, ma'am," I said quickly. "It's not that I don't believe."

"No?"

"No, ma'am. I believe, all right. That's the problem. It's not natural. The dead. It's dangerous to interfere."

She raised her eyebrows, considering the fact. "Dangerous . . ."

It was the wrong approach to take. By mentioning danger I'd only made the proposition more attractive.

"I shall go with you, ma'am," I said.

She had not expected this, was unsure whether to be annoyed or touched. In the end she was both. "No," she said quite sternly. "That won't be necessary. I'll be quite all right by myself." Then her voice softened. "It's your afternoon off, isn't it? Surely you have something lovely planned? Something preferable to accompanying me?"

I didn't answer. The plans I had were secret. After numerous letters backwards and forwards, Alfred had finally suggested he visit me in London. The months away from Riverton had left me lonelier than I'd expected. Despite Mr. Hamilton's comprehensive coaching, I'd found there were certain pressures being a lady's maid that I hadn't anticipated, especially with Hannah seeming not as happy as a young bride should. And Mrs. Tibbit's penchant for making trouble ensured that none of the staff was prepared to let down their guard long enough to enjoy a camaraderie. It was the first time in my life I had suffered from isolation. And though I was wary of reading the wrong sentiment into Alfred's attentions (sure enough, I had done that once before), I found myself longing to see him.

Nonetheless, I did follow Hannah that afternoon. My meeting with Alfred wasn't until later in the evening; if I went quickly I'd have time to make sure she arrived and then departed again in good condition. I'd heard enough stories about spiritualists to convince me it was the wisest course. Mrs. Tibbit's cousin had been possessed, she said, and Mr. Boyle knew of a fellow whose wife was fleeced and had her throat cut.

More than that, while I wasn't certain how I felt about spiritualists, I was certain enough about the type of people who were drawn to them. Only people unhappy in the present seek to know the future.

※

THERE was a thick fog out: gray and heavy. I followed Hannah along Aldwych like a detective on a trail, careful never to fall too far behind, careful she never slipped too long behind a cloud of fog. On the corner, a man in a trench coat was playing the mouth organ: "Keep the Home Fires Burning." They were everywhere, those displaced soldiers, in every alleyway, beneath every bridge, in front of every railway station. Hannah rummaged in her purse for a coin and dropped it in the man's cup before continuing on her way.

We turned into Kean Street and Hannah stopped in front of an elegant Edwardian villa. It looked respectable enough, but, as Mother was fond of saying, appearances could be deceptive. I watched as she checked the advertisement again and pressed a finger to the numbered doorbell. The door opened quickly and, without a glance behind, she disappeared inside.

I stood outside, wondering which level she was being led to. The third, I felt sure. There was something about the lamp glow that yellowed the frilled edges of the drawn curtains. I sat and waited near a one-legged man selling tin monkeys that ran up and down a piece of twine.

I waited over an hour. By the time she reappeared, the cement step on which I sat had frozen my legs and I was unable to stand quickly enough. I crouched, praying she wouldn't see me. She didn't; she wasn't looking. She was standing on the top step in a daze. Her expression was blank, startled even, and she seemed glued to the spot. My first thought was that the spiritualist had put a hex on her, held up one of those fob watches they showed in photographs and hypnotized her. My foot was all pins and needles so I couldn't rush over. I was about to call out when she took a deep breath, shook herself and started off quickly in the direction of home.

※

I WAS late meeting Alfred that foggy evening. Not by much, but enough that he looked worried before he saw me, hurt when he did.

"Grace." We greeted each other clumsily. He held out his hand to take mine at the same time as I reached for his. There was a clumsy moment where wrist hit against wrist, and he grabbed my elbow by mistake. I smiled nervously, reclaimed my own hand and tucked it under my scarf. "Sorry I'm late, Alfred," I said. "I was running an errand for the Mistress."

"Doesn't she know it's your afternoon off?" said Alfred. He was taller than I'd remembered, and his face more lined, but still, I thought him very nice to look at.

"Yes, but—"

"You should have told her what she could do with her errand."

His scorn did not surprise me. Alfred's frustrations with service were growing. In his letters from Riverton, distance had exposed something I hadn't seen before: there was a thread of dissatisfaction that ran through his descriptions of his daily life. And lately, his inquiries about London were peppered with quotes from books he'd been reading about classes and workers and trade unions.

"You're not a slave," he said. "You could have told her no."

296

"I know. I didn't think it would . . . The errand took longer than I thought."

"Oh well," he said, face softening so that he looked like himself again. "Not your fault. Let's make the most of it before we're back to the salt mines, eh? How about a spot to eat before the film?"

I was overwhelmed with happiness as we walked side by side. I felt grown-up and rather daring, out about town with a man like Alfred. I found myself wishing he would link his arm through mine. That people might see us and take us for a married couple.

"I looked in on your ma," he said, breaking my thoughts. "Like you asked."

"Oh, Alfred," I said. "Thank you. She wasn't too bad, was she?"

"Not too bad, Grace." He hesitated a moment and looked away. "But not too good, neither, if I'm honest. A nasty cough. And her back's been giving her grief, she says." He drove his hands into his pockets. "Arthritis, isn't it?"

I nodded. "It came on sudden when I was a girl. Got bad really fast. Winter's the worst."

"I had an aunt the same. Turned her old before her time." He shook his head. "Rotten luck."

We walked in silence a way. "Alfred," I said, "about Mother . . . Did she seem . . . Did she look to have enough, Alfred? Coal, I mean, and the like?"

"Oh, yes," he said. "No problems there. A nice pile of coal." He leaned to bump my shoulder. "And Mrs. Townsend makes sure she receives a nice parcel of sweets now and then."

"Bless her," I said, eyes filling with grateful tears. "And you too, Alfred. For going to see her. I know she appreciates it, even if she wouldn't say so herself."

He shrugged, said plainly, "I don't do it for your mother's gratitude, Gracie. I do it for you."

A wave of pleasure flooded my cheeks. I cupped one side of my face with a gloved hand, pressed it lightly to absorb the warmth.

"And how is everyone else?" I said shyly. "Back in Saffron? Is everybody well?"

There was a pause as he absorbed my subject change. "Well as can be expected," he said. "Downstairs that is. Upstairs is another matter."

"Mr. Frederick?" Nancy's last letter had suggested all was not right with him.

Alfred shook his head. "Gone all gloomy since you left. Must've had a soft spot for you, eh?" He nudged me and I couldn't help but smile.

"He misses Hannah," I said.

"Not that he'd admit it."

"She's as bad." I told him about the aborted letters I'd found. Draft after draft cast aside, but never sent.

He whistled and shook his head. "And they say we're s'posed to learn from our betters. Ask me, they could learn a thing or two from us."

I continued walking, wondering at Mr. Frederick's malaise. "Do you think if he and Hannah were to make it up between them . . . ?"

Alfred shrugged. "Don't know if it's that simple, to be honest. Oh, he misses Hannah, all right. No doubt about that. But there's more to it than that."

I looked at him.

"It's his motorcars, too. It's like he's got no purpose now the factory's gone. He spends all his time wandering the estate. He takes his gun and says he's looking for poachers. Dudley says it's all in his mind, that there are no poachers really, but still he goes on looking." He squinted into the fog. "I can understand that well enough. A man needs to feel utilized."

"Is Emmeline any consolation?"

He shrugged. "Turning into quite a little miss, if you ask me. She's got the run of the place with the Master as he is. He doesn't seem to mind what she does. Barely notices she's there, most times."

He kicked a small stone and watched as it bounced along, disappeared into the gutter. "No. It's not the same place any more. Not since you left."

I was savouring this comment when he said, "Oh," and dipped his hand into his pocket. "Speaking of Riverton, you'll never guess who I just saw. Just now when I was waiting for you."

"Who?"

"Miss Starling. Lucy Starling. Mr. Frederick's secretary as was."

A prickle of envy; his familiar use of her first name. Lucy. A slippery, mysterious name that rustled like silk. "Miss Starling? Here in London?"

"Lives here now, she says. A flat on Hartley Street, just round the corner."

"But what's she doing here?"

"Working. After Mr. Frederick's factory closed down she had to find another job and there's lots more of those in London." He handed me a piece of paper. White, warm, the corner folded where it had lain against the inside of his pocket. "I took down her address, told her I'd give it to you." He looked at me, smiled in a way that made my cheeks red all over again. "I'll rest easier," he said, "knowing you've a friend in London."

❦

I AM faint. My thoughts swim. Back and forth, in and out, across the tides of history.

The community hall. Perhaps that's where Sylvia is. There will be tea there. The ladies' auxiliary will be sure to have set up in the kitchenette, selling cakes and scones, and watery tea with sticks in place of spoons. I pick my way towards the small flight of concrete stairs. Steady as I go.

I step, misjudge, my ankle cuts hard against the rim of a concrete stair. Someone clutches my arm as I falter. A young man with dark skin, green hair and a ring right the way through his nostrils.

"You all right?" he says, his voice soft, gentle.

I cannot take my eyes from his nose-ring, cannot find the words.

"You're white as a sheet, darlin'. You here alone? You got some-one I should call?"

"There you are!" It is a woman. Someone I know. "Wandering off like that! I thought I'd lost you." She clucks like an old hen, plants her closed fists against her waist, only higher, so that she looks to be flapping fleshy wings. "What in heaven's name did you think you were doing?"

"Found her here," says green hair. "Almost fell on her way up the stairs."

"Is that right, you naughty thing," Sylvia says. "I turn my back one minute! You'll give me a heart attack if you're not careful. I don't know what you were thinking."

I begin to tell her, but stop. Realize that I cannot remember. I have the strongest sense that I was looking for something, that I wanted something.

"Come on," she says, both hands on my shoulders, steering me away from the hall. "Anthony's dying to meet you."

The tent is large and white with one flap tied back to permit entry. A painted fabric sign is strung above the entrance: *Saffron Green Historical Society*. Sylvia manoeuvres me inside. It is hot and smells like freshly mown grass. A fluorescent light tube has been fas-tened to the ceiling frame, humming as it casts its anaesthetic glow across the plastic tables and chairs.

"That's him there," Sylvia whispers, indicating a man whose or-dinariness renders him vaguely familiar. Gray-flecked brown hair, matching moustache, ruddy cheeks. He is in deep conversation with a matronly woman in conservative dress. Sylvia leans close. "Told you he was a good sort, didn't I?"

I am hot and my feet ache. I am confused. From nowhere, a de-licious urge to petulance. "I want a cup of tea."

Sylvia glances at me, quickly masks surprise. "Of course you do, ducky. I'll fetch you one, and then I've got a treat for you. Come and sit down." She bundles me over to sit by a hessian-covered board tiled with photographs, then disappears.

It is a cruel, ironical art, photography. The dragging of captured moments into the future; moments that should have been allowed to evaporate with the past; should exist only in memories, glimpsed through the fog of events that came after. Photographs force us to see people before their future weighed them down, before they knew their endings.

At first glance they are a froth of white faces and skirts amid a sepia sea, but recognition brings some into sharp focus while others recede. The first is the summer house, the one Teddy designed and had built when they took up residence in 1924. The photograph was taken that year, judging by the people in the foreground. Teddy stands near the incomplete stairs, leaning against one of the white marble entrance pillars. There is a picnic rug on the grassy escarpment nearby. Hannah and Emmeline sit on it, side by side. Both with the same faraway look in their eyes. Deborah stands at the front of the frame, tall body fashionably slumped, dark hair falling over one eye. She holds a cigarette in one hand. The smoke gives the impression of haze on the photo. If I didn't know better, I'd think there was a fifth person in the photo, hidden behind the haze. There's not of course. There are no photos of Robbie at Riverton. He only came the two times.

The second photograph has no people in it. It is of Riverton itself, or what was left of it after the fire swept through before the second war. The entire west wing has disappeared as if some mighty shovel descended from the sky and scooped out the nursery, the dining room, the drawing room, the family bedrooms. The remaining areas are charred black. They say it smoked for weeks. The smell of soot lingered in the village for months. I wouldn't know. By that time war was coming, Ruth was born, and I was on the threshold of a new existence.

The third photograph I have avoided recognizing, avoided assigning its place in history. The people I identify easily; the fact that they are dressed for a party. There were so many parties in those days, people were always dressing up and posing for photographs. They could be going anywhere. But they are not. I know where they are, and I know what is to come. I remember well what they wore. I remember the blood, the pattern it sprayed across her pale dress, like a jar of red ink dropped from a great height. I never managed to remove it completely; it wouldn't have made much difference if I had. I should simply have thrown it out. She never looked at it again, certainly never wore it.

In this photo they do not know; they are smiling. Hannah and Emmeline and Teddy. Smiling at the camera. It is Before. I look at Hannah's face, searching for some hint, some knowledge of impending doom. I don't find it, of course. If anything, it is anticipation I see in her eyes. Though perhaps I only imagine it because I know it was there.

There is someone behind me. A woman. She leans across to look at the same photograph.

"Priceless, aren't they," she says. "All those silly outfits they used to wear. A different world."

Only I perceive the shadow across their faces. Knowledge of what's to come spreads cold across my skin. No, it is not knowledge I feel; my leg is weeping where I bumped it, sticky liquid seeping down towards my shoe.

Someone taps my shoulder. "Dr. Bradley?" A man is bending towards me, his beaming face near mine. He takes my hand. "Grace? May I call you that? It's a pleasure to meet you. Sylvia's told me so much about you. It really is a pleasure."

Who is this man, speaking so loudly, so slowly? Shaking my hand so fervently? What has Sylvia told him of me? And why?

". . . It's English I teach for a living, but history's my passion. I like to consider myself a bit of a local history buff."

Sylvia appears through the tent's entrance, Styrofoam cup in hand. "Here you are then."

Tea. Just what I felt like. I take a sip. It is lukewarm; I can no longer be trusted with hot liquids. I have dozed off unexpectedly one too many times.

Sylvia sits in another chair. "Has Anthony told you about the testimonials?" She blinks mascara-clumped eyelashes at the man. "Have you told her about the testimonials?"

"Hadn't quite got round to it," he says.

"Anthony's videotaping a collection of personal stories from local people about the history of Saffron Green. It's to go to the Historical Society." She looks at me, smiles broadly. "He's got a funding grant and all. He's just been recording Mrs. Baker over there."

Once upon a time, people kept their stories to themselves. It didn't occur to them that folks would find them interesting. Now everybody's writing a memoir, competing for the worst childhood, the most violent father.

I suppose I should be glad. In my second life, after it all ended at Riverton, after the second war, I spent much of my time digging around discovering people's stories. Finding evidence, fleshing out bare bones. How much easier it would have been if everybody came replete with a record of their personal history. But all I can think of is a million tapes of the elderly ruminating on the price of eggs thirty years ago. Are they all in a room somewhere, a huge underground bunker, shelves from floor to ceiling, tapes lined up, walls echoing with trivial memories that no one has time to hear?

There is only one person whom I wish to hear my story. One person for whom I set it down on tape. I only hope it will be worth it. That Ursula is right: that Marcus will listen and understand. That my own guilt and the story of its acquisition will somehow set him free.

※

THE light is bright. I feel like a bird in an oven. Hot, plucked and watched. Why ever did I agree to this? Did I agree to this?

"Can you say something so we can test the levels?" Anthony is crouched behind a black item. A video camera, I suppose.

"What should I say?" A voice not my own.

"Once again."

"I'm afraid I really don't know what to say."

"Good," Anthony pulls away from the camera. "That's got it."

I smell the tent canvas, baking in the midday sun.

"I've been looking forward to speaking with you," he says, smiling. "Sylvia tells me you used to work at the big house."

"Yes."

"No need to lean towards the microphone. It'll pick you up just fine where you are."

I had not realized I was leaning and inch backward into the seat curve with the sense that I've been chastised.

"You worked at Riverton." It is a statement, no answer required, yet I cannot curb my urge to comply, to specify.

"I started in 1914 as a housemaid."

He is embarrassed, for himself or for me I do not know. "Yes, well . . ." He moves on swiftly. "You worked for Theodore Luxton?" He says the name with some trepidation, as if by invoking Teddy's specter he may be tarred by his ignominy.

"Yes."

"Excellent! Did you see much of him?"

He means did I hear much? Can I tell him what went on behind closed doors? I fear I shall be a disappointment. "Not much. I was his wife's lady's maid at the time."

"You must've had quite a bit to do with Theodore in that case."

"No. Not really."

"But I've read that the servants' hall was the hub of a household's gossip. You must have been aware of what was going on?"

"No." A lot of it came out later, of course. I read about it, along with everybody else, in the newspapers. Visits to Germany, meetings with Hitler. I never believed the worst charges. They were guilty of little more than an admiration for Hitler's galvanization of the working classes, his ability to grow industry. Never mind that it was off the backs of slave labor. Few people knew that then. History was yet to prove him a madman.

"The meeting in 1936 with the German ambassador?"

"I no longer worked at Riverton then. I left a decade earlier."

He stops; he is disappointed, as I knew he would be. His line of questioning has been unfairly cut. Then some of his excitement is restored. "1926?"

"1925."

"Then you must have been there when that fellow, that poet, what's-his-name, killed himself."

The light is making me warm. I am tired. My heart flutters a little. Or something inside my heart flutters; an artery worn so thin that a flap has come loose, is waving about, lost, in the current of my blood.

"Yes," I hear myself say.

It is some consolation. "All right. We can talk about that instead?"

I can hear my heart now. It is pumping wetly, reluctantly.

"Grace?"

"She's very pale."

My head is light. So very tired.

"Dr. Bradley?"

"Grace? Grace!"

Whooshing like wind through a tunnel, an angry wind that drags behind it a summer storm, rushing towards me, faster and faster. It is my past, and it is coming for me. It is everywhere; in my ears, behind my eyes, pushing my ribs . . .

"Is there a doctor? Someone call an ambulance!"

Release. Disintegration. A million tiny particles falling through the funnel of time.

"Grace? She's all right. You'll be all right, Grace, you hear?"

Horses' hooves on cobble roads, motorcars with foreign names, delivery boys on bicycles, nannies parading perambulators, skipping ropes, hopscotch, Greta Garbo, the Original Dixieland Jazz Band, Bee Jackson, the charleston, Chanel Number 5, *The Mysterious Affair at Styles*, F. Scott Fitzgerald . . .

"Grace!"

My name?

"Grace?"

Sylvia? Hannah?

"She just collapsed. She was sitting there and—"

"Stand back now, ma'am. Let us get her in." A new voice.

The slam of a door.

A siren.

Motion.

"Grace . . . it's Sylvia. Hold on, you hear? I'm with you . . . taking you home . . . you just hold on . . ."

Hold on? To what? Ah . . . the letter, of course. It is in my hand. Hannah is waiting for me to bring her the letter. The street is icy and the winter snow has just begun to fall.

In the Depths

❋

IT is a cold winter and I am running. I can feel my blood, thick and warm in my veins, pulsing quickly beneath my cold face. Icy air makes my skin stretch taut across my cheekbones, as if it has shrunk smaller than its frame, is stretched over a rack. On tenterhooks, as Nancy would say.

The letter I clutch tightly in my fingers. It is small, the envelope marked a little where its sender's thumb smudged still-wet ink. It is hot off the press.

It is from an investigator. A real detective with an agency in Surrey Street, a secretary at the door and a typewriter on his desk. I have been dispatched to collect it in person for it contains—with any luck—information far too inflammatory to be risked in the Royal Mail or over the telephone. The letter, we hope, contains the whereabouts of Emmeline, who has disappeared. It threatens to become a scandal; I am one of the few who have been trusted.

The telephone call came from Riverton three days ago. Emmeline had been staying the weekend with family friends at an estate in Oxfordshire. She gave them the slip when they went to town for church. There was a car waiting for her. It was all planned. There is rumored to be a man involved.

I am pleased about the letter—I know how important it is that we find Emmeline—but I am excited for another reason too. I am seeing Alfred tonight. It will be the first time since that foggy evening many months ago. When he gave me Lucy Starling's address, told me he cared for me, and late that night returned me to my door. We have exchanged letters in the months since with increased reliability (and increased fondness), and now, finally, we are to see each other again. A real, proper engagement. Alfred is coming to London. He has saved his wages and purchased two tickets to *Princess Ida*. It is a stage show. It will be my first. I have passed the signs for shows when I have walked along the Haymarket on errands for Hannah, or on one of my afternoons off, but I have never been to see one.

It is my secret. I do not tell Hannah—she has too much else on her mind—and I do not tell the other staff at number seventeen. Mrs. Tibbit's culture of unkindness has ensured they are all the sorts to tease, to poke cruel fun for the smallest reason. Once, when Mrs. Tibbit saw me reading a letter (from Mrs. Townsend, thank goodness, and not Alfred!), she insisted on seeing it herself. She said it was her duty to ensure that the under-staff (under-staff!) were not behaving improperly, keeping up improper liaisons. The Master would not approve.

She is right in one way. Teddy has become strict recently in matters of staff. There are problems at work, and although he is not by nature ill-tempered, it seems even the mildest man is capable of bad humor when pushed. He has become preoccupied with matters of germs and hygiene, has begun issuing bottles of mouth gargle to the staff, insisting we use it; it is one of the habits he's adopted from his father.

That is why the other servants are not to be told of Emmeline. One of them would be sure to tell, to score points from having been the one to inform.

When I reach number seventeen, I enter via the servants' staircase and hurry through, anxious not to draw undue attention from Mrs. Tibbit.

Hannah is in her bedroom, waiting for me. She is pale, has been pale since she received the call from Mr. Hamilton last week. I hand her the letter and she immediately tears it open. She scans what is

written. Exhales quickly. "They've found her," she says without looking up. "Thank God. She's all right."

She continues reading; inhales, then shakes her head. "Oh, Emmeline," she says under her breath. "Emmeline."

She reaches the end, drops the letter to her side and looks at me.
She presses her lips together and nods to herself. "She must be fetched
immediately, before it's too late." She returns the letter to its envelope.
She does it agitatedly, cramming the paper too quickly. She has been
like that lately, since she saw the spiritualist: nervous and preoccupied.

"Right now, ma'am?"

"Immediately. It's already been three days."

"Would you like me to have the chauffeur bring the motorcar
around?"

"No," says Hannah quickly. "No. I can't risk anyone finding
out." She means Teddy and his family. "I'll drive myself."

"Ma'am?"

"Well, don't look so surprised, Grace. My father made motorcars. There's nothing to it."

"Shall I fetch your gloves and scarf, ma'am?"

She nods. "And some for yourself."

"For myself, ma'am?"

"You're coming, aren't you?" says Hannah, looking up with
wide eyes. "We stand more chance of rescuing her that way."

We. One of the sweetest words. Of course I go with her. She
needs my help. I will still be back for Alfred.

※

H E is a filmmaker, a Frenchman, and he is twice her age. Worse yet,
he is already married. Hannah tells me this as we drive. We are going
to his film studio in north London. The investigator says this is
where Emmeline has been staying.

When we arrive at the address, Hannah stops the car and we
both sit for a moment, looking through the window. It is a part of

London neither of us has seen before. The houses are short and narrow, and made of dark brick. There are people in the street, gambling it turns out. Teddy's Rolls-Royce is conspicuously shiny. Hannah takes out the investigator's letter and checks the address again. She turns to me and raises her eyebrows, nods.

It is little more than a house. Hannah knocks at the door and a woman answers. She has blond hair wrapped around curlers and is dressed in a silk wrap, cream in color, but dirty.

"Good morning," says Hannah. "My name is Hannah Luxton. *Mrs.* Hannah Luxton."

The woman shifts her weight so that a knee appears through the gap in her gown. She widens her eyes. "Sure, honey," she says in an accent similar to Deborah's Texan friend. "Whatever you like. You here 'bout the audition?"

Hannah blinks. "I'm here about my sister. Emmeline Hartford?"

The woman frowns.

"A little shorter than me," says Hannah, "light hair, blue eyes?" She pulls a photograph from her bag, hands it to the woman.

"Oh, yeah, yeah," she says, handing the photograph back. "That's Baby all right."

Hannah exhales with relief. "Is she here? Is she all right?"

"Sure," the woman says.

"Thank goodness," Hannah says. "Well then. I'd like to see her."

"Sorry, sugar. No can do. Baby's in the middle of shooting."

"Shooting?"

"She's in the middle of shooting a scene. Philippe don't like to be disturbed once filming's started." The woman shifts her weight and the left knee replaces the right, peeking through where her gown parts. She tilts her head to the side. "You all can wait inside if you like?"

Hannah looks at me. I raise my shoulders helplessly, and we follow the woman into the house.

We are shown through the hall, up the stairs and into a small room with an unmade double bed in its center. The room's curtains are drawn so there is no natural light. In its place three lamps have been turned on, each shade draped with a red silk scarf.

Against one wall is a chair, and on the chair is a piece of luggage we recognize as Emmeline's. On one of the bedside tables is a man's pipe set.

"Oh, Emmeline . . ." says Hannah, and is unable to continue.

"Would you like a glass of water, ma'am?" I say.

She nods, automatically. "Yes . . ."

I don't fancy going back downstairs to find a kitchen. The woman who showed us in has disappeared and I don't know what might lurk behind closed doors. Instead, I find a tiny bathroom down the hall. The benchtop is covered with brushes and make-up pencils, powders and false eyelashes. The only cup I can see is a heavy mug with a grimy collection of concentric rings inside. I try to wash it clean, but the stains are resistant. I return to Hannah empty-handed. "I'm sorry, ma'am . . ."

She looks at me. Takes a deep breath. "Grace," she says, "I don't want to shock you. But I believe Emmeline might be living with a man."

"Yes, ma'am," I say, careful not to reveal my own horror in case it inflames hers. "It would appear so."

The door bursts open and we swing around. Emmeline is standing in the entrance. I am stunned. Her blond hair is curled up high on top, cupping her cheeks, and long black lashes make her eyes impossibly large. Her lips are painted in bright red and she is wearing a silk robe like the woman downstairs. Grown-up affectations all, and yet she looks younger somehow. It is her face, I realize, her expression. She lacks the artifice of adulthood: she is genuinely shocked to see us and unable to conceal it. "What are you doing here?" she says.

"Thank goodness," Hannah says, breathing a sigh of relief, rushing to Emmeline.

"What are you doing here?" Emmeline says again. By now she has regained her poise, droopy lids have replaced wide eyes, and the little round *o* of her lips has become a pout.

"We've come for you," says Hannah. "Hurry up and dress so we can leave."

Emmeline struts slowly to the dressing table, sinks onto the stool. She shakes a cigarette from its crumpled packet, pouts when it catches, then lights it. After she's exhaled a stream of smoke, she says, "I'm not going anywhere. You can't make me."

Hannah seizes her arm and pulls her to her feet. "You are and I can. We're going home."

"*This* is my home now," says Emmeline, shaking her arm free. "I'm an actress. I'm going to be a film star. Philippe says I have the look."

"I'm sure he does," says Hannah grimly. "Grace, gather Emmeline's bags while I help her dress."

Hannah releases Emmeline's robe and we both gasp. Underneath is a negligee, see-through. Pink nipples peek from beneath black lace. "Emmeline!" says Hannah as I turn away quickly to the suitcase. "What kind of film have you been making?"

"A love story," says Emmeline, wrapping the robe around her middle again and dragging on her cigarette.

Hannah's hands cover her mouth and she glances at me—round blue eyes, a mix of horror and concern and anger. It is far worse than either of us imagined. We are both lost for words. I hold out one of Emmeline's dresses. Hannah hands it to Emmeline. "Get dressed," she manages to say. "Just get dressed."

There is a noise outside, heavy feet on the stairs, and suddenly a man is at the door; a short, mustachioed man, stout and swarthy with an air of slow arrogance.

"Philippe," says Emmeline triumphantly, pulling free from Hannah.

"What is this?" he says in a heavy French accent. "What do you think you are doing?" he says to Hannah, striding to Emmeline's side, placing a proprietorial hand on her arm.

"Taking her home," Hannah says.

"And who," says Philippe, eyeing Hannah up and down, "are you?"

"Her sister."

This seems to please him. He sits on the end of the bed, pulls Emmeline down next to him, never taking his eyes from Hannah. "What's the rush?" he says. "Perhaps big sister will join Baby in some shots, eh?"

Hannah inhales quickly, then regains her composure. "Certainly not. We are both leaving this minute."

"I'm not," says Emmeline.

Philippe shrugs in the way only Frenchmen can. "It seems she does not wish to go."

"She hasn't a choice," says Hannah. She looks at me. "Have you finished packing, Grace?"

"Almost, ma'am."

Only then does Philippe notice me. "A third sister?" He raises an appraising eyebrow and I squirm beneath the unwarranted attention, as uncomfortable as if I were naked.

Emmeline laughs. "Oh, Philippe. Don't tease. That's only Grace, Hannah's maid."

Though I am flattered at his mistake, I am grateful when Emmeline tugs at his sleeve and he turns his gaze away.

"Tell her," Emmeline says to Philippe. "Tell her about us." She smiles at Hannah with the unchecked enthusiasm of a seventeen-year-old. "We've eloped, we're going to be married."

"And what does your wife think of that, monsieur?" says Hannah.

"He doesn't have a wife," says Emmeline. "Not yet."

"Shame on you, monsieur," says Hannah, voice quivering. "My sister is only seventeen."

As if spring-loaded, Philippe's arm pulls away from Emmeline's shoulders.

"Seventeen's old enough to be in love," says Emmeline. "We'll marry when I'm eighteen, won't we, Philly?"

Philippe smiles an awkward smile, wipes his hands on his trouser legs and stands.

"Won't we?" says Emmeline, voice rising a tone. "Like we talked about? Tell her."

Hannah tosses the dress into Emmeline's lap. "Yes, monsieur, do tell."

One of the lamps flickers and the light extinguishes. Philippe shrugs. "I, ah . . . I . . ."

"Stop it, Hannah," says Emmeline, voice trembling. "You're going to ruin everything."

"I'm taking my sister home," says Hannah. "And if you make this any more difficult than it already is, my husband will ensure you never make another film. He has friends in the police and the government. I'm sure they'd be very interested to know about the films you're making."

Philippe is very helpful after that; he collects some more of Emmeline's things from the bathroom and packs them in her bag, though not with as much care as I would like. He carries her bags to the car, and while Emmeline is crying and telling him how much she loves him and begging him to tell Hannah that they're to be married, he stays very quiet. Finally, he looks at Hannah, frightened by the things Emmeline is saying, and just what kind of trouble Hannah's husband could make for him, and he says, "I do not know what she talks about. She is crazy. She told me she was twenty-one."

❦

EMMELINE cries all the way home, hot angry tears. I doubt she hears a word of Hannah's lecture about responsibility and reputation and running away not being the answer.

"He loves me," is all she says when Hannah reaches the end. "Why did you have to come and ruin things?"

"Ruin things?" Hannah says. "I rescued you. You're lucky we got there before you got yourself into real trouble. He's already married. He lied to you so you'd make his disgusting films."

Emmeline stares at Hannah, her bottom lip trembling. "You just can't stand it that I'm happy," Emmeline says, "that I'm in love. That something wonderful has finally happened to me. Someone loves *me* the best."

Hannah doesn't answer. We have reached number seventeen and the chauffeur is coming to park the car.

As Hannah and Emmeline disappear into the house I hurry down the servants' stairs. I do not own a wristwatch, but feel sure it must be getting on for five. The stage show starts at half past the hour. I push through the door, but it is Mrs. Tibbit waiting for me, not Alfred.

"Alfred?" I say, out of breath.

"Nice fellow, him," she says, a sly smile tugging at her mole. "Pity he had to go so soon."

My heart sinks and I glance at the clock. "How long ago did he leave?"

"Oh, some time now," she says, turning back towards the kitchen. "Sat around here a while, watching the time tick by. Until I put him out of his misery."

"Out of his misery?"

"Told him he was wasting his time. That you were out on one of your *secret* errands for the Mistress and it was anyone's guess when you'd be back."

✳

I AM running again. Down Regent Street towards Piccadilly. If I go quickly perhaps I can catch him up. I curse that meddling witch, Mrs. Tibbit, while I go. What business had she telling Alfred I wouldn't be back? And to advise him I was running an errand for Hannah, on my day off too! It's as if she knew the very way to inflict the largest wound.

As Regent Street opens into Piccadilly, the noise and bustle escalate. The Saqui & Lawrence clocks are arranged at half past five—

end of business—and the circus is clogged with traffic: pedestrian and automotive. Gentlemen and businessmen, ladies and errand boys jostle for safe passage. I squeeze between a motorbus and a stalled motorized taxi, am almost flattened by a horse-drawn cart laden with fat hessian sacks.

Down the Haymarket I hurry, jumping over an extended cane, invoking the ire of its monocled owner. I stay close to the buildings where the pavement is less traveled until, breathless, I reach Her Majesty's Theatre. I lean against the stone wall directly beneath the playbill, scanning the laughing, frowning, speaking, nodding faces going by, waiting for my gaze to strike that familiar template. A thin gentleman and a thinner lady rush up the theatre stairs. He presents two tickets and they are swept inside. In the distance, a clock—Big Ben?—strikes the quarter-hour. Could Alfred still be coming? Has he changed his mind? Or am I too late and he's already in his seat?

I wait to hear Big Ben sound the hour, then another quarter-hour for good measure. No one has entered or left the theatre since the pair of well-dressed greyhounds. By now I am sitting on the stairs. My breath is caught and I am resigned. I will not be seeing Alfred this evening.

When a street cleaner risks a lewd smile at me, it is finally time to leave. I gather my shawl about my shoulders, straighten my hat and set off back for number seventeen. I will write to Alfred. Explain what happened. About Hannah and Mrs. Tibbit; I may even tell him the whole truth, about Emmeline and Philippe and the almost-scandal. For all his ideas about exploitation and feudal societies, Alfred is sure to understand. Isn't he?

❋

HANNAH has told Teddy about Emmeline and he is outraged. The timing couldn't be worse, he says: he and his father are on the verge of amalgamating with Briggs Bank. They'll be one of the biggest banking syndicates in London. The world. If word gets out about this filth, it will ruin him, ruin all of them.

Hannah nods and apologizes again, reminds Teddy that Emmeline is young and naive and gullible. That she will grow out of it.

Teddy grunts. He is grunting a lot these days. He runs a hand through his dark hair, which is turning gray. Emmeline has had no guidance, he says; that's the problem. Creatures that grow up in the wilderness turn out wild.

Hannah reminds him that Emmeline is growing up in the same place she did, but Teddy only raises an eyebrow.

He huffs. He doesn't have time to discuss it further; he has to get to the club. He has Hannah write down the filmmaker's address and tells her not to keep things from him in future. There is no room for secrets between married people.

The next morning, when I am tidying Hannah's dressing table, I find a note with my name at its top. She has left it for me; must have put it there after I dressed her. I unfold it, my fingers trembling. Why? Not with fear or dread or any of the usual emotions that make people tremble. It is with expectation, unexpectedness, excitement.

When I open it, however, it is not written in English. It is a series of curves and lines and dots, marked carefully across the page. It is shorthand, I realize as I stare at it. I recognize it from the books I found, years ago, back at Riverton, when I was tidying Hannah's room. She has left me a note in our secret language, a language I cannot read.

I keep the note with me all through the day while I clean, and stitch, and mend. But even though I make it through my chores, I am unable to concentrate. Half my mind is always occupied, wondering what it says, how I can find out. I look for books so that I might decode it—did Hannah bring them here from Riverton?—but I cannot find any.

A few days later, while I'm clearing tea, Hannah leans close to me and says, "Did you get my note?"

I tell her I did and my stomach tightens when she says, "Our secret," and smiles. The first smile I have seen in some time.

I know then it is important, a secret, and I am the only person she has trusted. I must either confess or find a way to read it.

※

DAYS later, it comes to me. I pull from beneath my bed *The Return of Sherlock Holmes* and let it fall open to a well-marked spot. There, between two favorite stories, is my special secret place. From amongst Alfred's letters, I pluck a small scrap of notepaper, kept for over a year. I am lucky I still have it; kept not because it contains her address, but because it is written in his hand. I used to take it out regularly: look at it, smell it, replay the day he gave it to me, but have not done so in months, not since he started to write his regular, more affectionate letters. I remove it from its safe-keeping: Lucy Starling's address.

I have never visited her before, have never needed to. My position keeps me busy and what little spare time I have is spent reading, or writing to Alfred. Besides, something else has stopped me contacting her. A small flame of envy, ridiculous but potent, sparked when Alfred spoke her first name so casually that evening in the fog.

As I reach the flat I'm racked with doubt. Am I doing the right thing? Does she still live here? Should I have worn my second, better dress? I ring the doorbell and an old lady answers. I am relieved and disappointed.

"I'm sorry," I say, "I was looking for someone else."

"Yes?" says the old lady.

"An old friend."

"Name?"

"Miss Starling," I say, not that it's any of her business. "Lucy Starling."

I have nodded farewell and am turning to leave when she says, somewhat slyly, "First floor. Second door on the left."

318

I go carefully along the hall. It is dark. The only window, above the stairwell, is grimy with dust from the road. Second on the left. I knock on the door. There is rustling behind it and I know she is home. I take a breath.

The door opens. It is her. Just as I remember.

She looks at me a moment. "Yes?" Blinks. "Do I know you?"

The landlady is still watching. She has climbed up the first few stairs to keep me in her sights. I glance quickly at her, then back at Miss Starling.

"My name is Grace. Grace Reeves. I knew you at Riverton Manor?"

Realization lights her face. "Grace. Of course. How lovely to see you." The in-between voice that used to set her apart amongst the staff at Riverton. She smiles, stands aside and gestures for me to come in.

I have not thought this far ahead. The idea of visiting at all came to me rather suddenly.

Miss Starling is standing in a little sitting room, waiting for me to sit so that she may do so.

She offers a cup of tea and it seems impolite to refuse. When she disappears into what I presume is a kitchenette, I allow my gaze to tiptoe over the room. It is lighter than the hall, and her windows, I notice, like the flat itself, are scrupulously clean. She has made the best of a modest situation.

She returns with a tray. Teapot, sugar bowl, two cups.

"What a lovely surprise," she says. In her gaze is the question she is too polite to ask.

"I've come to ask a favor," I say.

She nods. "What is it?"

"You know shorthand?"

"Of course," she says, frowning a little. "Pitman's and Gregg's."

It is the last opportunity I have to back out, to leave. I could tell her I made a mistake, put back my teacup and head for the door.

Hurry down the stairs, into the street and never return. But then I would never know. And I must. "Would you read something for me?" I hear myself say. "Tell me what it says?"

"Of course."

I hand her the note. Hold my breath, hoping I have made the right decision.

Her pale eyes scan, line by line, excruciatingly slowly it seems. Finally she clears her throat. "It says, *Thank you for your help in the unfortunate film affair. How would I have got on without you? T. was none too pleased . . . I'm sure you can imagine. I haven't told him everything, certainly not about our visit to that dreadful place. He doesn't take kindly to secrets. I know I can count on you, my trusted Grace, more like a sister than a maid.*" She looks up at me. "Does that make sense to you?"

I nod, I am unable to speak. More like a sister. A sister. I am suddenly in two places at once: here in Lucy Starling's modest sitting room, and far and long ago in the Riverton nursery, gazing longingly from the bookcase at two girls with matching hair and matching bows. Matching secrets.

Miss Starling returns the note, but makes no further comment on its contents. I realize, suddenly, that it may have raised suspicions, with its talk of unfortunate affairs and keeping secrets.

"It's part of a game," I say quickly, then slower, luxuriating in the falsehood. "A game we sometimes play."

"How nice," says Miss Starling, smiling unconcernedly. She is a secretary and is used to learning and forgetting the confidences of others.

We finish our tea chatting about London and the old days at Riverton. I am surprised to hear that Miss Starling was always nervous when she had to come downstairs. That she found Mr. Hamilton more imposing than Mr. Frederick. We both laugh when I tell her we were as nervous as she.

"Of me?" she says, patting the corners of her eyes with a handkerchief. "Of all the funny things."

When I stand to leave, she asks me to come again and I tell her I will. I mean it too. I wonder why I have not done so sooner: she is a kind person and neither of us has other contacts in London. She walks me to the door and we say goodbye.

As I turn to leave, I see something on her reading table. Lean closer to make sure.

A theatre program.

I'd have thought nothing of it, only the name is familiar.

"Princess Ida?" I say.

"Yes." Her own gaze drops to the table. "I went last week."

"Oh?"

"It was enormous fun," she says. "You really must go if you have the chance."

"Yes," I say. "I had planned to."

"Now that I think of it," she says, "it's really quite a coincidence you should come today."

"A coincidence?" Coldness spreading beneath my skin.

"You'll never guess who I went to the theatre with."

Oh, but I fear I will.

"Alfred Steeple. You remember Alfred? From Riverton?"

"Yes," I seem to say.

"It was really quite unexpected. He had a spare ticket. Someone canceled on him at the last minute. He said he was all set to go alone and then he remembered I was in London. We ran into each other over a year ago and he still remembered my address. So we went together; it was a shame to waste a ticket, you know what they cost these days."

Do I imagine the pink that spreads under her pale, freckled cheeks, makes her seem gauche and girlish, despite being at least ten years older than I?

Somehow I manage to nod goodbye as she closes the door behind me. In the distance a car horn sounds.

Alfred, my Alfred, took another woman to the theatre. Laughed with her, bought her supper, walked her home.

I start down the stairs.

While I was looking for him, searching the streets, he was here, asking Miss Starling to accompany him instead. Giving her the ticket intended for me.

I stop, lean against the wall. Close my eyes and clench my fists. I cannot rid my mind of this image: the two of them, arm in arm, smiling as they relive the evening's events. Just as I had dreamed Alfred and I would. It is unbearable.

A noise close by. I open my eyes. The landlady is standing at the bottom of the stairs, gnarled hand resting on the banister, spectacled eyes trained on me. And on her unkind face an expression of inexplicable satisfaction. Of course he went with her, her expression says, what would he want with the likes of you when he could have someone like Lucy Starling? You've got too big for your boots, aimed too high. You should've listened to your mother and minded your place.

I want to slap her cruel face.

I hurry down the remaining stairs, brush past the old woman and into the street.

And I vow never to see Miss Lucy Starling again.

❀

H A N N A H and Teddy are arguing about the war. It seems everyone across London is arguing about the war these days. Enough time has passed and, though the grief has not gone, will never go, distance is allowing people a more critical eye.

Hannah is making poppies out of red tissue paper and black wire, and I am helping. But my mind is not on my work. I am still afflicted with thoughts of Alfred and Lucy Starling. I am bewildered and I am cross, but most of all I am hurt that he could transfer his affections so easily. I have written him another letter, but I am yet to hear back. In the meantime, I feel strangely empty; at night, in my darkened room, I have been subject to the odd rush of tears. It is easier by day, I am better able to put such emotions aside, affix my servant's mask and try to be the best lady's maid I can. And I must. For without Alfred, Hannah is all I have.

The poppies are Hannah's new cause. It's to do with the poppies on Flanders fields, she says. The poppies in a poem by a Canadian medical officer who did not survive the war. It's how we're going to remember the war dead this year.

Teddy thinks it unnecessary. He believes those who died at war made a worthy sacrifice, but that it is time to move on.

"It wasn't a sacrifice," Hannah says, finishing another poppy, "it was a waste. Their lives were wasted. Those who died and those who came back: the living dead, who sit on the street corners with bottles of liquor and beggars' hats."

"Sacrifice, waste, same thing," says Teddy. "You are being pedantic."

Hannah says he is being obtuse. She doesn't look up as she adds that he would do well to wear a poppy himself. It might help stop the trouble downstairs.

There have been difficulties lately. They started after Lloyd George ennobled Simion for services during the war. Some of the servants were in the war themselves, or lost fathers and brothers, and don't think too much of Simion's war record. There is not a lot of love lost for folks like Simion and Teddy, who are seen to have made money from the deaths of others.

Teddy doesn't answer Hannah, or not fully. He mutters something about folks being ungrateful and how they should be pleased to have a job in these times, but he does pick up a poppy, twirling it by its black wire stem. He is quiet for a while, pretending absorption in the newspaper. Hannah and I continue to twist red tissue paper, to bind the petals onto stems.

Teddy folds his newspaper and tosses it onto the table beside him. He stands and straightens his jacket. He is off to the club, he says. He comes to Hannah's side and threads the poppy lightly into her hair. She can wear it for him, he says, it suits her better than it does him. Teddy bends and kisses her cheek, and then he strides across the room. As he reaches the door he hesitates as if he's remembered something, and he turns.

"There's one sure way to lay the war to rest," he says, "and that's to replace the lives that were lost with new ones."

It is Hannah's turn not to answer. She stiffens, but not so that anyone would notice who wasn't looking for the reaction. She does not look at me. Her fingers reach up and slip Teddy's poppy from her hair.

※

I N the autumn of 1921, an attempt is made on me. A friend of Estella's, Lady Pemberton-Brown, corners me at a country weekend and offers me a position. She begins by admiring my needlepoint, then tells me that a good lady's maid is hard to find these days and she would very much like me to come and work for her.

I am flattered: it is the first time my services have been sought. The Pemberton-Browns live at Glenfield Hall and are one of the oldest and grandest families in all of England. Mr. Hamilton used to tell us stories about Glenfield, the household against which every other English butler compared his own.

I thank her for her kind words, but tell her I couldn't possibly leave my current position. I tell her that I know my place, I know where I belong. With whom, to whom.

Weeks later, when we are back at number seventeen, Hannah finds out about Lady Pemberton-Brown. She calls me to the drawing room one morning and I know as soon as I enter that she is not pleased, although I don't yet know why. She is pacing.

"Can you imagine, Grace, what it's like to find out in the middle of a luncheon, with seven other women intent on making me look a fool, that an attempt has been made on my lady's maid?"

I inhale; am caught unawares.

"To be sitting amid a group of women and to have them start on about it, laughing if you please, acting all surprised that I didn't know. That such a thing could happen right under my nose. Why didn't you tell me?"

"I'm sorry, ma'am—"

"I should think so. I need to be able to trust you, Grace. I thought I could, after all this time, after all we've been through together . . ."

I have still not heard from Alfred. Weariness and worry lend my voice a jagged edge. "I told Lady Pemberton-Brown no, ma'am. I didn't think to mention it because I didn't think to accept."

Hannah stops, looks at me, exhales. She sits on the edge of the sofa and shakes her head. She smiles feebly. "Oh, Grace. I'm sorry. How perfectly beastly of me. I don't know what's come over me, behaving like this." She seems paler than usual.

She rests her forehead lightly in one of her hands and says nothing for a minute. When she lifts her head she looks straight at me and speaks in a low, quivering voice. "It's just so different to how I thought it would be, Grace."

She appears so feeble I am immediately sorry for having spoken sternly to her. "What is, ma'am?"

"Everything." She gestures halfheartedly. "This. This room. This house. London. My life." She looks at me. "I feel so ill equipped. Sometimes I try to trace back through my mind to see where I made the first wrong choice." Her gaze drifts towards the window. "I feel like Hannah Hartford, the real one, ran off to live her real life and left me here to fill her place." After a moment she turns back to me. "Do you remember earlier this year, Grace, when I saw the spiritualist?"

"Yes, ma'am." Tremors of misgiving.

"She didn't read for me in the end."

Relief, short-lived, as she continues.

"She couldn't. Wouldn't. She intended to: sat me down, had me draw a card. But when I gave it to her, she slid it back, reshuffled and had me draw again. I could tell by her face it was the same card again, and I knew which one it was. The death card." Hannah stands and paces across the room. "She didn't want to tell me, not at first. She tried my palm instead, wouldn't read that, either. She said she didn't know what it meant, that it was foggy, her vision was foggy, but she said one thing was sure." Hannah turns to face me. "She said death was hanging around me and I was to watch my step. Death past or death future, she couldn't tell, but there was a darkness."

It takes all the conviction I can muster to tell her she's not to let it bother her, that it was just as likely a ploy to get more money from her, to make sure she came back for further readings. After all, it's a safe bet in London these days that everyone's lost someone they love, especially those seeking the services of a spiritualist. But Hannah shakes her head impatiently.

"I know what it meant. I worked it out myself. I've been reading about it. It was a metaphorical death. Sometimes the cards speak in metaphors. It's me. I'm dead on the inside; I've felt it for a long time. As if I died and everything that's happening is someone else's strange and awful dream."

I don't know what to say. I assure her she isn't dead. That everything is real.

She smiles sadly. "Ah then. That's worse. If this is real life, I have nothing."

For once I know the perfect thing to say. *More like a sister than a maid.* "You have me, ma'am."

She meets my eyes then and takes my hand. Seizes it, almost roughly. "Don't leave me, Grace, please don't leave me."

"I won't, ma'am," I say, touched by her solemnity. "I never will."

"Promise?"

"I promise."

And I kept my word. For better and for worse.

RESURRECTION

※

DARKNESS. Stillness. Shadowy figures. This is not London; this is not the morning room at number seventeen Grosvenor Square. Hannah has vanished. For now.

"Welcome home." A voice in the dark, someone leaning over me.

I blink. And again, slowly.

I know the voice. It is Sylvia, and I am suddenly old, tired.

"You've been asleep for a long time. You gave us quite a scare. How do you feel?"

Displaced. Left over. Out of time.

"Would you like a glass of water?"

I must nod, because a straw is in my mouth. I sip. Lukewarm water. Familiar.

I am unaccountably sad. No, not unaccountably. I am sad because the scales have tipped and I know what's coming.

※

IT is Saturday again. A week has passed since the spring fair. Since my episode, as it is now known. I am in my room, in my bed. The curtains are open and the sun is shimmering in off the heath. It is morning and there are birds. I am expecting a visitor. Sylvia has been in and prepared me. I am propped like Miss Polly's dolly against a stack of pillows. The top sheet she has folded over neatly to form a wide smooth strip beneath my hands. She is determined to make me presentable. Bless her, she has even brushed out my hair. And this time I remembered to thank her.

There is a knock.

Ursula leans her head around the door, checks that I am awake, smiles. Her hair is pulled back today to reveal her face.

She is beside the bed now, head inclined, looking down at me. Those large dark eyes: eyes that belong in an oil painting.

"How are you?" she says, as everybody says.

"Much better. Thank you for coming."

She shakes her head rapidly from side to side; don't be silly, her gesture says. "I'd have come earlier. I didn't know until yesterday, when I called."

"It's as well you didn't. I've been in rather large demand. My daughter has been installed since it happened. I gave her quite a scare."

"I know. I saw her in the foyer." She smiles conspiratorially. "She told me not to excite you."

"God forbid."

She sits on the chair near my pillows, rests her shoulder bag on the floor beside.

"The film," I say. "Tell me how your film is coming along."

"It's almost ready," she says. "The final edit's done and we've almost finished the post-sound and the soundtrack."

"Soundtrack," I say. Of course they are to have a soundtrack. Tragedy should always play out against music. "What sort?"

"There are a few songs from the twenties," she says, "dance songs mainly, and some piano. Sad, beautiful, romantic piano, Tori Amos–style."

I must look blank, for she continues, scrabbling for musicians more my vintage.

"There's some Debussy, some Prokofiev."

"Chopin?"

She raises her eyebrows. "Chopin? No. Should there be?" Her face falls. "You're not going to tell me one of the girls was a Chopin nut, are you?"

328

"No," I say. "It was their brother—David—who played Chopin."

"Oh, thank goodness. He's not really a major character. He died a little too early to affect things."

This is debatable, but I don't debate it.

"What's it like?" I say. "Is it a good film?"

She bites her lip, exhales. "I think so. I hope so. I'm afraid I've lost perspective."

"Is it as you imagined?"

She considers. "Yes and no. It's difficult to explain." She exhales again. "Before I started, when it was all in my head, the project was full of unlimited potential. Now that it's on film, it feels bordered by limitations."

"I suspect that's the way with most endeavors."

She nods. "I feel such a responsibility to them, though; to their story. I wanted it to be perfect."

"Nothing's ever perfect."

"No." She smiles. "Sometimes I worry I'm the wrong person to tell their story. What if I've got it wrong? What do I know?"

"Lytton Strachey used to say ignorance was the first requisite of the historian."

She frowns.

"Ignorance clarifies," I say. "It selects and omits with placid perfection."

"Too much truth gets in the way of a good story, is that what you mean?"

"Something like that."

"But surely truth is the most important thing? Particularly in a biopic."

"What is truth?" I say, and I would shrug if I had the strength.

"It's what really happened." She looks at me as if I might finally have lost my marbles. "You know that. You spent years digging into the past. Searching for the truth."

"So I did. I wonder if I ever found it." I am slipping down

against the pillows. Ursula notices and lifts me gently by the upper arms. I continue before she can debate with me any further on semantics. "I wanted to be a detective," I say. "When I was young."

"Really? A police detective? What changed your mind?"

"Policemen make me nervous."

She grins. "That would have been a problem."

"I became an archaeologist instead. They're not so dissimilar when you think about it."

"The victims have just been dead longer."

"Yes," I say. "It was Agatha Christie who first gave me the idea. Or one of her characters. He said to Hercule Poirot, 'You would have made a good archaeologist, Mr. Poirot. You have the gift of recreating the past.' I read it during the war. The second war. I'd sworn off mystery stories by then, but one of the other nurses had it and old habits die hard."

Ursula smiles, then starts suddenly. "Oh! That reminds me. I brought something for you." She reaches into her shoulder bag and pulls out a small rectangular box.

It is the size of a book, but it rattles. "It's a tape set," she says. "Agatha Christie." She shrugs sheepishly. "I didn't realize you'd sworn off mysteries."

"Never mind that. It was a temporary swearing-off, a misguided attempt to shed my youthful self. I picked up where I left off the minute the war ended."

She points to the tape recorder on my bedside table. "Shall I put a tape in before I go?"

"Yes," I say. "Do."

She tears off the plastic packaging, removes the first tape and opens my Dictaphone. "There's one in here already." She holds the cassette to show me. It is the tape I am currently recording for Marcus. "Is it for him? For your grandson?"

I nod. "Just leave it on the table, if you don't mind; I'll need it later." And I will. Time is closing in on me, I can feel it, and I am determined to finish before it comes.

"Have you heard anything from him?" she says.

"Not yet."

"You will," she says firmly. "I'm sure of it."

I am too weary for faith, but nod anyway; her own is so fervent.

Ursula puts Agatha in place and returns the Dictaphone to the table. "There you are." She puts her bag over her shoulder. She is leaving.

I reach for her hand as she turns, clutch it in mine. So smooth. "I want to ask you something," I say. "A favor, before Ruth . . ."

"Of course," she says. "Anything." She is quizzical, has detected the urgency in my voice. "What is it?"

"Riverton. I want to see Riverton. I want you to take me."

She tightens her lips, frowns. I have put her on the spot.

"Please."

"I don't know, Grace. What would Ruth say?"

"She'd say no. Which is why I've asked you."

She looks towards the wall. I have troubled her. "Maybe I could bring you some of the footage we shot there instead? I could have it put on video—"

"No," I say firmly. "I need to go back." Still she looks away. "Soon," I say. "I need to go soon."

Her eyes return to mine and I know she will say yes even before she nods.

I nod back, thanking her, then I point to Ursula's cassettes. "I met her once, you know. Agatha Christie."

❋

IT was late in 1922. Teddy and Hannah were hosting a dinner at number seventeen. Teddy and his father had some business with Archibald Christie, something to do with an invention he was interested in developing.

They entertained so often in those early years of the decade. But I remember that dinner particularly for a number of reasons. One was the presence of Agatha Christie herself. She had only published one book at that time, *The Mysterious Affair at Styles*, but already Hercule Poirot had replaced Sherlock Holmes in my imagination.

Emmeline was there too. She'd been in London for a month. She was eighteen and had made her debut from number seventeen. There was no talk of finding her a husband as there had been with Hannah. Only four years had passed since the ball at Riverton and yet the times had changed. Girls had changed. They had liberated themselves from their corsets only to throw themselves at the tyranny of the "diet plan." They were all coltish legs, bound chests and smooth scalps. They no longer whispered behind their hands and hid behind shy glances. They joked and drank, smoked and swore with the boys. Waistlines had slipped, fabrics were thin and morals were thinner.

Maybe this accounted for the unusual dinner conversation that night, or perhaps it was Mrs. Christie herself. Not to mention the spate of recent newspaper articles on the subject.

"They'll both be hanged," said Teddy brightly. "Edith Thompson and Freddy Bywaters. Just like that other fellow who killed his wife. Earlier this year, in Wales. What was his name? Army fellow, wasn't he, Colonel?"

"Major Herbert Rowse Armstrong," said Colonel Christie.

Emmeline shuddered theatrically. "Imagine killing your very own wife, someone you're supposed to love."

"Most murders are done by people who purport to love each other," said Mrs. Christie crisply.

"People are becoming more violent on the whole," said Teddy, lighting a cigar. "A fellow only has to open the newspaper to see that. Despite the ban on handguns."

"This is England, Mr. Luxton," said Colonel Christie. "Home of the fox hunt. Obtaining firearms isn't difficult."

"I have a friend who always carries a handgun," Emmeline said airily.

"You do not," said Hannah, shaking her head. She looked at Mrs. Christie. "My sister has seen too many American films, I'm afraid."

"I do," Emmeline insisted. "This fellow I pal around with—who shall remain nameless—said it was as easy as buying a packet of cigarettes. He offered to get me one any time I like."

"Harry Bentley, I'll wager," said Teddy.

"Harry?" said Emmeline, flashing wide eyes rimmed with black lashes. "Harry wouldn't hurt a fly! His brother Tom, perhaps."

"You know too many of the wrong people," said Teddy. "Need I remind you that handguns are illegal, not to mention dangerous."

Emmeline shrugged. "I've known how to shoot since I was a girl. All the ladies in our family can shoot. Grandmama would have disowned us if we couldn't. Just ask Hannah: she tried to dodge the hunt one year, told Grandmama she didn't believe it was right to kill defenceless animals. Grandmama had something to say about that, didn't she, Hannah?"

Hannah raised her eyebrows and took a sip of red wine as Emmeline continued. "She said, 'Nonsense. You're a Hartford. Shooting's in your blood.' "

"Be that as it may," said Teddy. "There will be no handguns in this house. I can imagine what my constituents would make of my possessing illegal firearms!"

Emmeline rolled her eyes as Hannah said, "Future constituents."

"Do relax, Teddy," said Emmeline. "You won't have to worry about firearms if you go on like that. You'll give yourself a heart attack. I didn't say I was going to get a handgun. I was just saying that a girl can't be too careful these days. What with husbands killing wives and wives killing husbands. Don't you agree, Mrs. Christie?"

Agatha Christie had been watching the exchange with wry amusement. "I'm afraid I don't much care for firearms," she said. "Poisons are more my thing."

※

LATE in the evening, after the Christies had left, I pulled my copy of *The Mysterious Affair at Styles* from under my bed. It had been a gift from Alfred, and I was so absorbed with rereading his inscription that I barely registered the telephone ringing. Mr. Boyle must have answered the call and transferred it upstairs to Hannah. I thought nothing of it. It was only when Mr. Boyle knocked on my door and announced the Mistress would see me that I thought to worry.

Hannah was still dressed in her oyster-colored silk. Like liquid. Her pale hair was pressed in waves about her face and a strand of diamonds was pinned around the crown of her head. She was standing with her back to me and turned as I entered the room.

"Grace," she said, taking my hands in hers. The gesture worried me. It was too personal. Something had happened.

"Ma'am?"

"Sit down, please." She led me to sit by her on the sofa and then she looked at me, blue eyes round with concern.

"Ma'am?"

"That was your aunt on the telephone."

And I knew.

"I'm so sorry, Grace." She shook her head gently. "Your mother took a fall. There was nothing the doctor could do."

⁂

HANNAH arranged my transport back to Saffron Green. Next afternoon the car was brought round from the mews and I was packed into the back seat. It was very kind of her and much more than I expected; I was quite prepared to take the train. Nonsense, Hannah said, she was only sorry Teddy's upcoming client dinner prohibited her from accompanying me.

I watched out of the motorcar window as the driver turned down one street and then another, and London became less grand, more sprawling and decrepit, and eventually disappeared behind us. The countryside fled by, and the farther east we drove the colder it became. Sleet peppered the windows, turning the landscape bleary; winter had bleached the world of vitality. Snow-dusted meadows bled into the mauve sky, gradually giving way to the ancient wildwood of Essex, all gray-brown and lichen green.

We left the main road and followed the lane to Saffron through the cold and lonely fen. Silvery reeds quivered in frozen streams and Grandfather's beard clung like lace to naked trees. I counted the bends and, for some reason, held my breath, releasing it only after we had passed the Riverton turnoff. The driver continued into the village and delivered me to the graystone cottage on Market Street, wedged silently, as it had always been, between its two sisters. The driver held the door for me and set my small suitcase on the wet pavement.

"There you are then," he said.

I thanked him and he nodded.

"I'll collect you in five days," he said, "like the Mistress told me."

I watched the motorcar disappear down the lane, turn into Saffron High Street, and I felt a great urge to call him back, to beg him not to leave me here. But it was too late for that. I stood in the dim dusk looking up at the house where I had spent the first fourteen years of my life, the place where Mother had lived and died. And I felt nothing.

I'd felt nothing since Hannah told me. All the way on the journey back to Saffron I had tried to remember. My mother, my past, my self. Where do the memories of childhood go?

The streetlights came on—hazy yellow in the cold air—and sleet began again to fall. My cheeks were already numb and I saw the flecks in the lamplight before I felt them.

I collected my suitcase, took out my key and was climbing the stairs when the door flew open. My Aunt Dee, Mother's sister, stood in the doorway. She held a lamp that cast shadows on her face, making it appear older and surely more twisted than it really was. "There you are," she said. "Come inside then."

She took me into the sitting room first. She was using my old bed, she said, so I would have the sofa. I put my suitcase against the wall and she huffed defensively.

"I've made soup for supper. Might not be what you're used to in your grand London house, but it's always been good enough for the likes of me and mine."

"Soup would be lovely," I said.

We ate silently at Mother's table. Aunt sat at the head with the warmth of the stove behind her and I sat at Mother's seat near the window. Sleet had turned to snow, tip-tapping on the glass panes. The only other sound was the scraping of our spoons and an occasional crack from the stove fire.

"I s'pose you'd like to see your mother," my aunt said when we had finished.

She was laid out on her mattress, brown hair loose behind. I was used to seeing it tied back; it was very long and much finer than mine. Someone—my aunt?—had pulled a light blanket to her chin, as if she were sleeping. She looked grayer, older, more sunken than I remembered. It was difficult to make out the shape of her body. One could almost imagine that there was none, that she was disintegrating, piece by piece.

We went downstairs and my aunt made tea. We drank it in the sitting room and said very little. Afterwards I managed something about being tired from the journey and started making up the sofa. I spread the sheet and blanket my aunt had left for me, but when I reached for Mother's cushion it was not in its place. My aunt was watching.

"If you're looking for the cushion," she said, "I've put it away. Filthy, it was. Tatty. Found a big hole on the bottom. And her a seamstress!" She tut-tutted. "I'd like to know what she was doing with the money I was sending!"

And she left. Took herself up to bed in the room next to her dead sister. The floorboards above me creaked, the bed springs sighed, and then there was silence.

Resurrection

I lay in the dark, but I could not sleep. I was imagining my aunt casting her critical eye over Mother's things; Mother being caught unawares, unable to prepare, to put forward her best foot. I should have been the first to come. I should have arranged things, put on a good face on Mother's behalf. Finally, I wept.

※

W E buried her in the churchyard near the showgrounds. The vicar read quickly from the Bible, an eye on the sky—whether to the Lord or the weather, I couldn't tell. He spoke about duty and commitment and the direction they bring to life's journey.

An icy wind rushed towards me and whipped my skirts against my stockinged legs. I looked up to the darkening skies and noticed the figure on the hill, by the old oak tree. It was a man, a gentleman; I could tell that well enough. He was dressed in a long black coat and a stiff shiny hat. He carried a cane, or perhaps it was an umbrella, wrapped tightly. I didn't think much of it at first; I presumed he was a mourner visiting another grave. If it seemed strange that a gentleman, who must surely have his own estate, his own family cemetery, should be mourning amongst the town's graves, I didn't think it then.

As the vicar sprinkled the first handful of dirt on Mother's coffin, I glanced up to the tree again. The gentleman was still there. Watching us, I realized. The snow started to fall then and the man looked upwards so that his face was in the light.

It was Mr. Frederick. But he was changed. Like the victim of a fairy-tale curse, he was suddenly old.

The vicar drew to a hurried close, and the undertaker gave orders that the grave was to be filled quickly on account of the weather.

My aunt was by my side. "He's got a nerve," she said, and at first I thought she meant the undertaker, or else the vicar. But when I followed her gaze, she was looking at Mr. Frederick. I wondered how she knew who he was. I supposed Mother had pointed him out at one time or another when Aunt was visiting. "What a nerve. Showing his face here." She shook her head, tightened her lips.

Her words made no sense, but when I turned to ask what she meant she had already moved away, was smiling at the vicar, thanking him for his thoughtful service. I supposed she blamed the Hartford family for Mother's health problems, but the accusation was unfair. For while it was true that years of service had weakened Mother's back, it was her arthritis and pregnancy that finished the job.

Suddenly, all thought of my aunt evaporated. Standing by the vicar, black hat in his hands, was Alfred.

From across the grave, his eyes met mine and he raised his hand.

I hesitated, nodded jerkily so that my teeth chattered.

He started walking. Came towards me. I watched, as if to look away could cause him to disappear. Then he was at my side. "How are you holding up?"

I nodded again. It was all I could seem to do. In my mind, whirlpools of words spun too quickly for me to grasp. Weeks of waiting for his letter; of hurt, confusion, sadness; of lying awake composing imaginary scripts of explanation and reunion. And now, finally . . .

⁂

"ARE you all right?" he said stiffly, bringing a tentative hand towards mine, then thinking better of it, returning it to the brim of his hat.

"Yes," I managed to say, hand heavy where he hadn't touched it. "Thank you for coming."

"Course I came."

"You didn't have to go to any trouble."

"No trouble, Grace," he said, feeding his hat brim through his fingers.

These last words floated lonely between us. My name, familiar and brittle on his lips. I let my attention drift to Mother's grave; watched the undertaker hastily working. Alfred followed my gaze.

"I'm sorry about your ma," he said.

"I know," I said quickly. "I know you are."

"She was a hard worker."

"Yes," I said.

"I saw her only last week—"

I glanced at him. "Did you?"

"Brought her some coal Mr. Hamilton said could be spared."

"Did you, Alfred?" I said appreciatively.

"Been cold of a night, it has. Didn't like to think of your ma going cold."

I was filled with gratitude; it had been my guilty fear that Mother's passing had been brought about through neglect.

A hand clamped firmly on my wrist. My aunt was beside me. "That's over and done then," she said. "And a fine service too. Can't see she'd have anything to complain about."

Alfred was watching us.

"Alfred," I said, "this is my Aunt Dee, Mother's sister."

My aunt narrowed her eyes as she caught his gaze; a groundless suspicion that was native to her. "Charmed, I'm sure." She turned back to me. "Come on then, miss," she said, fixing her hat and tightening her scarf. "Landlord's coming first thing tomorrow and that house needs to be spotless."

I glanced at Alfred, cursed the wall of uncertainty still stretched between us. "Well," I said, "I suppose I'd best be—"

"Actually," said Alfred quickly, "I was hoping . . . that is, Mrs. Townsend thought you might like to come back up to the house for tea?"

❦

ALFRED and I walked through the village, side by side; soft flakes of snow, too light to fall, suspended on the breeze. For a time we walked without speaking. Footsteps muffled by the damp dirt road. Bells ringing as shoppers went in and out of doors. Occasional motorcars whirring down the lane.

As we neared the Bridge Road we began to speak of Mother: I recounted the day of the button in the string bag; the long-ago Punch and Judy visit; told him of my narrow escape from the Foundling Hospital.

Alfred nodded. "Brave of your ma, if you ask me. Can't have been easy, her all on her own."

"She never tired of telling me so," I said, with more bitterness than I intended.

"Shame about your da," he said as we passed Mother's street and the village turned abruptly to countryside. "Having to leave her like that."

At first I thought I had misheard. "My what?"

"Your da. Shame things didn't work out for the two of them."

My voice trembled against my best attempts to still it. "What do you know about my father?"

He shrugged ingenuously. "Only what your ma told me. Said she was young and she loved him, but in the end it was impossible. Something to do with his family, his commitments. She wasn't real clear."

"When did she tell you that?" My voice was thin as the floating snow.

"What?"

"About him. My father." I shivered into my shawl, pulled it tight around my shoulders.

"I took to visiting recently," he said. "She was all alone, what with you in London. Didn't seem much trouble on my part to keep her company once in a while. Have a natter about this and that."

"Did she tell you anything else?" Was it possible, after a lifetime of keeping secrets from me, Mother had opened up so easily at the end?

"No," said Alfred. "Not much. Nothing more about your da. To be honest, I did most of the talking; she was more a listener, don't you think?"

I was unsure what I thought. The whole day had been deeply unsettling. Burying Mother, Alfred's unexpected arrival, learning he and Mother had met regularly, had discussed my father. A topic closed to me from before I'd even thought to ask. I walked faster as we entered the Riverton gates, as if to walk free of the day.

I could hear Alfred behind me, hurrying to catch me up. I welcomed the clinging damp of the long dark driveway. Surrendered myself to a force that seemed to be pulling me inexorably on.

"I meant to write, Gracie," he said quickly. Small branches cracked underfoot, the trees seemed to eavesdrop. "To reply to your letters." He drew beside me. "I tried so many times."

"Why didn't you?" I said, walking on.

"I couldn't get the words right. You know how my head is. Since the war . . ." He lifted a hand and rapped lightly on his forehead. "Certain things I just can't seem to do no more. Not like before. Words and letters are one of them." He hurried to keep up with me. "Besides," he said, breath catching, "there were things I needed to say that could only be said in person."

The air was icy on my cheeks. I slowed. "Why didn't you wait for me?" I said softly. "The day of the theatre show?"

"I did, Gracie."

"But when I got back—it had only just gone five."

He sighed. "I left at ten before. We just missed each other." He shook his head. "I would've waited longer, Gracie, only Mrs. Tibbit said you must have forgot. That you'd gone on an errand and wouldn't be back for hours."

"But that wasn't true!"

"Why would she make it up, a thing like that?" said Alfred, confused.

I lifted my shoulders helplessly, let them fall. "It's what she's like."

We had reached the top of the driveway. There on the ridge stood Riverton, large and dark, the edges of evening beginning to enclose her. We paused unconsciously, stood a moment before continuing past the fountain and around towards the servants' entrance.

"I went after you," I said as we entered the rose garden.

"You didn't," he said, glancing at me. "Did you?"

I nodded. "I waited at the theatre until the last. I thought I could catch up with you."

"Oh, Gracie," Alfred said, stopping at the base of the stairs. "I'm so sorry."

I stopped too.

"I should never have listened to that Mrs. Tibbit," he said.

"You weren't to know."

"But I should have trusted you'd be back. It's just . . ." He glanced at the closed servants' door, tightened his lips, exhaled. "There was something on my mind, Grace. Something important I'd been wanting to talk to you about. To ask you. I was wound up tighter than a drum that day. Full of nerves." He shook his head. "When I thought you'd given me the flick, I was that upset I couldn't stand it any longer. Got out of that house as fast as I could. Started down the first street I came to and kept walking."

"But Lucy . . ." I said quietly, eyes on the fingers of my gloves. Watching as snowflakes disappeared on contact. "Lucy Starling . . ."

He sighed, looked beyond my shoulder. "I took Lucy Starling to make you jealous, Gracie. That I confess." He shook his head. "It was unfair of me to do it, I know that: unfair to you and unfair to Lucy." He reached out with a gloved finger and lifted my chin tentatively so that my eyes met his. "It was disappointment made me do it, Grace. All the way down from Saffron, I'd imagined seeing you, practiced what I was going to say when we met."

His hazel eyes were earnest. A nerve flickered in his jaw.

"What were you going to say?" I asked.

He smiled nervously.

The clatter of iron hinges and the servants' hall door swung open. Mrs. Townsend, large frame backlit, plump cheeks red from her seat by the fire.

"Here!" she chortled. "What are you two doing out there in the cold?" She turned back to those inside. "They're out in the cold! Didn't I tell you they was?" She returned her attention to us. "I said to Mr. Hamilton, 'Mr. Hamilton, blimey if I don't hear voices outside.' 'You're imagining things, Mrs. Townsend,' says he. 'What would they be wanting standing out in the cold when they could be in here where it's nice and warm?' 'I wouldn't know, Mr. Hamilton,' says I, 'but unless my ears deceive me, that's where they is.' And I was right." She called inside: "I was right, Mr. Hamilton." She extended her arm and waved us inside. "Well, come on then, you'll catch your deaths out there, the pair of you."

THE CHOICE

※

I HAD forgotten how dim it was downstairs at Riverton. How low the ceiling rafters, and how cold the marble floor. I had forgotten, too, the way the wintry wind blew in off the heath, whistled through the crumbling mortar of the stone walls. Not like number seventeen, where we had the latest insulation and heating.

"You poor dear," said Mrs. Townsend, pulling me towards her, squashing my head into her fire-warmed breasts. (What a loss for some child, never born, to miss the opportunity for such comfort. But that was the way then, as Mother knew too well: family was the first sacrifice of any career servant.) "Come and sit down," she said. "Nancy? Cup of tea for Grace."

I was surprised. "Where's Katie?"

They all exchanged glances.

"What is it?" I said. Nothing dreadful, surely. Alfred would have said—

"Up and married, didn't she," said Nancy with a sniff, before flouncing off into the kitchen.

My jaw dropped.

Mrs. Townsend lowered her voice and spoke quickly: "Fellow from up north that works in the mines. Met him in town while she was s'posed to be running an errand for me, silly girl. Happened awful fast. Won't surprise you to hear there's a wee one on the way." She straightened her apron, pleased with the effect her news was having on me, and glanced towards the kitchen. "Try not to mention it

344

round Nancy, though. She's green as a gardener's thumb, however much she insists she ain't!"

I nodded, stunned. Little Katie married? A mother-to-be?

As I tried to make sense of the remarkable news, Mrs. Townsend continued to fuss, insisting I take the seat nearest the fire, that I was too thin and too pale and would need some of her Christmas pudding to set me to rights. When she disappeared to collect me a plate, I felt the weight of attention upon me. I pushed Katie from my mind and inquired after things at Riverton.

They all fell silent, looked at one another, before Mr. Hamilton finally said, "Well now, young Grace, things are not quite as you might remember from your time."

I asked what he meant and he straightened his jacket. "It's a lot quieter these days. A slower pace."

"A ghost town, more like," said Alfred, who was fidgeting over by the door. He'd seemed agitated since we came inside. "Him upstairs wandering about the estate like the living dead."

"Alfred!" Mr. Hamilton reprimanded, though with less vigor than I would have expected. "You're exaggerating."

"I am not," said Alfred. "Come on, Mr. Hamilton, Grace is one of us. She can wear the truth." He glanced at me. "It's like I told you in London. After Miss Hannah left like that, His Lordship was never the same."

"He was upset all right, but it weren't just Miss Hannah leaving, the two of them on such bad terms," said Nancy. "It was losing his factory like that. And his mother." She leaned towards me. "If you could only see upstairs. We all do our best, but it isn't easy. He won't let us have tradesmen in for repairs—says the sound of hammers banging and ladders dragging across the floor drives him to distraction. We've had to close up even more of the rooms. Said he wouldn't be entertaining again, so it was no use us wasting time and energy maintaining them. Once he caught me trying to dust the library and he just about had my neck." She glanced at Mr. Hamilton and continued. "We don't even do the books any more."

"It's because there's no mistress to run the house," said Mrs. Townsend, returning with a plate of pudding, licking a smear of cream from her finger. "It's always the way when there's no mistress."

"He spends most of his time traipsing over the estate, chasing phantom poachers," Nancy continued, "and when he is inside, he's down in the gunroom, cleaning his rifles. It's frightening, if you ask me."

"Now, Nancy," said Mr. Hamilton, somewhat defeated. "It is not our place to question the Master." He removed his glasses to rub his eyes.

"Yes, Mr. Hamilton," she said. Then she looked at me, said quickly, "You should see him, though, Grace. You wouldn't recognize him. He's grown so old."

"I have seen him," I said then.

"Where?" said Mr. Hamilton with some alarm. He replaced his glasses. "Not out in the grounds, I hope? He wasn't wandering too near the lake?"

"Oh no, Mr. Hamilton," I said. "Nothing like that. I saw him in the village. In the cemetery. At Mother's funeral."

"He was at the funeral?" said Nancy, eyes wide.

"He was up on the hill nearby," I said, "but he was watching well enough."

Mr. Hamilton looked for corroboration. Alfred raised his shoulders, shook his head. "I didn't notice."

"Well, he was there," I said firmly. "I know what I saw."

"I expect he was just taking a stroll," said Mr. Hamilton without conviction. "Taking some air."

"He wasn't doing much walking," I said doubtfully. "He was just standing there, sort of lost, looking down on the grave."

Mr. Hamilton exchanged a glance with Mrs. Townsend. "Aye, well, he always was fond of your mother, when she worked here."

"Fond," said Mrs. Townsend, raising her eyebrows. "Is that what you call it?"

I looked between them. There was something in their expressions I couldn't understand. A knowingness to which I wasn't privy.

"And what of you, Grace?" said Mr. Hamilton suddenly. "Enough of us. Tell us about London? How is young Mrs. Luxton?"

I only half heard his questions. On the edges of my mind something was forming. Whisperings, and glances, and insinuations that had long fluttered singularly were now coming together. Forming a picture. Almost.

"Well, Grace?" said Mrs. Townsend impatiently. "Cat got your tongue? What of Miss Hannah?"

"Sorry, Mrs. Townsend," I said. "Must've been away with the fairies."

They were all watching me eagerly, so I told them Hannah was well. It seemed the proper thing to do. Where would I have begun to tell them otherwise? About the arguments with Teddy, the visit to the spiritualist, the frightening talk of being dead already? I spoke instead of the beautiful house, and Hannah's clothes, and the glittering guests they entertained.

"And what of your duties?" Mr. Hamilton said, straightening. "Quite a different pace in London. Lots of entertaining? I suppose you're part of a large staff?"

I told him that the staff was large, but not so proficient as here at Riverton, and he seemed pleased. And I told them about the attempt Lady Pemberton-Brown had made on me.

"I trust you told her what was what," said Mr. Hamilton. "Politely but firmly, as I've always instructed?"

"Yes, Mr. Hamilton," I said. "Of course I did."

"That's the girl," he said, beaming like a proud father. "Glenfield Hall, eh? You must be making quite a name for yourself if the likes of Glenfield Hall were trying to poach you. Still, you did the right thing. In our line of work, what have we if we don't have our loyalty?"

We all nodded agreement. All except Alfred, I noticed.

347

Mr. Hamilton noticed too. "I suppose Alfred's told you his plans?" he said, raising a silvery eyebrow.

"What plans?" I looked at Alfred.

"I was trying to tell you," he said, biting back a smile as he came to sit by me. "I'm leaving, Grace. No more yes, sir-ing for me."

My first thought was that he was leaving England again. Just when we had begun to make amends.

He laughed at my expression. "I'm not going far. I'm just leaving service. A mate of mine, from the war; we're setting up in business together."

"Alfred . . ." I didn't know what to say. I was relieved, but I was also worried for him. To leave service? The security of Riverton? "What kind of business?"

"Electrical. My mate's awful good with his hands. He's going to teach me how to install bells and the like. In the meantime I'm going to take on managing the shop. Going to work hard and save money, Gracie—I've already got some put away. One day I'm going to have my very own business, I'm going to be my own man. You'll see."

☙

A F T E R W A R D S , Alfred walked me back to the village. Cold night was falling fast and we went quickly to save from freezing. Though I was pleased with Alfred's company, relieved that we had mended our differences, I said little.

I was thinking of Mother. About the bitterness that always simmered beneath her surface; her conviction, expectation almost, that hers was a life of ill fortune. That was the Mother I remembered. And yet, for some time now I had begun to realize she was not always so. Mrs. Townsend remembered her affectionately; Mr. Frederick, interminably difficult to please, had been fond of her.

But what had happened to transform the young serving maid with her secret smile? The answer, I was beginning to suspect, was the key to unlocking many of Mother's mysteries. And its solution was nearby. It lurked like an elusive fish in my mind's reeds. I knew it was there, could sense it, glimpse its vague shape, but every time I got close, reached to grasp its shadowy form, it slipped away.

That it had something to do with my birth was certain: Mother had been open on that front. And I was sure my ghost of a father figured somewhere: the man she spoke of with Alfred, but never with me. The man she'd loved, but couldn't be with. What reason had Alfred given? His family? His commitments?

"Grace."

My aunt knew who he was, but she was as tight-lipped as Mother. Nonetheless, I knew well enough what she thought of him. My childhood was peppered with their whispered exchanges: Aunt Dee castigating Mother for her poor choices, telling her she'd made her bed and had no option now but to lie in it; Mother weeping as Aunt Dee patted her shoulder with brusque condolences: "You're better off," "It couldn't have worked," "You're well rid of that place." That place, I knew even as a girl, was the grand house on the hill. And I knew also that Aunt Dee's contempt for my father was equaled only by her disdain for Riverton. The two great catastrophes in Mother's life, she was fond of saying.

"Grace."

A disdain that extended to Mr. Frederick, it would seem. "He's got a nerve," she'd said when she spied him at the funeral, "showing his face now." I wondered how my aunt knew who he was, and what Mr. Frederick could possibly have done to make her scowl so?

I wondered, too, what he had been doing there. Fondness for an employee was one thing, but for His Lordship to appear at the town cemetery. To watch as one of his long-ago serving maids was buried.

❦

"GRACE." In the distance, through the tangle of my thoughts, Alfred was speaking. I glanced at him distractedly. "There's something I've been meaning to ask all day," he said. "I'm afraid if I don't ask now, I'll lose my nerve."

And Mother had been fond of Mr. Frederick too. "Poor, poor Frederick," she had said when his father and brother passed away. Not poor Lady Violet or poor Jemima. Her sympathy had extended directly and exclusively to Mr. Frederick.

But that was understandable, wasn't it? Mr. Frederick would have been a young man when Mother worked at the house; it was natural her sympathy would lie with the family member closest to her in age. Just as my sympathy lay with Hannah. Besides, Mother had seemed just as fond of Mr. Frederick's wife, Penelope. "Frederick wouldn't marry again," she'd said when I told her Fanny sought his hand. Her certainty, her despondency when I insisted it was so: surely these could only be explained by her closeness to her former mistress?

"I don't have a way with words, Gracie, you know that as well as I," Alfred was saying. "So I'm going to come right out with it. You know I'm going into business soon . . . ?"

I was nodding, somehow I was nodding, but my mind was elsewhere. The elusive fish was close. I could see the glimmer of its slippery scales, weaving through the reeds, out of the shadows . . .

"But that's just the first step. I'm going to save and save and one day, not too far away, I'm going to have a business with 'Alfred Steeple' on the front door, you see if I don't."

. . . and into the light. Was it possible Mother's upset was not the result of affection for her former mistress at all? But because the man she had cared for—still cared for—might be planning to marry again? That Mother and Mr. Frederick . . . ? That all those years ago, when she was in service at Riverton . . . ?

"I've waited and waited, Grace, because I wanted to have something to offer you. Something more than what I am now . . ."

But surely not. It would have been a scandal. People would have known. I would have known. Wouldn't I?

Memories, snatches of conversation, floated back. Was that what Lady Violet meant when she spoke to Lady Clementine of "that

despicable business?" Had people known? Had scandal erupted in
Saffron twenty-two years ago when a local woman was sent from the
manor in disgrace, pregnant by the son of her mistress?

But if so, why had Lady Violet welcomed me onto her staff?
Surely I'd have served as a not-so-welcome reminder of what had
gone before?

Unless my employment was some sort of recompense. The price
for Mother's silence. Was that why Mother had been so sure, so certain a position would be found for me at Riverton?

And then, quite simply, I knew. The fish swam into full sunlight, its scales glistening brightly. How had I not seen it before?
Mother's bitterness, Mr. Frederick's failure ever to remarry. It all made
sense. He had loved Mother too. That's why he had come to the funeral. That's why he watched me so strangely: as if he'd seen a ghost.
Had been glad to lose me from Riverton, had told Hannah he didn't
need me there.

"Gracie, I wonder . . ." Alfred took my hand.

Hannah. I was struck again by realization.

I gasped. It explained so much: the feeling of solidarity—sisterly,
surely?—we shared.

Alfred's hands tightened on mine, stopped me from falling.
"There now, Gracie," he said, smiling nervously. "Don't go getting
faint on me."

My legs buckled: I felt as if I'd broken into a million tiny particles, was falling like sand from a bucket.

Did Hannah know? Was that why she'd insisted I accompany
her to London? Had turned to me when she felt deserted on all other
fronts? Had begged me never to leave her? Had made me promise?

"Grace?" said Alfred, his arm supporting me. "Are you all
right?"

I nodded, tried to speak. Couldn't.

"Good," said Alfred. "Because I haven't said all I mean to quite
yet. Though I have a feeling you've guessed."

Guessed? About Mother and Mr. Frederick? About Hannah? No: Alfred had been talking. What about? His new business, his friend from the war . . .

"Gracie," said Alfred, bringing my hands together between us. He smiled at me, swallowed. "Would you do me the honor of becoming my wife?"

A flash of consciousness. I blinked. Couldn't answer. Thoughts, feelings, rushed through me. Alfred had asked me to marry him. Alfred, who I adored, was standing before me, face frozen in the previous moment, waiting for me to answer. My tongue formed words, but my lips would not oblige.

"Grace?" said Alfred, eyes wide with apprehension.

I felt myself smile, heard myself begin to laugh. I couldn't seem to stop. I was weeping too, cold, damp tears on my cheeks. It was hysteria, I suppose: so much had happened in the past few moments, too much to take in. The shock of realizing I was related to Mr. Frederick, to Hannah. The surprise and delight of Alfred's proposal.

"Gracie?" Alfred was watching me uncertainly. "Does that mean you'd like to? To marry me, I mean?"

To marry him. Me. It was my secret dream, yet now it was happening I found myself hopelessly unprepared. I had long since put such fancy down to youth. Stopped imagining it might ever really come about. That anyone would ask me. That Alfred would ask me.

Somehow, I nodded, managed to stop myself from laughing. Heard myself say: "Yes." Little more than a whisper. I closed my eyes, my head swirled. A little louder: "Yes."

Alfred whooped and I opened my eyes. He was grinning, relief seeming to lighten him. A man and woman walking down the other side of the street turned to look at us and Alfred called out to them, "She said yes!" And then he turned back to me, rubbed his lips together, trying to stop smiling so that he could speak. He gripped my upper arms. He was trembling. "I was hoping you'd say that."

I nodded again, smiled. So much was happening.

"Grace," he said softly. "I was wondering . . . Would it be all right for me to kiss you?"

I must have said yes, for next I knew he had lifted a hand to support my head, leaned towards me.

Time seemed to slow.

Then he linked his arm through mine, the first time he had ever done so, and we started down the street. We didn't speak, just walked silently, together. Where his arm crossed mine, pressed the cotton of my shirt against my skin, I shivered. Its warmth, its weight, a promise.

Alfred stroked my wrist with his gloved fingers and I thrilled. My senses were acute: as if someone had removed a layer of skin, enabling me to feel more deeply, more freely. I leaned a little closer. To think that in the space of a day so much had changed. I had gleaned Mother's secret, realized the nature of my bond to Hannah, Alfred had asked me to marry him. I almost told him then my deductions about Mother and Mr. Frederick, but the words died on my lips. There would be plenty of time later. The idea was still so new: I wanted to savor Mother's secret a little longer. And I wanted to savor my own happiness. So I remained silent and we continued to walk, arms linked, down Mother's street.

Precious, perfect moments that I have replayed countless times throughout my life. Sometimes, in my mind, we reach the house. We go inside and drink a toast to our health, are married soon after. And we live happily the rest of our days until we both reach a great age.

But that is not what happened, as well you know.

Rewind. Replay. We were halfway along the street, outside Mr. Connelly's house—maudlin Irish flute music on the breeze—when Alfred said, "You can give notice as soon as you get back to London."

I glanced sharply at him. "Notice?"

"To Mrs. Luxton." He smiled at me. "You won't need to be dressing her any longer once we're married. We'll move to Ipswich straight after. You can work with me, if you like. On the books. Or you could take in stitching, if you prefer?"

Give notice? Leave Hannah? "But Alfred," I said simply, "I can't leave my position."

"Of course you can," he said. Bemusement tugged at his smile. "I am."

"But it's different . . ." I grasped at words of explanation, words that would make him understand. "I'm a lady's maid. Hannah needs me."

"She doesn't need *you*, she needs a drudge to keep her gloves in order." His voice softened. "You're too good for that, Grace. You deserve better. To be your own person."

I wanted to explain to him. That Hannah would find another maid, certainly, but that I was more than a maid. That we were bonded. Tied. Since the day in the nursery when we were both fourteen, when I'd wondered what it might be like to have a sister. When I'd lied to Miss Prince for Hannah, so instinctively it had frightened me.

That I had made her a promise. When she begged me not to leave I'd given her my word.

That we were sisters. Secret sisters.

"Besides," he said. "We'll be living in Ipswich. You can hardly keep up work in London, can you?" He patted my arm good-naturedly.

I looked sideways at his face. So genuine. So sure. Empty of ambivalence. And I felt my arguments disintegrating, falling away, even as I framed them. There were no words to make him see, to make him understand in a moment what had taken me years to grasp.

And I knew then I could never have them both, Alfred and Hannah. That I would have to make a choice.

I unlinked my arm from his, told him I was sorry. I'd made a mistake, I said. A terrible mistake.

And then I ran from him. Didn't turn back, though I knew somehow he remained, unmoving, beneath the cold yellow streetlight. That he watched me as I disappeared down the darkened lane, as I waited miserably for my aunt to admit me and slipped, distraught, into the house. As I closed between us the doorway into what-might-have-been.

✳

T H E trip back to London was excruciating. It was long and cold and the roads were slippery with snow. But it was the company that made it particularly painful. I was trapped with myself in the motorcar's cabin, engaged in fruitless debate. I spent the entire journey telling myself I'd made the right choice, the only choice, to remain with Hannah as promised. And by the time the motor car pulled up at number seventeen, I had myself convinced.

I was convinced, too, that Hannah already knew of our bond. That she'd guessed, overheard folk whispering, had even been told. For surely it explained why she'd always turned to me, treated me as a confidante. Since the morning I'd bumped into her in the cold alleyway of Miss Dove's Secretarial School.

So now we both knew.

And the secret would remain, unspoken, between us.

A silent bond of dedication and devotion.

I was relieved I hadn't told Alfred. He wouldn't have understood my decision to keep it to myself. Would have insisted I tell Hannah: even demanded some sort of recompense. Kind, caring though he was, he wouldn't have perceived the importance of maintaining the status quo. Wouldn't have seen that no one else could know. For what if Teddy were to find out? Or his family? Hannah would suffer, I could be let go.

No, it was better this way. There was no choice.

PART FOUR

HANNAH'S STORY

✺

I T is time now to speak of things I didn't see. To push Grace and her concerns aside and bring Hannah to the fore. For while I was away, something had happened. I realized as soon as I laid eyes on her. Things were different. Hannah was different. Brighter. Secretive. More self-satisfied.

What had happened at number seventeen I learned gradually, as I did so much of what went on that final year. I had my suspicions, of course, but I neither saw nor heard everything. Only Hannah knew exactly what occurred and she had never been one for fervent confessions. They were not her style; she had always preferred secrets. But after the terrible events of 1924, when we were shut up together at Riverton, she became more forthcoming. And I was a good listener. This is what she told me.

-I -

I T was the Monday after my mother's death. I had left for Saffron Green, Teddy and Deborah were at work, and Emmeline was lunching with friends. Hannah was alone in the drawing room. She had intended to write correspondence, but her paper box languished on the sofa. She found she had little spirit for writing copious thank-you letters to the wives of Teddy's clients and was instead looking out over the street, guessing at the lives of the passers-by. She was so involved in her game she didn't see him come to the front door. Didn't hear

359

him ring the bell. The first she knew was when Boyle appeared at the morning-room door.

"A gentleman to see you, ma'am."

"A gentleman, Boyle?" she said distractedly, watching as a little girl broke free from her nanny and ran into the frosty park. When was the last time she had run? Run so fast she felt the wind like a slap on her face, her heart thumping so large in her chest that she almost couldn't breathe?

"Says he has something belonging to you that he'd like to return, ma'am."

How tiresome it all was. "Could he not leave it with you, Boyle?"

"He says not, ma'am. Says he has to deliver it in person."

"I really can't think that I'm missing anything." Hannah pulled her eyes reluctantly from the little girl and turned from the window. "I suppose you'd better show him in."

Mr. Boyle hesitated. Seemed to be on the verge of speaking.

"Is there something else?" said Hannah.

"No, ma'am," he said. "Only that the gentleman . . . I don't think he's much of a gentleman, ma'am."

"Whatever do you mean?" said Hannah.

"Only that he doesn't seem entirely respectable."

Hannah raised her eyebrows. "He's not in a state of undress, is he?"

"No, ma'am, he's dressed well enough."

"He's not saying obscene things?"

"No, ma'am," said Boyle. "He's polite enough."

Hannah gasped. "It's not a Frenchman; short with a moustache?"

"Oh no, ma'am."

"Then tell me, Boyle. What form does this lack of respectability take?"

Boyle frowned. "I couldn't say, ma'am. Just a feeling I got."

Hannah gave the appearance of considering Boyle's feeling, but her interest was piqued. "If the gentleman says he has something belonging to me, I had best have it back. If he gives any sign of wanting respectability, Boyle, I'll ring for you directly."

⁂

SHE didn't recognize him at first. She had only known him briefly, after all; one winter, almost a decade before. And he had changed. He had been a boy when she knew him at Riverton. With smooth, clear skin, wide brown eyes and a gentle manner. And he had been still, she remembered. It was one of the things that had infuriated her. His self-possession. The way he came into their lives with no warning, goaded her into saying things she oughtn't, and proceeded, with such ease, to woo their brother from them.

The man who stood before her in the morning room was tall, dressed in a black suit and a white shirt. It was ordinary enough clothing, but he wore it differently from Teddy and the other businessmen Hannah knew. His face was striking, but lean: hollows below his cheekbones and shadows beneath his dark eyes. She could see the lack of respectability to which Boyle referred, and yet she was at just as much of a loss to articulate it.

"Good morning," she said.

He looked at her, seemed to look right inside her. She'd had men stare before, but something in the focus of his gaze caused her to blush. And when she did, he smiled. "You haven't changed."

It was then she knew him. Recognized his voice. "Robbie Hunter," she said incredulously. She looked him over again, this new knowledge coloring her observation. The same dark hair, the same dark eyes. Same sensuous mouth, always slightly amused. She wondered how she'd missed them before. She straightened, stilled herself. "How nice of you to come." The moment the words were out, she regretted their ordinariness and longed to pull them back.

He smiled; rather ironically, it seemed to Hannah.

"Won't you sit down?" She indicated Teddy's armchair and Robbie sat perfunctorily, like a schoolboy obeying a mundane instruction unworthy of defiance. Once again she had an irksome sense of her own triviality.

He was still looking at her.

She checked her hair lightly with the palms of both hands, made sure the pins were all in place, smoothed the pale ends against her neck. She smiled politely. "Is there something amiss, Mr. Hunter? Something I need to fix?"

"No," he said. "I've carried an image in my mind, all this time . . . You're still the same."

"Not the same, Mr. Hunter, I assure you," she said, as lightly as she could. "I was fifteen when last we met."

"Were you really so young?"

There was that lack of respectability again. Oh, it wasn't so much what he said—it was a perfectly ordinary question, after all—it was something in the way he said it. As if he concealed a double meaning she couldn't grasp. "I'll ring for tea, shall I?" she said, and regretted it immediately. Now he would stay.

She stood and pressed the bell button, then hovered by the mantel, straightening objects and collecting herself, until Boyle was at the door.

"Mr. Hunter will be joining me for tea," said Hannah.

Boyle looked at Robbie suspiciously.

"He was a friend to my brother," Hannah added, "in the war."

"Ah," said Boyle. "Yes, ma'am. I'll have Mrs. Tibbit fetch up tea for two." How deferential he was. How conventional his deference made her seem.

Robbie was looking around, taking in the morning room. The Art Deco furnishings that Elsie de Wolfe had selected ("the latest thing") and that Hannah had always tolerated. His gaze drifted from the octagonal mirror above the fire to the gold and brown diamond-print curtains.

"Modern, isn't it?" Hannah said, striving for flippancy. "I'm never quite sure I like it, but I believe that's the point of modernity."

Robbie seemed not to hear. "David spoke of you often," he said. "I feel that I know you. You and Emmeline and Riverton."

Hannah sank onto the edge of the chair at the mention of David. She had schooled herself not to think of him, not to open the box of tender memories. And yet here sat the one person with whom she might be able to discuss him. "Yes," she said, "tell me about David, Mr. Hunter." She steeled herself. "Was he . . . did he . . ." She pressed her lips together, looked at Robbie. "I've often hoped he forgave me."

"Forgave you?"

"I was such a prig that last winter, before he left. We weren't expecting you. We were used to having David to ourselves. I was rather stubborn, I fear. I spent the entire duration ignoring you, wishing you weren't there."

He shrugged. "I didn't notice."

The door opened and Boyle appeared with the salver of tea. He laid it on the table by Hannah and stood back.

"Mr. Hunter," said Hannah, aware that Boyle was lingering, eyeing Robbie. "Boyle said you had something to return to me."

"Yes," Robbie said, reaching into his pocket. Hannah nodded to Boyle, assured him everything was in hand, his presence no longer required. As the door closed, Robbie withdrew a piece of cloth. It was tatty, with threads loose, and Hannah wondered how on earth he thought this might belong to her. As she watched she realized it was an old piece of ribbon, once white, now brown. He peeled the ribbon open, fingers shaking, and held it towards her.

Her breath caught in her throat. Wrapped inside was a tiny book.

She reached over and plucked it gingerly from its shroud. Turned it over in her hands to look at its cover, though she knew well enough what it would say. *Journey Across the Rubicon*.

"I gave this to David. For luck."

He nodded.

Her eyes met his. "Why did you take it?"

"I didn't."

"David would never have given this away."

"No, he wouldn't, he didn't, I was only ever its messenger. He wanted it returned; the last thing he said was, 'Take it to Nefertiti.' And I have."

Hannah didn't look at him. The name. Her own secret name. He didn't know her well enough. She closed her fingers around the little book, dropped the lid on memories of being brave and untamed and full of prospect, lifted her head to meet his gaze. "Let's speak of other things."

Robbie nodded slightly and pushed the ribbon back into his pocket. "What do people speak of when they meet again like this?"

"They ask each other what they've been doing," said Hannah, tucking the tiny book inside her escritoire. "Where their lives have taken them."

"Well then," Robbie said. "What have you been doing, Hannah? I can see well enough where life has taken you."

Hannah straightened, poured a cup of tea and held it out to him. The cup jiggled against its saucer in her hand. "I've married. A gentleman called Theodore Luxton, you might have heard of him. He and his father are bankers. They work in the City."

Robbie was watching her, but gave no indication that Teddy's name was familiar to him.

"I live in London, as you know," Hannah continued, trying to smile. "Such a wonderful city, don't you think? So much to see and do? So many interesting people . . ." Her voice trailed off. Robbie was distracting her, watching her as she spoke with the same disconcerting intensity he'd offered all those years ago in the library. "Mr. Hunter," she said with some impatience. "Really. I must ask you to stop. It's quite impossible to—"

"You're right," he said softly. "You have changed. Your face is sad."

She wanted to respond, to tell him he was wrong. That any sadness he perceived was a direct consequence of having her brother's memory resurrected. But there was something in his voice that stopped her. Something that made her feel transparent, uncertain, vulnerable. As if he knew her better than she knew herself. She didn't like it, but she knew somehow it would do no good to argue.

"Well, Mr. Hunter," she said, standing stiffly. "I must thank you for coming. For finding me, returning the book."

Robbie followed her lead, stood. "I said I would."

"I'll ring for Boyle to show you out."

"Don't trouble him," said Robbie. "I know the way well enough."

He opened the door and Emmeline burst through, a whirl of pink silk and shingled blond hair. Her cheeks glowed with the joy of being young and well connected in a city and a time that belonged to the young and well connected. She collapsed onto the sofa and crossed one long leg over the other. Hannah felt old suddenly, and strangely faded.

"Phew. I'm pooped," Emmeline said. "I don't suppose there's any tea left?"

She looked up and noticed Robbie.

"You remember Mr. Hunter, don't you, Emmeline?" said Hannah.

Emmeline puzzled for a moment. She leaned forward and rested her chin on the palm of her hand, wide blue eyes blinking as she gazed at his face.

"David's friend?" said Hannah. "From Riverton?"

"Robbie Hunter," said Emmeline, smiling slowly, delightedly, hand dropping into her lap. "Of course I do. By my count, you owe me a dress."

※

At Emmeline's insistence, Robbie stayed for dinner. It was unthinkable, she said, that he be allowed to leave when he had only just arrived. So it was that Robbie joined Deborah, Teddy, Emmeline and Hannah in the dining room of number seventeen that night.

Hannah sat on one side of the table, Deborah and Emmeline on the other, Robbie the foot to Teddy's head. They made amusing book-ends, Hannah thought: Robbie the young bohemian, and Teddy, after four years working with his father, a caricature of affluence and influence. He was still a handsome man—Hannah had noticed some of his colleagues' young wives making eyes at him, little use it would do them—but his face was fuller and his hair was grayer. His cheeks, too, had taken on the blush of bountiful living. He leaned back against his chair.

"So. What is it you do for a crust, Mr. Hunter? My wife tells me you're not in business." That an alternative existed no longer occurred to him.

"I'm a writer," said Robbie.

"Writer, eh?" said Teddy. "Write for *The Times*, do you?"

"I did," said Robbie, "amongst others. Now I write for myself." He smiled. "Foolishly, I thought I'd be easier to please."

"How fortunate," said Deborah breezily, "to have the time to give oneself over to one's leisure. I wouldn't recognize myself if I wasn't rushing hither and yon." She began a monologue on her organization of a recent fashion parade, and smiled wolfishly at Robbie.

Deborah was flirting, Hannah realized. She looked at Robbie. Yes, he was handsome, in a languid, sensuous sort of way: not at all Deborah's usual type.

"Books, is it?" said Teddy.

"Poetry," said Robbie.

Teddy raised his eyebrows dramatically. " 'How dull it is to stop, to rust unburnished rather than to sparkle in use.' "

Hannah winced at the mishandled Tennyson.

Robbie met her eye and grinned. " 'As though to breathe were life.' "

"I've always loved Shakespeare," said Teddy. "Your rhymes anything like his?"

"I'm afraid I pale by comparison," said Robbie. "But I persist nonetheless. Better to lose oneself in action than to wither in despair."

"Quite so," said Teddy.

As Hannah watched Robbie, something she had glimpsed came into focus. Suddenly she knew who he was. She inhaled. "You're R. S. Hunter."

"Who?" said Teddy. He looked between Hannah and Robbie, then to Deborah for clarification. Deborah lifted her shoulders affectedly.

"R. S. Hunter," said Hannah, eyes still searching Robbie's. She laughed. She couldn't help it. "I have your collected poems."

"First or second?" said Robbie.

"*Progress and Disintegration*," said Hannah. She hadn't realized there was another.

"Ah," said Deborah, eyes widening. "Yes, I saw a write-up in the paper. You won that award."

"*Progress* is my second," said Robbie, looking at Hannah.

"I should like to read the first," Hannah said. "Tell me the name, won't you, Mr. Hunter, so I may purchase it."

"You can have my copy," said Robbie. "I've already read it. Between you and me, I find the author quite a bore."

Deborah's lips curled into a smile and a familiar glint appeared in her eye. She was assessing Robbie's worth, cataloguing the list of people she could impress if she produced him at one of her soirées. By the keen way she rubbed her glossy red lips together, his value was high. Hannah felt a surprising jolt of possession then.

"*Progress and Disintegration*?" said Teddy, winking at Robbie. "You're not a socialist, are you, Mr. Hunter?"

Robbie smiled. "No, sir. I have neither possessions to redistribute, nor the desire to acquire them."

Teddy laughed.

"Come now, Mr. Hunter," said Deborah. "I suspect you're having fun at our expense."

"I'm having fun. I hope it's not at your expense."

Deborah smiled in a way she thought beguiling. "A little birdie tells me you're not quite the stray you'd have us think."

Hannah looked at Emmeline, smirking behind her hands; it wasn't difficult to deduce the identity of Deborah's little birdie.

"What are you talking about, Deb?" said Teddy. "Out with it."

"Our guest has been teasing us," said Deborah, voice rising triumphantly. "For he isn't *Mr.* Hunter at all, he's *Lord* Hunter."

Teddy lifted his eyebrows. "Eh? What's that?"

Robbie twisted his wineglass by its stem. "It's true enough my father was Lord Hunter. But the title isn't one I use."

Teddy eyed Robbie over his plate of roast beef. Denying a title was something he couldn't understand. He and his father had campaigned long and hard for Lloyd George's ennobling. "You sure you're not a socialist?" he said.

"Enough politics," said Emmeline suddenly, rolling her eyes. "Of course he's not a socialist. Robbie's one of us, and we didn't invite him so we could bore him to death." She fixed her gaze on him, rested her chin on the palm of her hand. "Tell us where you've been, Robbie."

"Most recently?" said Robbie. "Spain."

Spain. Hannah repeated it to herself. How wonderful.

"How primitive," said Deborah, laughing. "What on earth were you doing there?"

"Fulfilling a promise made long ago."

"Madrid, was it?" said Teddy.

"For a time," said Robbie. "On my way to Segovia."

Teddy frowned. "What's a fellow do in Segovia?"

"I went to the Alcázar."

Hannah felt her skin prickle.

"That dusty old fort?" said Deborah, smiling broadly. "I can't think of anything worse."

"Oh no," said Robbie. "It was remarkable. Magical. Like stepping into a different world."

"Do tell."

Robbie hesitated, searching for the right words. "Sometimes I felt that I could glimpse the past. When evening came, and I was all

368

alone, I could almost hear the whispers of the dead. Ancient secrets swirling by."

"How ghoulish," said Deborah.

"Why would you ever leave?" said Hannah.

"Yes," said Teddy. "What brought you back to London, Mr. Hunter?"

Robbie met Hannah's eyes. He smiled, turned to Teddy. "Providence, I suspect."

"All that traveling," said Deborah, cranking up her flirtation. "You must have some of the gypsy in you."

Robbie smiled, but he didn't answer.

"Either that or our guest has a guilty conscience," said Deborah, leaning towards Robbie and lowering her voice playfully. "Is that it, Mr. Hunter? Are you on the run?"

"Only from myself, Miss Luxton," he said.

"You'll settle down," said Teddy, "as you get older. I used to have a bit of the travel bug myself. Entertained notions of seeing the world, collecting artifacts and experiences." By the way he ran his flat palms over the tablecloth on either side of his plate, Hannah knew he was about to launch into a lecture. "A man accumulates responsibilities as he gets older. Gets set in his ways. Differences that used to thrill when he was younger start to irritate. Take Paris, for instance; I was there recently. I used to adore Paris, but the whole city is going to the dogs. No respect for tradition. The way the women dress!"

"Dear Tiddles," laughed Deborah. "So un-chic."

"I know you're fond of the French and their fabrics, Deb," said Teddy, "and for you single women it's all a bit of fun. But there's no way a wife of mine would be allowed to gad about like that!"

Hannah couldn't look at Robbie. She focused attention on her plate, moved her food about and set her fork to rest.

"Traveling certainly opens one's eyes to different cultures," Robbie was saying. "I came across a tribe in the Far East in which the men carved designs into their wives' faces."

Emmeline gasped. "With a knife?"

Teddy swallowed a lump of half-masticated beef, enthralled. "Why on earth?"

"Wives are considered mere objects of enjoyment and display," said Robbie. "Husbands think it their God-given right to decorate them as they see fit."

"Barbarians," said Teddy, shaking his head, signaling to Boyle to refill his wine. "And they wonder why they need us to civilize them."

⁂

HANNAH didn't see Robbie again for weeks after that. She thought he'd forgotten his promise to lend her his book of poetry. It was just like him, she suspected, to charm his way into a dinner invitation, make empty promises, then vanish without honoring them. She was not offended, merely disappointed in herself for being taken in. She would think of it no more.

Nonetheless, a fortnight later, when she happened to find herself in the H–J aisle of the little bookstore in Drury Lane, and her eyes happened to alight on a copy of his first poetry collection, she bought it. She had appreciated his poetry, after all, long before she realized him to be a man of loose promises.

Then Pa died, and any lingering thoughts of Robbie Hunter's return were put aside. With news of her father's sudden death, Hannah felt as if her anchor had been severed, as if she had been washed from safe waters and was at the whim of tides she neither knew nor trusted. It was ridiculous, of course. She hadn't seen Pa for such a long time: he had refused to see her since her marriage and she'd been unable to find the words to convince him otherwise. Yet despite it all, while Pa lived she had been tied to something, to someone large and sturdy. Now she was not. She felt abandoned by him: they had often fought, it was a part of their peculiar relationship, but she had always known he loved her specially. And now, with no word, he was gone. She started to dream at night of dark waters, leaking ships, relentless ocean waves. And in the day she began to dwell once more upon the spiritualist's vision of darkness and death.

Perhaps it would be different when her sister moved permanently to number seventeen, she told herself. For it had been decided after Pa's death that Hannah would serve as guardian of sorts for Emmeline. It was just as well they keep an eye on her, Teddy said, after the unfortunate business with the filmmaker. The more Hannah thought about it, the more she looked forward to the prospect. She would have an ally in the house. Someone who understood her. They would sit up late together, talking and laughing, sharing secrets the way they had when they were younger.

When Emmeline arrived in London, however, she had other ideas. London had always agreed with Emmeline and she threw herself further into the social life she adored. She attended costume balls every night—"White Parties," "Circus Parties," "Under the Sea Parties"—Hannah could never keep count. She drank too much and smoked too much, and considered the night a failure if she couldn't find a shot of herself in the society pages the next day.

Hannah found Emmeline one afternoon entertaining a group of friends in the morning room. They had shifted the furniture to the edges of the walls and the expensive Berlin rug lay by the fire in a haphazard roll. A girl in flimsy jade green chiffon, whom Hannah had never met, sat on the rolled rug smoking lazily, dropping ash, watching as Emmeline tried to teach a baby-faced young man with two left feet to foxtrot.

"No, no," Emmeline said, laughing. "There are four counts, Harry darling. Not three. Here, take my hands and I'll show you." She restarted the gramophone. "Ready?"

Hannah picked her way around the room's rim. She was so distracted by the casualness with which Emmeline and her friends had colonized the place (her room, after all) that she had quite forgotten what it was she came for. She made a pretence of digging around in the writing bureau as Harry collapsed on the sofa, saying, "Enough. You're going to kill me, Emme."

Emmeline fell next to him, threw her arm around his shoulders. "Have it your way, Harry darling, but you can hardly expect me to dance with you at Clarissa's party if you don't know the steps. The foxtrot is all the rage and I intend to dance it all night long!"

All night long was right, thought Hannah. More and more, Emmeline's late nights were becoming early mornings. Not content with dancing the night away at Claridge's, drinking some sort of brandy and Cointreau concoction they called *sidecars*, she and her friends had taken to continuing the party at someone's house. More often than not, a someone who was unknown to them. "Gate-crashing" they called it: touring along Mayfair in evening dress until they found a party to join. Even the servants were beginning to talk. The new housemaid had been clearing the entrance hall when Emmeline swept in at half past five the other morning. Emmeline was just lucky that Teddy didn't know. That Hannah made sure he didn't.

"Jane says Clarissa's serious this time," said the girl in jade chiffon.

"Think she'll actually go through with it?" said Harry.

"We'll see tonight," said Emmeline. "Clarissa's been threatening to bob her hair for months." She laughed. "More fool her if she does: with that bone structure she'll look like a German drill sergeant."

"Are you taking gin?" said Harry.

Emmeline shrugged. "Or wine. Hardly matters. Clarissa intends to throw it all in together so people can dip their cups."

A bottle party, thought Hannah. She'd heard of those. Teddy liked to read her reports from the newspaper when they were at the breakfast table. He'd lower the paper to attract her attention, shake his head with weary disapproval and say, "Listen to this. Another of those parties. Mayfair, this time." Then he'd read the article, word by word, taking great pleasure, it seemed to Hannah, in describing the uninvited guests, the indecent decorations, the raids by police. Why couldn't young people behave as they had when they were young, he'd say? Have balls with supper, servants pouring wine, dance cards.

Hannah was so horrified by Teddy's insinuation that she herself was no longer young that, although she thought Emmeline's behavior a little like dancing on the graves of the dead, she never said as much to her.

And she took particular care to ensure Teddy didn't know Emmeline attended such parties. Much less helped to organize them. Hannah became very good at inventing excuses for Emmeline's nocturnal activities.

But that night, when she climbed the stairs to Teddy's study, armed with an ingenious half-truth about Emmeline's dedication to her friend Lady Clarissa, he was not alone. As she neared his closed door, Hannah heard voices. Teddy's and Simion's. She was about to turn, to come back later, when she heard her father's name. She held her breath and crept towards the door.

"You have to feel sorry for him, though," said Teddy. "Whatever you think of the man. Dying like that, a hunting accident, a country fellow like him."

Simion cleared his throat. "Well now, Teddy, between you and me, it seems there was more to it than that." A meaningful pause. A lowered voice, words Hannah couldn't make out.

Teddy inhaled quickly. "Suicide?"

Lies, Hannah thought, her breath grown hot. Terrible lies.

"It seems so," said Simion. "Lord Gifford tells me one of the servants—the elderly fellow, Hamilton—found him out on the estate. The staff were doing their best to cover the details—I've told you before, there's no servant holds a torch to the British servant in matters of discretion—but Lord Gifford reminded them it was his job to protect the family's reputation and that he needed the facts to do so."

Hannah heard glass scraping against glass, the burbling of sherry being poured.

"And what did Gifford say?" Teddy said. "What made him think it was . . . intentional?"

Simion sighed philosophically. "The man had been in a bad way for some time. Not all men are suited to the rough and tumble of business. He'd become morose, gun-happy. The servants had taken to following him when he left the house, just to make sure . . ." He struck a match and the faint waft of cigar smoke reached Hannah. "Let's just say, the way I understand it, this 'accident' was some time coming."

There was a break in conversation as both men pondered this pronouncement. Hannah held her breath, listened for footsteps.

Having observed the obligatory moment's silence, Simion continued with renewed energy. "Lord Gifford has worked his magic, though—no one'll ever know the difference—and there's no reason not to seize the silver lining." There was a squeak of leather as he rearranged himself in his chair. "I've been thinking, it's about time you took another stab at politics. The business has never been better, you've kept your nose clean, gained a reputation amongst Conservatives as a sensible type. Why not seek nomination for the seat of Saffron?"

Teddy's voice was shiny with the glimmer of hope. "You mean move out to Riverton?"

"It's yours now, and country people do love their lord of the manor."

"Father," Teddy said breathlessly, "you're a genius. I'll call Lord Gifford immediately. See if he'll have a word with the others on my behalf." The telephone cradle rattled. "It's not too late is it?"

"Never too late for business," said Simion. "Or politics."

Hannah pulled away then. She had heard enough.

- II -

Robbie came back. He gave no explanation for his absence, simply sat down in Teddy's armchair as if no time had passed and presented Hannah with his first volume of poetry. She was about to tell him she already owned a copy when he drew another book from his coat pocket.

"For you," he said, handing it to her.

Hannah's heart skipped when she saw its title. It was James Joyce's *Ulysses*, and it was banned everywhere.

"But where did you—?"

"A friend in Paris."

Hannah ran her fingertips over the word *Ulysses*. It was about a married couple, she knew, and their moribund physical relationship. She had read—rather, Teddy had read her—extracts from the news-paper. He'd called them filth and she had nodded agreement. In truth, she'd found them strangely affecting. She could imagine what Teddy would have said if she'd told him so. He'd have thought her ill, recommended she see a doctor. And perhaps she was.

Yet, though thrilled to have the opportunity to read the novel, she wasn't certain how she felt about Robbie bringing it for her. Did he think she was the type of woman for whom such topics were ordinary fare? Worse: was he making a joke? Did he think her a prude? She was about to ask him when he said, very simply and very gently, "I'm sorry about your father."

And before she could say anything about *Ulysses*, she realized she was crying.

❋

No one thought much of Robbie's visits. Not at first. Certainly there was no suggestion that anything improper was passing between him and Hannah. Hannah would've been the first to deny it if there had. It was known to everyone that Robbie had been a friend to her brother, had been with him at the end. If he seemed a little irregular, less than respectable, as she knew Boyle continued to maintain, it was easily enough put down to the terrible mystery of war.

Robbie's visits followed no pattern, his arrival was never planned, but Hannah started looking forward to them, waiting for them. Sometimes she was alone, sometimes Emmeline or Deborah was with her; it didn't matter. For Hannah, Robbie became a lifeline. They spoke of books and travel. Far-fetched ideas and faraway places. He seemed to know so much about her already. It was almost like having David back.

Perhaps if Hannah had been less preoccupied she would have noticed she was not the only one for whom Robbie's visits had come to hold attraction. Might have observed that Deborah was spending more time at home. But she did not.

It came as a complete surprise one morning, in the drawing room, when Deborah put aside her crossword puzzle and said, "I'm throwing a little soirée to launch the new Chanel fragrance next week, Mr. Hunter, and wouldn't you know it? I've been so busy organizing I haven't had time even to think about finding myself a partner." She smiled, all white teeth and red lips.

"Doubt you'll have trouble," said Robbie. "Must be heaps of fellows looking for a ride on society's golden wave."

"Of course," said Deborah, mistaking Robbie's irony. "All the same, it's such late notice."

"Lord Woodall would be sure to take you," said Hannah.

"Lord Woodall is abroad," Deborah said quickly. She smiled at Robbie. "And I couldn't possibly go alone."

"Going stag is all the rage, according to Emmeline," said Hannah.

Deborah appeared not to have heard. She batted her lids at Robbie. "Unless . . ." She shook her head with a coyness that didn't suit her. "No, of course not."

Robbie said nothing.

Deborah pursed her lips. "Unless you'd accompany me, Mr. Hunter?"

Hannah held her breath.

"Me?" Robbie said, laughing. "I don't think so."

"Why not?" said Deborah, "We'd have a great old time."

"I know nothing of fashion," said Robbie. "I'd be a fish out of water."

"I'm a very strong swimmer," said Deborah. "I'll keep you afloat."

"All the same," said Robbie. "No."

Not for the first time, Hannah's breath caught in her throat. He had a lack of propriety quite unlike the affected vulgarity of Emmeline's friends. His was genuine and, Hannah thought, quite stunning.

Suitably rebuked, Deborah shook the newspaper onto her lap and gave the appearance of resuming her crossword.

Robbie smiled at Hannah, that smile of his that made her feel guilty somehow, complicit. Deliciously so. She couldn't help herself, she smiled back.

Deborah looked up sharply, glanced between them. Hannah recognized the expression: Deborah had inherited it, along with her lust for conquest, from Simion. Her lips thinned around the bitter taste of defeat. "You're a wordsmith, Mr. Hunter," she said coldly. "What's a seven-letter word starting with *b* that means an error of judgment?"

❦

At dinner a few nights later, Deborah took revenge for Robbie's blunder.

"I noticed Mr. Hunter was here again today," she said, spearing a pastry puff.

"He brought a book he thought might interest me," Hannah said.

Deborah glanced at Teddy, who was sitting at the head, dissecting his fish. "I just wonder whether Mr. Hunter's visits might be unsettling the staff."

Hannah laid down her cutlery. "I can't see why the staff would find Mr. Hunter's visits unsettling."

"No," said Deborah, drawing herself up. "I rather feared you wouldn't. You've never really been one for taking responsibility where the household is concerned." She spoke slowly, enunciating each word. "Servants are like children, Hannah dear. They like a good routine, find it almost impossible to function without. It's up to us, their betters, to provide them with one." She leaned her head to the side. "Now, as you know, Mr. Hunter's visits are unpredictable. By his own

377

admission, he doesn't know the first thing about polite society. He doesn't even telephone ahead so you can give notice. Mrs. Tibbit gets herself into quite a flap trying to provide tea for two when she's only been prepared for one. It's really not fair. Don't you agree, Teddy?"

"What's that?" He looked up from his fish.

"I was just saying," Deborah said, "how regrettable it is that the staff have been unsettled lately."

"Staff unsettled?" said Teddy. It was, of course, his pet fear, inherited from his father, that the servant class would one day revolt.

"I'll speak to Mr. Hunter," said Hannah quickly. "Ask him to telephone ahead in future."

Deborah appeared to consider this. "No," she said, shaking her head. "I'm afraid it's too little too late. I think perhaps it would be best if he were to cease visiting at all."

"Bit extreme, don't you think, Deb?" Teddy said, and Hannah felt a wave of warm affection for him. "Mr. Hunter's always struck me as harmless enough. Bohemian, I'll grant you, but harmless. If he calls ahead, surely the staff—"

"There are other issues to consider," Deborah snapped. "We wouldn't want anyone getting the wrong idea, would we, Teddy?"

"Wrong idea?" Teddy said, frowning. He began to laugh. "Oh Deb, you can't mean that anyone would think Hannah and Mr. Hunter . . . That my wife and a fellow like him . . . ?"

Hannah closed her eyes lightly.

"Of course I don't," Deborah said sharply. "But people love to talk, and talk isn't good for business. Or politics."

"Politics?" Teddy said.

"Mother said you're having another go," said Deborah. "How can people trust you to keep your electorate in check if they suspect you're having trouble keeping your *wife* in check?" She delivered herself a triumphant forkful of food.

Teddy looked troubled. "I hadn't thought of it like that."

"And neither should you," Hannah said quietly. "Mr. Hunter was my brother's good friend. He visits so that we may speak of David."

"I know that, old girl," said Teddy with an apologetic smile. He shrugged helplessly. "All the same, Deb has a point. You understand, don't you? We can't have people getting the wrong end of the stick."

※

DEBORAH stuck to Hannah like glue after that. Having suffered Robbie's rejection, she wanted to be sure he received the directive; more importantly, that he realized from whom it came. Thus the next time Robbie visited, he once again found Deborah on the drawing-room sofa with Hannah.

"Good morning, Mr. Hunter," Deborah said, smiling broadly while she plucked knots from the fur of her Maltese, Bunty. "How lovely to see you. I trust you're well?"

Robbie nodded. "You?"

"Oh, fighting fit," said Deborah.

Robbie smiled at Hannah. "What did you think?"

Hannah pressed her lips together. The proof copy of *The Waste Land* was sitting beside her. She handed it to him. "I loved it, Mr. Hunter. It moved me immeasurably."

He smiled. "I knew it would."

Hannah glanced towards Deborah, who widened her eyes pointedly. "Mr. Hunter," said Hannah, tightening her lips, "there's something I need to discuss with you." She pointed to Teddy's seat.

Robbie sat, looked at her with those dark eyes.

"My husband," began Hannah, but she didn't know how to finish. "My husband . . ."

She looked at Deborah, who cleared her throat and pretended absorption in Bunty's silky head. Hannah watched a moment, transfixed by Deborah's long, thin fingers, her pointed nails . . .

Robbie followed her gaze. "Your husband, Mrs. Luxton?"

Hannah spoke softly. "My husband would prefer that you no longer call without purpose."

Deborah pushed Bunty off her lap, brushed her dress. "You understand, don't you, Mr. Hunter?"

Boyle came in then carrying the tea salver. He laid it on the table, nodded to Deborah, then left.

"You will stay for tea, won't you?" said Deborah, in a sweet voice that made Hannah's skin crawl. "One last time?"

With Deborah as conductor, they managed an awkward conversation about the collapse of the coalition government and the assassination of Michael Collins. Hannah was hardly listening. All she wanted was a few minutes alone with Robbie in which to explain. She also knew it was the last thing Deborah would permit.

She was thinking this, wondering whether she would ever have the opportunity to speak with him again, realizing just how much she'd come to depend on his company, when the door opened and Emmeline came in from lunching with friends.

Emmeline was particularly pretty that day: she'd had her hair set into blonde waves and was wearing a new scarf in a new color—burnt sienna—that made her skin glow. She flew through the door as was her way, sending Bunty scuttling beneath the armchair, and sank casually into the corner of the sofa, resting her hands dramatically on her stomach.

"Phew," she said, oblivious to the room's tension. "I'm as stuffed as a Christmas goose. I truly don't think I'll ever eat again." She lolled her head to the side. "How's tricks, Robbie?" She didn't wait for an answer. She sat up suddenly, eyes wide. "Oh! You'll never guess who I met the other night at Lady Sybil Colefax's party. I was sitting there, talking with darling Lord Berners—he was telling me all about the dear little piano he's had installed in his Rolls-Royce—when who should arrive but the Sitwells! All three Sitwells. They were ever so much funnier in the flesh. Dear Sachy with his clever jokes, and Osbert with those little poem things with the funny endings—"

"Epigrams," Robbie mumbled.

"He's every bit as witty as Oscar Wilde," Emmeline continued. "But it was Edith who was most impressive. She recited one of her poems and it brought the whole lot of us to tears. Well, you know what Lady Colefax is like—an absolute snob for brains—I couldn't help myself, Robbie darling, I mentioned that I knew you and they just about died. I dare say they didn't believe me, they all think I've a talent for invention—I can't think why—but you see? You simply have to come to the party tonight to prove them wrong."

She drew breath and in one swift movement withdrew a cigarette from her bag and had it lit. She exhaled a rush of smoke. "Say you'll come, Robbie. It's one thing to have people doubt one when one's lying, quite another when one's speaking the truth."

Robbie paused a moment, considering her offer. "What time should I collect you?" he said.

Hannah blinked. She'd expected him to decline as he always did when Emmeline tossed him one of her invitations. She'd thought Robbie felt the same way about Emmeline's friends as she did. Perhaps his disdain did not extend to the likes of Lord Berners and Lady Sybil. Perhaps the lure of the Sitwells was too much to resist.

❦

F O R a time it continued thus: Hannah saw Robbie when he came to collect Emmeline and there was little Deborah could do to change things. Once, when she made a last-ditch attempt to have him banished, Teddy shrugged and said it seemed only proper that the mistress of the house entertain guests who called for her younger sister. Would she have the fellow sit by himself in the drawing room?

Hannah tried to satisfy herself with precious snatched moments, but found herself thinking about Robbie between times. He'd never been forthcoming about what he did when they weren't together. She didn't even know where he lived. So she started imagining; she'd always been good at games of imagination.

She managed, rather conveniently, to ignore the fact that he was spending time with Emmeline. What did it matter anyway? Emmeline had an enormous group of friends. Robbie was just one more.

Then one morning, when she was sitting at the breakfast table with Teddy, he flicked his hand against his open newspaper and said, "What do you think of that sister of yours, eh?"

Hannah braced, wondering what disgrace Emmeline had caused this time. She took the paper as Teddy passed it across the table.

It was only a small photograph. Robbie and Emmeline leaving a nightclub. A good shot of Emmeline, Hannah had to concede, chin lifted, laughing as she pulled Robbie by the arm. His face was less obvious. He was in shadow, had looked away at the critical moment.

Teddy took it back and read the accompanying text aloud: "*The Honorable Miss E. Hartford, one of society's most glamorous young ladies, is pictured with a dark stranger. The mystery man is said to be the poet R. S. Hunter. A source says Miss Hartford has hinted an engagement announcement is not too far away.*" He laid the paper down, took a forkful of devilled egg. "Quite the dark horse, isn't she? Didn't think Emmeline was the sort to keep a secret," he said. "Could be worse, I suppose. Could have set her cap at that Harry Bentley." He dabbed his thumb at the corner of his moustache, wiped away a clot of egg. "You'll talk to him, though, won't you? Make sure everything's above board. I don't need a scandal."

＊

W H E N Robbie came to collect Emmeline the following night, Hannah received him as usual. They spoke for a time as they always did, until finally Hannah could stand it no longer.

"Mr. Hunter," she said, walking to the fireplace. "I must ask. Do you have something you wish to speak with me about?"

He sat back, smiled at her. "I have. And I thought I was speaking to you."

"Something else, Mr. Hunter?"

His smile faltered. "I don't think I follow."

"Something you wanted to ask me about?"

"Perhaps if you told me what it is you think I should be saying," said Robbie.

Hannah sighed. She collected the newspaper from the writing bureau and gave it to him.

He scanned it and handed it back. "So?"

"Mr. Hunter," Hannah said in a quiet voice. She didn't want the servants to hear if they happened to be in the entrance hall. "I am my sister's guardian. If you wish to become engaged, it really would be polite for you to discuss your intentions with me first."

Robbie smiled, saw that Hannah was not amused and coached his lips back into repose. "I'll remember that, Mrs. Luxton."

She blinked at him. "Well, Mr. Hunter?"

"Well, Mrs. Luxton?"

"Is there something you would like to ask me?"

"No," said Robbie, laughing. "I have no intention of marrying Emmeline. Not now. Not ever. But thank you for asking."

"Oh," said Hannah simply. "Does Emmeline know that?"

Robbie shrugged. "I don't see why she'd think otherwise. I've never given her reason."

"My sister is a romantic," said Hannah. "She forms attachments easily."

"Then she'll have to unform them."

Hannah felt sympathy for Emmeline then, but she felt something else too. She hated herself as she realized it was relief.

"What is it?" Robbie said. He was very close. She wondered when he'd moved to stand so close.

"I'm worried about Emmeline," Hannah said, stepping back a little, her leg grazing the sofa. "She imagines your feelings are more than they are."

"What can I do?" said Robbie. "I've already told her they're not."

"You must stop seeing her," said Hannah quietly. "Tell her

383

you're not interested in her parties. It won't be too much of a hardship for you, surely. You've said yourself you have little to speak of with her friends."

"I don't."

"Then if you don't feel anything for Emmeline, be honest with her. Please, Mr. Hunter. Break it off. She'll come to harm otherwise and I can't allow that."

Robbie looked at her. He reached out and, very gently, straightened a lock of her hair that had come loose. She was frozen to the spot, was aware of nothing but him. His dark eyes, the warmth coming from his skin, his soft lips. "I would," he said. "This minute." He was very close now. She was aware of his breath, could hear it, feel it on her neck. He spoke softly. "But how would I ever see you?"

⚘

THINGS changed after that. Of course they did. They had to. Something implicit had become explicit. For Hannah the darkness had started to recede. She was falling in love with him, of course, not that she realized it at first. She'd never been in love before, had nothing with which to compare. She'd been attracted to people, had felt that sudden, inexplicable pull, had felt it once with Teddy. But there is a difference between enjoying someone's company, thinking them attractive, and finding oneself helplessly in love.

The occasional meetings she had once looked forward to, snatched while Robbie waited for Emmeline, were no longer enough. Hannah longed to see him elsewhere, alone, somewhere they might speak freely. Where there wasn't the constant risk that someone else might join them.

Opportunity came one evening in early 1923. Teddy was in America on business, Deborah at a country-house weekend, and Emmeline out with friends at one of Robbie's poetry readings. Hannah made a decision.

She ate dinner alone in the dining room, sat in the morning

room afterwards and sipped coffee, then retired to her bedroom. When I came to dress her for bed, she was in the bathroom, sitting on the edge of the elegant claw-foot tub. She was wearing a delicate satin slip; Teddy had brought it back from one of his trips to the Continent. In her hands was something black.

"Would you like to take a bath, ma'am?" I said. It was unusual, but not unheard of, for her to bathe after dinner.

"No," said Hannah.

"Shall I bring you your nightdress?"

"No," she said again. "I'm not going to bed, Grace. I'm going out."

I was confused. "Ma'am?"

"I'm going out. And I need your help."

She didn't want any of the other servants to know. They were spies, she said matter-of-factly, and she wanted neither Teddy nor Deborah—nor Emmeline, for that matter—to know she'd been anywhere but home all evening.

It worried me to think of her out alone at night, keeping such a thing from Teddy. And I wondered where she was going, whether she would tell me. Despite my misgivings, however, I agreed to help. Of course I did. It was what she'd asked of me.

Neither of us spoke as I helped her into a dress she'd already chosen: pale blue silk with a fringe that brushed her bare knees. She sat in front of the mirror, watching as I pinned her hair tight against her head. Plucking at the fronds of her dress, twirling her locket chain, biting her lip. Then she handed me a wig: black, sleek and short, something Emmeline had worn months before to a fancy-dress party. I was surprised—wigs were not her habit—but I fitted it, then stepped back to observe. She looked like a different person. Like Louise Brooks.

She picked up a bottle of perfume—another of Teddy's gifts—Chanel N°5, brought back from Paris the year before, then changed her mind. Returned the bottle to its place and regarded herself. It was then I saw the piece of notepaper on her bureau: *Robbie's Reading,* it said. *The Stray Cat, Soho, Saturday, 10 p.m.* She grabbed the paper, stuffed it into her clutch bag and snapped it shut. Then, in the mirror, her eyes met mine. She said nothing; she didn't have to. I wondered why I hadn't guessed. Who else would have her this alert? This jittery? So full of expectation?

I went ahead, making sure the servants were all downstairs. And then I told Mr. Boyle I'd noticed a stain on the glass pane in the entrance vestibule. I hadn't, but I couldn't have any of the staff hearing the front door open for no reason.

I went back upstairs and signaled to Hannah, standing at the turn of the stairs, that the way was clear. I opened the front door and through she went. On the other side we stopped. She turned to me, smiled.

"Be careful, ma'am," I said, silencing my rumblings of foreboding.

She nodded. "Thank you, Grace. For everything."

And she disappeared into the night air, silently, shoes in her hands so as not to make the slightest noise.

✻

HANNAH found a taxi on a street around the corner and gave the driver the address of the club in which Robbie was reading. She was so excited she could hardly breathe. She had to keep tapping her heels on the floor of the taxi to convince herself it was really happening.

The address had been easy enough to obtain. Emmeline kept a journal into which she clipped pamphlets and advertisements and invitations, and it hadn't taken Hannah long to find it. She needn't have bothered as it turned out. Once she'd told the taxi driver the name, he needed no further instruction. The Stray Cat was one of Soho's better-known clubs, a meeting spot for artists, drug dealers, business tycoons and bright young members of the aristocracy, bored and idle, keen to shake off the shackles of their birth.

He pulled up the cab and told her to be careful, shook his head as she paid him. She turned to thank him, and watched as the club's reflected name slid off his black cab as he disappeared into the night.

Hannah had never been to such a place before. She stood where she was, took in the plain brick exterior, the flashing sign and the crowds of laughing people spilling onto the street outside. So this was what Emmeline meant when she talked about the clubs. This was where she and her friends came to play in the evenings. Hannah shivered into her scarf, kept her head down and went inside, refusing the valet's offer to take her wrap.

It was tiny, little more than a room, and it was warm, full of jostling bodies. The smoky air smelled sweetly of gin. She stayed near the entrance, close to a pillar, and scanned the room, looking for Robbie.

He was onstage already, if stage it could be called. A small patch of bare space between the grand piano and the bar. He was sitting on a stool, cigarette on his lips, smoking lazily. His jacket was hanging on the back of a nearby chair and he wore only his black suit trousers and a white shirt. His collar was loose and so was his hair. He was flicking through a notebook. In front of him, the audience lounged around small round tables. Others had crowded onto bar stools or draped themselves against the edges of the room.

Hannah saw Emmeline then, sitting in the middle of a table of friends. Fanny was with her, the old lady of the group. (Married life had proven something of a disappointment for Fanny. With the children appropriated by a rather tedious nurse and a husband who spent his time dreaming up new ailments to suffer, there was little to keep her interest. Who could blame her for seeking adventure at the side of her young friends?) They tolerated her, Emmeline had told Hannah, because she was so genuine in her pursuit of fun, and besides, she was older and could get them out of all sorts of trouble. She was especially good at sweet-talking police when they were caught in after-hours raids. They were all drinking cocktails in Martini glasses, and one of them ran a line of white powder on the table. Ordinarily, Hannah would have worried for Emmeline, but tonight she was in love with the world.

Hannah inched closer to the pillar, but she needn't have bothered. They were so engrossed with one another they had little time to look beyond. The fellow with the white powder whispered something to Emmeline and she laughed wildly, freely, her pale neck exposed.

Robbie's hands were shaking. Hannah could see the notebook quivering. He rested his cigarette across an ashtray on the bar beside him and began, giving no introduction. A poem about history, and mystery, and memory: "The Shifting Fog." It was one of her favorites.

Hannah watched him; it was the first opportunity she'd ever had to gaze at him, to let her eyes roam his face, his body, without him knowing. And she listened. The words had touched her when she'd read them, but to hear him speak them was to see inside his own heart.

He finished, and the audience clapped, and someone called out, and there was laughter, and he looked up. At her. His face didn't betray him, but she knew he saw, recognized her despite her disguise.

For a moment they were alone.

He looked back at his notebook, turned a few pages, fumbled a bit, settled on the next poem.

And then he spoke to her. Poem after poem. About knowing and unknowing, truth and suffering, love and lust. She closed her eyes and with every word she felt the darkness disappearing.

Then he was finished and the audience was applauding. The bar staff swept into action, mixing American cocktails and pouring shots, and the musicians took their seats, broke into jazz. Some of the drunk, laughing people improvised a dance floor between the tables. Hannah saw Emmeline wave to Robbie, beckon him to join them. Robbie waved back and pointed to his watch. Emmeline jutted her bottom lip, an exaggerated gesture, then whooped and waved as one of her male friends dragged her up to dance.

Robbie lit another cigarette, shrugged into his jacket and tucked his notebook into the inside pocket. He said something to a man behind the bar and headed across the room towards Hannah.

In that moment, as time slowed and she watched him walking,

drawing closer, she was faint. She experienced vertigo. As if she were standing on the top of an enormous cliff, in a strong wind, unable to do anything but fall.

Without a word, he took her hand and led her out of the door.

※

I T was three in the morning when Hannah crept down the servants' stairs of number seventeen. I was waiting for her, as I'd promised, my stomach a knot of nerves. She was later than expected, and darkness and disquiet had conspired to fill my mind with awful scenes.

"Thank goodness," Hannah said, slipping through the door as I opened it. "I was worried you'd forget."

"Of course not, ma'am," I said, offended.

Hannah floated through the servants' hall and tiptoed into the main house, shoes in hand. She'd started up the stairs to the second floor when she realized I was still following. "You don't need to see me to bed, Grace. It's far too late. Besides, I'd like to be alone."

I nodded, stopped where I was, stood on the bottom step in my white nightie like a forgotten child.

"Ma'am," I said quickly.

Hannah turned. "Yes?"

"Did you have a nice time, ma'am?"

Hannah smiled. "Oh, Grace," she said. "Tonight my life began."

- III -

T H E Y always met at his place. She had often wondered where he lived, but her imaginings had never brought her close. He had a little barge called the *Sweet Dulcie* and he kept it moored at the Thames Embankment, usually near Chelsea Bridge. He had bought it from a dear friend, he told her, in France after the war, and had sailed it back to London. It was a sturdy little thing and, despite appearances, quite capable of a voyage on the open sea.

The inside was surprisingly well appointed: wood-paneled, a tiny box kitchen hung with copper pots and a sitting area with a pull-down bed beneath a bank of curtained windows. There was even a shower and water-closet recess. That he lived somewhere so unusual, so different to anywhere she'd been before, only added to the adventure. There was something delicious, she thought, about captured moments of intimacy in such a secret place.

It was easy enough to arrange. Robbie would come to collect Emmeline, and while he waited would slip Hannah a note with a time and a date and the bridge by which he'd be moored. Hannah would scan the note, nod agreement, and they would meet. Sometimes it was impossible—Teddy would require her presence at an event or Estella would volunteer her for this committee or that. On such occasions, she had no way of telling him. It pained her to imagine him waiting in vain.

But most of the time she did make it. She would tell the others she was meeting a friend for lunch, or going shopping, and she would disappear. She was never gone for long. She was careful about that. Anything beyond a morning or an afternoon was liable to raise suspicions. Illicit love makes people devious and she soon became adept: came to think quickly on her feet if she were seen somewhere unexpected, by someone unexpected. One day she ran into Lady Clementine on Oxford Circus. Where was her driver? asked Lady Clementine. She'd come out on foot, said Hannah. It was such beautiful weather they were having and she'd felt like a walk. But Lady Clementine hadn't come down in yesterday's shower. She narrowed her eyes and nodded, told Hannah to be sure and be careful as she went. The street had eyes and ears.

The street, perhaps, but not the river. At least, not the sort of eyes and ears that Hannah had to fear. The Thames was different then. A working waterway, full of the bustle and traffic of commerce: coal ferries en route to factories, barges transporting dry goods, fishing boats bearing cargo to market; and along the canal towpaths, great gentle Clydesdales pulling painted longboats, trying to ignore the cheeky swooping gulls.

Hannah loved it on the river. She couldn't believe she'd lived in London for years and never discovered the city's heart. She had strolled across the bridges, of course, some of them at least; been chauffeur-driven to and fro on many occasions. But she had paid scant attention to the seething life below.

And so they met. She would leave number seventeen and make her way to whichever bridge his note had named. Sometimes it was an area she knew, other times it took her to a foreign part of London. She would find the bridge, descend the embankment and scan the river for his little blue boat.

He was always waiting. When she drew near, he would reach out, take her hand in his and help her aboard. They'd go down into the cabin, away from the busy, noisy world and into their own.

⚘

SOMETIMES, afterwards, they would lie together, lulled by the gentle rocking of the boat. Telling each other about their lives. They spoke, as lovers do, of poetry, and music, and the places that Robbie had been and she longed to see.

One wintry afternoon, when the sun was low in the sky, they climbed the narrow stairs onto the upper deck and into the wheelhouse. A fog had come in and with it the gift of privacy. In the distance, on another reach of the river, something was burning. They could smell the smoke from where they sat and, as they watched, the flames grew higher and brighter.

"It must be a barge," said Robbie. Something exploded as he spoke, and he flinched. A bright shower of sparks filled the air.

Hannah watched as a cloud of golden light consumed the fog. "How dreadful," she said. "But how beautiful." It was like one of Turner's paintings, she thought.

Robbie seemed to read her mind. "Whistler used to live on the

391

Thames," he said. "He loved to paint the shifting fog, the effects of light. Monet too, he was here for a while."

"You're in good company, then," said Hannah, smiling.

"My friend who used to own the *Dulcie* was a painter," said Robbie.

"Really? What's his name? Would I know his work?"

"Her name is Marie Seurat."

Hannah felt a flicker of envy then, thinking of this phantom woman who had lived on her own boat, made a life as a painter, known Robbie when she, Hannah, had not.

"Did you love her?" she said, preparing herself for his answer.

"I was very fond of her," he said, "but alas, she was rather attached to her lover, Georgette." He laughed, watching Hannah's face. "Paris is a very different place."

"I'd love to go there again," said Hannah.

"We will," said Robbie, taking her hand in his. "One day, we will."

✤

ONE drizzly day in April they lay curled up together, listening to the gentle slap of the water against the boat's hull. Hannah was watching the clock on the wall, counting off the time before she had to leave. Finally, when the unfaithful minute hand reached the hour, she sat up. Retrieved her pair of stockings from the end of the bed and began to drag the left one on. Robbie walked his fingers along the base of her spine.

"Don't go," he said.

She bunched her right stocking and slipped it over her foot.

"Stay."

She was standing now. Dropping her slip over her head, straightening it around her hips. "You know I would. I'd stay forever if I could."

"In our secret world."

"Yes," she smiled, knelt on the edge of the bed and reached out to stroke the side of his face. "I like that. Our own world. A secret world. I love secrets." She exhaled, she'd been thinking about this for some time. Wasn't sure why she wanted so keenly to share it with him. "When we were children," she said, "we used to play a game."

"I know," said Robbie. "David told me about The Game."

"He did?"

Robbie nodded.

"But The Game is secret," said Hannah automatically. "Why did he tell you?"

"You were about to tell me yourself."

"Yes, but that's different. You and I . . . It's different."

"So tell me about The Game," he said. "Forget that I already know."

She looked at the clock. "I really should be going."

"Just tell me quickly," he said.

"All right. Just quickly."

And she did. She told him about Nefertiti and Charles Darwin, and Emmeline's Queen Victoria, and the adventures they went on, each more extraordinary than the one before.

"You should have been a writer," he said, stroking her forearm.

"Yes," she said seriously. "I could have made my escapes and adventures at the sweep of a pen."

"It's not too late," he said. "You could start writing now."

She smiled. "I don't need to now. I escape to you."

※

SOMETIMES he bought wine and they would drink it from old glass tumblers. They would eat cheese and bread, and listen to romantic music on the tiny gramophone that had accompanied him from France. Sometimes, when the lace curtains were drawn, they would dance. Oblivious to the boat's confined space.

One such afternoon he fell asleep. She drank the rest of her wine, then for a time she lay next to him, tried to match her breaths to his, succeeded finally in catching his rhythm. But she couldn't sleep, the novelty of lying next to him was too great. The novelty of him was too great. She knelt on the floor and watched his face. She'd never seen him sleeping before.

He was dreaming. She could see the muscles around his eyes tightening at whatever was playing on his closed lids. The twitching grew fiercer as she watched. She thought she should wake him. She didn't like to see him like this, his beautiful face contorted.

Then he started to call out and she was worried someone on the embankment might hear. Might come to their aid. Might contact someone. The police, or worse.

She laid her hand on his forearm, ran her fingers lightly over the familiar scar. He continued to sleep, continued to call out. She shook him gently, said his name. "Robbie? You're dreaming, my love."

His eyes flashed open, round and dark, and before she knew what was happening she was on the floor, he on top of her, his hands around her neck. He was choking her, she could barely breathe. She tried to say his name, tell him to stop, but she couldn't. It only lasted a moment, then something in him clicked and he realized who she was. Realized what he was doing. He recoiled. Jumped off.

She sat up then, inched quickly backwards until her back hit the wall. She was looking at him, shocked, wondering what had come over him. Who he had thought she was.

He was standing against the far wall, hands pressed against his face, shoulders curved. "Are you all right?" he said, without looking at her.

She nodded, wondered whether she was. "Yes," she said, finally.

He came to her then, knelt beside her. She must have flinched, for he held his hands up by his shoulders and said, "I won't hurt you." He reached out, lifted her chin to see her throat. "Jesus," he said.

"It's all right," she said, more firmly this time. "Are you—?"

He held a finger to her lips. He was still breathing quickly. He shook his head absently, and she knew he wanted to explain. Couldn't.

He cupped the side of her face with his hand. She leaned into his touch, eyes locked with his. Such dark eyes, full of secrets he wouldn't share. She longed to know them all, determined to earn them from him. And when he kissed her throat, oh, so lightly, she swooned, as she always did.

She had to wear scarves for a week after that. But she didn't mind. In some way it pleased her to have his mark. It made the times between more bearable. A secret reminder that he really did exist, that they existed. Their secret world. She would look at it sometimes, in the mirror, the way a new bride looks repeatedly at her wedding ring. Reminding herself. She knew he would have been horrified if she'd told him.

※

L O V E affairs, in their beginnings, are all about the present. But there is a point in each—an event, an exchange, some other unseen trigger—which forces the past and the future back into focus. For Hannah, this was it. There were other sides to him. Things she hadn't known before. She'd been too full of the wonderful surprise of him to look beyond immediate happiness. The more she thought about this aspect of him, of which she knew so little, the more frustrated she became. The more determined to know everything.

One cool afternoon in September, they were sitting together on the bed watching the embankment through the window. There were people walking this way and that, and they'd been giving them names and imagined lives. They'd been quiet for a while, had been content just to watch the passing procession from their secret position, when Robbie hopped out of bed.

She remained where she was, rolled over to watch him as he sat himself on the kitchen chair, one leg curled beneath him, head bent over his notebook. He was trying to write a poem. Had been trying all day. He'd been distracted while he was with her. Had been unable to play their game with any enthusiasm. She didn't mind. In some way she couldn't explain, his distraction made him more attractive.

She lay on the bed, watching his fingers clutching his pencil, directing it in flowing circles and loops across the page, only to stop, hesitate, then backtrack fiercely across its previous path. He tossed the notebook and pencil onto the table and rubbed his eyes with his hand.

She didn't say anything. She knew better than that. This was not the first time she'd seen him like this. He was frustrated, she knew, by his own failure to find the right words. Worse, he was frightened. He hadn't told her, but she knew. She'd watched him, and she had read about it: at the library and in newspapers and journals. It was a trait of what the doctors were calling shell shock. The increased unreliability of memory, the numbing of the brain by traumatic experiences.

He took his hand from across his eyes and reached once more for the pencil and paper. Started again to write, stopped, scratched it out.

She longed to make it better, to make him forget. Would give anything to make it stop; his relentless fear that he was losing his mind.

※

AND then it was winter again. He set the boat's little firebox against the wall by the kitchen. They sat on the floor, watching the flames flicker and hiss in the grate. Their skin was warm and they were drowsy with red wine and warmth and each other.

Hannah took a sip of wine and said, "Why won't you talk about the war?"

He didn't answer; instead he lit a cigarette.

She'd been reading Freud on repression and had some idea that if she could get Robbie to speak about it, perhaps he would be cured. She held her breath, wondered if she dared to ask. "Is it because you killed somebody?"

He looked at her profile, took a drag of his cigarette, exhaled and shook his head. Then he started to laugh softly, without humor. He reached out to lay his hand gently along the side of her face.

"Is that it?" she whispered, still not looking at him.

He didn't answer and she took another tack.

"Who is it you dream about?"

He removed his hand. "You know the answer to that," he said. "I only ever dream of you."

"I hope not," said Hannah. "They're not very nice dreams."

He took another drag of his cigarette, exhaled. "Don't ask me," he said.

"It's shell shock, isn't it?" she said, turning to him. "I've been reading about it."

His eyes met hers. Such dark eyes. Like wet paint; full of secrets.

"Shell shock," he said. "I've always wondered who came up with that. I suppose they needed a nice name to describe the unspeakable for the nice ladies back home."

"Nice ladies like me, you mean," said Hannah. She was put out. Was not in the mood to be fobbed off. She sat up and slipped her petticoat over her head. Started to pull her stockings on.

He sighed. She knew he didn't want her to leave like this. Angry with him.

"You've read Darwin?" he said.

"Charles Darwin?" she said, turning to him. "Of course. But what does Charles Darwin have to do with—"

"Adaptation. Survival is a matter of successful adaptation. Some of us are better at it than others."

"Adaptation to what?"

"To war. To living by your wits. The new rules of the game."

Hannah thought about this. A large boat went by, setting the barge to rocking.

"I'm alive," Robbie said plainly, firelight flickering on his face, "because some other bugger isn't."

So now she knew.

She wondered how she felt about it. "I'm glad you're alive," she said, but she felt a shiver from deep down inside. And when his fingers stroked her wrist she withdrew it despite herself.

"That's why nobody talks about it," he said. "They know that if they do, people will see them for what they really are. Members of the devil's party moving amid the regular people as though they still belong. As if they're not monsters returned from a murderous rampage."

"Don't say that," said Hannah sharply. "You're not a murderer."

"I'm a killer."

"It's different. It was war. It was self-defense. Defense of others."

He shrugged. "Still a bullet through some fellow's brain."

"Stop it," she whispered. "I don't like it when you talk like that."

"Then you shouldn't have asked."

※

S H E didn't like it. She didn't like to think of him that way, and yet she found she couldn't stop. That someone she knew—someone she knew intimately, whose hands had run gently, lightly, over her body, whom she trusted implicitly—should have killed . . . Well, it changed things. It changed him. Not for the worse. She didn't love him any less. But she looked at him differently. He had killed a man. Men. Countless, nameless men.

She was thinking that one afternoon, watching him as he prowled about the barge. He had his trousers on, but his shirt was still draped across a chair. She was watching his lean muscled arms, his bare shoulders, his beautiful, brutal hands, when it happened.

Footsteps on the deck above.

They both froze, stared at each other; Robbie lifted his shoulders.

There was a knock. Then a voice, "Hello, Robbie? Open up. It's just me."

Emmeline's voice.

Hannah slid off the side of the bed and quickly gathered her clothing.

Robbie held his finger to his lips and tiptoed to the door.

"I know you're in there," said Emmeline. "There's a lovely old man on the towpath who said he saw you come in and that you haven't been out all afternoon. Let me in, it's bloody freezing out here."

Robbie signaled to Hannah to hide in the water closet.

Hannah nodded, tiptoed across the cabin, snibbed the door quickly behind her. Her heart was pounding against her ribcage. She fumbled with her dress, pulled it over her head and knelt to peer through the keyhole.

Robbie opened the door. "How'd you know where to find me?"

"Charmed, I'm sure," said Emmeline, ducking her head and sauntering into the center of the cabin. Hannah noticed she was wearing her new yellow dress. "Desmond told Freddy, Freddy told Jane. You know how those kids are." She paused and ran her wide-eyed gaze over everything. "How utterly divine, Robbie darling! What a wonderful hidey-hole. You must have a party . . . A very *cozy* party." She raised her brows when she saw the tangle of sheets on the bed and turned back to Robbie, smiling as she assessed his state of undress. "I haven't interrupted anything?"

Hannah inhaled.

"I was sleeping," said Robbie.

"At a quarter to four?"

He shrugged, found his shirt and put it on.

"I wondered what you did all day. Here was I thinking you'd be busy writing poetry."

"I was. I do." He rubbed his neck, exhaled angrily. "What do you want?"

Hannah winced at the harshness of his voice. It was Emmeline's mention of poetry: Robbie hadn't written in weeks. Emmeline didn't seem to notice any unkindness. "I wanted to know if you were coming tonight. To Desmond's place."

"I told you I wasn't."

"I know that's what you said, but I thought you might have changed your mind."

"I haven't."

There was a silence as Robbie glanced back towards the door and Emmeline looked longingly around the cabin. "Perhaps I could—"

"You have to go," said Robbie quickly. "I'm working."

"But I could help out," she used her bag to lift the edge of a dirty plate, "tidy up or—"

"I said no." Robbie opened the door.

Hannah watched as Emmeline forced her lips into a breezy smile. "I was joking, darling. You didn't really think I'd have nothing better to do on a lovely afternoon than clean house?"

Robbie didn't say anything.

Emmeline strolled towards the door. Straightened his collar. "You're still coming to Freddy's tomorrow?"

He nodded.

"Pick me up at six?"

"Yeah," said Robbie, and he closed the door behind her.

Hannah came out of the bathroom then. She felt dirty. Like a rat slinking out of its hole.

"Perhaps we should leave it a while?" she said. "A week or so?"

"No," said Robbie. "I've told Emmeline not to drop around. I'll tell her again. I'll make sure she understands."

Hannah nodded, wondered why she felt so guilty. She reminded herself, as she always did, that it had to be this way. That Emmeline wasn't being harmed. Robbie had long ago explained that his feelings were not romantic. He said she'd laughed and wondered why on earth he ever imagined she thought otherwise. And yet. Something in Emmeline's voice, a strain beneath the practised flippancy. And the yellow dress. Emmeline's favorite . . .

Hannah looked at the wall clock. There was still half an hour before she had to leave. "I might go," she said.

"No," he said. "Stay."

"I really—"

"At least a few minutes. Give Emmeline time to find her way."

Hannah nodded as Robbie came towards her. He ran a hand over each side of her face to grip the back of her neck, then pulled her lips to his.

A sudden, jagged kiss that caught her off balance and silenced, utterly, the niggling voices of misgiving.

※

A WET afternoon in December; they were sitting in the wheelhouse. The boat was moored near Battersea Bridge, where the willows wept into the Thames.

Hannah exhaled slowly. She had been waiting for the right moment to tell him. "I won't be able to meet for two weeks," she said. "It's Teddy. He has guests from America for the next fortnight and I'm expected to play the good wife. Take them places, entertain them."

"I hate to think of you like that," he said. "Fawning all over him."

"I certainly don't fawn all over him. Teddy wouldn't know what was happening if I did."

"You know what I mean," said Robbie.

She nodded. Of course she knew what he meant. "I hate it too. I'd do anything so that I never had to leave you."

"Anything?"

"Almost anything." She shivered as a scud of rain blew into the wheelhouse. "Arrange to see Emmeline sometime next week; let me know when and where we can meet, after New Year?"

Robbie reached across the wheel to pull closed the window. "I want to break it off with Emmeline."

"No," said Hannah suddenly. "Not yet. How will we see each other? How will I know where to find you?"

"Wouldn't be a problem if you lived with me. We'd always be able to find one another. Wouldn't be able to lose each other."

"I know, I know," she reached for his hand. "But until then . . . How can you think of breaking it off?"

He pulled away, the window was stuck, wouldn't budge. "You were right," he said. "She's becoming too attached."

"Leave that," said Hannah, "you're getting wet."

Finally it gave way, slammed closed. Robbie sat down again, hair dripping. "Far too attached."

"Emmeline's ebullient," said Hannah, taking a towel from the cupboard behind her, reaching out to dry his face. "It's just her way. Why? What makes you say that?"

Robbie shook his head impatiently.

"What is it?" said Hannah.

"Nothing," said Robbie. "You're right. It's probably nothing."

"I know it's nothing," said Hannah firmly. And in that moment she believed it. Would have said it even if she didn't. Love is like that: insistent, sure, persuasive. It silences easily all whispers of misgiving.

The rain was heavy now. "You're cold," said Hannah, wrapping the towel around his shoulders. She knelt before him, rubbing his bare arms dry. "You'll catch a chill." She didn't meet his eyes when she said, "Teddy wants us to move back to Riverton."

"When?"

"March. He's going to have it restored, build a new summer house. It's all he's thought about for weeks." She spoke drily. "He imagines himself quite the country squire."

"Why didn't you tell me before?"

"I didn't want to think of it," she said helplessly. "I kept hoping he'd change his mind." She threw her arms around him with sudden fierceness. "You have to keep contact with Emmeline. I can't invite you to stay, but she can. She's bound to have friends up for weekends, country parties."

He nodded, wouldn't meet her eyes.

"Please," said Hannah. "For me. I have to know you're coming."

"And we'll become one of those country-house couples?"

"Yes," she said.

"We'll play the same games as countless couples before us. Sneak around in the night, pretend to be distantly acquainted in the day?"

"Yes," she said quietly.

"That's not our game."

"I know."

"It's not enough," he said.

"I know," she said again.

☙

NINETEEN twenty-three became 1924, and one evening, with Teddy away on business and Deborah and Emmeline engaged with various friends, they arranged to meet. The boat was moored in a part of London Hannah had never entered. As the taxi wended its way deeper into the tangled East End, she watched out of the windows. Night had fallen and for the most part there was little to see: gray buildings; horse-drawn carts with lanterns suspended over their top; occasional red-cheeked children in woollen jumpers, tossing jacks, rolling marbles, pointing at the taxi. Then, down one street, the shock of colored lights, people thronging, music.

Hannah leaned forward, said to the driver, "What is this? What's happening here?"

"New Year festival," he said in a heavy cockney accent. "Bloody barmy, the lot of 'em. Middle o' winter; should be inside."

Hannah watched, fascinated, as the taxi crawled down the street towards the river. Lights had been strung between buildings so that they zigzagged right the way along. A band of men playing fiddles and a piano accordion had gathered quite a crowd, clapping and laughing. Children wove between adults, dragging streamers and blowing whistles; men and women mingled around great metal drums, roasting chestnuts, drinking ale from mugs. The taxi driver had to hit his horn and call out at them to clear the way. "Mad, the lot of 'em," he said as the taxi emerged at the other end of the street and turned the corner into a darkened road. "Stark raving."

Hannah felt as if she'd passed through a sort of fairyland. When the driver pulled up finally at the docks, she ran breathlessly to find Robbie who had been waiting for her.

Robbie was resistant, but Hannah pleaded, convinced him finally to accompany her back to the festival. They got out so little, she said, and when might they have the opportunity again to visit a party together? No one would know them here. It was safe.

She led the way from memory, half convinced she'd be unable to find it again. Half convinced the festival would have disappeared like a fairy ring in a children's tale. But soon enough the frenetic strains of the violin band, children's whistles, jovial shouts, and she knew it lay ahead.

Moments later they turned the corner into wonderland, began to wander down the street. The cool breeze brought with it mingling wafts of roasting nuts, sweat and good cheer. People hung out of windows, calling to those below, singing, toasting the new year, farewelling the old. Hannah watched wide-eyed, held tightly to Robbie's arm, pointing this way and that, laughing with delight at the people who'd started dancing on a makeshift floor.

They stopped to watch, joined the growing crowd, found seats together on a plank of wood stretched across timber boxes. A large woman with red cheeks and masses of dark curling hair perched on a stool by the fiddlers, singing and slapping a tambourine against her padded thigh. Whoops from the audience, shouts of encouragement, flowing skirts whipping past.

Hannah was enthralled. She'd never seen such revelry. Oh, she'd attended her fair share of parties, but compared to this they seemed so orchestrated. So tame. She clapped, laughed, squeezed Robbie's hand vehemently. "They're wonderful," she said, unable to shift her eyes from the couples. Men and women of all shapes and sizes, arms linked as they swirled and stomped and clapped. "Aren't they wonderful?"

The music was infectious. Faster, louder, seeping through each pore, flowing into her blood, making her skin tingle. Driving rhythm that tugged at her core.

Then Robbie's voice in her ear. "I'm thirsty. Let's go, find something to drink."

She hardly heard, shook her head. Realized she'd been holding her breath. "No. No, you go. I want to watch."

He hesitated. "I don't want to leave you."

"I'll be fine." Vaguely aware as his hand held firm a moment, then detached from hers. No time to watch him go, too much else to see. To hear. To feel.

She wondered later whether she should have noticed something in his voice. Whether she should have realized then that the noise, the activity, the crowds were pressing in on him so that he could hardly breathe. But she didn't. She was captivated.

Robbie's place was soon filled, someone else's warm thigh pressed against hers. She glanced sideways. A short, stocky man with red whiskers, a brown felt hat.

The man caught her eye, leaned close, cocked his thumb towards the dance floor. "Take a spin?"

His breath was tinged with tobacco. His eyes were pale, blue, trained on her.

"Oh . . . No," she smiled at him. "Thank you. I'm with someone." She looked over her shoulder, scanned for Robbie. Thought she saw him through the darkness on the other side of the street. Standing by a smoking barrel. "He won't be long."

The man tilted his face. "Come on. Just a little one. Keep the both of us warm."

Hannah peered behind again. No sign now of Robbie. Had he said where he was going? How long he would be?

"Well?" The man. She turned back to him. Music was everywhere. It reminded her of a street she'd seen in Paris years before. On her honeymoon. She bit her lip. What would it hurt, just a little dance? What purpose life if not to seize at opportunity? "All right," she said, taking his hand. Smiling nervously. "Though I'm not sure I know how."

The man grinned. Pulled her up, dragged her into the center of the swirling crowd.

And she was dancing. Somehow, in his strong grip, she knew the steps. Knew them well enough. They skipped and turned, swept up in the current of the other couples. Violins sang, boots stomped, hands clapped. The man linked an arm through hers, elbow to elbow, and round they spun. She laughed, couldn't help herself. She'd never felt such rushing freedom. She turned her face towards the night sky; closed her eyes, felt the kiss of cold air on her warm lids, warm cheeks. She opened them again, looked for Robbie as they went. Longed to dance with him. Be held by him. She stared into the sea of faces—surely there hadn't been so many before?—but she was spinning too fast. They were a blur of eyes and mouths and words.

"I . . ." She was out of breath, clapped her hand to her bare neck. "I have to stop now. My friend will be back." She tapped the man's shoulder as he continued to hold her, continued to spin. Said, right into his ear: "That's enough. Thank you."

For a moment she thought he wasn't going to stop, was going to continue, round and round, never letting her go. But then she felt a loss of momentum, a rush of dizziness, and they were near the bench again.

It was full now of other spectators. Still no Robbie.

"Where's your friend?" said the man. He'd lost his hat in the dance, ran his hand through a mat of red hair.

"He'll be here," said Hannah, scanning strange faces. Blinking to rid herself of giddiness. "Soon."

"No sense sitting out in the meantime," said the man. "You'll catch a chill."

"No," said Hannah. "Thank you, but I'll wait here."

The man gripped her wrist. "Come on. Keep a fellow company."

"No," said Hannah, firmly this time. "I've had enough."

The man's grip loosened. He shrugged, ran his fingers over his whiskers, his neck. Turned to leave.

Suddenly, out of the darkness, movement. A shadow. Upon them.

Robbie.

An elbow in her shoulder and she was falling.

A shout. His? The man's? Hers?

Hannah collapsed into a wall of onlookers.

The band continued; the clapping and stomping too.

From where she fell she glanced upwards. Robbie was on the man. Fist pounding. Pounding. Again. Again. Again.

Panic. Heat. Fear.

"Robbie!" she called. "Robbie, stop!"

She pushed her way through endless people, grabbing at anything she could.

The music had stopped and people had gathered to the fray. Somehow she pressed between them, made her way to the front. Clutched at Robbie's shirt. "Robbie!"

He shook her off. Turned briefly towards her. Eyes blank, not meeting hers. Not seeing hers.

The man's fist met Robbie's face. And he was atop.

Blood.

Hannah screamed. "No! Let him be. Please, let him be." She was crying now. "Somebody help."

She was never sure exactly how it ended. Never learned the fellow's name who came to her assistance, to Robbie's assistance. Pulled the whiskered man off; dragged Robbie to the wall. Fetched glasses of water, then of whisky. Told her to take her old man home and put him to bed.

Whoever he was, he'd been unsurprised by the evening's events. Had laughed and told them it wouldn't be a Saturday night—or a Friday, or a Thursday, for that matter—if a couple of lads didn't set one against the other. And then he'd shrugged, told them Red Wycliffe wasn't a bad sort—he'd seen a bad war, that was all, hadn't been the same since. Then he'd packed them off, Robbie leaning on Hannah for support.

They attracted hardly a glance as they made their way along the street, leaving the dancing, the merriment, the clapping behind them.

Later, back at the barge, she washed his face. He sat on a low timber stool and she knelt before him. He'd said little since they'd left the festival and she hadn't wanted to ask. What had overcome him, why he'd pounced, where he'd been. She'd guessed he was asking himself the same sorts of questions, and she was right.

"What might have happened?" he said eventually. "What might have happened?"

"Shhh," she said, pressing the damp flannel against his cheekbone. "It's over."

Robbie shook his head. Closed his eyes. Beneath his thin lids, his thoughts flickered. Hannah barely heard him when he spoke. "I'd have killed him," he whispered. "So help me God, I'd have killed him."

※

THEY didn't go out again. Not after that. Hannah blamed herself; berated herself for not listening to his protestations, for insisting they go. The lights, the noise, the crowds. She had read about shell shock: she should have known better. She resolved to care better for him in future. To remember all he'd been through. To treat him gently. And never to mention it again. It was over. It wouldn't happen again. She'd make sure of it.

A week or so later they were lying together, playing their game, imagining they lived in a tiny isolated village at the top of the Himalayas, when Robbie sat up and said, "I'm tired of this."

Hannah propped herself on one side. "What would you like to do?"

"I want it to be real."

"So do I," Hannah said. "Imagine if—"

"No," Robbie said. "Why can't we make it real?"

"Darling," said Hannah gently, running a finger along his right cheekbone, across his recent scar. "I don't know whether the fact had slipped your mind, but I'm already married." She was trying to be light-hearted. To make him laugh, but he didn't.

"People get divorced."

She wondered who these people were. "Yes, but—"

"We could sail somewhere else, away from here, away from everyone we know. Don't you want to?"

"You know I do," said Hannah.

"With the new law you only have to prove adultery."

Hannah nodded. "But Teddy hasn't been adulterous."

"Surely," Robbie said, "in all this time that we've . . ."

"It isn't his way," said Hannah. "He's never been particularly interested." She ran a finger over his lips. "Not even when we were first married. It wasn't until I met you that I realized . . ." She paused, leaned to kiss him. "That I realized."

"He's a fool," said Robbie. He looked at her intensely and ran his hand lightly down her arm, from shoulder to wrist. "Leave him."

"What?"

"Don't go to Riverton," he said. He was sitting now, had hold of her wrists. God, he was beautiful. "Run away with me."

"You're not being serious," she said uncertainly. "You're teasing."

"I've never been more serious."

"Just disappear?"

"Just disappear."

She was silent for a minute, thinking.

"I couldn't," she said. "You know that."

"Why?" He released her wrists roughly, left the bed and lit a cigarette.

"Lots of reasons . . ." She thought about it. "Emmeline—"

"Fuck Emmeline."

Hannah flinched. "She needs me."

"I need you."

And he did. She knew he did. A need both terrifying and intoxicating.

"She'll be all right," said Robbie. "She's tougher than you think."

He was sitting at the table now, smoking. He looked thinner than she remembered. He was thinner. She wondered why she hadn't noticed before.

"Teddy would find me," she said. "His family would."

"I wouldn't let them."

"You don't know them. They couldn't bear the scandal."

"We'd go somewhere they wouldn't think to look. The world's a big place."

He looked so fragile sitting there. Alone. She was all he had. She stood by him, cradled him in her arms so that his head rested against her stomach.

"I can't live without you," he said. "I'd rather die." He said it so plainly she shivered, disgusted herself by deriving some pleasure from his words.

"Don't say that," she said.

"I need to be with you," he said simply.

※

AND so, she let him plan it. Their great escape. He'd stopped writing poetry, his notebook only ever pulled out now to sketch escape ideas. She even helped sometimes. It was a game, she told herself, just like the others they'd always played. It made him happy, and besides, she often got swept up in the planning herself. Which faraway places they could live in, what they might see, the adventures they might have. A game. Their own game in their own secret world.

She didn't know, couldn't know, where it would all lead.

If she had, she told me later, she'd have kissed him one last time, turned and run as fast and as far as she could.

THE BEGINNING OF THE END

I T hardly needs to be said: sooner or later secrets have a way of making themselves known. Hannah and Robbie managed to keep theirs long enough: right through 1923 and into the beginning of 1924. But, as with all impossible love affairs, it was destined to end.

Downstairs, the servants had started to talk. It was Deborah's new maid, Caroline, who lit the match. She was a snoopy little miss, come from serving at the house of the infamous Lady Penthrop (rumored to have tangled with half the eligible lords in London). She'd been let go with a glowing recommendation, extracted, alongside a pretty sum, after catching her mistress in one too many compromising positions. Ironically, she needn't have bothered: she didn't need the reference when she came to us. Her reputation preceded her and it was her snooping rather than her cleaning that inclined Deborah to employ her.

There are always signs if one knows where to look, and know where to look she did. Scraps of paper with strange addresses plucked from the fire before they burned, ardent notes hidden in the escritoire, shopping bags that contained little more than old ticket stubs. And it wasn't difficult to get the other servants talking. Once she invoked the specter of Divorce, reminded them that if scandal broke they'd likely find themselves without employment, they were pretty forthcoming.

She knew better than to ask me, but in the end she didn't need to. She learned Hannah's secret well enough. I blame myself for that:

I should have been more alert. If I hadn't had my mind on other things, I would have noticed what Caroline was up to, I could have warned Hannah. But I'm afraid at that time I was not a good lady's maid, was sadly remiss in my responsibilities to Hannah. I was distracted, you see; I'd suffered a disappointment of my own. From Riverton had come news of Alfred.

Thus, the first either of us knew was the evening of the opera, when Deborah came to Hannah's bedroom. I'd dressed Hannah in a slip of pale French silk, neither white nor pink, and was just fixing her hair into curls about her face when there came the knock at the door.

"Almost ready, Teddy," said Hannah, rolling her eyes at my reflection. Teddy was religiously punctual. I drove a hairpin into a particularly errant curl.

The door opened and Deborah swanned into the room, dramatic in a red dress. She sat on the end of Hannah's bed and crossed one leg over the other, a flurry of red silk.

Hannah's eyes met mine. A visit from Deborah was unusual. "Looking forward to *Tosca*?" said Hannah.

"Immensely," said Deborah. "I adore Puccini." She withdrew a make-up compact from her bag and flicked it open, arranged her lips so they made a figure eight and stabbed at the corners for lipstick smears. "So sad, though, lovers torn apart like that."

"There aren't many happy endings in opera," said Hannah.

"No," said Deborah. "Nor in life, I fear."

Hannah pressed her lips together. Waited.

"You realize, don't you," said Deborah, smoothing her brows in the little mirror, "that I don't give a damn who you're sleeping with when my fool of a brother has his back turned."

Hannah's eyes met mine again. Shock made me fumble with the hairpin, drop it on the floor.

"It's my father's business I care about."

"I didn't realize the business had anything to do with me," said

Hannah. Despite her casual voice, I could hear her breath had grown shallow and quick.

"Don't play dumb," Deborah said, snapping her compact closed. "You know your part in all of this. People trust us because we represent the best of both worlds. Modern business approaches, with the old-fashioned assurance of your family heritage. Progress and tradition, side by side."

"Progressive tradition? I always suspected Teddy and I made rather an oxymoronic match," said Hannah.

"Don't be smart," Deborah said. "You and yours benefit from the union of our families just as much as we do. After the mess your father made of his inheritance—"

"My father did his best." Hannah's cheeks flushed hotly.

Deborah raised her brows. "Is that what you call it? Running his business into the ground?"

"Pa lost his business because of the war. He was unlucky."

"Of course," Deborah said, "terrible things, wars. So many unlucky people. And your father, such a decent man. So determined to hang on, turn his business around. He was a dreamer. Not a realist, like you." She laughed lightly, came to stand behind Hannah, forcing me aside. She leaned over Hannah's shoulder and addressed her reflection. "It's no secret he didn't want you to marry Teddy. Did you know he came to see my father one night? Oh, yes. Told him he knew what he was up to and he could forget about it, that you'd never consent." She straightened, smiled with subtle triumph as Hannah looked away. "But you did. Because you're a smart girl. Broke your poor father's heart, but you knew as well as he that you had little other choice. And you were right. Where would you be now if you hadn't married my brother?" She paused, raised an overplucked brow. "With that poet of yours?"

Standing against the wardrobe, unable to cross to the door, I wished to be anywhere else. Hannah, I saw, had lost her flush. Her body had taken on the stiffness of one preparing to receive a blow.

"And what of your sister?" said Deborah. "What of little Emmeline?"

"Emmeline has nothing to do with this," said Hannah, voice catching.

"I beg to differ," said Deborah. "Where would she be if it weren't for my family? A little orphan whose daddy lost the family's fortune, put a bullet through his own head. Whose sister is carrying on with one of her boyfriends. Why, it could only be worse if those nasty little films were to resurface!"

Hannah's back stiffened.

"Oh yes," said Deborah. "I know all about them. You didn't think my brother kept secrets from me, did you?" She smiled and her nostrils flared. "He knows better than that. We're family."

"What do you want, Deborah?"

Deborah smiled thinly. "I just wanted you to see, to understand how much we all have to lose from even the whiff of scandal. Why it has to stop."

"And if it doesn't?"

Deborah sighed, collected Hannah's bag from the end of the bed. "If you won't stop seeing him of your own accord, I'll make certain that you can't." She snapped the bag shut and handed it to Hannah. "Men like him—war-damaged, artistic—disappear all the time, poor things. No one thinks anything of it." She straightened her dress and started for the door. "You get rid of him. Or I will."

※

AND with that, the *Sweet Dulcie* was no longer safe. Robbie, of course, had no idea, not until Hannah sent me with a letter: an explanation and a location where they could meet, one last time.

He was taken aback to see me in Hannah's stead, and none too pleased. He took the letter warily, scanned the embankment to check I was alone, then began to read. His hair was disheveled and he hadn't shaved. His cheeks were shadowed, as was the skin around his smooth lips, which were moving softly, speaking Hannah's words. He smelled unwashed.

I had never seen a man in such a natural state, didn't quite know where to look. I concentrated instead on the river behind him. When he got to the end of the letter, his eyes met mine and I saw how dark they were, and how desperate. I blinked, looked away, left as soon as he said he'd be there.

They met for the final time that winter in the Egyptian room at the British Museum. It was a rainy morning in March 1924. And while I pretended to read articles about Howard Carter, Hannah and Robbie sat at opposite ends of a bench before the Tutankhamun display. Speaking at times—though the words that passed between them I didn't learn till later—and looking for all the world like strangers who shared nothing more than an interest in Egyptology.

⚘

A FEW days later, at Hannah's behest, I was helping Emmeline pack for her move to Fanny's house. Emmeline had spread across two rooms while at number seventeen, and there was little doubt that without help she had no hope of being ready in time. Thus I was plucking Emmeline's winter accessories from the shelves of soft toys given her by admirers when Hannah came to check on our progress.

"You're supposed to be helping, Emmeline," said Hannah. "Not leaving Grace to do everything."

Hannah's tone was strained, had been that way since the day in the British Museum, but Emmeline didn't notice. She was too busy flicking through her journal. She'd been at it all afternoon, sitting cross-legged on the floor, poring over old ticket stubs and sketches, photographs and ebullient youthful scrawlings. "Listen to this," she said, "from Harry. *Do come to Desmond's else it'll be just we three fellows: Dessy, yours truly and Clarissa.* Isn't he a scream? Poor Clarissa, she really shouldn't have bobbed her hair."

Hannah sat on the end of the bed. "I'm going to miss you."

"I know," said Emmeline, smoothing a crinkled page of her journal. "But you do understand I can't come to Riverton with you all. I'd simply die of boredom."

"I know."

"Not that it will be boring for you, darling," Emmeline said suddenly, realizing she might have caused offense. "You know I don't mean that." She smiled. "It's funny, isn't it, the way things turn out?"

Hannah raised her eyebrows.

"I mean, when we were girls, you were always the one who longed to get away. Remember you even talked about becoming an office girl?" Emmeline laughed. "I forget, did you ever go so far as to ask Pa's permission?"

Hannah shook her head.

"I wonder what he would have said," said Emmeline. "Poor old Pa. I seem to remember being awfully angry when you married Teddy and left me with him. I can't quite remember why." She sighed happily. "Things have turned out, haven't they?"

Hannah pressed her lips together, searched for the right words. "You're happy in London, aren't you?"

"Do you need to ask?" said Emmeline. "It's bliss."

"Good." Hannah stood to leave, then hesitated, sat again. "And you know that if anything should happen to me—"

"Abduction by Martians from the red planet?" said Emmeline.

"I'm not fooling, Emme."

Emmeline cast her eyes skywards. "Don't I know it. You've been a sourpuss all week."

"Lady Clementine and Fanny would always help. You know that, don't you?"

"Yes, yes," said Emmeline. "You've said it all before."

"I know. It's just, leaving you alone in London—"

"You're not leaving me," said Emmeline. "I'm staying. And I'm not going to be alone, I'll be living with Fanny." She flourished her hand. "I'll be fine."

"I know," said Hannah. Her eyes met mine, she pulled them away quickly. "I'll leave you to it, shall I?"

Hannah was almost at the door when Emmeline said, "I haven't seen Robbie lately."

Hannah stiffened, but she didn't look back. "No," she said, "now that you mention it, he hasn't been around for days."

"I went to look for him, but his little boat wasn't there. Deborah said he'd gone away."

"Did she?" said Hannah, back rigid. "Where did she say he'd gone?"

"She didn't." Emmeline frowned. "She said you might know."

"How should I know?" said Hannah, turning. She avoided my eyes. "I shouldn't worry. He's probably off writing poetry somewhere."

"He wouldn't have just left. He'd have told me."

"Not necessarily," said Hannah. "He was like that, don't you think? Unpredictable. Unreliable." She lifted her shoulders, dropped them again. "Anyway, what does it matter?"

"It might not matter to you, but it does to me. I love him."

"Oh, Emme, no," said Hannah softly. "No, you don't."

"I do," said Emmeline. "I always have. Ever since he first came to Riverton and he bandaged my arm for me."

"You were eleven," said Hannah.

"Of course, and it was just puppy love then," said Emmeline. "But it was the beginning. I've compared every man I've met since to Robbie."

Hannah pressed her lips together. "What about the filmmaker? What about Harry Bentley, or the half-dozen other young men you've been in love with this year alone? You've been engaged to at least two of them."

"Robbie's different," said Emmeline quietly.

"And how does he feel?" Hannah said, not daring to look at her sister. "Has he ever given you reason to believe he might feel the same way?"

"I'm sure he does," Emmeline said. "He's never once missed an opportunity to come out with me. I know it's not because he likes my friends. He's made no secret of the fact he thinks they're a bunch of spoiled and idle kids." She nodded resolutely. "I'm sure he does. And I love him."

"No," said Hannah with a firmness that took Emmeline by surprise. "He's not for you."

"How do you know?" said Emmeline. "You barely know him."

"I know his type," said Hannah. "Blame the war. It took perfectly normal young men and returned them changed. Broken." I thought of Alfred, the night on the stairs at Riverton when his ghosts had come for him, then I forced him from my mind.

"I don't care," said Emmeline stubbornly. "I think it's romantic. I should like to look after him. Fix him."

"Men like Robbie are dangerous," said Hannah. "They can't be fixed. They are as they are." She exhaled, frustrated. "You have so many other suitors. Can't you find it in your heart to love one of them?"

Emmeline shook her head stubbornly.

"I know you can. Promise you'll try?"

"I don't want to."

"You must."

Emmeline looked away from Hannah then, and I saw something new in her expression: something harder, more immovable. "It's really no concern of yours, Hannah," she said flatly. "I don't need you to help make my decisions. You were married at my age and Lord knows you didn't consult anyone on that decision."

"It's hardly the same thing—"

"I don't need a big sister watching over everything I do. Not any more." Emmeline exhaled and turned again to face Hannah. Her voice was lighter. "Let's agree, shall we, that from this point on we'll let one another live the life she chooses? What do you say?"

Hannah, it turned out, had little to say. She nodded agreement, and closed the door behind her.

※

ON the eve of our departure for Riverton, I packed the last of Hannah's dresses. She was sitting by the windowsill, watching over the park as the last of the day's light faded. The streetlights were just coming on when she turned and said to me, "Have you ever been in love, Grace?"

Her question startled me. Its timing. "I . . . I couldn't say, ma'am." I laid her fox-tail coat along the base of the steamer trunk.

"Oh, you'd know if you had," she said.

I avoided her gaze. Tried to sound indifferent; hoped that it would cause her to change the subject. "In that case, I'd have to say no, ma'am."

"Probably a lucky thing." She turned back to the window. "True love, it's like an illness."

"An illness, ma'am?" I certainly felt sick enough then and there.

"I never understood it before. In books and plays. Poems. I never understood what drove otherwise intelligent, right-thinking people to do such extravagant, irrational things."

"And now, ma'am?"

"Yes," she said softly. "Now I do. It's an illness. You catch it when you least expect. There's no known cure. And sometimes, in its most extreme, it's fatal."

I let my eyes close briefly. My balance faltered. "Not fatal, ma'am, surely?"

"No. You're probably right, Grace. I exaggerate." She turned to me and smiled. "You see? I'm a case in point. I'm behaving like the heroine in some awful penny novelette." She was quiet then, but must have continued to think along the same lines, for after a while she tilted her head quizzically and said, "You know, Grace, I always thought that you and Alfred . . . ?"

"Oh no, ma'am," I said quickly. Too quickly. "Alfred and I were never more than friends." The hot sting of a thousand needles in my skin.

"Really?" She pondered this. "I wonder what made me think otherwise."

"I couldn't say, ma'am."

She watched me, fumbling with her silks, and she smiled. "I've embarrassed you."

"Not at all, ma'am," I said. "It's just that . . ." I clutched at conversation. "I was just thinking of a recent letter I received. News from Riverton. It's a coincidence you should ask after Alfred just now."

"Oh?"

"Yes, ma'am." I couldn't seem to stop. "Do you remember Miss Starling that used to work for your father?"

Hannah frowned. "That thin lady, with the mousy hair? Used to tiptoe about the house with a leather satchel?"

"Yes, ma'am, that's her." I was outside myself then, watching and listening as somehow I gave every appearance of carelessness. "She and Alfred were married, ma'am. Just this last month past. They're living in Ipswich now, running his electrical business." I closed her trunk and nodded, kept my gaze low. "Now if you'll excuse me, ma'am, I believe Mr. Boyle needs me downstairs."

I closed the door behind me and I was alone. I clamped my hand to my mouth. Clenched my eyes shut. Felt my shoulders shaking, moist clicks in my throat.

I crumpled against the wall, longing to disappear into the floors, the wall, the air. And I felt nothing. No shame. No duty. For what did it matter? What did any of it matter any more?

Then somewhere downstairs, a crash. Plates and cutlery.

A breath caught in my throat. My eyes opened. The present rushed upon me, refilled me.

Of course it mattered. Hannah mattered. Now more than ever she needed me. The move back to Riverton, being without Robbie.

I pushed away from the wall, smoothed my skirt and straightened my cuffs. Wiped my eyes.

I was a lady's maid. Not a petty housemaid. I was relied upon. Could not be given to episodes of such imprudent abandon.

I breathed out. Deeply. Purposefully. Nodded to myself and walked large, definite steps down the hall.

And as I climbed the stairs to my room, I forced closed the horrid door in my mind through which I'd briefly glimpsed the husband, the hearth, the children I might have had.

RIVERTON REVISITED

✳

URSULA has come as promised. We are driving along the winding lane towards the village of Saffron Green. Any moment now we'll take a bend and there'll be tourist signs welcoming us to Riverton. I glance at Ursula's face while she drives; she smiles at me, then returns her attention to the road. Any misgivings she might have had about the wisdom of our excursion, she has pushed aside. Sylvia wasn't pleased, but she agreed not to tell Matron, to stall Ruth if need be. I suspect I am giving off the stench of last opportunities.

The metal gates are open. Ursula turns the car into the driveway and we weave our way towards the house. It is dark, the tunnel of trees is strangely still, strangely silent, as it always was, listening for something. We turn the last corner and the house is upon us. Just as it has been so many times before: my first day at Riverton, fourteen years old and green as a gardener's thumb; the day of the recital, rushing from Mother's, full of expectation; the evening of Alfred's proposal; the morning in 1924 when we returned to Riverton from London. Today is a homecoming, of sorts.

There is a concrete car-parking space nowadays, after the driveway and before the Eros and Psyche fountain. Ursula winds her window down as we approach the toll booth. She has a word with the guard, who waves us through. On account of my obvious frailty, she is given special dispensation to drop me off before finding a parking space. She drives around the turning circle—bitumen now, rather than gravel—and stops the car at the entrance. There is a little iron

422

garden seat by the portico, and Ursula leads me to it, settles me, then returns to the car park.

I am sitting there, thinking of Mr. Hamilton, wondering how many times he answered the Riverton front door before his heart attack in the spring of 1934, when it happens.

"Good to see you back, young Grace."

I squint up into the watery sun (or is it my eyes that are watery?) and there he stands, on the top step.

"Mr. Hamilton," I say. I am hallucinating, of course, but it seems churlish to ignore an old comrade, no matter he's been dead sixty years.

"We've been wondering when we might see you again. Mrs. Townsend and I."

"You have?" Mrs. Townsend passed away soon after him: a stroke in her sleep.

"Oh, aye. We always like it when the young ones return. We get a little lonely, just the two of us. No family to serve. Just a lot of hammering and knocking and dirty boots." He shook his head and cast his eyes upwards to take in the arch of the portico. "Aye, the old place has seen a lot of changes. Just wait till you see what they've done with my pantry." He smiles at me, down his long burnished nose. "And tell me, Grace," he said gently. "How are things with you?"

"I'm tired," I say. "I'm tired, Mr. Hamilton."

"I know you are, lassie," he says. "Not long now."

"What's that?" Ursula is by my side, pushing her parking ticket into her purse. "Are you tired?" Concern knots her brow. "I'll see about renting a wheelchair. They've put lifts in as part of the renovation."

I tell her perhaps that might be best, and then I sneak a glance back at Mr. Hamilton. He is no longer there.

※

INSIDE the entrance hall a sprightly woman dressed like the wife of a 1940s country squire welcomes us and announces that our entrance fee includes the tour she's about to start. Before we can demur, we are herded into a group with seven other unwitting visitors: a couple of daytrippers from London, a schoolboy researching a local history assignment, and a family of four American tourists—the adults and son in matching running shoes and T-shirts that read *I escaped the tower!*, the teenage daughter, tall, pale and dour, dressed all in black. Our tour leader—Beryl, she says, tweaking her name badge to verify the fact—has lived in the village of Saffron Green all her life and we are to ask her anything we'd like to know.

The tour starts downstairs. The hub of any English country house, says Beryl with a practiced smile and a wink. Ursula and I take a lift installed where the coat cupboard used to be. By the time we reach the bottom, the group is already crowded around Mrs. Townsend's kitchen table, laughing as Beryl reads through a comic list of traditional English dishes of the nineteenth century.

The servants' hall looks much as it did, yet it is unaccountably different. It's the lighting, I realize. Electricity has silenced the flickering, whispering spaces. We were without for a long time at Riverton. Even when Teddy had the place wired in the mid-twenties it was nothing like this. I miss the dimness, though I suppose it wouldn't do to keep it lit as was, even for historical effect. There are laws about that sort of thing now. Health and safety. Public liability. No one wants to be sued because a daytripper accidentally misses his step on a poorly lit staircase.

"Follow me," chirps Beryl. "We'll take the servants' exit to the back terrace, but don't worry, I won't make you put on uniforms!"

✻

W E are on the lawn above Lady Ashbury's rose garden. It looks, surprisingly, much as it always did, though ramps have been constructed between the tiers. They have a team of gardeners now, says Beryl, employed continuously on grounds maintenance. There's a lot to look after: the gardens themselves, the lawns, the fountains, other various estate buildings. The summer house.

The summer house was one of the first changes Teddy made when Riverton fell to him in 1923. It was a crime, he said, that such a beautiful lake, the jewel in the estate, had been allowed to fall into disuse. He envisaged boating parties in the summertime, planetary-observation parties in the evenings. He had plans drawn immediately and by the time we came from London in April 1924 it was almost complete, the only hold-ups a tardy shipment of Italian limestone and some spring rain.

It was raining the morning we arrived. Relentless, drenching rain that started as we drove through the outer villages of Essex and didn't let up. The fens were full, the forest soggy, and when the motorcars crawled up the muddy Riverton driveway, the house wasn't there. Not at first glance. So shrouded was it by low-lying fog that it only appeared gradually, as if an apparition. When we drew close enough, I wiped the palm of my hand against the misty motor-car window and peered through the cloud towards the etched glass of the nursery window. I had an almost overwhelming sense that somewhere inside that great dark house Grace of five years ago was busy preparing the dining room, dressing Hannah and Emmeline, receiving Nancy's latest wisdom. Here and there, then and now, simultaneously, at the capricious whim of time.

The first motorcar stopped and Mr. Hamilton materialized from the front portico, black umbrella in hand, to help Hannah and Teddy alight. The second car continued on to the rear entrance and stopped. I attached my raincoat to my hat, nodded to the driver and made a run for the servants' hall entrance.

Perhaps it was the fault of the rain. Perhaps if it had been a clear day, if the sky had glittered blue and sunlight had smiled through the windows, the house's decline would not have been so shocking. For though Mr. Hamilton and his staff had gone to their best efforts—had been cleaning around the clock, said Nancy—the house was in poor condition. It was a tall order to make up so promptly for years of Mr. Frederick's determined neglect.

It was Hannah who was most affected. Naturally enough, I suppose. Seeing it in its demoralized state brought home to her the loneliness of her father's last days. Brought back, too, the old guilt: her failure to mend the bridges between them.

"To think he lived like this," she said to me that first evening as I readied her for bed. "All the while I was in London and I didn't know. Oh, Emmeline made jokes every so often, but I never for a minute imagined . . ." She shook her head. "To think, Grace. To think of poor old Pa being so unhappy." She was silent for a moment, then said, "It goes to show, doesn't it, what happens when a person isn't true to their own nature?"

"Yes, ma'am," I said, unaware that we were no longer speaking of Pa.

※

TEDDY, though surprised by the extent of Riverton's decline, was not perturbed. He had planned a full renovation anyway.

"Just as well to bring the old place into the twentieth century, eh?" he said, smiling benevolently at Hannah.

They'd been back a week by then. The rain had cleared and he was standing at one end of her bedroom, surveying the sunlit room. Hannah and I were sitting on the chaise longue, sorting through her dresses.

"As you like," was her noncommittal answer.

Teddy looked at her, his face a sketch of bewilderment: wasn't it exciting to restore her family home? Didn't all women relish the opportunity to put their feminine stamp on a place? "I'll spare no expense," he said.

Hannah looked up and smiled patiently, as one might at an overeager shop assistant. "Whatever you think best."

Teddy, I'm sure, would have liked it if she'd shared his enthusiasm for the renovation project: meeting with designers, debating the merits of one fabric over another, delighting in the acquisition of an exact replica of the King's own hall stand. But he didn't make a fuss. He was used, by now, to misunderstanding his wife. He just shook his head, stroked hers and dropped the subject.

❧

HANNAH, while not interested in the renovations, displayed a surprising elevation of mood when we returned to Riverton. I had expected that leaving London, leaving Robbie, would devastate her, had prepared myself for the worst. But I was wrong. If anything, she was of lighter spirit than usual. While the renovations were taking place she spent much time outside. She took to strolling over the estate, rambling all the way to the back meadows and returning for lunch with grass seeds on her skirt and a glow in her cheeks.

She had given Robbie up, I thought. Love it might have been, but she had decided she would live without. You will think me naive, and I was. I had only my own experience to guide me. I had given Alfred up, had returned to Riverton and adjusted to his absence, and I supposed Hannah had done the same. That she too had decided her duty lay elsewhere.

One day I went looking for her; Teddy had won the Tory nomination for the seat of Saffron and there was a lunch organized with Lord Gifford. He was due in thirty minutes and Hannah was still on one of her walks. I found her, finally, in the rose garden. She was sitting on the stone stairs beneath the arbor—the same that Alfred sat upon that night, all those years before.

"Thank goodness, ma'am," I said, out of breath as I approached. "Lord Gifford will be here any minute and you're not dressed."

Hannah smiled over her shoulder at me. "I could have sworn I was wearing my green dress."

"You know what I mean, ma'am. You've yet to dress for lunch."

"I know," she said. She stretched her arms out to the side and rolled her wrists. "It's just such a beautiful day. It seems a shame to sit inside. I wonder if we might convince Teddy to dine on the terrace?"

427

"I don't know, ma'am," I said. "I don't think Mr. Luxton would like that. You know how he is with insects."

She laughed. "You're right, of course. Ah well, it was a thought." She stood up, gathered her writing pad and a pen into her arms. On top was an envelope without a stamp.

"Would you like me to have Mr. Hamilton post that for you, ma'am?"

"No," she said, smiling and hugging the writing pad to her chest. "No, thank you, Grace. I'll go into town this afternoon and post it myself."

So you see why I supposed her happy. And she was. She was. But not because she'd given Robbie up. I was wrong there. Certainly not because she'd rediscovered a flame for Teddy. And not because she was back in her family home. No. She was happy for another reason. Hannah had a secret.

✻

BERYL leads us now through the Long Walk. It is a bumpy ride in the wheelchair, but Ursula is careful. When we reach the second kissing gate there is a sign attached. Beryl explains that the bottom of the south garden is closed for renovation. They're working on the summer house, so we won't be able to look closely today. We can go as far as the Icarus fountain, but not beyond. She swings the gate and we begin to file through.

✻

THE party was Deborah's idea. It was as well to remind people that, just because Teddy and Hannah were no longer in London, they hadn't slipped off the social scene. Teddy thought it a splendid proposal. The main renovations were almost complete and it was an excellent opportunity to show them off. Hannah was surprisingly acquiescent. Beyond acquiescent: she took a hand in organizing it. Teddy, surprised but pleased, knew better than to ask questions. Deborah, unused to having to share the plan-making, was less impressed.

"But surely you don't want to concern yourself with all the details," she said as they sat down to tea one morning.

Hannah smiled. "On the contrary. I've a great many ideas. What do you think of Chinese lanterns?"

It was at Hannah's urging that the party turned from an intimate affair for a select few into the huge extravaganza it became. She produced guest lists and suggested they bring a dance floor in for the occasion. The midsummer's night party had once been a Riverton institution, she told Teddy; why shouldn't they resurrect it?

Teddy was delighted. Seeing his wife and sister work together was his fondest dream. He gave Hannah free rein and she took it. She had her reasons. I know that now. It is so much easier to go unnoticed in a large energetic crowd than a small gathering.

꙰

URSULA wheels me slowly around the Icarus fountain. It has been cleaned. The blue tiles glimmer and the marble gleams where it never did before, but Icarus and his three mermaids are still frozen in their scene of watery rescue. I blink and the two ghostly figures in white petticoats lounging on the tiled rim disappear.

"I'm the king of the world!" The young American boy has clambered onto the harpist mermaid's head and is standing with his arms outstretched.

Beryl sweeps the scowl from her face and smiles with determined pleasantness. "Come down from there now, lad. The fountain was built to be looked at, not clambered over." She waggles her finger towards the little path that leads to the lake. "Take a walk along there. You can't go beyond the barricade, but you'll be able to glimpse our famous lake."

The youngster jumps from the fountain rim and lands with a thud at my feet. He shoots me a glance of diffident scorn, then scuttles on his way. His parents and sister follow him down the path.

It is too narrow for the wheelchair, but I need to see. It is the same path I followed that night. I ask Ursula to help me walk. She looks at me uncertainly.

"Are you sure?"

I nod.

She wheels me to the entrance of the path and I lean against her as she hoists me up. We stand a moment as Ursula catches our balance, then we go slowly. Little stones beneath my shoes, long grass reeds brushing along my skirt, dragonflies hovering, then dipping in the warm air.

We pause as the American family files back towards the fountain. They are lamenting loudly the restorative process.

"Everything in Europe's under scaffold," says the mother.

"They should give us a refund," says the father.

"The only reason I came on this trip was to see where he died," says the girl in the heavy black boots.

Ursula smiles wryly at me and we proceed. The sound of hammers becomes louder as we go. Finally, after numerous pauses, we reach the barricade where the path terminates. It's in the same place as the other barricade, all those years ago.

I hold onto it and look towards the lake. There it is, rippling lightly in the distance. The summer house is hidden, but the sounds of construction are clear. It reminds me of 1924, when the builders rushed to have it finished for the party. Vainly, as it turned out. The limestone had been held up by a shipping dispute in Calais and, much to Teddy's chagrin, did not arrive in time. He had hoped to have his new telescope in place so that party guests could come down to the lake and take a look at the night sky. Hannah was the one to reassure him.

"Never mind," she said. "Better to wait until it's finished. You can have another party then. A proper observation party." You notice she said "you," not "we." Already she had ceased to see herself in Teddy's future.

"It's probably for the best," Hannah continued. She inclined her head to the side. "In fact, it might not be a bad idea to put barricades along the path to the lake. Stop people from wandering too close. It could be dangerous."

Teddy frowned. "Dangerous?"

"You know builders," said Hannah. "They're just as likely to have left some other part unfinished. Best to wait until you've had time to give it a proper going-over."

Oh yes, love can make a person devious. She convinced Teddy easily enough. Raised the specter of lawsuits and ghastly publicity. Teddy had Mr. Boyle arrange for signs and barricades to keep the guests from the lake. He'd have another party in August for his birthday. A luncheon party in the summer house, with boats, and games, and striped canvas tents. Just like the painting by that French fellow, he said; what was his name?

He never did have the party, of course. By August 1924 the last thing on anyone's mind, except Emmeline's, was throwing a party. But hers was a particular kind of social exuberance then, a reaction to the horror and the blood, rather than despite it.

The blood. So much blood. Who'd have imagined there could be so much? I can see the spot on the lake's bank from here. Where they stood. Where he stood just before . . .

My head lightens, my legs fail. Ursula's arms grip mine, keep me steady.

"Are you all right?" she says, dark eyes worried. "You're very pale."

My thoughts are swimming. I'm hot. Dizzy.

"Would you like to go inside for a bit?"

I nod.

Ursula leads me back along the path, settles me in the wheelchair and explains to Beryl that she needs to take me to the house.

It's the heat, says Beryl knowingly, her mother's just the same. Such unseasonable warmth. She leans towards me and smiles so that her eyes disappear. "That's it, isn't it, pet, the heat."

431

I nod. There is no use arguing. Where to begin explaining, it is not the heat that oppresses me, but the weight of ancient guilt?

✹

U R S U L A takes me to the drawing room. We don't go all the way inside; we can't. They have strung a red cord right the way across, four feet from the doorway. I suppose they can't have everyone wandering through, dragging their dirty fingers along the back of the sofa. Ursula parks me against the wall and sits beside on a bench installed for observers.

Tourists straggle by, pointing at the elaborate table setting, ooh-ing and aahing at the tiger skin on the back of the chesterfield. None of them seems to notice that the room is thick with ghosts.

✹

I T was in the drawing room that the police held their interviews. Poor Teddy. He was so bewildered. "He was a poet," he told the po-lice, clutching a blanket around his shoulders, still in his dinner suit. "He knew my wife when they were younger. Nice enough fellow: artistic, but harmless. He mostly went about with my sister-in-law and her group."

The police interviewed everyone that night. Everyone except Hannah and Emmeline. Teddy made sure of that. It was unfortunate enough they'd witnessed such a thing, he told the police officers; they didn't need to relive it. Such was the Luxton family's influence, I suppose, the officers acceded.

It was of little consequence so far as they were concerned. It was very late at night and they were anxious to get back to their wives and their warm beds. They'd heard all they needed to. It was not such an unusual story. Deborah had said it herself, there were young men all over London, all over the world, who found the adjustment back to ordinary life an ill fit after everything they'd seen and done at war.

✹

432

O U R tour group has found us. Beryl bids us rejoin the party and leads us to the library.

"One of the few rooms not destroyed by the fire of 1938," she says, clip-clipping purposefully down the hall. "A blessing, I assure you. The Hartford family owned a priceless collection of antique books. Over nine thousand volumes."

I can vouch for that.

Our motley group follows Beryl into the room and spreads out. Assorted necks crane to take in the domed glass ceiling and the shelves of books reaching all the way into the loft. Robbie's Picasso is gone now. In a gallery somewhere, I suppose. Gone are the days when every English house had works of the great masters hanging freely on the walls.

It was here that Hannah spent much of her time after Robbie died: full days curled up in a chair in the silent room. Reliving the recent past. For a time I was the only one she'd see. She spoke obsessively, compulsively, of Robbie, recounting to me the details of their affair. Each account ending with the same lament.

"I loved him, you know, Grace," she would say. Her voice so soft I almost didn't hear.

"I know you did, ma'am."

"I just couldn't . . ." She would look at me then, eyes glazed. "It just wasn't quite enough."

Teddy accepted her withdrawal to begin with—it seemed a natural consequence of having seen what she'd seen—but as the weeks passed, her failure to acquire the stiff upper lip that was her nation's renown perplexed him.

Everyone had an opinion as to how she should behave, what should be done to restore her spirits. There was a round-table discussion one night, after supper.

"She needs a new hobby," said Deborah, lighting a cigarette. "I don't doubt it was a shock to see a man top himself, but life goes on."

"What sort of hobby?" said Teddy, frowning.

"I was thinking mah-jongg," said Deborah, flicking ash into a dish. "A good game of mah-jongg, has the ability to take one's mind off just about anything."

Estella, who'd stayed on at Riverton to "do her bit," agreed that Hannah needed distraction, but had her own ideas as to what kind: she needed a baby. What woman didn't? Couldn't Teddy see what he could do to give her one?

Teddy said he'd do what he could. And, mistaking Hannah's compliance for consent, he did.

❦

T o Estella's delight, three months later the doctor declared Hannah pregnant. Far from taking her mind off things, however, she seemed to grow more detached. She told me less and less of her affair with Robbie, and eventually stopped calling me to the library at all. I was disappointed but, more than that, worried: I had hoped confession would free her somehow from her self-imposed exile. That by telling me everything about their liaison, she might find her way back to us. But it was not to be.

On the contrary, she withdrew from me further; she took to dressing herself, looking at me strangely, almost angrily, if I so much as offered assistance. I tried to talk her out of it, remind her it wasn't her fault, she couldn't have saved him, but she only looked at me, a bemused expression on her face. As if she didn't know of what I spoke or, worse, doubted my reasons for saying such a thing.

She drifted about the house those last months like a ghost. Nancy said it was like having Mr. Frederick back again. Teddy became even more concerned. After all, it wasn't just Hannah at risk now. His baby, his son, the Luxton heir deserved better. He called in doctor after doctor, all of whom, recalling the war, diagnosed shock and said it was only natural after what she'd seen.

One of them took Teddy aside after his consultation and said, "Shock all right. Very interesting case; completely out of touch with her environment."

"How do we fix it?" said Teddy.

The doctor shook his head ruefully. "What I wouldn't pay to know."

"Money's no object," said Teddy.

The doctor frowned. "There was another witness?"

"My wife's sister," said Teddy.

"Sister," said the doctor, noting it on his pad. "Good. Close, are they?"

"Very," said Teddy.

The doctor pointed his finger at Teddy. "Get her here. Talking: that's the way with this sort of hysteria. Wife needs to spend time with someone else who experienced the same shock."

Teddy took the doctor's advice and repeated invitations were sent to Emmeline, but she wouldn't come. She couldn't. She was too busy.

It was true: Emmeline had thrown herself back into her whirlwind social life in London. She became the life of the party, starred in a number of films—love films, horror films; she found her niche playing the misused femme fatale.

It was a shame, society types whispered eagerly, that Hannah couldn't bounce back the same way. Strange that she should take it so much harder than her sister. It was Emmeline, after all, who'd been going around with the fellow.

※

EMMELINE took it hard enough, though. Hers was just a different way of coping. She laughed louder and she drank harder. Rumor had it, the day she was killed on the Braintree Road, police found open bottles of brandy in the motorcar. The Luxtons had that hushed up. If there was one thing money could buy, back in those days, it was the law. Perhaps it still can; I wouldn't know.

They didn't tell Hannah at first. Estella thought it too risky and Teddy agreed, what with the baby being so close to term. Lord Gifford made statements on Teddy and Hannah's behalf.

Teddy came downstairs the night after the accident. He looked out of place in the drab servants' hall, like an actor who'd walked onto the wrong stage set. He was so tall he had to duck his head to avoid knocking it on the ceiling beam above the last step.

"Mr. Luxton," said Mr. Hamilton. "We didn't expect—" His voice tapered off and he leaped to action, turning to us, clapping silently, then raising his hands and motioning as if conducting an orchestra in a very fast piece of music. Somehow we formed a line and stood, hands behind our backs, waiting to see what Teddy would say.

What he said was simple. Emmeline had been involved in an unfortunate motorcar accident that had taken her life. Nancy clutched my hand behind my back.

Mrs. Townsend shrieked and sank onto her chair, hand across her heart. "The poor dear love," she said. "I'm all atremble."

"It's been a terrible shock for all of us, Mrs. Townsend," said Teddy, looking from one servant to the next. "There is, however, something I have to ask of you."

"If I may speak on behalf of the staff," said Mr. Hamilton, ashen-faced, "we're only too happy to assist in any way we can at this terrible time."

"Thank you, Mr. Hamilton," said Teddy, nodding gravely. "As you all know, Mrs. Luxton has suffered awfully over the other business at the lake. I believe it would be kindest if we kept this most recent tragedy from her for the time being. It doesn't do to upset her further. Not while she's with child. I'm sure you'll all agree."

The staff stayed silent as Teddy continued.

"I'd ask then that you refrain from mentioning Miss Emmeline or the accident. That you make a special effort to ensure newspapers are not left lying about where she might see them."

He paused, glanced at each of us in turn.

"Do you understand?"

Mr. Hamilton blinked to attention then. "Ah, yes. Yes, sir."

"Good," said Teddy. He nodded quickly a few times, realized there was nothing left to say and left with a grim smile.

After Teddy had disappeared, Mrs. Townsend turned, round-eyed, to Mr. Hamilton. "But . . . does he mean not to tell Miss Hannah at all?"

"It would seem that way, Mrs. Townsend," said Mr. Hamilton. "For the time being."

"But her own sister's death—"

"Those were his instructions, Mrs. Townsend." Mr. Hamilton exhaled and pinched the bridge of his nose. "Mr. Luxton is Master of this house just as surely as Mr. Frederick was before him."

Mrs. Townsend opened her mouth to debate the point, but Mr. Hamilton cut her off. "You know as well as I that the Master's instructions must be observed." He removed his glasses and polished them fiercely. "Never matter what we think of them. Or him."

Later, when Mr. Hamilton was upstairs serving supper, Mrs. Townsend and Nancy approached me in the servants' hall dining room. I was at the table mending Hannah's silver dress. Mrs. Townsend sat one side, Nancy the other. Like two guardsmen arrived to accompany me to the gallows.

With a glance to the stairs, Nancy said, "You have to tell her."

Mrs. Townsend shook her head. "It isn't right. Her own sister. She should know."

I wove my needle into the silver thread reel and set my stitching down.

"You're her maid," said Nancy. "She's fond of you. You have to tell her."

"I know," I said quietly. "I will."

✣

NEXT morning I found her, as I expected to, in the library. In an armchair on the far side, looking through the huge glass doors towards the churchyard. She was intent on something in the distance and didn't hear me approach. I came up close and stood quietly beside the matching chair. Early sunlight floated through the glass and bathed her profile, giving her an almost ethereal look.

"Ma'am?" I said softly.

Without shifting her gaze, she said, "You've come to tell me about Emmeline."

I paused, surprised, wondered how she knew. "Yes, ma'am."

"I knew you would. Even though he's told you not to. I know you well after all this time, Grace." Her tone was difficult to read.

"I'm sorry, ma'am. About Miss Emmeline."

She nodded slightly, but she didn't take her eyes from that distant point in the churchyard. I waited for a while, and when it seemed clear she didn't want company, I asked if there was anything I could bring her. Tea perhaps? A book? She didn't answer at first, appeared not to have heard. And then, seemingly out of the blue, she said, "You can't read shorthand."

It was a statement, not a question, so I did not answer.

I found out later what she meant, why she spoke to me then of shorthand. But not for many years. On that morning I was still innocent of the part my deception had played.

She shifted slightly, retracted her long bare legs closer to the chair. Still didn't meet my eyes. "You may go, Grace," she said, her voice tinged with a coldness that made my eyes sting.

※

BERYL brings us to the room that was Hannah's at the end. I wonder at first whether I'll be able to continue. But it is different now. It has been repainted and refurnished with a Victorian suite that was not amongst the original furniture at Riverton. It is not the same bed on which Hannah's baby was born.

Most people thought it was the baby that killed her. Just like Emmeline's birth had killed their own mother. So sudden, they said, shaking their heads. So sad. But I knew better. It was a convenient excuse.

An opportunity. True enough, it wasn't an easy birth, but she had no will left. What happened on the lake, Robbie's death and Emmeline's so soon after, killed her long before the baby got itself stuck in her pelvis.

I had started in the room with her, but as the contractions came harder and faster and the baby began to force its way out, she had surrendered more and more to delusion. Had stared at me, fear and anger in her face, shouted at me to leave, that it was all my fault. It was not uncommon for birthing women to lose their grasp, the doctor explained as he bid me do as she ask, to give themselves over to fantasy.

But I couldn't leave her, not like that. I retired from her bedside, but not from the room. As she lay on the bed and the doctor started to cut, I watched from the door and I saw her face. As she laid back her head, she breathed a sigh that looked an awful lot like relief. Release. She knew that if she didn't fight it, she could go. It would all be over.

No, it wasn't a sudden death; she'd been dying for months.

⚜

AFTERWARDS, I was broken. Bereft. In an odd way, I had lost myself. That is what happens when you give your life and service to another person. You're bound to them. Without Hannah, I was without function.

I had no capacity for feeling. Was emptied, just as surely as if someone had slit me open like a dying fish and scraped out everything inside. I performed perfunctory duties, though with Hannah gone there were few enough of those. I stayed a month like that, steering myself from one interchangeable location to another. Until one day I told Teddy I was leaving.

He wanted me to stay; when I refused he begged me to reconsider, for Hannah's sake if not for his, for her memory. She had been fond of me, didn't I know? Would want me to be a part of her daughter's life, of Florence's life.

But I couldn't. I had no heart for it. I had no heart. I was blind to Mr. Hamilton's disapproval, Mrs. Townsend's tears. Had little concept of my own future, other than to know for certain it didn't lie at Riverton.

How indescribably frightening it would have been, leaving Riverton, leaving service, if I'd had any sensation left. Better for me that I hadn't: fear might have triumphed over grief and tied me forever to the house on the hill. For I knew nothing of life outside service. Was panicked by independence. Wary of going places, doing the simplest things, making my own decisions.

I rented a little room in Marble Arch, though, and proceeded to live. I took what jobs I could—cleaning, waiting at table, stitching—resisted closeness, left when people started to ask too many questions, wanted more of me than I was able to give. In such occupation, I passed a decade. Waiting, though I didn't know it, for the next war. And for Marcus, whose birth would do what my own daughter's could not. Return to me what had been emptied by Hannah's death.

In the meantime, I thought little of Riverton. Of all I had lost.

Let me rephrase: I refused to think of Riverton. If I found my mind, in a quiet moment of inactivity, roaming the nursery, lingering by the stairs in Lady Ashbury's rose garden, balancing on the rim of the Icarus fountain, I quickly sought occupation.

But I did wonder about that little baby, Florence. My half-niece, I suppose. She was a pretty little thing. Hannah's blond hair, but not her eyes. Big, brown eyes, they were. Perhaps they changed as she grew. That can happen. But I suspect they stayed brown, like her father's. For she was Robbie's daughter, wasn't she?

※

I HAVE given it quite some thought over the years. It is possible, of course, that despite Hannah's failure to fall pregnant to Teddy all those years, she fell swiftly and unexpectedly in 1924. Stranger things have happened. But at the same time, isn't it too convenient an explanation? Teddy and Hannah shared a bed infrequently in the latter years of their marriage, but Teddy had been anxious for a child at the beginning. For Hannah not to fall suggests, doesn't it, that there was a problem with one of them? And as she proved with Florence, Hannah was able to conceive.

Isn't it more likely then that Florence's father was not Teddy? That she was conceived on the lake? That after months of being apart, when Hannah and Robbie met that night, in the near-finished summer house, they were unable to resist? The timing, after all, was right. Deborah certainly thought so. She took one look at those big dark eyes and her lips tightened. She knew.

Whether it was she who told Teddy, I don't know. Perhaps he worked it out for himself. Whatever the case, Florence didn't stay long at Riverton. Teddy could hardly be expected to keep her: a constant reminder of his cuckolding. The Luxtons all agreed it was best he put the whole sorry affair behind him. Settle down to running Riverton Manor, staging his political comeback.

I heard they sent Florence to America, that Jemima agreed to take her as sister to Gytha. She had always longed for more than one. Hannah would've been pleased, I think; would've preferred to imagine her daughter growing up a Hartford than a Luxton.

※

T H E tour ends and we are delivered to the entrance hall. Despite Beryl's keen encouragement, Ursula and I bypass the gift shop.

I wait again on the iron seat while Ursula fetches the car. "I won't be long," she promises. I tell her not to worry, my memories will keep me company.

"Come again soon?" Mr. Hamilton says from the doorway.

"No," I say. "I don't think so, Mr. Hamilton."

He seems to understand, smiles briefly. "I'll tell Mrs. Townsend you said goodbye."

I nod and he disappears, dissolves like watercolor into a dusty streak of sunlight.

Ursula helps me into the car. She has bought a bottle of water and opens it for me when I am buckled into my seat. "Here you are," she says, feeding a straw into the spout and wrapping my hands around its cold sides.

She starts the engine and we drive slowly out of the car park. I am aware, vaguely, as we enter the dark leafy tunnel of the driveway, that it's the last time I will take this particular journey, but I don't look back.

We drive in silence for a time, until Ursula says, "You know, there's one thing that's always niggled me."

"Mmm?"

"The Hartford sisters saw him do it, right?" She sneaks a sideways glance at me. "But what were they doing down by the lake when they should have been up at the party?"

I do not answer and she glances at me again, wondering if perhaps I have not heard.

"What did you decide?" I say. "What happens in the film?"

"They see him disappear, follow him to the lake and try to stop him." She shrugs. "I looked everywhere, but I couldn't find police interviews with either Emmeline or Hannah, so I had to sort of guess. It made the most sense."

I nod.

"Besides, the producers thought it more suspenseful than if they stumbled on him accidentally."

I nod.

"You can judge for yourself," she says. "When you see the film."

I had once thought to attend the film's premiere, but somehow I know it is beyond me now. Ursula seems to know too.

"I'll bring you a copy as soon as I can," she says.

"I'd like that."

She turns the car into the Heathview entrance. "Uh-oh," she says, eyes widening. She places a hand on mine. "Ready to face the music?"

Ruth is standing there, waiting. I expect to see her mouth sucked tight around her disapproval. But it isn't. She is smiling. Fifty years dissolve and I see her as a girl. Before life had a chance to disappoint her. She is holding something; waving it. It is a letter, I realize. And I know who it is from.

SLIPPING OUT OF TIME

✻

HE is here. Marcus has come home. In the past week he's been to see me every day. Sometimes Ruth comes with him; sometimes it's just the two of us. We don't always talk. Often he just sits beside me and holds my hand while I doze. I like him to hold my hand. It is the most companionable of gestures: a comfort from infancy to old age.

I am beginning to die. Nobody has told me, but I see it in their faces. The pleasant, soft expressions, the sad, smiling eyes, the kind whispers and glances that pass between them. And I feel it myself.

A quickening.

I am slipping out of time. The demarcations I've observed for a lifetime are suddenly meaningless: seconds, minutes, hours, days. Mere words. All I have are moments.

✻

MARCUS brings a photograph. He hands it to me and I know before my eyes focus which one it is. It was a favorite of mine, is a favorite of mine, taken on an archaeological dig many years before. "Where did you find this?" I say.

"I've had it with me," he says sheepishly, running a hand through longish sun-lightened hair. "All the time I was away. I hope you don't mind."

"I'm glad," I say.

"I wanted a photo of you," he says. "I always loved this one, when I was a kid. You look so happy."

"I was. The very happiest." I look at the photo some more, then hand it back. He positions it on my bedside table so that I can see it whenever I care to look.

❋

I WAKE from dozing and Marcus is by the window, looking out over the heath. At first I think Ruth is in the room with us, but she is not. It is someone else. Something else. She appeared a little while ago. Has been here ever since. No one else can see her. She is waiting for me, I know, and I am almost ready. Early this morning I taped the last for Marcus. It is all done now and all said. The promise I made is broken and he will learn my secret.

Marcus senses I have woken. He turns. Smiles. His glorious broad smile. "Grace." He comes away from the window, stands by me. "Would you like something? A glass of water?"

"Yes," I say.

I watch him: his lean shape housed in loose clothing. Jeans and a T-shirt, the uniform of today's youth. In his face I see the boy he was, the child who followed me from room to room, asking questions, demanding stories: about the places I'd been, the artifacts I'd unearthed, the big old house on the hill and the children with their game. I see the young man who delighted me when he said he wanted to be a writer. Asked me to read some of his work, tell him what I thought. I see the grown man, caught in grief's web, helpless. Unwilling to be helped.

I shift slightly, clear my throat. There is something I need to ask him. "Marcus," I say.

He looks sideways from beneath a lock of brown hair. "Grace?"

I study his eyes, hoping, I suppose, for the truth. "How are you?"

To his credit he doesn't dismiss me. He sits, props me against my pillows, smooths my hair and hands me a cup of water. "I think I'm going to be all right," he says.

❋

URSULA comes. She kisses my cheek. I want to open my eyes; to thank her for caring about the Hartfords, for remembering them, but I can't. Marcus looks after things. I hear him, accepting the video tape, thanking her, assuring her I'll be glad to see it. That I've spoken highly of her. He asks if the premiere went well.

"It was great," she says. "I was nervous as anything, but it went off without a hitch. Even had a good review or two."

"I saw that," says Marcus. "A *very* good write-up in the *Guardian.* 'Haunting,' didn't they say, 'subtly beautiful'? Congratulations."

"Thank you," says Ursula, and I can picture her shy, pleased smile.

"Grace was sorry she couldn't make it."

"I know," says Ursula. "So was I. I'd have loved her to be there." Her voice brightens. "My own grandmother came, though. All the way from America."

"Wow," says Marcus. "That's dedication."

"Poetic actually," says Ursula. "She's the one who got me interested in the story. She's a distant relation to the Hartford sisters. A second cousin, I think. She was born in England, but her mother moved them to the States when she was little, after her father died in the First World War."

"That's great she was able to come and see what she inspired."

"Couldn't have stopped her if I'd wanted to," says Ursula, laughing. "Grandma Florence has never taken no for an answer."

Ursula comes near. I sense her. She picks up the photograph on my bedside table. "I haven't seen this before. Doesn't Grace look beautiful? Who's this with her?"

Marcus smiles; I hear it in his voice. "That's Alfred."

There is a pause.

"My grandmother is not a conventional woman," says Marcus, fondness in his voice. "Much to my mother's disapproval, at the grand age of sixty-five she took a lover. Evidently she'd known him years before. He tracked her down."

445

"A romantic," says Ursula.

"Yeah," says Marcus. "Alfred was great. They didn't marry, but they were together almost twenty years. Grace used to say she'd let him go once before and she didn't believe in making the same mistake twice."

"That sounds like Grace," says Ursula.

"Alfred used to tease her: he'd say it was just as well she was an archaeologist. The older he got, the better she liked him."

Ursula laughs. "What happened to him?"

"He went in his sleep," Marcus says. "Nine years ago. That's when Grace moved in here."

※

A WARM breeze drifts in from the open window, across my closed eyelids. It is afternoon, I think.

Marcus is here. He's been here some time. I can hear him, near me, scratching away with pen and paper. Sighing every so often. Standing up, walking to the window, the bathroom, the door.

It is later. Ruth comes. She is at my side, strokes my face, kisses my forehead. I can smell the floral of her Coty powder. She sits.

"Are you writing something?" she says to Marcus. She is tentative. Her voice strained.

Be generous, Marcus; she's trying.

"I'm not sure," he says. There's a pause. "I'm thinking about it."

I can hear them, breathing. Say something, one of you.

"Inspector Adams?"

"No," says Marcus quickly. "I'm considering doing something new."

"Oh?"

"Grace sent me some tapes."

"Tapes?"

"Like letters, but recorded."

"She didn't tell me," Ruth says quietly. "What does she say?"

"All sorts of things."

"Does she . . . does she mention me?"

"Sometimes. She talks about what she does each day, but also about the past. She's lived an amazing life, hasn't she?"

"Yes," says Ruth.

"A whole century, from domestic service to a doctorate in archaeology. I'd like to write about her." A pause. "You don't mind, do you?"

"Why would I mind?" says Ruth. "Of course I don't. Why would I mind?"

"I don't know . . ." I can hear Marcus shrug. "Just had a feeling you might."

"I'd like to read it," says Ruth firmly. "You should write it."

"It'll be a change," says Marcus. "Something different."

"Not a mystery."

Marcus laughs. "No. Not a mystery. Just a nice safe history."

Ah, my darling. But there is no such thing.

※

I AM awake. Marcus is beside me in the chair, scribbling on a notepad. He looks up.

"Hello there, Grace," he says, and he smiles. He puts his notepad aside. "I'm glad you're awake. I wanted to thank you."

Thank me? I raise my eyebrows.

"For the tapes." He is holding my hand now. "The stories you sent. I'd forgotten how much I liked stories. Reading them, listening to them. Writing them. Since Rebecca . . . It was such a shock . . . I just couldn't . . ." He takes a deep breath, gives me a little smile. Begins again. "I'd forgotten how much I needed stories."

Gladness—or is it hope?—hums warmly beneath my ribs. I want to encourage him. Make him understand that time is the master of perspective. A dispassionate master, breathtakingly efficient. I must make some attempt for he says softly, "Don't speak." He lifts a

447

hand, strokes my forehead gently with his thumb. "Just rest now, Grace."

I close my eyes. How long do I lie like that? Do I sleep?

When I open my eyes again I say, "There is one more." My voice is hoarse from lack of use. "One more tape." I point to the chest of drawers and he goes to look.

He finds the cassette stacked by the photographs. "This one?"

I nod.

"Where's your cassette player?" he says.

"No," I say quickly. "Not now. For later."

He is momentarily surprised.

"For after," I say.

He doesn't say, after what? He doesn't need to. He tucks it in his shirt pocket and pats it. Smiles at me and comes to stroke my cheek.

"Thank you, Grace," he says softly. "What am I going to do without you?"

"You're going to be all right," I say.

"Do you promise?"

I don't make promises, not any more. But I use all my energy to reach up and clutch his hand.

❦

I T is dusk: I can tell by the purple light. Ruth is at my bedroom door, a bag under her arm, eyes wide with concern. "I'm not too late, am I?"

Marcus gets up and takes her bag, gives her a hug. "No," he says. "Not too late."

We're going to watch the film, Ursula's film, all of us together. A family event. Ruth and Marcus have organized it and seeing them together, making plans, I'm not about to interfere.

Ruth comes to kiss me, arranges a chair so she can sit by my bed.

Another knock at the door. Ursula.

Another kiss on my cheek.

"You made it." This is Marcus, pleased.

"I wouldn't miss it," says Ursula. "Thanks for asking me."

She sits on my other side.

"I'll just drop the blinds," says Marcus. "Ready?"

The light dims. Marcus drags a chair to sit beside Ursula. Whispers something that makes her laugh. I am enveloped by a welcome sense of conclusion.

The music starts and the film begins. Ruth reaches over and squeezes my hand. We are watching a car, from a great distance, as it winds along a country road. A man and a woman side by side in the front seat, smoking. The woman wears sequins and a feather boa. They reach the Riverton driveway and the car winds its way to the top, and there it is. The house. Huge and cold. She has captured perfectly its vast and melancholy glory. A footman comes to greet them and we are in the servants' hall. I can tell by the floor. The noises. Champagne flutes. Nervous excitement. Up the stairs. The door opens. Across the hall, out onto the terrace.

It is uncanny. The party scene. Hannah's Chinese lanterns flickering in the dark. The jazz band, clarinet squealing. Happy people dancing the Charleston . . .

⚜

THERE is a terrible bang and I am awake. It is the film, the gunshot. I have fallen asleep and missed the ultimate moment. Never mind. I know how this film ends: on the lake of Riverton Manor, witnessed by two beautiful sisters, Robbie Hunter, war veteran and poet, kills himself.

And I know, of course, that's not what really happened.

THE END

✺

FINALLY. After ninety-nine years my end has come for me. The final thread that tethered me has released and the north wind blows me away. I am fading at last to nothing.

I can hear them still. Am vaguely aware that they are here. Ruth is holding my hand. Marcus is lying across the end of the bed. Warm upon my feet.

There is someone else in the window. She steps forward, finally, out of the shadow, and I am looking into the most beautiful face. It is Mother, and it is Hannah, and yet it is not.

She smiles. Holds out her hand. All mercy and forgiveness and peace.

I take it.

I am by the window. I see myself on the bed: old and frail and white. My fingers rubbing together, my lips moving, but finding no words.

My chest rises and falls.

A rattle.

Release.

Ruth's breath catches in her throat.

Marcus looks up.

But I am already gone.

I turn around and I don't look back.

My end has come for me. And I do not mind at all.

THE TAPE

TESTING. One. Two. Three. Tape for Marcus. Number four. This is the last tape I will make. I am almost at the end and there is no going beyond.

TWENTY-FIRST of June 1924. Summer solstice and the day of the Riverton midsummer's night party.

Downstairs, the kitchen was abuzz. Mrs. Townsend had the stove fire raging and was barking orders at three village women hired to help. She smoothed her apron over her generous middle and surveyed her minions as they basted hundreds of tiny quail.

"A party," she said, beaming at me as I hurried by. "And it's about time." She swiped with her wrist at a strand of hair already escaped from her topknot. "Lord Frederick—rest that poor man's soul—wasn't one for parties, and he had his reasons. But in my humble opinion, a house needs a good party once in a while; remind folks it exists."

"Is it true," said the skinniest of the village women, "Prince Edward is coming?"

"Everyone that's anyone will be here," said Mrs. Townsend, pointedly plucking a hair off a quiche. "Those that live in this house are known to the very best."

By ten o'clock Dudley had trimmed and rolled the lawn, and the decorators had arrived. Mr. Hamilton positioned himself mid-terrace, arms swinging like an orchestra conductor.

451

"No, no, Mr. Brown," he said, waving to the left. "The dance floor needs to be assembled on the west side. There's a cool fog blows up from the lake of an evening and no protection on the east." He stood back, watching, then huffed. "No, no, no. Not there. That's for the ice sculpture. I made that quite clear to your other man."

The other man, perched atop a stepladder stringing Chinese lanterns from the rose arbor to the house, was in no position to defend himself.

I spent the morning receiving those guests who'd be staying the weekend, couldn't help catching their excitement. Jemima, on holiday from America, arrived early with her new husband and baby Gytha in tow. Life in the United States agreed with her: her skin was golden and her body plump. Lady Clementine and Fanny came together from London, the former glumly resigned to the prospect that an outdoor party in June would almost certainly bring on arthritis.

Emmeline arrived after luncheon with a large group of friends and caused quite a stir. They'd driven in convoy from London and tooted their horns all the way up the driveway before turning circles around Eros and Psyche. On one of the car bonnets was perched a woman dressed in bright pink chiffon. Her ivory scarf drifted behind her neck. Nancy, en route to the kitchen with the luncheon trays, stood, horrified, when she realized it was Emmeline.

There was precious little time, however, to be wasted tut-tutting about the decline of the nation's youth. The ice sculpture had come from Ipswich, the florist from Saffron, and Lady Clementine was insisting on high tea in the morning room, for old time's sake.

Late afternoon the band arrived, and Nancy showed them through the servants' hall onto the terrace. Six tall, thin men with instruments slung over their shoulders and faces Mrs. Townsend declared as black as Newgate's knocker.

"To think," she said, eyes wide with fearful excitement, "the likes of them at Riverton Manor. Lady Ashbury will be turning in her grave."

"Which Lady Ashbury?" said Mr. Hamilton, inspecting the hired waiting staff.

"All of them, I dare say," said Mrs. Townsend.

Finally, afternoon tilted on its axis and began its slide towards evening. The air cooled and thickened, and the lanterns began to glow, green and red and yellow against the dusk.

I found Hannah at the burgundy-room window. She was kneeling on the sofa peering down towards the south lawn, watching the party preparations, or so I thought.

"Time to get dressed, ma'am."

She startled. Exhaled tensely. She'd been like that all day: jumpy as a kitten. Turning her hand first to this task, then to that, never leaving any more complete than she had found it.

"Just a minute, Grace." She lingered a moment, the setting sun catching the side of her face, spilling red light across her cheek. "I don't think I ever noticed what a pretty view it is," she said. "Don't you think it's pretty?"

"I do, ma'am."

"I wonder that I never noticed before."

In her room, I set her hair in curlers, an undertaking more easily said than done. She refused to stay still long enough for me to pin them tightly, and I wasted a good deal of time unwinding and starting again.

With the curlers in place, or good enough, I helped her dress. Silver silk, shoestring straps falling into a low-cut V at the back. It hugged her figure, fell to an inch below her pale knees.

While she pulled at the hem, straightening it, I fetched her shoes. The latest from Paris: a gift from Teddy. Silver satin with fine ribbon straps. "No," she said. "Not those. I'll wear the black."

"But, ma'am, these are your favorites."

"The black are more comfortable," she said, leaning forward to pull her stockings on.

"But with your dress, it's a shame—"

"I said black, for God's sake; don't make me say it again, Grace."

I drew breath. Returned the silver and found the black.

Hannah apologized immediately. "I'm nervous. I shouldn't take it out on you. I'm sorry."

"That's all right, ma'am," I said. "Natural to be excited."

I unrolled the curlers and her hair sat in blonde waves around her shoulders. I parted it on the side and brushed it across her forehead, catching the hair with a diamond clasp.

Hannah leaned forward to attach pearl drop earrings, winced and then cursed as she caught her fingertip in the clip.

"You're rushing, ma'am," I said gently. "You must go carefully with those."

She handed them to me. "I'm all thumbs today."

I was draping ropes of pale pearls around her neck when the evening's first car arrived, crunching the gravel on the driveway below. I straightened the pearls so they fell between her shoulderblades, rested in the small of her back.

"There now," I said. "You're ready."

"I hope so, Grace." She raised her eyebrows, scanned her reflection. "Hope there's nothing I've overlooked."

She used her fingertips to brush rapidly the edges of her brows, stroking them into line. She straightened one of her pearl strands, lowered it a little, raised it again, exhaled noisily.

Suddenly, the squeal of a clarinet.

Hannah gasped, clapped a hand to her chest. "My!"

"Must be exciting, ma'am," I said cautiously. "All your plans finally coming to fruition."

Her eyes met mine sharply. She seemed as if about to speak, yet she didn't. She pressed her red-stained lips together. "I have something for you, Grace. A gift."

I was perplexed. "It's not my birthday, ma'am."

She smiled, quickly pulled open the small drawer of her dressing table. She turned back to me, fingers closed. She held it by the chain high above my hand, let it collapse into my palm.

"But, ma'am," I said. "It's your locket."

"Was. Was my locket. Now it's yours."

I couldn't return it fast enough. Unexpected gifts made me nervous. "Oh no, ma'am. No, thank you."

She pushed my hand away firmly. "I insist. To say thank you for all you've done for me."

Did I detect the note of finality even then?

"I only do my duty, ma'am," I said quickly.

"Take the locket, Grace," she said. "Please."

Before I could argue further, Teddy was at the door. Tall and slick in his black suit; comb marks channelling his oiled hair, nerves furrowing his broad brow.

"Ready?" he said to Hannah, fretting with his moustache ends. "That friend of Deborah's is downstairs, Cecil what's-his-name, the photographer. He wants to take family shots before too many guests arrive." He knocked the doorframe twice with his open palm and continued down the hall saying, "Where on earth is Emmeline?"

Hannah smoothed her dress over her waist. I noticed her hands were shaking. She smiled anxiously. "Wish me luck."

"Good luck, ma'am."

She surprised me then, coming to me, kissing my cheek. "And good luck to you, Grace."

She squeezed my hands around the locket and hurried after Teddy.

✻

I WATCHED for a while from the upstairs window. Gentlemen and ladies—in green, yellow, pink—arriving on the terrace, sweeping down the stone stairs onto the lawn. Jazz music floating on the air; Chinese lanterns flickering in the breeze; Mr. Hamilton's hired waiters balancing huge silver trays of sparkling champagne flutes on raised hands, weaving through the growing crowds; Emmeline, shimmering in pink, leading a laughing fellow to the dance floor to perform the Shimmy shake.

I turned the locket over and over in my hands, glanced at it every so often. Did I notice then the faint rattle from within? Or was I too preoccupied, wondering at Hannah's nerves? I hadn't seen her that way for a long time, not since the early days in London, after her visit to the spiritualist.

"There you are." Nancy was at the door, cheeks flushed, out of breath. "One of Mrs. Townsend's women has collapsed with exhaustion and there's no one to dust the strudels."

❦

I T was midnight before I finally climbed the stairs to bed. The party was still raging on the terrace below, but Mrs. Townsend had sent me away as soon as she could spare me. It seemed Hannah's twitchiness was contagious, and a busy kitchen was no place for fumbling.

I climbed the stairs slowly, feet throbbing: years as a lady's maid had caused them to soften. An evening in the kitchen was all it took to blister them. Mrs. Townsend had given me a little parcel of bicarbonate of soda and I intended to soak them in a warm bath.

There was no escaping the music that night: it permeated the air, impregnating the stone walls of the house. It had grown more raucous as the evening wore on, matching the spirits of the party-goers. I could feel the frenzied drumbeat in my stomach even as I reached the attic. To this day, jazz turns my blood to ice.

At the top landing I considered going straight to set the bath running, but decided to fetch my nightgown and toiletries first.

A pool of the day's hot air hit my face when I opened my bedroom door. I pulled the electric switch and hobbled to the window, swinging the sash open.

I stood for a moment, savoring the burst of cool, breathing its faint aroma of cigarette smoke and perfume. I exhaled slowly. Time for a long, warm bath, then the sleep of the dead. I collected my soap from the dressing table beside me, then limped towards the bed for my nightgown.

It was then I saw the letters. Two of them. Propped against my pillow.

One addressed to me; one with Emmeline's name on the front. The handwriting was Hannah's.

I had a presentiment then. A rare moment of unconscious clarity. I knew instantly that the answer to her odd behavior lay within.

I dropped my nightgown and picked up the envelope marked *Grace*. With trembling fingers I tore it open. I smoothed the sheet of paper. My eyes scanned and my heart sank.

It was written in shorthand.

I sat on the edge of the bed, staring at the piece of paper, as if, through sheer force of will, its message would become clear.

Its indecipherability only made me more certain its contents were important.

I picked up the second envelope. Addressed to Emmeline. Fingered its rim.

I deliberated only a second. What choice did I have?

So help me God, I opened it.

❦

I WAS running: sore feet forgotten, blood pulsing, heartbeat in my head, breath catching in time with the music, down the stairs, through the house, onto the terrace.

I stood, chest heaving, scanning for Teddy. But he was lost. Somewhere amid the jagged shadows and the blurred faces.

There was no time. I would have to go alone.

I plunged into the crowd, skimming faces—red lips, painted eyes, wide laughing mouths. I dodged cigarettes and champagne glasses, beneath the colored lanterns, around the dripping ice sculpture towards the dance floor. Elbows, knees, shoes, wrists whirled by. Color. Movement. Blood pulsing in my head. Breath catching in my throat.

Then, Emmeline. Atop the stone staircase. Cocktail in hand,

head tipped back to laugh, strand of pearls draped from her neck to lasso that of a male companion. His coat draped about her shoulders.

Two would have more chance than one.

I stopped. Tried to catch my breath.

She righted herself, regarded me from beneath heavy lids. "Why, Grace," she said with careful enunciation, "is that the prettiest party dress you could find?" She threw her head back with laughter.

"I must speak with you, miss . . ."

Her companion whispered something; she smacked his nose playfully.

I tried to breathe. ". . . a matter of urgency . . ."

"I'm intrigued."

". . . please . . ." I said. "In private . . ."

She sighed dramatically, removed her pearls from the fellow's neck, squeezed his cheeks and pouted. "Don't go far now, Harry darling."

She tripped on her heel, squealed, then giggled, stumbling the rest of the way down the stairs. "Tell me all about it, Gracie," she slurred as we reached the bottom.

"It's Hannah, miss . . . she's going to do something . . . something dreadful, at the lake . . ."

"No!" said Emmeline, leaning so close I could smell respired gin. "She's not going to take a midnight swim, is she? How s-s-scandalous!"

". . . I believe she's going to take her life, miss—that is, I know it's what she intends . . ."

Her smile slipped, eyes widened. "Huh?"

". . . I found a note, miss." I handed it to her.

She swallowed, swayed, her voice leapt an octave. "But . . . Have you . . . Teddy—?"

"No time, miss."

Then I took her wrist and dragged her into the Long Walk.

❦

458

H E D G E S had grown to meet overhead and it was pitch black. We ran, stumbled, kept our hands to the side, brushing leaves to find the way. With each turn the party sounds grew more dreamlike.

We were in the Egeskov Garden when Emmeline's heel snagged and she tumbled.

I almost tripped over her, stopped, tried to help her up.

She swept my hand aside, clambered to her feet and continued running.

There was a noise then in the garden and it seemed that one of the sculptures was moving. It giggled, groaned: not a sculpture at all, but a pair of amorous escapees. They ignored us and we ignored them.

The second kissing gate was ajar and we hurried into the fountain clearing. The full moon was high and Icarus and his mermaids glowed ghostly in the white light. Without the hedges, the band's music and the whooping of the party were loud again. Strangely nearer.

With the aid of moonlight we went faster along the small path towards the lake. We reached the barricade, the sign forbidding entrance and, finally, the water's edge.

We both stopped in the shelter of the path's nook, breathing heavily, and surveyed the scene before us. The lake glistened silently beneath the moon. The summer house, the rocky bank, were bathed in silvery light.

Emmeline inhaled sharply.

I followed her gaze.

On the pebbly bank were Hannah's black shoes. The same I'd helped her into hours before.

Emmeline gasped, stumbled towards them. Beneath the moon she was very pale, her thin figure dwarfed by the large man's jacket she wore.

A noise from the summer house. A door opening.

Emmeline and I both looked up.

A person. Hannah. Alive.

Emmeline gulped. "Hannah," she called, her voice a hoarse blend of alcohol and panic, echoing off the lake.

Hannah stopped stiff, hesitated; with a glance to the summer house she turned to face Emmeline. "What are you doing here?" she called, voice tense.

"Saving you?" said Emmeline, beginning to laugh wildly. Relief, of course.

"Go back," said Hannah quickly. "You must go back."

"And leave you here to drown yourself?"

"I'm not going to drown myself," said Hannah. She glanced again at the summer house.

"Then what are you doing? Airing your shoes?" Emmeline held them aloft before dropping them again to her side. "I've seen your letter."

"I didn't mean it. The letter was a . . . a joke." Hannah swallowed. "A game."

"A game?"

"You weren't meant to see it until later." Hannah's voice grew surer. "I had an entertainment planned. For tomorrow. For fun."

"Like a treasure hunt?"

"Sort of."

My breath caught in my throat. The note was not in earnest. It was part of an elaborate game. And the one addressed to me? Had Hannah intended me to help? Did that explain her nervous behavior? It wasn't the party, but the game she wanted to go well?

"That's what I'm doing now," said Hannah. "Hiding clues."

Emmeline stood, blinking. Her body jerked as she hiccoughed. "A game," she said slowly.

"Yes."

Emmeline started to laugh hoarsely, dropped the shoes onto the ground. "Why didn't you say so? I adore games! How clever of you, darling."

"Go back to the party," said Hannah. "And don't tell anyone you saw me."

Emmeline twisted an imaginary button on her lips. She turned on her heel and tripped her way over the stones towards the path. She scowled at me as she got close to my hiding spot. Her make-up had smudged.

"I'm sorry, miss," I whispered. "I thought it was real."

"You're just lucky you didn't ruin everything." She eased herself onto a large rock, settled the jacket around her. "As it is I've a swollen ankle and I'll miss more of the party while I rest. I'd better not miss the fireworks."

"I'll wait with you. Help you back."

"I should think so," said Emmeline.

We sat for a minute, the party music reeling on in the distance, interspersed occasionally with a whoop of excited revelry. Emmeline rubbed her ankle, pressed it onto the ground every so often, transferring her weight.

Early morning fog had started to gather in the fens, was shifting out towards the lake. There was another hot day coming, but the night was cool. The fog kept it so.

Emmeline shivered, held open one side of her companion's coat, rifled through the large inside pocket. In the moonlight, something glistened, black and shiny. Strapped to the coat's lining. I inhaled: it was a gun.

Emmeline sensed my reaction, turned to me, wide-eyed. "Don't tell me: first handgun you've ever seen. You are a babe in the wood, Grace." She pulled it from the coat, turned it over in her hands, held it out to me. "Here. Want to hold it?"

I shook my head as she laughed, wishing I had never found the letters. Wishing, for once, that Hannah hadn't included me.

"Probably best," Emmeline said, hiccoughing. "Guns and parties. Not a good mix."

She slipped the gun back into her pocket, continued to rummage, locating finally a silver flask. She unscrewed the lid and tossed her head back, drank for a long time.

"Darling Harry," she said, smacking her lips together. "Prepared for every event." She took another swig and tucked the flask back into the coat. "Come on then. I've had my pain relief."

I helped her up, my head bent over as she leaned on my shoulders. "That should do it," she said. "If you'll just . . ."

I waited. "Ma'am?"

She gasped and I lifted my head, followed her gaze back towards the lake. Hannah was at the summer house and she wasn't alone. There was a man with her, cigarette on his bottom lip. Carrying a small suitcase.

Emmeline recognized him before I did.

"Robbie," she said, forgetting her ankle. "My God. It's Robbie."

※

EMMELINE limped clumsily onto the lake bank; I stayed behind in the shadows. "Robbie!" she called, waving her hand. "Robbie, over here."

Hannah and Robbie froze. Looked at one another.

"What are you doing here?" Emmeline said excitedly. "And why on earth have you come the back way?"

Robbie drew heavily on his cigarette.

"Come on up to the party," Emmeline said. "I'll find you a drink."

Robbie glanced across the lake into the distance. I followed his gaze, noticed something metallic shining on the other side. A motorbike, I realized, nestled where the lake met the outer meadows.

"I know what's happening," Emmeline said suddenly. "You've been helping Hannah with her game."

Hannah stepped forward into the moonlight. "Emme—"

"Come on," said Emmeline quickly. "Let's all go back to the house and find Robbie a room. Find some place for your suitcase."

"Robbie's not going to the house," said Hannah.

"Why, of course he is. He's not going to stay down here all night, surely," said Emmeline with a silvery laugh. "It might be June, but it's rather cold, darlings."

Hannah glanced at Robbie and something passed between them.

Emmeline saw it too. In that moment, as the moon shone pale on her face, I watched as excitement slid to confusion, and confusion arrived horribly at realization. The months in London, Robbie's early arrivals at number seventeen, the way she had been used.

"There is no game, is there?" she said softly.

"No."

"The letter?"

"A mistake," Hannah said.

"Why'd you write it?" said Emmeline.

"I didn't want you to wonder," said Hannah. "Where I'd gone." She glanced at Robbie. He nodded slightly. "Where we'd gone."

Emmeline was silent.

"Come on," said Robbie cagily, picking up the suitcase and starting for the lake. "It's getting late."

"Please understand, Emme," said Hannah. "It's like you said, each of us letting the other live the life they want." She hesitated: Robbie was motioning her to hurry. She started walking backwards. "I can't explain now, there's no time. I'll write: tell you where we are. You can visit." She turned, and with one last glance at Emmeline, followed Robbie around the foggy edge of the lake.

Emmeline stayed where she was, hands dug into the coat's pockets. She swayed, shuddered as someone walked over her grave.

And then.

"No." Emmeline's voice was so quiet I could barely hear. "No." She yelled out, "Stop."

Hannah turned, Robbie tugged her hand, tried to keep her with him. She said something, started back.

"I won't let you go," said Emmeline.

Hannah was close now. Her voice was low, firm. "You must."

Emmeline's hand moved in her coat pocket. She gulped. "I won't."

She withdrew her hand. A flash of metal. The gun.

Hannah gasped.

Robbie started running towards Hannah.

My pulse pumped against my skull.

"I won't let you take him," said Emmeline, hand wobbling.

Hannah's chest moved up and down. Pale in the moonlight. "Don't be stupid, put it away."

"I'm not stupid."

"Put it away."

"No."

"You don't want to use it."

"I do."

"Which of us are you going to shoot?" said Hannah.

Robbie was by Hannah now and Emmeline looked from one to the other, lips trembling.

"You're not going to shoot either," said Hannah. "Are you?"

Emmeline's face contorted as she started to cry. "No."

"Then put the gun down."

"No."

I gasped as Emmeline lifted a shaky hand, pointing the gun at her own head.

"Emmeline!" said Hannah.

Emmeline was sobbing now. Great hulking sobs.

"Give it to me," said Hannah. "We'll talk more. Sort it out."

"How?" Emmeline's voice was thick with tears. "Will you give him back to me? Or will you keep him the way you have all of them. Pa, David, Teddy."

"It's not like that," said Hannah.

"It's my turn," said Emmeline.

Suddenly there was a huge bang. A firework exploded. Every-

464

one jumped. A red glow sprayed across their faces. Millions of red specks spilled across the lake surface.

Robbie covered his face with his hands.

Hannah leaped forward, seized the gun from Emmeline's slackened fingers. Hurried backward.

Emmeline was running towards her then, face a mess of tears and lipstick. "Give it to me. Give it to me or I'll scream. Don't you leave. I'll tell everyone. I'll tell everyone you've gone and Teddy will find you and—"

Bang! A green firework exploded.

"Teddy won't let you get away, he'll make sure you stay, and you'll never see Robbie again and—"

Bang! Silver.

Hannah scrambled onto a higher part of the lake bank. Emmeline followed, crying. Fireworks exploded.

Music from the party reverberated off the trees, the lake, the summer-house walls.

Robbie's shoulders were hunched, hands over his ears. Eyes wide, face pale.

I didn't hear him at first, but I could see his lips. He was pointing at Emmeline, yelling something at Hannah.

Bang! Red.

Robbie flinched. Face contorted with panic. Continued to yell.

Hannah hesitated, looked at him uncertainly. She had heard what he was saying. Something in her bearing collapsed.

The fireworks stopped; burning embers rained from the sky.

And then I heard him too.

"Shoot her!" he was yelling. "Shoot her!"

My blood curdled.

Emmeline froze in her tracks, gulped. "Hannah?" Voice like a frightened little girl. "Hannah?"

"Shoot her," he said again. "She'll ruin everything." He was running towards Hannah.

Hannah was staring. Uncomprehending.

"Shoot her!" He was frantic.

Her hands were shaking. "I can't," she said finally.

"Then give it to me." He was coming closer now, faster. "I will."

And he would. I knew it. Desperation, determination were loud on his face.

Emmeline jolted. Realized. Started running towards Hannah.

"I can't," said Hannah.

Robbie grabbed for the gun; Hannah pulled her arm away, fell backwards, scrambled further onto the escarpment.

"Do it!" said Robbie. "Or I will."

Hannah reached the highest point. Robbie and Emmeline were converging on her. There was nowhere further to run. She looked between them.

And time stood still.

Two points of a triangle, untethered by a third, had pulled further and further apart. The elastic, stretched taut, had reached its limit.

I held my breath, but the elastic did not break.

In that instant, it retracted.

Two points came crashing back together, a collision of loyalty and blood and ruin.

Hannah pointed the gun and she pulled the trigger.

※

THE aftermath. For, oh, there is always an aftermath. People forget that. Blood, lots of it. Over their dresses, across their faces, in their hair.

The gun dropped. Hit the stones with a crack and lay immobile.

Hannah stood wavering on the escarpment.

Robbie's body lay on the ground below. Where his head had been, a mess of bone and brain and blood.

I was frozen, my heart beating in my ears, skin hot and cold at the same time. Suddenly, a surge of vomit.

Emmeline stood frozen, eyes tightly closed. She wasn't crying, not any more. She was making a horrible noise, one I've never forgotten. She was wheezing as she inhaled. The air catching in her throat on every breath.

Moments passed, I don't know how many, and a way off, behind me, I heard voices. Laughter.

"It's just down here a little farther," came the voice on the breeze. "You wait until you see, Lord Gifford. The stairs aren't finished—damned French and their shipping hold-ups—but the rest, I think you'll agree, is pretty impressive."

I wiped my mouth, ran from my hiding spot onto the lake edge.

"Teddy's coming," I said to no one in particular. I was in shock of course. We were all in shock. "Teddy's coming."

"You're too late," Hannah said, swiping frantically at her face, her neck, her hair. "You're too late."

"Teddy's coming, ma'am." I shivered.

Emmeline's eyes snapped open. A flash of silver-blue shadow in the moonlight. She shuddered, righted herself, indicated Hannah's suitcase. "Take it to the house," she said hoarsely. "Go the long way."

I hesitated.

"Run."

I nodded, took the bag and ran towards the woods. I couldn't think clearly. I stopped when I was hidden and turned back. My teeth were chattering.

Teddy and Lord Gifford had reached the path's end and stepped out onto the lake bank.

"Dear God," said Teddy, stopping abruptly. "What on earth—?"

"Teddy, darling," said Emmeline. "Thank God." She turned jerkily to face Teddy and her voice leveled. "Mr. Hunter has shot himself."

THE LETTER

Tonight I die and my life begins.

I tell you, and only you. You have been with me a long time on this adventure, and I want you to know that in the days that follow, when they are combing the lake for a body they will never find, I am safe.

We go to France first, from there I cannot say. Hopefully, I will see Nefertiti's head mask!

I have given you a second note addressed to Emmeline. It is a suicide note for a suicide that will never take place. She must find it tomorrow. Not before. Look after her, Grace. She will be all right. She has so many friends.

There is one final favor I must ask of you. It is of the utmost importance. Whatever happens, keep Emmeline from the lake tonight. Robbie and I leave from there. I cannot risk her finding out. She won't understand. Not yet.

I will contact her later. When it is safe.

And now to the last. Perhaps you've already discovered the locket I gave you is not empty? Concealed inside is a key, a secret key to a safe box in Drummonds on Charing Cross. The box is in your name, Grace, and everything inside it is for you. I know how you feel about gifts, but please, take it and don't look back. Am I too presumptuous in saying it is your ticket to a new life?

Goodbye, Grace. I wish you a long life full with adventure and love. Wish me the same . . .

I know how good you are with secrets.

468

Acknowledgments

❀

I would like to thank the following:

First and foremost, my best friend, Kim Wilkins, without whose encouragement I would never have started, let alone finished.

Davin for his endurance, empathy and unwavering faith.

Oliver for expanding the emotional boundaries of my life and for curing me of writer's block.

My family: Warren, Jenny, Julia and, in particular, my mother Diane, whose courage, grace and beauty inspire me.

Herbert and Rita Davies, dear friends, for telling the best stories. Be brilliant!

My fabulous literary agent, Selwa Anthony, whose commitment, care and skill are peerless.

Selena Hanet-Hutchins for her efforts on my behalf.

The sf-sassies for writerly support.

Everybody at Allen & Unwin, especially Annette Barlow, Catherine Milne, Christa Munns, Christen Cornell, Julia Lee and Angela Namoi.

All at Pan Macmillan UK, especially Maria Rejt for her judicious editorial eye.

Julia Stiles for being everything I hoped an editor would be.

Dalerie and Lainie for their assistance with Oliver (was ever a little boy so loved?), and for giving me the precious gift of time.

The lovely people at Mary Ryan's for adoring books and making great coffee.

Acknowledgments

For matters of fact: thank you to Mirko Ruckels for answering questions about music and opera, Drew Whitehead for telling me the story of Miriam and Aaron, Elaine Rutherford for providing information of a medical nature, and Diane Morton for her extensive and timely advice on antiques and customs, and for being an arbiter of good taste.

Finally, I would like to mention Beryl Popp and Dulcie Connelly. Two grandmothers, dearly loved and missed. I hope Grace inherited a little from each of you.

Author's Note

✺

WHILE the characters of *The House at Riverton* are fictitious, the milieu in which they move is not. The socio-historical location of the novel is one that has always fascinated me: nineteenth century had just given way to twentieth, and the world as we now know it was beginning to take shape. Queen Victoria died, and with her, old certainties were consigned to the grave: the aristocratic system began to crumble, humanity suffered battle on a scale undreamed of, and women were freed somewhat from rigid preexisting expectations of social function.

When a writer seeks to evoke a historical period of which they have no personal experience, it is necessary, of course, to carry out research. It is impossible for me to list here every source consulted; however, I would like to mention a few without which the book would have been the poorer. Cressida Connolly's *The Rare and the Beautiful*, Anne de Courcy's *1939: The Last Season* and *The Viceroy's Daughters*, Victoria Glendinning's *Vita*, Mary S. Lovell's *The Mitford Girls*, Laura Thompson's *Life in a Cold Climate* and Channel 4's *The Edwardian Country House* television series provided colorful illustrations of country-house life in the early part of the twentieth century.

More broadly, Lucasta Miller's *The Brontë Myth*, Noel Carthew's *Voices from the Trenches: Letters to Home*, Thorstein Veblen's *The Theory of the Leisure Class*, Margaret Macmillan's *Paris 1919*, Max Arthur's *Forgotten Voices of the Great War*, Stephen Inwood's *A History of London*, Alison Adburgham's *A Punch History of Manners and*

471

Modes, the Reader's Digest *Yesterday's Britain*, W. H. Rivers's "The Repression of War Experience," Bruce Bliven's "Flapper Jane," F. M. L. Thompson's "Moving Frontiers and the Fortunes of the Aristocratic Townhouse" and Michael Duffy's website firstworldwar.com were all very useful.

Along with such secondary sources, Beverley Nichols's *Sweet and Twenties*, Frances Donaldson's *Child of the Twenties*, Daphne du Maurier's *Myself When Young*, *Punch* magazine and *The Letters of Nancy Mitford and Evelyn Waugh* edited by Charlotte Mosley provided rich and textured first-hand accounts of literary lives in the 1920s. I would also like to mention Esther Wesley's account of "Life Below Stairs at Gayhurst House," which appears on the Stoke Goldington Association website. For information on Edwardian etiquette I turned, as have countless young ladies before me, to *The Essential Handbook of Victorian Etiquette* by Professor Thomas E. Hill and to *Manners and Rules of Good Society or Solecisms to be Avoided*, published by "A Member of the Aristocracy" in 1924.

I am also indebted to the precious historical information contained and preserved in novels and plays written during the period. In particular, I would like to acknowledge the following authors: Nancy Mitford, Evelyn Waugh, Daphne du Maurier, F. Scott Fitzgerald, Michael Arlen, Noël Coward and H. V. Morton. I would also like to mention a few contemporary storytellers whose works fed my fascination for the socio-historical period: Kazuo Ishiguro's *Remains of the Day*, Robert Altman's *Gosford Park* and, of course, the UK television production *Upstairs Downstairs*.

I have long been interested, as a reader and a researcher, in novels, like *The House at Riverton*, that utilize tropes of the literary Gothic: the haunting of the present by the past; the insistence of family secrets; return of the repressed; the centrality of inheritance (material, psychological and physical); haunted houses (particularly haunting of a metaphorical nature); suspicion concerning new technology and changing methods; the entrapment of women (whether physical or social) and associated claustrophobia; character doubling; the unreliability of memory and the partial nature of history; mysteries and the unseen; confessional narrative; and embedded texts. I have included here some examples in case there are readers who share such interests and would like to read further: Thomas H. Cook's *The Chatham School Affair,* A. S. Byatt's *Possession,* Margaret Atwood's *The Blind Assassin,* Morag Joss's *Half Broken Things* and Barbara Vine's *A Dark-Adapted Eye.*

Finally, having taken the liberty of acknowledging so many references and interests, I claim all bent truths and errors of fact as my own.